WITH
L R a
LIBRARY

W9-AES-249

WITHDRAWN

THE THIRD CHOICE

BOOKS BY ELIZABETH JANEWAY

THE THIRD CHOICE
LEAVING HOME
THE QUESTION OF GREGORY
DAISY KENYON
THE WALSH GIRLS

The
Third
Choice

Elizabeth
Janeway

1959

DOUBLEDAY & COMPANY, INC., GARDEN CITY, N.Y.

Carl A. Rudisill Library
LENOIR RHYNE COLLEGE

813.54
9 25 +

37 810
July 1959

Four lines from "Sailing to Byzantium" from *Collected Poems of W. B. Yeats*, copyright, 1906, by The Macmillan Company. Reprinted by permission of Mrs. Yeats, The Macmillan Company, New York, and The Macmillan Company of Canada.

All of the characters in this book
are fictitious, and any resemblance
to actual persons, living or dead,
is purely coincidental.

Library of Congress Catalog Card Number 59–9784
Copyright © 1959 by Elizabeth Janeway
All Rights Reserved
Printed in the United States of America
Designed by Diana Klemin

THE THIRD CHOICE

1

Of course I can remember a hundred things earlier than the Christmas when I was eleven, but I don't remember anything before as happening, so to speak, to me. To the me who is still here and still feels things the same way, with the same perceptions. What I do remember —gusts of emotion, pictures, sensations—happened not to this "me" but to a discontinuous process, to a thing that came and went and flared into consciousness and died down again like a flame. By that Christmas, however, I had become a person, the same person I am now; which is an odd thing to consider when I remember that the year when I was eleven was dated 1906. No one but myself, perhaps, would quite believe that I was the same person then that I am now, contemplating the number of things (or people) I must seem to have been in these fifty years. But I do believe it, because I can shut my eyes and go back over the links between then and now, and there isn't any break in them. And I can feel my skin creep and my hair prickle just the way they did when I waked on Christmas night and heard the voices.

I didn't recognize them. One reason was that in my family we didn't talk about things. We pushed them into the background, into closets, where they grew towery and shadowy and turned into skeletons. It was hard to find out what had originally been pushed inside from the looming menace behind the closet door which everyone felt and ignored. Even the pusher was apt to forget, after a while, and then all that anyone could know would be that another area of taboo had grown up.

Besides, I'd been put to sleep in the sewing room, and when I woke I didn't know where I was. Some cousins of my mother's had come to spend Christmas and their son Harry was asleep in my bed. I resented this deeply, and I don't think my parents were any too pleased, but blood was a lot thicker then than it is now. This particular branch of the Burney family was unsuccessful (my father called the whole connection "The Blessed Burneys" in a tone of sarcasm as scathing as he ever could manage), and they were en route from Springfield, Massachusetts, where Harry Senior had failed in business, to what promised to be a re-enactment of this process in Kansas City, Missouri. Naturally, Harry Senior's fortunes were one of the things we didn't talk about. We took them in for a week, hastily relabeled some Christmas presents, ordered a larger turkey, put Harry Senior and his wife Ella in the guest room, their daughter Flossie in with my sister Mary, and Harry in my room. That left the old bed in the sewing room for me. Harry was nine and his nose ran and he whined. It rubbed me raw to think of him in my room. It still does.

The sewing room lay off the kitchen and was intended, I think, to be something as grand as a servants' dining room, but the servants we had weren't up to this. We had one girl living in and a part-time man who did heavy work and washed windows and kept the grounds up, and a part-er-time laundress. They all ate in the kitchen and this room off it became a catch-all, and when it had caught a large old table with a scarred top and the sewing machine and a dressmaker's dummy, it became the sewing room. A little woman whose name I've forgotten—was it Miss Roberts?—came twice a year, spring and fall, and made and altered clothes for Mother and Mary and me. There was an old bed there which accommodated Miss Roberts, if that's her name, when she was in residence, and a bureau stuffed with patterns and scraps of material and pinking shears and papers of pins. I don't know where poor Miss Roberts put her clothes, I'm sure. And that's where I spent Christmas 1906.

It was the middle of the night when I woke. The bed sagged after a different fashion from my own. The door opened the wrong way round and the light from outside came in at a strange angle. People were talking in the kitchen, people who did not know or had forgotten where I was. As I floated to the surface of sleep a man stopped speaking and there was a pause. Then a voice that I never remembered hearing before said, "I didn't know you felt that way."

The man's voice spoke again and this time I knew it for my father's. "What difference would it have made if you'd known?" he asked.

CHAPTER ONE

"What difference?" said the other voice, and as it spoke, terror came up in me like bubbles in champagne, bringing with it to the surface the knowledge that this presence behind the strange door, overheard in the strange room, was no stranger. "How do I know? How can I tell what difference? Even now? It seems to me——"

"Jenny," my father broke in, "I didn't mean to be cruel, I didn't mean——"

"It seems to me," my mother went on without paying any attention to him, "as if you had gone away, and someone else was standing there in your clothes, in your body, and as if I had gone away, and someone else is here in my clothes and my body. Who are these people? Where did they come from?"

"Jenny, don't! You misunder——"

"They look like my hands but I don't think they can be. He looks like my husband, but that must just be a joke—oh, a cruel joke! Why don't you laugh? A stranger, a very smart stranger, has put you on like a glove and has come——"

At this point I sat up in bed and screamed. I thought then—and perhaps I was right—that if my mother had gone on for one more second she would have made it all come true: the spell she was casting would have worked, and she would truly have changed them forever and ever. The scream ripped out of me to stop her, to frustrate in the final moment that very smart stranger and that lost woman who were waiting, at the turning point of change, to step into the bodies which had made me. I screamed. I was in time—or so it seemed, at any rate, for they came running in to me, both of them, and of course I would have known their voices anywhere. "What is it, what is it?" cried my mother. But I was too shaken to answer and could only sit chattering my teeth like a monkey.

"She must have had a dream," said my father.

"Did you, Baby?" asked my mother. I nodded my head against her warm breast. "Poor baby," she said, and stroked my hair. "It's all gone now. I'm here. Daddy's here. Matthew, this room's awfully cold. The cold must have waked her. Were you cold, Baby?"

"Yes," I said, sniveling. "Awfully cold. I hate that old Harry."

"Now, now," said my mother, and I thought a lecture on manners was coming, but she let it go at that. She must have been tired. Could I feel—can I feel—her weariness in the arms that held me, that animal warmth of affection, her heart beating against me, dead now these twenty years? "Come," she said, "come into my bed and I'll snuggle you warm as toast."

"What about Daddy?" I asked, for her bed was Daddy's bed too, of course, and sacred. When I was little I had peeked in once or twice and seen them in it together, but I didn't do that any more.

"Daddy can stay here," she said. "Matthew, if you get the Indian blanket out of the den you'll be warm enough, I should think." She waited a minute, but my father didn't say anything, and she went on, "Come on, Little Mouse, find your slippers and robe. You're too big for me to carry."

"Can't Daddy carry me?" I asked in a whine that rivaled Harry's. Neither of them answered this for a moment, but then my father came over to the bed and took me out of my mother's arms. I clung to him—the room was icy—and he carried me out through the kitchen, where I blinked and hid my head in his neck against the light, and through the dining room and the hall and up the stairs, past the closed mysterious doors of the rooms where the invasion of Burneys lay sleeping. I tried to see what the grandfather's clock in the hall said—half past something, but I couldn't tell for sure. Then he put me down on the big bed. I clung round his neck, pulling him down toward me. I would have liked to say something, but I didn't know what, and could only hope my embrace was saying it for me.

"Get under the covers," said my mother, and I let him go. He straightened up and said, "Good night, Puss. No more dreams, now."

"Here are your night things," said my mother. I watched her hold them out, I watched him take them, in the light from the hall. The big bed was cold and I was shaking a little. "Good night," said my mother.

"Good night," said my father, noncommittally, and went out. The bed began to warm up a little. There were soft sounds as my mother got undressed in the dark. By the time she got into bed I was ready to doze off as the lovely warmth of her body reached me.

I just managed to say, before I slid down into sleep, "Won't Pearl be surprised in the morning when she thinks it will be me in the bed and it's Daddy."

"Go to sleep," said my mother, and I did.

What do you suppose they were talking about? I've never known, and no speculation has got me anywhere. There have been years, decades, when I've forgotten the whole thing. And then, suddenly, the scene comes back and what they said, what I heard, takes on a reality so intense that it reduces any guesses about what I didn't hear to sheer banality. Had she found a letter from another woman? Was he reproaching her for being cold? All I have to do is to frame such questions: and I know at once that they are not merely wrong, but irrelevant, outside the right frame of reference. And then I say to myself, What difference does it make, anyway? Isn't what I do know enough? He had been cruel, unintentionally. When she learned how he felt, she had been astonished to the point where she saw him as a stranger, and twenty years of their common life shimmered and shivered as if "marriage" had dropped two letters and become "mirage." And this was for me the first date of my adulthood, when my parents revealed themselves as human and the cloak of myth fell away; Christmas night, 1906, when my first salty taste of loneliness told me I was an individual, embarked irrevocably on my solitary journey.

1906! Sometimes I wonder when my parents found out about their parents, what they heard, what flash first taught them the shape of the world and showed them how the copybook maxims they had learned were wrong. And how they were right, too, of course. And then I wonder about their parents.

You can go back so fast, down under the surface in the private world of affection and revelation given and received, history breaking over your head like a wave that is hardly felt. Down there is where the stories are written and the mythology dreamed, down there is where we confront what cannot happen but has; where we feel ourselves fail and our lives break in two, lose our way, and—unable to turn back, unable to see ahead—still somehow devise the impossible third choice which will allow life to go on living us. Down there is where we are made human. I have a right to say this, for I have lived a great deal of history in these fifty years, I've met kings and presidents and prime ministers and poets, I've been rich and poor and caged and free, I've been bored in romantic places and tormented at home, I have succeeded brilliantly in failing, and I know.

2

Lorraine de Koning was driving a Cadillac up the Merritt Parkway in Connecticut. It was a nearly mechanical occupation with traffic at a minimum on a weekday afternoon. Thoughts bounced in and out of her head but none of them stayed for long; the smooth concrete miles lulled them all to sleep.

The maples were faintly red along their branches, the willows carried a yellow haze. Every now and then, back in a swampy patch, a shrub shone with thin white bloom. The sunlight fell palely from a pale sky. It was almost spring.

Lorraine thought, What a silly performance!

A moment passed, the turn for Route 25 flashed by. Then she asked herself, What's a silly performance? Spring? Or these trips of mine?

At the next exit, passing an old station wagon with a mattress lashed on top, she decided that perhaps both things were silly. They were both irrational, at any rate, each the product of some nameless, mindless drive. Certainly, for a city dweller like herself, spring was a great fake. If you noticed at all that it had arrived it was either because of department store advertisements, or because of something out of the past, some remembered poets' propaganda from the years when you thought you had to believe all that. "I don't now," she said aloud. "I don't believe in it."

The landscape did not care. It had been neatly laid out by the Parkway Commission's gardeners, but it was budding and blooming away as if no human intervention had disturbed it. All over the world, thought Lorraine, this green is creeping up, through the meadows and woods, and nothing, *nothing*, can stop it. Well, to be strictly accurate, all over the North Temperate Zone—— But this geographical precision did not make her feel any less uneasy.

A mindless drive.

Why do I come up every week? She almost always manages to exasperate me!

Well, I can't leave her there all alone.

Don't be silly. You know it isn't just duty that brings you. Anyway, it's her choice to be alone. She doesn't want her friends to come. Which is certainly exasperating of her.

I come because—because I want to. Isn't that enough? Because I get something, I suppose.

What do you mean, you suppose? You know you get something——

This was funny. All alone in the car, Lorraine laughed, remembering the scene between them when just this question had come up. It was the third time she had driven out to visit after her aunt had been moved from the hospital to the nursing home in the country. "My dear child," Mrs. Belchamber had said, "I hope you aren't doing this out of duty. Or because you are sorry for me. It's no doubt exceedingly selfish of me, but if I thought I had become someone's duty, even with my advanced years to justify it, I should be very upset."

Lorraine let the advanced years go hang. "You mean you would be very angry," she said.

"Being angry is upsetting," said her aunt.

Lorraine took a breath and rose to the occasion. "I come because I enjoy myself with you," she said firmly. "I have for twenty-five years. When Faith and I were little, having you come to stay was always like having a party."

Her aunt looked at her solemnly. Lorraine, pleased with herself, felt that she had made a pretty speech, and a touching one. And it was true, no matter how sentimental it sounded. "Just fancy!" said Mrs. Belchamber. "Twenty-five years! We're both getting on!"

What I got that time, thought Lorraine, still laughing to and at herself, was my comeuppance. She really is impossible—which is another thing that's been true for twenty-five years. Longer, probably, when I remember the tone that always came into Mother's voice when someone asked about her beautiful sister. Impossible. And yet, every week, up I come. Aunt Di, I think you're a witch. How she'd love that! How——

Suddenly, shockingly, a horn blasted behind her. Her eyes, which had not left the highway, communicated to her brain that the heavy car was tearing down the concrete at seventy miles an hour with nothing in command but habit. She felt very cold as she came back into her body, and everything seemed to take a long time to happen. In the mirror she became able to see that an open sport car was on her heels, it contained two young men in tweed caps, they despised Cadillacs, they wanted to pass her at ninety, no doubt they despised women too. In the wave of emotions that went through her, terror came first, and then, suddenly, fury: she was lightheaded with it. She pushed the accelerator down, her hands grew competent on the wheel, the speedometer climbed to seventy-five, to eighty, to eighty-five, a gap opened behind her——

You fool! she said to herself. On the right lumbered an ancient sedan. She was past it in a flash. Behind her, the young man at the wheel of the sport car cut in his supercharger, it snarled and sang, he was coming up, he was going to pass on her right, he cut over and for a moment hung there next to her, she could see him out of the corner of her eye. There was another slow car ahead on the right. She could—— No. She thought she would never get her foot off the gas in time, brake down; but there was just room, he cut ahead of her with a scream of tires, the car swaying, the Cadillac would have been over if she'd tried to do it. They pulled ahead, and as they did, the young man who was not driving turned and called something at her she could not hear. He was masked by the goggles he wore, anonymous, hostile, stupid, the world's danger, irrational violence, mindless drive—— He thumbed his nose at her.

And she found herself again laughing helplessly. He had got the best of her, just as Aunt Di had. What could she do but laugh? She pulled to the right, she settled down with the conventional in the slow lane. But as she drove, a kind of wonder grew. What got into me? she thought. How did I come to do that? Heavens, I hope Herbert never finds out! For her husband was almost passionately law-abiding.

Don't be silly, she assured herself. How could he possibly find out! No, of course. But it was such a funny thing for me to do! I got so mad! They made me so mad, those two characters in their caps! But I never get mad. I was as mad as—as Bobby in a tantrum. I was so mad I almost didn't let them by.

Oh no, that's silly. You let them by, said the other voice within her. Then, suddenly exasperated, it went on, Why must you scold so, anyway? You scold all the time, I get so tired of it. Why can't you just relax and—and *be?* And not think and worry and nag at yourself? Why——

It was as if a gray veil had been thrown across the light. The day darkened, grew colder. She was back in the familiar, unhappy place of argument within herself, argument that was always the same, that never came out anywhere new. She knew it all by heart. It had been going on forever and ever. Of course there were days when it was better than others, days when she was reconciled to herself, or at least didn't notice the clumsy creature. But there were other days when she felt as if she were a bear-leader, sentenced for life to drag after herself on a chain incompetence, misunderstanding, and a kind of ponderous, incurable naïveté that made her afraid to ask questions, condemned her to put up with boredom, and marked her out at once as someone odd. Odd—but dull.

How I hate unhappy women! she said to herself now. You have a husband, you have children, you have money—— What in the world do you want? Positive thinking, you ass? But the grayed landscape, the faint sour taste of life were unchanged by anger or irony. And Lorraine had almost ceased to think that they might be. It was, in a way, rather like being color-blind.

She was coming to her turn. Twenty minutes now to the convalescent home and Aunt Di. Did she want to get there? Did she, a little, dread to get there? She swung down to the state highway and started north.

It was a pretty drive now, through real countryside, the landscape gardened here only by the passing generations who had worked it and lived in it. The road was narrow and the tires of the big car sang as she swung it around the curves. The air was faintly fragrant, cold in her nostrils. Everything seemed clear and defined—the trees, still bare; the houses—a few old ones, a few new ones, most of them nondescript, speaking of a life that vibrated narrowly within familiar limits; the deserted stall beside the road where someone sold "Honey" in the summer and "Apples" in the fall; the small old cemetery with its stones leaning wistfully toward each other; the gas station where the attendant had grown lonesome and was talking determinedly to a man driving a green truck. All the world was going about its business.

Lorraine observed it as if through a glass. The figures at the gas station, the woman in the car who had stopped by a mailbox and was reaching in—they all shared some secret Lorraine had never learned, they were immersed in life. When she spoke to them they turned—and their eyes went blank, they knew she was different, on the outside of things. Pretend as she might, try as she might, she was a spy, an observer, an intruder, clumsy, tone-deaf, color-blind. How often she had seen it, how well she knew it! And how often she had thought (it was so easy and deceiving to think): But this is silly! It's not true, I'm making it up! Really, I'm no different, really I'm like everyone else! All I need do is——

And that was the end. Think, dream, say it to yourself, imagine that all you needed to do was to say the right word, smile the right way, look into someone's eyes, reach out and find the glass that cut you off dissolved to mist: but it was not so. There was no magic word, no simple act of conversion, no rebirth that would take her (like Alice) through the glass, to where the sun *really* shone, colors danced, and sounds rang on her suddenly opened ears. She knew. She knew, too, that it was wiser not to try, not to hope. There were the children, no glass between her and them. She had that, at least. And there was Aunt Di, impossible, exasperating Aunt Di, whose eyes never went blank when they looked at her, Aunt Di waiting now for her niece's weekly visit in Dr. Rushmore's exceedingly expensive nursing home.

Which loomed ahead now, doing its best to look like a country house. Two things, however, denied this statement—its size and its hospital neatness. Lorraine left her car in the parking lot, collected the books and magazines she'd brought out for her aunt, and went up the wide steps to the pillared entrance. The shrubbery, the planting, the lawns, all hinted "institution," and the rubberized tile floor of the hall—noise-absorbing, easy to clean—confirmed it. I do hate this place, thought Lorraine. It's a machine. "Hello," she said to the little nurse who popped out of a room to the right. "How's my aunt?"

"Oh—Mrs. de Koning. It's hard to see you against the light. Why, Mrs. Belchamber's just fine, thanks. Is she expecting you? Shall I take you up?"

"Don't bother. I told her I'd be out today."

"That's good. They do love company. End of the hall to the right."

"Yes, I know." Lorraine went up the stair (shallow, carefully un-carpeted to allow ancient or merely convalescent feet to climb easily) and turned right down the hall. It was obtrusively quiet. The shut doors she passed implied that they were shut on secrets. So they are, she thought, on pain and discomfort and all the nuisance of sickness and aging, on everything we bundle out of our houses and pay someone else to face. We have bowdlerized our lives. At the last door she stopped, raised her hand to knock, paused, made a face at her hesitation, and knocked—all in one second.

Silence. Lorraine waited. Still silence. Shall I go get the nurse? Shall I knock again? Yes, of course. She did so and the silence continued.

Damn! she thought, and turned away from the shut door (the door shut on what?) to look hopefully down the hall. Not a soul. Of course she could call the nurse—and then what would she say? "She doesn't answer." "Did you look in?" the nurse would ask. "No, I didn't. I didn't want to. I didn't dare to." Is that what she would answer? She opened the door.

Fresh flowers, fresh chintz, afternoon sunshine pouring in through the corner windows, all very country house—and pulled out, to front the view, a hospital bed. In it, in profile, leaning back on piled pillows, an old woman. She *is* almost an old woman, Lorraine said to herself. I always forget. She's just asleep, of course. A red leather portfolio lay across her lap and Lorraine could see her aunt's strong black writing marching steadily across the paper as if she had never hesitated for one moment over any word, any thought. "Aunt Di," she said to the closed eyes, the slightly sunken cheeks, the darkness in the eye sockets, the fine lines in the fine soft skin. "Aunt Di!"

A little pool of time collected, drop by drop. Then Mrs. Belchamber opened her eyes, turned her head toward the sound of the voice that had waked her—and all illusion of old age vanished at once. "Why, Lorraine!" she said. "I was asleep."

"Indeed you were," said her niece and kissed her aunt carefully on the cheek, thus hiding her face where, she feared, some remnant of her uncertain emotion might linger. As always, Mrs. Belchamber smelled faintly, deliciously, of the very same scent that Lorraine remembered from those "party visits" of a quarter of a century earlier.

Her aunt opened her eyes wider and stretched her shoulders and neck. She shut the portfolio on her lap and put it on the table next to her. "I'm annoyed with myself," she said. "I intended to sleep, but I also intended to wake up fifteen minutes before you came and have Tucker wash my face for me. It's a fine how-do-you-do if I can't wake up when I want to any more."

"I'm early," said Lorraine. "We're having dinner tonight with what Herbert calls 'important people,' and I promised him I'd come home in time to rest and get ready without rushing."

"Who are they?" asked her aunt promptly.

"Mr. and Mrs. Gerard Grantley Miller."

"I never heard of them."

"Well, I won't tell Herbert that. Actually, they haven't been in New York long. They come from Indiana or somewhere"—she was taking off her gloves, dropping her jacket, putting the books she had brought on a table as she talked—"and I suppose they may well be the toast of Terre Haute. We went there for cocktails a couple of weeks ago, and they had pounds and pounds of caviar sitting in a swan made out of ice. I felt as if I'd got into the movies. Shall I ring for Miss Tucker? Or can I get you a washcloth and all?"

"Oh, do. And my cologne. And see if you can't find something bigger than that horrid little kidney-shaped spit-basin for the water. I don't mind brushing my teeth in it, but it's inadequate for washing purposes, and I can't seem to persuade Tucker so."

Lorraine went and rooted in the bathroom, which was hospitally and antiseptic, thinking as she did of her aunt's big mirrored dressing room and bath in her country house twenty miles away. For three months now, since she broke her hip, Mrs. Belchamber had been dependent on other people for baths and bedpans and hairbrushing and all the other physical necessities. To accept this and to ignore it seemed to Lorraine as praiseworthy as accepting the pain her aunt had endured. Of course one could do it, but to do it without, as it were, noticing it—this was heroic. Mrs. Belchamber, however, looking not at all heroic, made her toilet with the neatness of a cat, frowned into a hand mirror that lay on the bed table, and said, "Well, that's better. Now I feel human. What a silly thing to say when you think of all the centuries when humanity didn't wash! Tell me your news. How are the children?"

"The children are fine," said Lorraine at once, for the one person within her who moved easily at the direction of instinct was the children's mother. "Bobby has learned to tie his shoes—well, he tied them once. And he brought home a painting from school called 'Upstairs, Downstairs,' which is interesting because of course we don't have either an upstairs or a downstairs in the apartment. It's a line of houses in a murky night with lighted windows here and there. Very sinister. I asked him why 'Upstairs, Downstairs' (you're not supposed to ask, but I do now and then), and he said, 'Because it is!' So now I shan't ask for a while. Jane. Let me see. I took Jane to the zoo yesterday, and when the leopards growled at her, she growled right back. Do you think I have macabre children? I'm beginning to feel rather like a Charles Addams mama."

"Not more macabre than other people's. You and Faith—do you remember that I once gave you squirrel coats when you were very small?"

"Yes, I do. Only Mother—well, frankly, Mother didn't think they were suitable, not for Boston. I'm very much afraid that we were only allowed to wear them when you took us out, Aunt Di. Except that Faith used to take hers to bed. I wanted to, but being two years older, I couldn't."

"Lorraine, I'm not at all sure that I didn't give those coats to you partly to plague your poor mother. There were times when she picked up echoes from your father's family and worried about the right people and the wrong people, and I would think back to our childhood—— Never mind. I don't suppose they were at all suitable coats, I just thought you would like them. Do you remember by any chance what Faith said about hers?"

"No, I don't. Knowing Faith, she either said nothing at all, or else far too much. I used to feel the obligation of being her older sister very heavily, and thank everyone for her. I've forgotten about the coats, though."

"She said, 'Oh, Aunt Di, how lovely and soft,' or something proper like that, and I beamed, and then she asked what kind of fur, and I told her squirrel, and she said, 'How many?'"

"Oh, Aunt Di!"

"And I had a vision of dozens of dead little squirrels with their toes turned up waiting to be made into coats—and I suppose she did too, but it didn't seem to bother her in the least. There was nothing macabre about your parents, Lorraine. Faith thought that up all by herself. How is Herbert? What does he think about the stock market?"

"I'll tell him to call you and chat about the stock market, you know I'm absolutely hopeless about business. He's had a cold, but it's better now. He's—as usual." She didn't meet her aunt's eye, but she was sure Mrs. Belchamber was studying her. I am really very fond of Herbert, she wanted to say, but if she did it would sound as if she were arguing, and why should she have to argue about being fond of Herbert? *Of course* she was fond of Herbert. "He's very busy. He said last night he may have to fly to Europe soon, to France and Switzerland."

"Will you go with him?"

"Not if it's all business."

"Lorraine, I forbid you to miss a trip you want because of me! Do you hear me? You've been as good as gold to come out to me like this, and I don't want you to imagine that I don't appreciate it, but if I thought you were staying home for me—you know what I said about being a duty—I should never forgive you. Do you hear me?"

"Yes, darling, and I'll go if it's sensible for me to, but not if it's all factories and investments and evenings with experts on arbitrage. I'd be bored to tears. He won't be away long, a month or six weeks, probably. I'll see."

"You need a change."

Lorraine was silent. She felt her heart swing out and away. A change, yes. Who shall I change with? It swung back, it was a pendulum, it could not alter its arc, or escape. "Listening to Herbert talk business wouldn't be much of a change. Perhaps I'll take a trip on my own. When you're well again, Aunt Di, I'll take you to Haiti. Doris Pierson says it's wonderful."

"All right," said her aunt, and just then a maid appeared with a tea tray. Lorraine poured the tea, and they went on chatting about acquaintances they didn't care about and plans they didn't believe in, until the light in the room began to deepen and thicken and the two women grew silent. Mrs. Belchamber lay quite still. Her gaze went through the window, through the honey-colored light out-side, and on and on as if searching the depths of the sky; as if, by lying very quietly and waiting, she might receive some message from the world outside which her accident had denied to her. Her accept-ance, this achievement of patience by someone who was not patient, touched Lorraine again, and this time so unbearably that she sprang up and went to the window herself, as if she could intercept and relay some word, some sign to the woman in the bed; and standing there, remembered how she had once used to stand by a window, to yearn through it for a message——

"Twilight in April always makes me homesick," she said. "I wish I knew for what. I suppose just for being young, for waiting. I re-member——"

After a minute Mrs. Belchamber turned her eyes to her niece and said, "Yes?"

"I remember leaning out of a window in a spring twilight—later than this, though, both in spring and in the twilight, it was darker, it's still almost light—and thinking of all the things I might do, all the lives I might live, wondering which of them would come true. It was a piercing sensation. I was pierced with longing. It hurt physically."

"I suppose we've all done that," said her aunt.

"I didn't think I was unique!" Lorraine blinked, for her eyes were suddenly wet.

"Child, child," said her aunt, "I didn't mean to hurt——" And there came a knock on the door. It stopped her, but just for a second; she went on rapidly, "I remember too. I've been remembering. Come in!"

Lorraine blinked again as the door opened. She felt oddly precari-ous, as if she were wearing someone else's glasses; the walls had an air of slanting in, the door of opening oddly, its shape distorted. Had the glass about her dissolved for a moment? It was frightening! The present, the past when she had ached for a future which was now but which was also never, all the possible-impossible worlds that she had missed so narrowly, pressed in on her. She was not sure for a moment how old she was or what New England landscape lay outside these windows in this possible-impossible room, only that she was here, Lorraine Forbes, a candle flame blown oddly by gusts from no center, but here—— Forbes! Why, she thought, turning from the window, gripping its sill, watching the door open, how many years is it since I have thought of myself by my maiden name? She put her hand to her forehead as if she were dizzy. I must get back, I must get back to now!

Her aunt's voice said, "Oh, Dr. Savage! Good afternoon." And even this, thought Lorraine, was strange. Her aunt's voice carried within it some shift in quality, and she looked not at the man in the doorway, but at Mrs. Belchamber, and saw that she was afraid. Afraid! Aunt Di! Lorraine stared at the new doctor whom she had not met, who had come through the door and had this amazing effect on her aunt; but he seemed to her quite uninteresting, and not at all the kind of person to impress her cosmopolitan aunt: a provincial doctor, who must be expected to think in terms that were rigidly, defensively, middle-class, who would be concerned never to miss a trick nor to give anything away; who neither in this world nor at Judgment Day could hope to inherit the earth.

"Oh, I beg your pardon," he said. "I didn't know you had company."

"I'm just going," said Lorraine.

"Well, don't for a minute," Mrs. Belchamber told her. "This is Dr. Savage. My niece, Mrs. de Koning. Dr. Savage and the Yale faculty have been holding a séance over the latest X-rays of my hip."

Lorraine sat down on the window sill. "Why didn't you tell me?" she asked. "Oh, how do you do, Dr. Savage."

"Because I had nothing to tell except that it's taking too long to heal, and we both know that. Perhaps he will tell us—something—now."

Oh, my poor dear! thought Lorraine, she is afraid to ask him directly! She could never remember seeing her aunt afraid before. Mrs. Belchamber folded her hands carefully, and Lorraine realized that this was to prevent their trembling. Pity, an unfamiliar emotion when related to her aunt, rose within her and made her clumsy. Does she need me? she thought. Shall I go and take her hand? Oh, but how could I help? cried withdrawal and fear. I am only I, how could she need me?

The doctor said, "How do you do, Mrs.—de Koning?" When Lorraine nodded, he sat down, pulling a chair up beside the bed in a matter-of-fact businesslike way. He was holding a manila envelope. "I've got the X-rays here, Mrs. Belchamber. I've been over them with Dr. Ingoldsby and Dr. Littell, and I'd like to show you——"

"No thank you," said Mrs. Belchamber.

"I beg your pardon?" He did not sound as if he were used to being interrupted.

"My dear man," said Mrs. Belchamber, and her voice had strengthened, she spoke with deliberate frivolity, "I can't read an X-ray! I leave that to you and Dr. Ingoldsby and Dr. Littell, and anyone else you want to chat with. Don't show me, tell me. When are you going to let me get up? When can I get out of here and go home? I put in five hundred new tulips last fall, and I want to see them."

"Yes," said Dr. Savage. "I see. Well." He lifted the manila envelope as if he thought it more relevant to the conversation than Mrs. Belchamber's tulips, but he put it down again, shifted in his chair, and started over. "We've been over these, then, and—— Well—the truth of the matter, Mrs. Belchamber, is that we aren't sure. Now I know that's not what you want to hear, or what a doctor's supposed to say——"

"Please forget what I want to hear. I want to hear what you know. I want to hear the truth."

"Naturally, naturally." He nodded his head, a big head covered with dark curly hair. The gesture was oddly histrionic. He is acting out being a doctor, thought Lorraine, how strange! She was not sure whether to feel mistrustful, or sorry for him. "That's what I—ah—want to tell you," he went on. "The truth is that we don't feel in a position to take any chances on this fracture of yours. You wouldn't want us to, I'm sure. Frankly, at the moment the evidence just isn't definite. Frankly, what we want to do is to wait—oh, perhaps three weeks—and take pictures regularly during that time. What we'd like to do, Mrs. Belchamber, to put it as clearly as I can, is to check on the rate of healing, if you see what I mean."

"I'm able to follow you, thank you."

"You see, not only was the whole thing, the whole experience, a shock for you, but it was a special shock to the area of the hip and the pelvis. And because we've had to introduce extraneous material (the pin, you know, to hold the bone together), there continues to be a certain element of shock. What we are anxious to determine is the ability of the body to incorporate this extraneous material—to heal, that is." He paused, as if this were the place for Mrs. Belchamber to speak, and she had somehow missed her cue. But she lay very still, watching him warily. Lorraine was suddenly amused and proud of her. She did not give him an inch. He moved uneasily in his chair, and his voice was slightly strained as he went on with what must be (she decided) a prepared speech, a presentation. "It may be—it may be that a little later on Dr. Ingoldsby and Dr. Littell, and some of the other senior men who are interested in the case, will come to the conclusion that we ought to help the process by introducing a little more mechanical aid. It may be that you need a little more of a brace in there than the first pin is providing."

"You mean you will want to operate on my hip?" asked Mrs. Belchamber.

"Well, yes. It's possible."

"Then won't you please do it right away and get it over with? I've been in a hospital bed, here or in New Haven, for ninety-three days, Dr. Savage, and though I'll give up my tulips and stay for another ninety-three days if I have to, I'd do it much more cheerfully if I could see an end to it."

"Well, now, Mrs. Belchamber," he said, and he had become both hearty and patronizing as if he now felt much more sure of himself since she had asked him a question, "well now, that's the difficulty. I know how you must feel but, you see, medicine isn't like arithmetic, there isn't a precise answer to every question. Perhaps we ought to operate on your hip, but then, perhaps it won't be necessary. I'm sure you don't want to rush into a major operation——"

"You're quite wrong, I'd rush into it tomorrow."

He raised his voice a little. "—an operation until we're sure we're right to do it. If I—— If Dr. Ingoldsby or Dr. Littell or I could tell you, 'Yes, Mrs. Belchamber, we'll do this or that, it will cause you some discomfort but in ninety-three days we'll have you back on your feet,' why, we'd like nothing better. But at the moment we can't tell you that. All we——"

"You mean that an operation mightn't do any good?"

"Oh, it would do some good, of course it would. On the other hand there's a chance that it might—ah—tend to reduce your freedom of movement. If we can just watch the hip a few more weeks, we may establish——"

"Reduce the freedom of movement! Does that mean that I'd be bedridden? For the rest of my life?"

"Oh no. Oh no indeed! In fact, I want to get you into a wheel chair next week. There is healing, there's no doubt about it. It's a question of deciding what's the best way to give you sufficient support without sacrificing mobility, whether the operation will be justified, or whether nature will do better than the doctors can. You see——"

"Do be quiet," said Mrs. Belchamber. Dr. Savage, stopped in full flight, sat for a moment with his mouth open. Lorraine got up and went over to the bed. Her aunt's hands opened and then clenched, and in the silence, where the word "wheel chair" reverberated, she shut her eyes and her face became at once that aging mask which Lorraine had seen when she arrived. She breathed for a moment strongly through her mouth. At the hiss of her breath, Lorraine did touch her hand and Dr. Savage got up and said unhappily, "I'm afraid it's been a shock——"

"I am so angry," said Mrs. Belchamber. Her eyes opened and she was indeed angry, they crackled with fury. Lorraine pulled her hand back as if she'd touched something too hot. "I'm angry at you and myself and the beautiful bay mare who threw me and dragged me, and the clumsy sympathetic louts who shook me up so badly getting me to the hospital. I'm angry at you, Lorraine, and you, Dr. What's-your-name, and every nurse and maid and janitor and gardener in this damned institution who's walking around on two feet. I'm angry enough to cry and scream and sit up and get out of bed and try to walk as if this were Lourdes and I could make my own miracle. No, I won't do it, I won't ruin all the work and time that's passed since it happened, but don't think I couldn't, don't think it's you that's stopping me, don't ever think I'm not angry enough to. Angry! I could throw this vase through the window and that tea cup at the maid who should have come for it an hour ago. I'm angry enough to make a spectacle of myself, and not care, and I'm doing it, and I know it. Go home, Lorraine. Go away, Dr. Thing, Dr. Savage. You can come back tomorrow, or the day after, or next week, and tell me any more clichés that have occurred to you and Dr. Ingoldsby, but right now I don't want to look at your face. I'm rude and unreasonable—yes, and I know that too!—but I'm an old woman (God knows I feel it today!), and I intend to be as rude and unreasonable as I want. Lorraine, ring for the nurse. Call me up tomorrow. But both of you go now. There's little enough that's left to me that I want and that I can have, but I can have privacy still, and I want it now! Go away!"

"Darling——" Lorraine tried.

"No," said Mrs. Belchamber. "Go away. You can't help me, and you know it. Can you walk for me? Can you ride for me again on a frosty morning? All you can do for me is sell the horses when the doctor tells you it's time to give up hope. Like a fool——"

"Mrs. Belchamber, I——" the doctor began.

"Like a fool, I'll wait for the official decision, though I can see that it doesn't matter and isn't important. But I want to wait alone! Leave me alone! I can manage. I can manage anything but sympathy."

"Aunt Di," said Lorraine, "I'm so sorry! Please——" But her aunt shut her eyes as if she could command the two of them to vanish by shutting them out of her sight. Lorraine waited helplessly for a minute and then, seeing nothing else to do, rang the bell for the nurse, gathered up her possessions, and went to the door. "I'll call you first thing," she said. There was no answer. She went out the door into the hateful corridor where the reality of pain was trapped and denied, and in a moment the doctor followed.

"We should have known, I suppose," she said to him as they walked toward the stairs, "when it didn't heal faster."

But he did not at once answer her; she looked up at him in mild surprise. His face was a puzzle, but he was not acting now: jaw set, mouth pulled in so that the corners were almost prim—— Why, she thought, *he's* angry too! He's as angry as she is! Oh dear! And just then he carefully opened his set lips and said, "Don't you think you ladies may be a little apt to jump to conclusions? Nobody said she wouldn't walk again."

"I'm so sorry," said Lorraine helplessly (Really, I seem to be saying nothing else! she thought), "of course you didn't say it, but it's what you meant, isn't it?"

"Of course it isn't what I meant!" He stopped. He was surprised at his own vehemence. He looked up and down the corridor to see if he had been overheard.

"But then you should go back and tell her!"

"Tell her! What was I doing? I told her!" He took a deep breath, he lowered his voice by an obvious effort of will; clutching his envelope of X-rays he glared down at Lorraine and said in a stony rumble, "No doubt my clichés weren't as clear as they might have been, but what I meant to convey was that we wouldn't know anything for three weeks or so. I see I was wrong."

Desperately, innocently, trying to understand, Lorraine stared into his face. But she could not see, through the curtain of his anger, whether or not he was telling her the truth; and the very fact of her questioning gaze worked against her. He grew angrier, since she did not at once accept his words. "I'm sorry I'm so obtuse," he said.

For one moment of increased puzzlement, she stared on, until she realized that he had simply used the wrong word. Of course many people did. He meant "obscure." At once she turned her eyes away in embarrassment. He's not educated, she thought, that's why he was acting before, and why he's unsure of himself. It was the most natural thing in the world for her to think this; though if you had told her that she was a snob she would have been stunned. But it changed the whole quality of her feeling about him. Condescension, completely unconscious and allowing him all the technical skill in the world or even commending him for having gained it but condescension nonetheless, flooded her. He was not a gentleman. He was someone for whom allowances must be made. She made them at once. "Why you're not at all!" she said, never hearing her tone go false. "I'm sure that what you said was perfectly clear and it's we who are stupid. But you shouldn't be angry because we don't quite understand, should you?"

He blinked at her. His mouth set again. "Please forgive me," he said with heavy sarcasm, "if *I've* said anything that has offended you. I'm sure I wouldn't want to do that. Your aunt——" He caught himself.

"My aunt is impossible," said Lorraine quickly. "I do apologize for her. She hurt your feelings, I know. It was——"

"I assure you, Mrs. de Koning, she didn't——"

"It was the shock, you see. She thought, I thought, you meant that it was all over for her. It was just the shock. You do understand, don't you?" She looked at him appealingly.

But it was no good. "Oh yes, I understand," he said huffily. But it was apparent that he didn't and wasn't going to try.

Familiar frustration rose within her: she was not explaining herself right. She was not getting through to him. And yet she must try, and go on trying—— "She'll apologize herself next time you see her, I know."

His lips were so tight that he gave the effect of having to unpin them to speak. "Dr. Ingoldsby will be in touch with your aunt," he said. "I've been very glad to help, of course, but I'm sure she'll be happier in the hands of someone that she has complete confidence in." He paused for a moment, but not for quite long enough for her to take in this circumlocution. "Good afternoon," he said, and started down the stairs.

"You mean," said Lorraine, "that you won't see her again?" She was so surprised that she forgot to be gracious and condescending, and came right out with it.

This clear speaking seemed to shock him. "Naturally," he said, "if I thought any purpose would be served, I'd be happy——"

"Oh, but a purpose would be!" Goodness, she thought, I'm catching his clichés now myself! "I mean, you really would help. I don't think you quite understand, Dr. Savage. She—it's not very nice, but it's true, and I'd better tell you. She doesn't think much of Dr. Ingoldsby. In fact—well—she thinks he's a fool."

For a second there was a hint in Dr. Savage's too expressive face that he might share this view. Then he said rapidly, "Dr. Ingoldsby is my senior and a very respected man. His experience——"

"Oh, I know. But that's what she thinks, just the same. No doubt it's as—as silly as what she said to you. Only, she'd be shattered if you just vanished without a word, I know she would. I don't think she realizes what a—well, what a temper she has." She looked down at him, standing a step or two below her on the stairs. He was looking up with just a shade of uncertainty in his face. She had a feeling that he had begun to listen to her, and that now was the time to drive her point home. "People don't always realize that they do have tempers, I think. Do they?" And she smiled at him with what she intended to be gentle, friendly mockery that would undermine any resentment he still felt.

It was a mistake. Watching, she saw him stiffen. Before her eyes he turned into a wooden Indian. The right color, too, for a flush spread over his already florid face. "Is that so?" he said, and it was a proper wooden-Indian tone, through stiff pinned-back lips. Now she too, not only her aunt, had offended him!

It had a queer effect on her. Looking at this angry man whom, against all her intention, she had only made angrier, she experienced a sense of failure and inadequacy so devastating that it left her dizzy. She had only to turn her hand to an action for it to go wrong! She had got herself at cross-purposes with life and all her efforts at living, at doing, at being, only made things worse. The very air about her was killing, green things withered, a small personal desert surrounded her that no one could reach across, that nothing could bridge. Dr. Savage—Indian-visaged, angry, on the verge of turning away, bearing forever a memory of her ineptitude, insensitivity, condescension—Dr. Savage became in this moment the symbol of all her distress. She would have to remember him always, now. She would carry forever the scar of his upturned face.

"I'm sorry," she said. "Never mind. Of course you must do what you want. I'm sorry." With a gesture of helplessness she turned her back on him and stood looking down at her clumsy hands, waiting for him to go.

He did not at once do so. "It's not—" he began, "it's not what I want, Mrs.—Mrs. de Koning. It's what is best for your aunt. I—— If she doesn't trust me——" He stopped.

Lorraine didn't say anything. What I do is wrong, she thought. I mustn't do anything.

"If she doesn't trust me," he said, "I can't be much good to her." He waited again. "Isn't that the position?"

"I don't know. You must do what you think best."

"But——"

"I'm sorry. I was wrong to interfere. I don't want to. You must have—other difficult patients. I'm sure you will know what to do. I—— Good-by. Thank you."

Another, a longer pause followed. Even not doing anything isn't right, thought Lorraine. Now I've just got him all mixed up. But there wasn't anything better to do that she could think of. She did not turn, she just waited. He could think her resentful, or hyper-sensitive, or slightly mad, it didn't matter as long as he went.

Finally he said, "Very well. If that's what you want. Good-by."

I don't want anything, she thought, I don't come into it. But she did not say it for even this would be too much, would involve her again in argument. If what she did was wrong she must simply remove herself and let things happen as they might. She waited, she waited—and then his steps went down the stairs, he crossed the hall, the door closed behind him almost with a slam, and he was gone. Even then she waited, for he must get in his car, start it, drive away. She did not want ever to see him again.

At last she followed him down the stairs and out. The light was changing, it was almost dusk and she had the long drive to New York ahead. I will be late, she thought, remembering the ordeal of the evening at the Millers' to be got through. But in the dead pause that surrounded and becalmed her she found this, though probable, quite unimportant. Indeed, it gave her a sort of reverse self-assurance. She had, she felt, stumbled at last on absolute truth, she had touched bottom. Everything she did was wrong: at least she knew where she stood. Her future was really quite clear, for she had only to make sure, at every opportunity, that she did nothing, touched nothing, let life flow past without disturbing it in any way.

You should make yourself a little heraldic device, she said to herself, with a motto on it: I will refrain. Remember that now, I will refrain.

CHAPTER

3

There is a wisdom of the body that knows things before the mind does. Drained by rage and apparently shattered by astonishment, having shouted and screamed at my unfortunate niece and that ill-bred, red-faced, muddy-minded young man (poor young man!), I lie here and realize that something (not I) knew all along what he told me today. I bought this notebook three weeks ago, intending to use it for memoranda on all that must be done in the house and the garden before I go home. (Will I ever go home?) I ordered it for the future and the practical present—and didn't use it. My lists of things to do are still written on scratch paper. Then last night——

Last night and this morning I wrote in it. Last night I looked up and saw, facing me, not the future nor the present, but the past. Last night something said to me, Look back, neither the future nor the practical present will fill this book, you are finished and part of the past. And today he came and told me so.

I should write that again and again and again. Finished. Over. No more to come. For terribly, dangerously, I don't believe it. I *know* it, but I don't believe it. I'd filled up my life with activity and buttressed it with "friends," all furiously, spuriously, active too. I'd made up a routine that took me from here to there and back, with a stay in Paris or London arranged a year ahead, reservations made and not to be questioned, my fellow circuit riders alerted, engagements planned, I thought I was busy. But now I see that it wasn't busy-ness, it was momentum left over from the full years when I had really lived at a center of things, it was habit.

Is it only anger that prompts me to write that? No. No, it's more like caution. Dr. What's-his-name—poor man, what *is* his name!—Dr. Savage said three weeks. Very well. Three weeks.

In three weeks I may have to begin filling up my life again with the circumscribed artificial diligence of the crippled. But I'll wait (with the taste of anger and despair in my mouth, it's a coppery taste), I'll wait three weeks. And every day will conspire to teach me resignation. Must I learn it? Must I? Be thankful for casual visitors and a jaunt in a wheel chair, a decorous drive and tea, at the end of it, with another old pussy? I, who have never been resigned in my life?

What has the past to say? Let me consult the blank page, the empty crystal ball. Let it fill with the smoke and storm of living.

At eleven, then, I first looked about me and saw the world, but it took me two years to act upon it. At thirteen I changed my name.

My father was more upset than my mother at this gesture, although it was my mother's mother that I'd been named for. Gertrude Burney Cummings, that was my name. I abandoned this unattractive persona the summer before I entered high school.

My mother, as I say, was quite unperturbed. This seems to me now remarkable, even though I have known for some time that she was a remarkable woman. She explained it to my father as a childish fancy of a kind that she knew all about. I bristled at "childish," but she went on, smiling at both of us, to recall how she herself had had an imaginary companion and confidante for years and years. "Anna Mary Rosenkeeler," she said, "that was what I called her, and she went to school with me until I was nearly grown. Where do you suppose I got her name from? I can't think! Isn't it awful?"

"Diana isn't awful," I said stiffly. "It's pretty."

"You'll grow out of it," said my mother cheerfully.

"Oh!" I said angrily, and my father groaned.

"She's going to have a nice mess on her hands when she does grow out of it and wants to change back," he informed us. Being a lawyer, he thought of this kind of thing. "How's she to be registered at high school? As Gertrude or Diana? They'll want to see her birth certificate, I suppose."

"Why as Gertrude of course," said my mother. And so I was, but it made no difference. "I use my middle name," I said to teachers and principals and clerks and pupils alike, sacrificing the "Burney" ruthlessly. "I am called Diana." Some of them said "Oh?" sarcastically, and some of them said, "What a pretty name," but none of them said, "No, you're not, you're called Gertrude." And I have never been called Gertrude since.

How long ago that was, really! Much longer than any other fifty years. How different life was in those first years of the century! Why we even *felt* differently, physically, I mean, our ancient sense of touch has changed. We were swaddled in clothes then, camisoles and petticoats and long drawers down to our ankles in winter with cotton stockings pulled over them, skirts hung from the shoulders on waists, middy blouses with dickeys in front to cover our skin to the neck, and over it all, flowing down our backs—hair. Hair that had to be brushed and braided or brushed into curls or just brushed.

There was actually an article of clothing, a kind of petticoat for babies and small children, called a "gertrude." As I recall, they were apt to be made of flannel and embroidered.

After clothes, we were swaddled in people. Not only did visiting Burneys descend upon us for Christmas, we in turn visited cousins, aunts, family friends. A holiday at the shore meant a stay with fat Aunt Carolyn and Uncle Paul and corned beef and cabbage which we never ate any other time. The mountains were always Grandma Cummings's mountains in Vermont. At home entertainment meant playing parlor games en masse, complicated ones with paper and pencil, or card games like Hearts and Old Maid. Mary and I were expected to walk to school together and, besides, to call for the Browning girls on the way. Going to church we called for the Filleys, the Brownings were Lutheran.

I can almost smell that life, recreating it, and any number of household objects float into my mind—Boston ferns in brass pots, rose Canton china in a glass-fronted cabinet, a horsehair sofa at one aunt's house that prickled the backs of my knees in summer when I was allowed to wear short socks, a velvet photograph album—and boredom, boredom, boredom! Boredom so acute it was like a disease. Even now in this terrible place, I've not been so bored as I was in my youth, bored as a steady diet, bored day in and day out with everyone and everything, all the too many objects and the too close friends and the too frequent visitors, and everything done together in a ritual chorus with no solo parts. If I write another word about it, I'll be bored again, so I shall just cry—Down with Togetherness!—and go on to point out that this wasn't peculiar to our family or the result of anything that anyone did. It was the way things were.

In fact, my parents were themselves individualists and loved and trusted us as individuals too. Though my father believed in rules as a lawyer must, he still felt that the ultimate sanction for any rule lay in the individual heart. My mother was addicted, almost guiltily, to the pleasures of solitude. She was capable of walking about the house for days with a book in her hand and falling into it at any lull in the conversation as an alcoholic falls into drink. But this made no difference to our communal upbringing. My mother fought her desire to be alone, she would put down her book and play parcheesi in the middle of a sentence. Whenever she remembered (and she tried hard to remember) she'd ask me where I was going or where I'd been, with whom, what they had worn, what we had eaten, if I'd asked Mrs. This how her married daughter Alice That liked living in Trenton——

Poor darling, she couldn't have wanted to know any more than I wanted to tell her, I can see that now. She was training me: this was the way women had to live, crocheting these odds and ends into a pattern of life. She wanted me to know how, to learn early, to do it instinctively because it was easier that way. I thought at the time she wanted me to like it, to be resigned. I know better now, she didn't, a little bit of her was never resigned, but I didn't know it then, and I was unkind to her. She bore it well, very well. She loved me, she understood how I felt, she sympathized. But everything she had been taught told her that we were both wrong, and that it was her duty to teach, and mine to learn, the conventional duties of women.

We didn't make a very good job of it, I'm afraid. I remember one particularly furious exit of mine from some games-playing session when, swaddled and hampered and pin-pricked into rebellion, I stalked from the parlor crying, "I am going to my room to *pray!*" which did at least gain me privacy. When I got there I paced up and down like a cat in a cage. Escape, I thought, escape! I thought of it all the time, it ran like an underground river beneath everything I did and said and thought. Everything I heard or read was related to it. Everyone I met was judged in its terms: Had they escaped, or had they settled down to stodge through life in the most familiar groove?

And yet, you know, I had no vision of where I was going to escape to. Those were still the years of the Dollar Princesses, and of Graustarkian romances. I wasn't interested, I thought such things terribly tawdry. I didn't want to marry the Duke of Marlborough or Rupert of Hentzau, no not I! In fact, I didn't want to marry anybody, I wanted to *be* somebody. My heart, swelling within my bosom, my eyes, searching the skies for portents, all my furious hidden self, was determined to get out, but to get out by myself, and to become the biggest, the best, the most brilliant and famous—— What? I didn't know.

I only knew that I didn't belong where I was.

It was hardly a secret! Years later my mother and I spoke a little of that time, and my memories shifted and turned in a new distortion of perspective. She'd taken me to Hot Springs. I didn't mind, one place was like another to me just then. We were sitting under a tree beside the first tee of the golf course that hot afternoon, watching a family foursome tee off. "Oh dear," said my mother, under her breath, "that angry young girl! How she reminds me of you!"

She was a scrawny child with her hair cut like a boy's (this was 1929) and I can't say I was flattered at the comparison. And yet as she walked off there was something in her stride——

"You were always walking away from us," said my mother. "Just like that. Look at her shoulders. If anyone tries to catch her she'll go faster." She was quite right, the younger brother caught up for a minute and the girl at once increased her pace. My mother laughed. "I must have followed you down Sherman Avenue a thousand times if I've done it once. Sometimes I still dream of your back."

"I'm sorry I was difficult," I said.

"Difficult!" she repeated and paused, weighing the word. "Yes, you were difficult." She fanned herself gently, but she wasn't satisfied. "You were impossible!" she burst out. "There were days when I had all I could do to keep my temper, days when I really had to leave the room or I'd have—I'd have——"

"What?" I asked, beginning in spite of myself to feel a real interest in the conversation.

"Shaken you. Shaken you till your teeth rattled!" She laughed again and I managed a smile for, physically speaking, I could have picked her up and spanked *her* any time after I got my growth when I was twelve.

"Why didn't you?" I said, lifting the putter I'd brought out with me in order to look as if I had some purpose in life and sighting along it at two old gentlemen panting along the fairway on the slope across the road.

"Well," she said, ignoring physical possibilities, "I suppose I respected whatever it was that drove you. In a way I was proud of you, for wanting so much and not being satisfied. I didn't know what to do about it, but at least I knew that shaking you wouldn't help."

"I didn't know what to do about it myself," I said, staring back across the years at that raging greedy child—unresigned, unresigned. My nerves prickled a little and I shifted restlessly. How pain calls to pain and anger to anger! I can feel it now as I felt it then, how I clung to indifference, how uneasy I was.

Then she played her trump card. I wonder if she knew it? She was always a sly and unpredictable opponent at games, taking her unexpected tricks modestly when you could have sworn you had every one accounted for. "Your father," she said, "wanted to send you to college. But you remember that, of course."

I was flabbergasted. "Never!" I said, and now I was really awake and aware. "I never remember hearing one word about college! You're making it up."

"Diana," she said, "what are you talking about! Why, he wrote to several colleges, Vassar and Smith and that one down in Pennsylvania, and they sent what-you-may-call-thems, booklets——"

"Catalogues."

"Catalogues, yes, and you went through them with me——"

"Mother, I promise you I don't remember one iota of this!"

"Well," said my mother, "you did. And once when a Miss Knox—— Now, which college was she from? Well, it doesn't matter now. At any rate, she came to New York and I took you in to the city to meet her and talk about your going there. Don't you remember that? It was at some women's club, we had tea in a big room, it was late summer, I think, and everything slip-covered, there was no one else there——"

"My soul," I said, "yes I do. I remember. She was tall and bony and had hair like gray spinach under a net. I liked her. Her name wasn't Knox."

"It was Knox," said my mother positively.

"And she wanted to know what I was reading, and when I told her Homer, she said some of it in Greek. It astounded me. I had thought Greek was smooth and flowing and this was all Ks."

"Just think!" said my mother. "If you had gone to college, you would have learned Greek!" And there we sat, the Homestead rising behind us and the golf course shimmering in the heat, contemplating a lost future in which I would have known Greek. What a silly little memory to crack the shell of my indifference! But she'd managed it. Perhaps she's managed it again, I suppose it's not too late for me to learn Greek even now.

No, I'd better not joke. In three weeks, it might not be a joke. In three weeks a cripple might seriously consider the uses of study for passing the time. In three weeks.

I have never believed in a neat pattern of life, of getting what we pay for and paying for what we get. There's no coin to count the payment in, for one thing. And yet, I suppose you could say that for a long time I got more than I paid for, though it didn't seem so at the time. I thought I paid.

But now the currency has been devalued. I must pay almost everything for very little.

Or else learn to value that little more highly; which, I suppose, is resignation, what I started talking to myself about.

So I come round to where I began, and find the past as ambiguous as any sibyl. It will tell you the truth if you can understand the truth. I was difficult, I was impossible, I had to get out—— Well, they knew it! My mother was proud of my intransigeance, my father offered me an escape. And what thanks did they get from me, storming into my teens? I forgot, I never noticed, I had to be told twenty years later that their forethought and patience had existed at all. I buried the very memory of the help I refused, I made my own escapes—my tantrums, my solitary walks, the poetry I learned, and my new name, which made it all possible. For how could any Gertrude have done what I did, have broken so many bonds, pulled things apart and not cared? I never learned Greek, no; and I had more sense than to call myself by Diana's Greek name, for in our little town in Westchester

"Artemis" would have been a joke, too much for anyone. But Diana served me well, stalking alone through the wild woods with her hounds at her heel, her arrows ready. I was Diana.

What am I now? My God, what am I now?

Peter Savage, having turned past the gateposts where a small dignified sign said, "The Elms. Dr. Charles F. Rushmore," opened the driver's window of his battered black sedan and began to sing. His song was simple, the tune a mere series of thumps and bumps. "Oh, I will go and have a drink, Oh, I will go and have a drink," he sang, "Oh, I will go and have a drink, And spit right in their eye." He repeated this as he wound down the road to the state highway, and then added, "Oh, the old bitch and the young bitch, and the old bitch and the young bitch, the old bitch and the young bitch, I'll spit right in your eye." By the time he reached the stop sign, he had begun to feel better, and as he turned toward New Haven he reduced his song to a hum.

It would be a great pleasure to throw up the case, no doubt about it, and give the bitches back to Ingoldsby. Particularly if it was true that the old one already thought he was an ass. "Oh, Ingoldsby, oh, Ingoldsby, You bastard, Dr. Ingoldsby!" he roared suddenly, interrupting the comforting monotone of his hum. Dr. Ingoldsby was fifty-nine. He parted his hair in the middle. He gave the effect, like Herbert Hoover, of wearing a stiff collar. He lived in a well-to-do suburb of New Haven and often drove from there the half hour or so necessary to dine in Fairfield County, in the rich, rich suburbs of New York. When you called him at home whoever answered the phone said, "Dr. Ingoldsby's residence." Savage suspected that half the time this answer was given not by the maid but by Mrs. Ingoldsby. "You bastard, bastard Ingoldsby," he sang now, with gusto and refreshment.

Let Ingoldsby tell the old bitch he was going to operate, and that she would probably never be able to walk without a crutch. Savage had a clear and satisfying vision of Ingoldsby sitting on a chair by her bed with his fingers in his ears, while she let fly. Ten to one he wouldn't do the operation himself: it was a long and tedious one

that could have no dramatic success. The most it could do would be
to cripple her rather less than more. It was not the kind of operation
he liked to do, certainly not on a patient already distrustful. But
getting someone else in would not save him from having to listen to
the old bitch, nor his fingers in his ears from hearing—— Dr. Thing.
You and your clichés. Dr. What's-Your-Name. I don't want to look at
your face.

"The old bitch, the old bitch," he sang (it would drown out her
voice in time), "The old bitch and the young bitch, The old bitch
and the young bitch, I'll spit right in your eye. I'll give you Dr.
Ingoldsby, That pompous bastard Ingoldsby, You can have Dr.
Ingoldsby, And spit right in his eye. Oh, Ingoldsby, oh, Ingoldsby,
Da dum, da dum, da Ingoldsby, I hope you sprain his etiquette, And
ruffle his toupee. Da dum, da dum——"

There would be a good big fee for that operation.

He could trade in the car.

Johnny and Helen could each go to camp for a month. Maybe
they could even find someone Norma would trust with the others
and get a real vacation at the shore themselves, without any of the
kids. Which would be practically the first time that had happened
since their honeymoon.

The old bitch, the old bitch——

Ingoldsby deserves her.

Hell, he'll have her anyway, he won't let go of her no matter what
she calls him. If I get out he'll just get someone else, Donaldson,
maybe. Why should Donaldson have the dough?

Jesus, I could have killed her, though!

Well, that was nearly true. And being so, it broke through both
the argument and the song, and left him driving in silence, hoping
for a neon sign saying Bar and Grill. But he wasn't likely to find one
this side of the parkway.

She looked right at him and she took the lid off. She looked right
at him and what did she see? Not the doctor, the respectable professional man, but the slum kid out of Waterbury, the one who'd
changed his name, the French Canuck, born in Quebec. What's-
your-name, she had called him. The kid who'd sweated his way up
without any breaks and eight other Canuck kids in the family to hold
him back, who'd worked nights, worked summers, looked forward

to a Sunday afternoon off as if it was a trip to the Promised Land—
and then been beaten. Known himself beaten. Because he *had* been
beaten, and he'd given up. He wasn't any hero, any self-made man.
It was nice to think so, Norma thought so and he let her, but it
wasn't true. If it hadn't been for the war, he wouldn't have been a
doctor.

Jesus——

One year in Medical School and he'd given up. Between football
and driving a laundry truck he'd got through college, but they didn't
give you room and board and find you a job that paid twenty bucks
a week at Med. School. You worked. And if you worked nights,
weekends, vacations, at anything you could find—male nurse, assistant
to a vet (they gave him a room there but he couldn't say so for fear of
jokes), counter man in a diner, salesman of everything from awnings
to vacuum cleaners, punch press operator, pin boy, and half a hundred
more—if you worked like that to live, when did you work to learn?
One year in Medical School and he knew he couldn't get through
the second. And when he lifted his head that summer, after he'd
given up and got drunk and slept for a week, he heard the draft
coming. And he thought he'd beat it by enlisting, and they gave him
his choice because he did, and he picked the Navy—and the way he
got through Med. School was that the God damn Navy sent him.
Like a gentleman. Like an officer and a gentleman, because in spite of
the laundry truck he had a B.A. and that first year in Med. But not
like a hero, not like a self-made man.

He hadn't escaped from Waterbury and the wooden tenements
that smelled of rot, the privies in the back yards, the old woman
with the cataracts over both eyes who was his grandmother, his father
who dragged his left foot after the accident in the brass mill, his
mother who never learned English—— No. The Navy had rescued
him. On his own, he'd never have made it. On his own—he might be
a pharmacist, he might be managing a bowling alley, he might be
still selling vacuum cleaners or awnings, but the one thing he could be
absolutely certain of was that he wouldn't be Dr. Peter Savage.

It was a silly thing to think of and sweat over once you'd made it
and were safe in respectability, and he didn't think of it often, but
the old woman had really galled him today. And then the young
one—first she'd been all over the place with that la-de-da voice, telling

him his own business and then all of a sudden getting her feelings hurt because he'd answered her back without kowtowing—— Jesus! She was good-looking enough (too thin and too tall, though), but she was a rich bitch too. They thought they owned the earth, God damn it! Some time he'd like to show them! They thought they knew it all, and they were so God damn ignorant! Ingoldsby's rich patients— they made him sick. "You lousy bitch, you lousy bitch," he sang again in an angry rasp, "I'd like to get you into bed, I'd like to get you into bed, You lousy, lazy bitch. I'll lay you till you ask for more, I'll lay you till you ask for more, I'll lay you till you ask for more, you lazy, lousy bitch!"

Knowing he sounded like a juvenile delinquent, but knowing also that this old jog-trot tune had helped him to get through bad times since he'd been in grammar school, he sang variations on this theme for several miles. Some verses were more colorful than others, so colorful, indeed, that he found it wise to forget them as soon as he'd shouted them out at the passing scenery. But they took the froth off the top of his anger. By the time he was close enough to the city to find a bar he felt reasonably calm, and what he asked the bartender as he went in was not for a drink, but where the telephone was.

Among the messages from the answering service, however, was one to call Dr. Ingoldsby. God damn it! thought Savage. Did the old bitch call and kick about me so fast? Or could the young one have? Damnation. He stood staring at the wall in the booth for a minute and then opened the door, went to the bar, and ordered a double rye.

Ingoldsby.

Why did he get me in on this anyway? He knows I'm no Ivy League character from a Better Family.

Listen, Dr. Ingoldsby. I'm sorry my face and my presentation didn't send the old bitch, but I'm no soft-soap artist——

Yah, he knows that. The old bastard. He probably knows the number of the house I was born in, and that the cellar flooded every April, and that my name was Pierre Sauvage till third year of High. So what in hell am I doing farting around on the case anyway?

You can call up and find out.

Yeah, sure. Fat chance he'll give you the time of day.

The old bastard! I will call him up. Let's see which of them called him!

CHAPTER FOUR

He finished his drink in a gulp, went back to the booth and dialed.

"Dr. Ingoldsby's residence," said the thin female voice that answered, and Savage said it right along with her—but fortunately under his breath.

"Dr. Savage speaking," he said. "Dr. Ingoldsby called me. Is he there?"

"Oh—Dr. Savage. Just one moment, please. I'll see if Dr. Ingoldsby can speak."

"Tell him to send it in Morse if he can't," said Savage—but also under his breath. He waited, sweating a little, watching a girl with a pony tail playing the pinball machine. A skinny kid with luxuriant hair sat on a stool and watched her, holding two glasses of beer. The girl finished her game, gestured at her score, took her glass of beer and drank. The boy got off the stool and prepared to play. He drank from his glass, handed it to her, and she climbed onto the stool. She had nice hard little buttocks under her tight wool skirt.

"Savage?" said Dr. Ingoldsby's voice. "Ingoldsby here. How are you, my boy?"

Savage nearly dropped the phone. Then he clutched it tighter than ever. What's the old bastard up to? he thought. "Okay, thanks. You wanted me?"

"Yes. Are you at home, or the hospital?"

I'm in a booth in a bar with a whisky breath and more to come, Savage did not even whisper. "No sir. I stopped to pick up messages on the way back from a call, and yours was there. I thought I'd see——"

"Ah, that was thoughtful. Nothing urgent though. I thought I remembered that you were going out to Charlie Rushmore's this afternoon, and I wondered how the lady out there took the news. The news that there isn't any news, that is."

Now does that mean she called, or does it mean she didn't? Savage wondered. Well, ask him! said the whisky. "Did she call you?" he blurted out.

"Call me? Why no." Savage could have kicked himself. "Was she going to call me?"

"I—I'm really not sure just what she was going to do. I thought she might have."

"Oh?" Ingoldsby waited.

Savage waited too, but it wasn't any good. He knew the old bastard could outwait him. God damn it! "I'm afraid she didn't take the news too well," he said stonily. You sure have your ass in a sling, he added to himself, and nobody put it there but you!

"Well, it's too bad," said Ingoldsby. "I should have warned you. I just hoped perhaps—— But that's our Mrs. Belchamber, I'm afraid. I'm sure you did everything you could."

Having taken the words of justification out of Savage's mouth, he waited again.

Savage chewed his lip. If he told Ingoldsby now he wanted to get off the case, it would sound as if he'd bungled things so badly that he had to get out. "She has a temper, I guess," he said cautiously.

Ingoldsby laughed. His laugh was always a little shrill. "She really blew you up, did she?" he asked.

"You might say that," said Savage, sweating.

"Well, now you've been blown up by an expert. You got the point across, though? That we want to wait a bit?"

"I hope so."

"Hm."

"Oh, she understands. It was just—well, the wheel-chair idea threw her a bit, I guess."

"I suppose it did. Well, if you'd ridden to hounds with the best hunt in England and shown jumpers in the Garden, it might upset you too."

It would upset me if I'd only raised a family of nine kids, like my mother, Savage thought but managed not to say. "Did she really," he brought out instead.

"She did, she did," Ingoldsby caroled, apparently taking Savage's interest for granted. "She was just going south last winter when this happened, had one of the horses out for a last canter before she went off to Hobe Sound when bango! there she was with a broken hip. It's sad, Savage, an active woman like that, years still before her, very sad. She has a tongue, I know she has a tongue, but still it's very sad."

"Yeah. Yes it is. It's always a shame when someone has to quit."

"I'm so glad you see it that way. It's generous of you, my boy. She was a beauty, you know, great beauty. Still attractive, I'd say, even at her age."

Since she was just two years older than Ingoldsby, Savage choked a little at this. Indeed, the idea of Ingoldsby as a connoisseur of women was funny to begin with. However, he managed to say, "Yes indeed."

"Glad you think so. Never know about you young fellows, what style you prefer. But she really was a stunner, they tell me. Another reason why the wheel chair can't be too welcome. Ah well. I'm very sorry she put you through it today, and it was remiss of me not to suggest that she might. I'm afraid I was just too optimistic. She put us all through it when she first came in, you know—Littell, too. Why, the air was blue! But she's been a good girl lately, and I hoped that perhaps that first time was all we'd have to face. It won't last long, though. I'll go out in a day or two and pick up the pieces, mend the fences. By next week, when you might run out again (we ought to have some more plates then), she'll be entirely over it, I'm sure, entirely over it. Be as sweet as sugar, I expect."

So now, Savage asked himself, how could he say he wouldn't go out next week or any week? Without seeming like a sulky kid, or a hopeless bungler? He chewed his lip, he glared at the girl with the pony tail (who didn't notice), he glared at the narrow back of her young man, twisted into a scoliosis curve as he bent over the pinball machine, but all he could do was rumble with useless resentment, "That will be a pleasant change."

Ingoldsby laughed delightedly, as if this were the wittiest thing he'd heard in weeks. "Now, now! Now, now!" he said. "Leave that to the patient! Seriously, Savage, I'm very grateful to you, very grateful to you indeed. And I do apologize for the old dear. Believe it or not, she can be an old dear. I'm really very attached to her. I admit she takes a little getting used to, but she's not at all an unintelligent woman, you know, very stimulating mind, very stimulating indeed. I appreciate your bearing the brunt of this today, I really do. Between the two of us, I'm pretty sure we can handle her—keep her happy, that is, as well as see that she gets the treatment she needs. I know I can depend on you for that! In fact, Savage, I should say that I feel very secure with you, very secure, and I want you to know it. Don't pay any attention to this little blowup, there's a dear fellow. I'll call you after I've seen her again, and we'll chat. Thank you, thank you, good-by!" And he was gone, vanished as if he really were the pixie he sounded like.

"You son of a bitch," said Savage, with deep conviction, into the telephone. "You old bugger. You prize, prime, super-bastard." And, adding a few remembered French-Canadian expressions of which his father had been fond, he hung up, went back to the bar, and ordered another double rye.

Because he could see now why Dr. Ingoldsby had decided to use a slum boy from Waterbury as a consultant to his rich, cranky patients: he was such a contrast to gentlemanly Dr. Ingoldsby. Even the crankiest, even the touchiest, even an opinionated old shrew who already thought Ingoldsby an ass, was unlikely to be wooed away by the slum boy. If he was a little rough, a little crude, a little clumsy, Dr. Ingoldsby profited by the comparison. He came along after the slum boy and picked up the pieces, mended the fences. In fact, Dr. Ingoldsby had sounded distinctly pleased to hear that his patient had blown up at his colleague, it made him feel secure. No wonder! Dr. Ingoldsby would now smooth things over. He would refer to his colleague, no doubt, as a rough diamond: "A bit of a rough diamond, but a dear boy, really——" and the rough diamond was not likely to charm any of Dr. Ingoldsby's rich patients away.

Neither would he be likely to pick up many rich patients of his own. He would always be glad, therefore, to have this nice little supplemental income by grace of Dr. Ingoldsby. He'd be willing to take the rough side of an old woman's tongue. He'd be very useful.

Looking down into his glass as if it mirrored the future, Savage saw himself as Ingoldsby's dear boy, called in, brains picked, crudities excused, facing a certain kind of humiliation over and over again. He took a good long look at it and he didn't like it at all. There were names for that kind of thing: kowtowing to the old bastard, listening to his chirps, invited to dinner, no doubt, communing with Mrs. Ingoldsby—— Jesus! They weren't pretty names. He knew them in English, he knew them in patois, he knew them in Navy-pidgin.

And then he finished his drink and had another think, standing and looking at himself in the spotted mirror back of the bar, and that came out somewhere else.

Who in hell do you think you are? he said to the face that looked back. You're up out of Waterbury. You've got one brother in the mills and another dead in a gutter, run over drunk. You've got one, and a sister, you know better than to ask about. Who in hell are you to pick and choose and retch about kowtowing to Ingoldsby? Let the boys who got sent to Yale and Harvard and Columbia and Cornell, all expenses paid, let them feel so God damn delicate. You ever notice any of them turning down a fee? Who in hell are you, you God damn fool? If that old bastard wants to give you some fees, you take his dirty fees!

And remember this, kid, when he asks you to dinner. Thirty years ago you didn't know a house as grand as his existed. You'd never seen one. Twenty years ago, driving that laundry truck at college, you'd have been lucky if his cook gave you a cup of coffee. Ten years ago you married a pretty Irish girl, and now you've got five kids. You're going to turn down fees, you stupid son of a bitch? Like hell you are! You're going to take what you have to take, and like it. That's what you're going to do.

And now you're going to pay for your drinks and go home to dinner and behave yourself. Norma doesn't like you to drink, and Norma's damn well right. You go home and behave yourself and try to learn when you're well off. Suppose you put in some time saying "Yes, Mrs. Belchamber, no, Mrs. Belchamber. Yes, Dr. Ingoldsby, no, Dr. Ingoldsby." Suppose you're not going to get the niece to bed and show them all, nor spit in anybody's eye? You're going to get paid for it, kid, you're going to get paid for it. Just remember that.

Only he's going to have to pay me enough, the old bastard. He's not going to get me cheap. If dough's all I'm going to get, I'm going to get plenty!

CHAPTER

5

The dream held her like a vise. It had total meaning: to be saved, one had to get down to the river. But to do that, it was necessary to come out in the open and cross a hundred yards or so of gravel and shale. It would have to be done fast, before——

No. The light was faded. It seemed to come from very far away, farther than the sun, but it was clear. There was no doubt that any movement away from the swelling red-earth escarpment would be seen.

Run. Run to be saved. Run to the river.

No. Menace. Don't move. Slink back.

Danger soon here. Only a question of time before eyes look over the edge of the bluff.

Danger certain there! Movement means target.

Run.

Don't move.

Menace swelled up, it was crushing, no room to breathe——

Lorraine opened her eyes. For a moment, between dream and waking, that empty blasted landscape hung clear before her: another time, or another planet, but all as clear as memory, the bluff at her back, the empty desert running down to the life-giving, unattainable river——

You are a dream, she said to it. But she was still shaking with terror. I know you, she said, you have nothing to do with me. You are a picture in an old book. Where? I will remember, you will vanish. Yes. Central Asia. Alexander's legions mutinied, there were horsemen in the hills, with bows, who picked them off. You are just an old story, read years ago in an old book, when I was a child. You have nothing to do with me.

She shut her eyes again, determined to think herself back to reality, out of the dream. It's morning, she told herself, still early but morning and soon I will get up, with errands to do and all the everyday things to see to——

But reality shimmered. The dream of the desert still wavered behind it, the terror of emptiness that was not empty, where alien eyes watched. The desert—— She gathered her poor scraps of courage, she tried to face it rationally, saying, That story always frightened me. Why that one, I wonder? Running before men on horses. Alone in the desert to be hunted. Running like a chicken over dry earth and pebbles that scattered under your feet, falling, your face stinging, bleeding, getting up and running, the arrow past your head twanging, bouncing, skittering on the ground before you——

Stop it! Eyes open, she stared round the room. Reason failed. The dream was too strong. It was all around her, even here. The desert, the desert, and an enemy concealed: terror bled out of it into the present, the meaning spoke from the dream and was here, was now, was yesterday—— She saw again the angry doctor last night, staring up at her; felt again the barrier that cut her off from him, from everyone. For a moment, it had given her strength. Last night, touching bottom, she had felt almost proud to be alone in the desert, inhuman, different, and resigned to the difference. But now, staring at this familiar room where she lived so much of her life, she was proud no longer. The dream had come to warn her. It had succeeded. She was terrified.

What am I to do? she thought. I'm clumsy, alone, frightened. If I can't be resigned to it, what shall I do? I was clumsy and stupid with the doctor. Aunt Di is an invalid, and yet I get from her more than I give. I was frightened when her door was shut and she didn't answer me, and she was only taking a nap. I was so angry at the young men in the sport car who wanted to pass me that I raced them and almost got all of us into an accident. Everything I did yesterday was wrong! So I decided that I must try to do nothing.

But the dream says *that* is wrong. The dream says that to retreat to the desert is to be hunted and frightened.

Then what am I to do? The question opened like an abyss at her feet. What am I to do? To have to act, and not to be able to—— She felt torn in two.

Begin to live, said a voice. It rang in her head, it astonished her so that she almost didn't hear what it said.

Then automatically she answered its echo: But I don't know how! When I try, I go wrong. Don't I? Don't I?

The voice was silent. It had spoken once, in the back of her head, like a bell tolling one solemn note. It was not the usual fretful voice that argued and nagged, her boring, exasperating, inept second self. She knew *that* Lorraine too well. This was something new. Begin to live, it had said—and gone.

How can I? she thought hopelessly. And yet—— No, it was not quite hopeless. For the dream and the desert had vanished in the second that the voice spoke. She was alone, she was suddenly conscious of exhaustion as if she had been only pretending to sleep all night, suspended in a hammock of anguished nerves, but she was really here, in her room, in her life. She was her single self.

As she had not been, she felt suddenly, for years. There was that young girl whom she had remembered yesterday, leaning out of a window into the future. *She* had been single, facing a hundred choices, a thousand chances. *She* had wanted to begin to live. What had happened to her? How had she got mixed up, frightened, divided, lost in the desert? Last night she had tried to resign herself to being lost. This morning, waked with nightmare barring the road.

Begin to live, said the voice, far away now, fainter. Not a command, thought Lorraine. A chance, perhaps? Could I? Could I not be afraid, could I dive through my fear and swim in life? Find not desert but the river—— She was drifting again toward sleep, so tired now, but for once not frightened, not divided. The early morning light wavered. The city turned in its sleep, plagued by fear and desolation, hugging warmth and riches to its breast. The lonely ones began to get up, made coffee, stared in the bathroom mirror at the familiar unlucky face, vowed to start again, vowed resignation, vowed to bear or not to bear what was unbearable. Far away a siren cried. In the other bed Herbert sighed and snored and turned over. The curtains blew, the light moved on the ceiling in slanting silver bars. There was no more desert, the curtains blew like a curtain of rain, soft rain, here— where? Somewhere there were parrots, parrots flying through warm rain, absurd, and those foolish birds whose beaks are too big for them. They flew awkwardly, holding their heads too high, to balance the beaks. Someone she knew swam that way, head held awkwardly, too high—— Herbert swam, the toucans (yes, toucans) flew, for two can play at that game, the curtain of silver rain wavered forward and covered her gently with a promise of green, and she slept again.

"Are you all right?" said Herbert at breakfast, folding the *Times*, ready to stand up, go, begin his day.

"Why yes," said Lorraine without thinking. Then she looked at him. Why did he ask that? "I didn't sleep too well," she said, scrupulously.

"I'm sorry." But it didn't seem to be what he had wanted to know.

"Oh, it's all right. I—had a bad dream, it woke me. But I went back to sleep."

"We had to rush so last night I didn't have time to ask about your aunt. Is she all right?"

Oh dear, she thought, that's it, there's another thing I did wrong yesterday. The Millers had to wait dinner for us. "I'm sorry I was late. The—— It was that, you see. The doctor came in when I was there. I don't really know." She heard the clumsy words with annoyance but could not stop them.

Herbert looked at her patiently. "My dear," he said, "no one on earth could know anything from that series of phrases. Start over again. You were late getting home because the doctor came to see your aunt while you were there. Is that right?"

"I was just leaving." She smoothed her hair back nervously.

"Yes?"

"He had some X-rays. They may operate. On her hip."

"I didn't think they'd operate on her elbow. I'm sorry to hear it, very sorry. When do they plan it?"

"They aren't sure. Aren't sure they're going to do it, even. They want to take X-rays some more and watch it a while."

"Good heavens, they've been watching it for three months! Why can't they make up their minds?"

"This is a new doctor."

"Oh? What happened to old Thingummy, Ingoldsby?"

"This man's working with him. He's on the Yale faculty."

"What's his name?"

"Oh dear. She introduced us. Doctor, Doctor—— I'm sorry. I don't remember."

"My dear child!"

"I'm sorry, I was upset. About her, I mean."

"I know what you mean, and I sympathize, but I can only say it wasn't very sensible to be so upset you didn't get the fellow's name. If it's in his hands now, I'd like to have some way of checking on him."

In the dining room, which looked east over Park Avenue and enjoyed the morning sun, the curtains blew and the light shifted on the ceiling. Lorraine thought, I am frightened again. I got free for a moment and now I am frightened. I can go on being frightened, I can stammer and say things wrong and make myself stupid. Or—— Or I can try to stop. I can stop. She took a breath. She looked at Herbert. She thought, I must begin sometime, and said, "It was silly of me. But I want to talk to her today, anyway, and I'll get his name for you."

Herbert blinked. "Yes, do that. How is she otherwise?"

"Very well." Inside Lorraine something laughed, crowed, clapped its hands. What a tiny triumph! she told herself sternly. Nevertheless, it was a beginning. She had looked at fear and dived through it. Fear had once been a wave on the south shore at Nantucket when she was nine and she had dived through it and been triumphant—— "She would like to talk to you about the stock market."

"Oh?"

"Yes. At any rate, she asked me what you thought and I didn't know, so——"

"I know very well you don't know. I'm sorry. Go on."

"So I said you would call her and chat."

"I'll be delighted." He sat on, though five minutes ago he had been ready to leave. He was studying her.

She thought, This is no time to be frightened. I did it. I began. This is a time to relax and be calm. But his look was disturbing. He had felt it, he had noticed something new. She had dived safely through fear and he had seen—— A new fear, icy, touched her. "More coffee?" she said quickly.

"Please," said Herbert.

Lorraine pushed the buzzer. In a moment a maid appeared. "More coffee for Mr. de Koning, please, Norah," said Lorraine. The maid took his cup and went out.

"Don't we have a coffeepot?" asked Herbert.

Lorraine stared at him. "Of course we have a coffeepot. How do you suppose they make——"

"No, I mean a silver one. She should put the coffee in, and bring it in."

"It wouldn't stay hot."

"She could put it in when you rang."

"It would take longer. Besides——"

"It would look better."

"Besides it's a nuisance to keep it clean——"

"And naturally you don't want them to work at anything. Let them pour it in the kitchen, it saves them steps. It's a wonder they don't serve the plates out there like a boardinghouse." I know what he is doing, thought Lorraine, and I must stop it somehow. But the fear had risen. It froze her—and he wanted it to.

Norah came back with his cup and set it down. Herbert lifted it. There was a ring of coffee in the saucer. "Take this back, please," he said. "You've spilled it."

"I'm sorry, Mr. de Koning. One minute and I'll wipe it——"

"No you won't wipe it. Take it outside. Get a clean cup and saucer. Fill the clean cup with fresh coffee. Bring it in, if you can, without spilling it."

"Yes sir."

"Mrs. de Koning will tell you how she wishes coffee served in the future."

"Yes sir." She took the cup and went to the pantry door. "It will take ten minutes to make fresh coffee, sir." She started through.

Herbert swung around in his chair. "What does that mean?" he said.

"Fresh coffee. You said to fill it with fresh coffee." Norah's face was quite expressionless, but she had dropped the "sir."

Lorraine made herself speak. "Mr. de Koning didn't mean a fresh pot of coffee, Norah. He just meant another cup out of the first, out of what's already made."

"I'm afraid there isn't any more out of what's already made, madam. This was the last."

After a tiny pause Lorraine said, "Then make another pot at once, please. Thank you."

When she had gone Herbert said, "Surely there must be pots large enough to make sufficient coffee for breakfast for two, and a bit over. Perhaps you could order one."

"It's an eight-cup pot that I have," said Lorraine. "They drink it too, you know."

"Indeed they must."

"I'll see they make more tomorrow."

"Thank you."

Lorraine shut her eyes. A tempest in a coffeepot, she wanted to say, but the fear had reached her heart. Act—but she could not act. Begin—but her new will was paralyzed. If she could only distract Herbert, she might gain a moment to catch her breath, harden her resolve. She forced herself to smile at him, to ask, "Who are the Armenians who were at the Millers' last night? What was their name, Evepian? He was very interesting, I thought, he told me reams of Armenian history."

"Azepian is the name. You wouldn't have trouble with names if you'd concentrate more while you're being introduced."

"I'll try."

"He's with one of the Swiss banks."

"Oh really? I thought they lived in Cairo."

"He left, naturally, when Nasser took over."

"I see. Did you know that Mount Ararat is in Armenia? I didn't. I always thought it was in the Sinai Peninsula. Did you know that Armenian is an Indo-European language just as much as English?"

"I'm glad that for once you found someone who interested you. Usually you sit like a statue and say Yes or No."

"I should think anyone would be interested in Armenian history."

"Even you."

She smiled again. She had to. "Yes, even me. You must admit, Herbert, that some of the wives are hard to take. All they talk about is where to get clothes, or who's been seen with whom, or where to go for a holiday, or where not to. We spent forty minutes on Peter Townsend and Margaret last night, and forty on how spoiled and dreadful Ischia is now, only movie people go there, and where to get blouses in Rome—— Ugh!"

"If it bored you, why didn't you introduce another subject?"

She looked down into her own coffee cup. There was a swallow left and she drank it.

"I'm serious," said Herbert. "You complain about being bored. Very well. Talk yourself. Talk about something that interests you, do it well enough, and others will be glad to listen. You could have gone on talking about Armenian history to Mrs. Azepian, couldn't you?"

"I'd have been stranded like the Ark on Ararat. She could barely speak English."

"You used to speak perfectly reasonable French. Why didn't you try that on her?"

She bent her head. Empty cup, empty plate with a crust of toast, half-used pat of butter. Desolation, symbols of the desert and defeat. "I don't know, Herbert."

"Maybe you don't, but I do. You won't be bothered, that's why. That's why there isn't enough coffee, it's why you can't remember names, it's why Bobby was rude, last Sunday, when I wanted to take him out. It's why going anywhere with you is——" he stopped.

She knew what he looked like. The muscles in his jaw stood out with the effort of stopping himself. She didn't have to look. She didn't have to ask him to finish the sentence. She knew. Tears came up in her eyes, hopeless, helpless tears. She clenched her teeth, she stared at her empty cup, her empty plate, her crumpled napkin, willing herself not to let them fall.

"So now you're crying," he said.

"I'm sorry. I'm not," she managed to say.

"Oh for God's sake! What difference does it make whether you are or not? You will be, in a minute, if you aren't yet. I can't talk to you—not about yourself and the mess you make of things, not about my work, not even about the people I introduce you to. Interesting people, I would have thought, with more to talk about than Mount Ararat or Armenian history. Armenian history! He was in Cairo when Nasser and Naguib threw Farouk out, if you want to talk about history! All right, some of the wives are dull. Who do you think you are? Queen Elizabeth?"

Her hands were shaking so that she had to catch them up to her breast. *I will not cry!* she said to herself. But to stop the tears she almost had to stop breathing, she had to clench herself together and huddle, she couldn't speak.

"What do I do to you?" said Herbert. "Look at you. You'd think I'd whipped you! I only suggested you'd find your life more fun if you made an effort to meet people halfway. What's wrong with that? It's true, isn't it?"

"Yes, Herbert, it's true," she whispered. Two tears escaped and ran down her cheeks.

"Here come the tears," said Herbert. He stood up. "Well, it's a delightful way to begin the day, hysterics at breakfast. It's a great send-off."

"I don't—mean to——"

He waited. "Mean to what?"

"To do this. I hate it."

"I don't exactly enjoy it." He stood at the end of the table. She could feel his eyes on her. His look had a palpable weight—weight of menace. It reared above like a wave, she *must* go through it, but she could not lift her eyes—— You must, you must, she told herself. Herbert. Herbert, my husband, who loves me—— She forced her head up, she met his eyes. He said, "Should you go to an analyst?"

She could not speak.

"For Christ's sake! I don't mean you're crazy! But if you have hysterics at breakfast when I ask you why you get bored——"

She was trembling all over. She got up and put her napkin on the table. She went blundering out of the dining room. "Lorraine!" said Herbert behind her.

She went with all swiftness through the bedroom and into the bathroom because it had a lock on the door. She locked it. Herbert was just behind her. He knocked. "Lorraine!"

She was panting as if she'd been running. She didn't answer.

"For God's sake, Lorraine! Open the door! My God! There are three servants in this apartment! Open it! What are they going to think? Do you want the children to see you in this condition? Or to see me banging at a locked door? Open it!"

The children. Lorraine could feel her heart clenching and clenching and clenching——

"Lorraine, please! Look, I'm sorry, dear, I didn't mean to upset you!"

"It's all right," she managed to say.

"What?"

"It's all right. Give me a minute. I'll open the door." Another breath. Another. She forced herself to turn, to unlock the door, to open it, to face him. He was very white. They stared at each other unbelievingly for a moment: two strangers, meeting on a road, who had known each other well long, long ago. How gray his hair has turned, thought Lorraine.

"Lorraine—— Darling——" he said, and took her in his arms.

She clung to him. Herbert. Reality. Wasn't he all she had of reality? She was breathing in gasps still.

"My poor darling," he said. "Don't shake so! I'm sorry, I'm sorry! Please stop, dear, please stop! There, there!"

"You were against me," she said. "You wanted to frighten me."

"No, no, never! You misunderstood! I want to help you. I'm not against you, you mustn't think like that! I want to help!"

She clung to him, longing to believe him; she wanted to tell him how badly she needed help, how she was lost and alone in the desert, how she knew it and was desperate to find her way out—— No. Analyst. He would repeat the word. She could not trust him. Before he had called her "darling" he had worried about the servants. They were in each other's arms, his voice was hoarse with emotion, she had reached the end of her rope—— She could not trust him! He had felt her attempt at courage, and had at once tried to break her. If she knew anything at all, if she was in any state except that where an analyst was a last-ditch hope, she knew that.

Coldly, calculatingly, slyly, she released herself from his embrace. "I'm so sorry," she said. "This is terrible! You'll be late."

"I don't care about that!" he said. She weighed his tone, it was over-vehement. "What I care about is you. I want you to be—all right."

The sad and universal cry, she thought. But he is lying. "Yes, Herbert."

"Will you think about what I said?"

She looked over his shoulder. He wanted her to meet his eyes, he wanted her gaze to be impressed by his, he wanted her to submit. He had always wanted this, she saw. Poor Herbert! she thought, surveying him with impartial clarity. It's little enough he wants! If only I had loved him, I might have done it. But I don't. What a strange way to find it out! What a strange time! For there, in the doorway, was Norah, carrying a cup of coffee. "Here is your coffee," said Lorraine. "Put it down there, Norah. Thank you."

Now it was Herbert who stood frozen with anger, embarrassment, resentment on his face. I suppose it will touch me again, thought Lorraine, that I will be frightened. This is like last night, I am touching bottom again. But at the moment she had the strength of despair. Norah left. Herbert swung around, saw the empty doorway, went over to his bureau and began to brush his hair hard.

He said, as he put the brushes down, "I'm late."

"I know," she agreed.

"I don't want coffee now."

"All right."

"You didn't answer me."

"Didn't I? What did you ask me?"

"I—asked you to think about what I said." He was watching her in the mirror, but he did not turn around.

She looked back at his reflection. "I'll think about everything," she said.

"Do that." Only then did he turn and face her. But she was able to look back expressionlessly thinking, My enemy; thinking, My husband. Herbert, my enemy.

He made an inarticulate sound, came over and kissed her cheek, and went out.

When enough time had passed for her to be sure that he had left the apartment, she went and got the cup from where Norah had left it, sat down at her dressing table, and slowly, thoughtfully, began to drink the coffee.

CHAPTER

6

For indeed she did have to think. She had reached some kind of turning point, and she knew it. Despair gave her this moment of curious calm, but even she was aware that there was something odd about it. Herbert had said "analyst," and perhaps Herbert was right. If she could not find her own way out of the desert, if she could not manage herself, if she could not begin to live and grow whole—then Herbert would be right. She would never be whole unless she was taken apart, like a stopped clock, mended and put back together by other hands than her own.

Who am I? she thought. What am I? staring at the coffee cup on the dressing table as if it were a crystal ball. What has happened, how did I get here? Everything around her seemed alien, the room where she had slept for six years, since Bobby was born and they had moved to this larger apartment, her own face in the mirror. She felt no attachment to anything here—nor to anywhere else. Since her father's death two years ago there had been nowhere on earth that she could mean when she said the word "home." Unless she meant this room, this apartment, this marriage; out of which, here, this morning, Herbert had said "analyst."

She gripped the edge of the dressing table. It was going to begin. Something was going to happen. A wave, *the* wave of terror was rising behind her. She wanted to scream. She wanted to shut her eyes——

You will not! she said to herself, and fixed her gaze on the white, set face looking back at her from the mirror. You will not be a coward any longer. You will face it, whatever it is, hang on, look at it. You will face fear. Face the desert. Face the enemy.

And stared at her own face.

The wave rose. The voices began. You are afraid of life, said one. Afraid of people. Afraid to mix with them, test yourself against them.

Afraid to compete with them and be beaten. Afraid to compete with them and win. Afraid they will hate you and threaten you.

You are afraid of love. Afraid of people. Afraid to mix with them and love them and give yourself to them, afraid to give yourself away and be betrayed. Why are you so afraid?

Herbert—she tried to answer. But it was her own face she saw. The waves reared higher, nearer. Who are you afraid of? said the voice. She wanted to shut her eyes again and submit, but she made herself hang on, wait, listen—just another minute, another second, just this moment, wait, wait—— Courage was a word she'd forgotten, but she made herself wait.

You are afraid of yourself, said the voice, and the wave broke over her and everything shouted together inside her head. You, you, you, frighten yourself! You, you, you, make the desert! You, you, you, choose to be clumsy, choose to be stupid, choose to be frightened! You are your enemy and the eyes in the desert that hate and betray you. You, you, you——

She clutched the table, she faced the truth at last. The enemy stared at her watchfully from the mirror. This was her betrayer, this hysterical creature who asked to be bullied, who stammered and stuttered and mopped and mowed, clumsy, clowning—— The Murderee, she named her suddenly; and felt terror lift a little from her heart as if, by defining and naming the enemy within, she had gained at least a little power over her. It was the Murderee who mocked at all resolutions and good intentions, who put the wrong thing to say in her mouth and stifled the right one. It was the Murderee, afraid and provocative at once, who hated the world and asked to be punished by it to justify her hate. This was the enemy with whom she had struggled!

And this was the enemy who now, caught in the grip of the wave, pulled her down into its buffeting. Falling through nightmare, she knew this chaos for the world of the Murderee, a world where every nerve, every cell, lived in constant dread, where a frightened creature, feeling herself defenseless, gibbered, huddled, or struck out blindly at the surrounding threats for nothing surrounded her but threats. She had been here before, in terrible dreams; but now it was true. This, this was the Murderee, this was her full power, this was the destruction which had crippled Lorraine and blasted the world around her, which by a great effort she had kept locked away. No more, no more! For once, she was free. As Lorraine saw and named her enemy at last, the bonds broke, the power within reared up, tore loose, and took shaking, wrenching, paralyzing control.

Nothing happened, and everything happened. The pact of sacrifice, sustained through the unlived years, dissolved. The creature was free, the creature was herself, it claimed her and was claimed. Torn apart and remarried, she was flooded by the invasion of her secret self.

When Lorraine found herself once more, she was staring again in the mirror. The same face looked back. And yet, it would never be the same face again. This was a face that had seen under the neat, careful cover of sanity into the burning, incoherent, insatiable rage of desire out of which humanity had dragged itself; and seen that it still existed. The cruelty, desire and rage so frighteningly loose in the world—Herbert at breakfast, her furious aunt, the angry doctor—they were matched by her own desire, her greed, her fury and lust for power, her cruelty and callousness. It was there underneath. It had flamed up into consciousness from the old, cold caverns where it flickered, and it could never be forgotten, nor its mark wiped out. This is I, said Lorraine to that white, unchanged, but forever changed face. This is what I am.

The wave had passed over, it ebbed, she had gone through it, faced fear, she knew her enemy. But what good had it done? Here she was, beached on the shore of life, caught in her own trap, for how could she get free of herself? She looked away from the mirror, she stretched out her hand. Yes, it was hers. It wore her ring. This was herself, her room, her home. The little square gold and glass traveling clock that had been her grandmother's struck ten.

What a queer time to die, thought Lorraine, at ten o'clock in the morning. Because that was death. I went through the wave and I died—— She sat still, listening to these melodramatic words, she who had always turned away from melodrama and extremes, she who had been brought up to decent reserve and hearty health, whose childhood fears had been laughed at, kindly but relentlessly. But the words echoed. For once, on another morning, half her life ago, she had sat facing death.

I don't want to remember! she thought. But it was too late. Another room appeared around her, the study of her headmistress, Miss

Meadows, on a bright morning, where that kind, relentless, hearty, healthy woman was telling her that her mother was dead. The same sun glinted off the glass paperweight on her desk as glinted now off the gilt clock which ticked the present away to join the past. There was the same emptiness in both rooms, that one, this one; and Lorraine, at sixteen, had stared at Miss Meadows unbelievingly, expressionlessly, feeling nothing. "A terrible thing," Miss Meadows kept saying unwillingly as if it cost her a great deal to admit this death into her regulated world. "A terrible, terrible thing. The squall caught them just outside the harbor. Four boats out of seven capsized. The Coast Guard said it was the worst——" But her words faded here, gave place to the picture, the sloop over, drowned by her sail, the gray water rearing (it was too late, too late in the year to be sailing those chancy northern waters), and Lorraine put her hand out to hold it off, the wave, her mother's face; and began to make noises in her throat that brought Miss Meadows to her feet, calling for someone to help the poor Forbes girl.

Now, setting her teeth, Lorraine told herself, it happened. It happened and everything changed in ways I didn't understand, and that couldn't be undone. Things changed that I didn't expect to, and other things stayed the same, without rhyme or reason. There was the funeral, and school went on, and next summer we'd planned to go abroad and couldn't because it was the blitz, but couldn't go back to the island, either, ever, so Faith and I were sent to a riding camp on a ranch, and then Daddy bought the place in East Hampton because it wasn't New England. And no one ever talked about it, not even Faith and I together. But it happened.

And this has happened—now, this morning, whatever melodramatic name I want to call it—a crise de nerfs, a fit of hysterics, the beginning of a breakdown, a traumatic shock. It doesn't matter what I call it. But everything is changed again, and all the things I believed yesterday aren't so. Herbert doesn't love me and I don't love him. He bullies me and I help him to do it, have been helping him for years. It's grotesque, it's horrible, it has to stop. Well, at least I know it.

But can I stop it? Because I will have to do it alone, and it won't be easy. I've made myself into a cripple. I've chosen to be frightened and stupid and incoherent and clumsy, and those are hard habits to break. Herbert's right about a lot. I couldn't be bothered, I don't talk to people. I *could* have tried French on the Armenian woman last night and remembered the doctor's name. I will have to change myself. And Herbert won't help me. He is angry when I'm stupid, but he was angrier, he was frightened, this morning when I tried not to be. I think he needs me to bully. All that control of his—is it there because he really is strong, or does he need to conquer me and bully me to prove he is strong, and to stay in control? He will fight me, I think.

Well, fight back, said the face in the mirror. We are one, now. I will help. We used to be strong, don't you remember? How you swam and laughed and rode, all those long summers of your youth, and never doubted yourself? Don't you remember how you leaned out toward the future and longed for it, how life seemed exciting in the fall, and how Christmas glittered every year, how brown your arms were in August, and the boy who kissed you at the beach club, around behind the bathhouse, and how his mouth tasted of salt? Remember the weekends home from college, and the dances, you were never awfully brilliant at the dances but they were often fun and sometimes wonderful, and remember Jemmy, dear Jemmy, the golden retriever who was always so glad to see you that he tried to knock you down and scratched at your door at night to be let in and sleep by the bed, grunting and thumping his tail? Remember, remember what it's like to be happy and how the world can fit round you?

But it was all so far away! I remember, thought Lorraine, but it was like remembering another life, it was all gone, there was nothing left, nothing to help her now, nothing to fight Herbert with out of that simple and superficial past. And I may forget, she thought, forget what I know now, that I must fight. I will be frightened again, and clumsy, and say the wrong thing, and look up to see him watching me with his eyes hard and his jaws locked together. I can't get out of the desert and be saved just by wanting to be. Oh, I see it this morning, I see it all, it's as clear and as queer as if Dali had painted it, Herbert and I gesturing at each other in the middle of a wasteland that runs off to a horizon a hundred miles away, not a shred of green anywhere. I know I have to get out. But I'll lose the picture, I'll get muddled, and when I try to act it will go wrong. Won't I get frightened again then? Won't I give up?

Thinking this, she turned her head and heard the sounds of every-day life going on outside her shut door. They burst in on her, demanding attention. This was the real world, not a dream! Norah was running the vacuum cleaner in the hall, the cook was waiting to go over the menu (and waiting, Lorraine supposed, in a rigid state of indignation over the coffee incident at breakfast). The nursemaid, Hilda, would soon be taking Jane out to the park. The television set had been flickering, the repairman would have to be called. She was supposed to lunch with two women and discuss the Junior League lecture program for next year, and go on to play bridge at Cynthia Hayman's. There was her day, her life, all planned and set and waiting——

And when she came home from her bridge game, it would be time for Herbert to arrive; to arrive, and to look at her measuringly, to ask again, "Have you thought over what I said?" She felt herself begin to tremble already—and suddenly she knew that she could not go through with this planned day, whatever became of her planned and waiting life. Suddenly she was not quiveringly afraid of the necessity for doing something different, she was bursting, eager, to do it, she could not stand it if she did not do it! Suddenly the decision was made. She took a breath and straightened her shoulders, she thought, Well, now, what shall it be? What shall I do instead of arranging a lecture program and playing bridge? What will be some *use*?

At once, a woman's voice that she had heard months ago across a luncheon table came back to her. "—the children's clinic," she was saying. "There just never are enough helpers. When I think of the hours people waste on shopping and bridge——" Lorraine had felt a faint stirring of guilt as she listened. Surely she could give a morning or an afternoon a week? She had made a note of the woman's name and then had never done anything about it. But she could find her, certainly, in the telephone book.

She sat on for a moment testing this astounding resolve. It was more than astounding, really. It was absurd. She remembered her father's voice describing one of his sisters with humor so dry it was hard to be sure it was there: "Margaret? Oh, Margaret can't manage her own life, so she devotes herself to living for others." Aunt Margaret still, presumably, ventured forth from Louisburg Square on her missions of mercy, all in black, small, wispy, and incorruptible—

though she had once taken tea with the Cardinal. Lorraine had never found her very sympathetic, for she had no conversation except about her causes, and if one inquired after them, one was handed a pamphlet and expected to subscribe.

Half past ten, said the clock suddenly, in its small golden chime of a voice. Lorraine looked at it blindly. Temptation rose. It was perhaps not really necessary to turn into Aunt Margaret, to go dashing off to live for others. A little voice—Was it the Murderee reawakening?—said, You don't have to do this, you know. You can sit still, go to lunch, do what Herbert asked and diddle him over it, go to the analyst and let *me* talk, use the analyst, make him an excuse and an ally for not facing dangerous life. You don't really have to indulge in this absurdity, make a show of yourself, people will laugh, won't Herbert laugh? Isn't it really neurotic, aren't you playing at being a martyr?

Lorraine stumbled to her feet and went to the telephone.

CHAPTER

7

I must differentiate anger from despair. The first can be useful. I can teach myself to live on it. Oh, I wouldn't choose it for my diet, it's a coarse aliment, but I can live on rage. Despair will kill me. What am I now? I wrote. It stands out on the page and mocks me. I wish I dared cross it out, for there is no answer that can please me to set down. But let me, at any rate, answer— An angry old woman and not, God help me, a desperate one. Anger still looks out, still sees the world around it even if the colors change. But despair bows its head and huddles into itself, everything shimmers and shifts, nothing is real but one's own silly, boring emotions and sensations, the world is reduced to a horrid solipsism. Dear Lord, help me to stay angry!

I must write a note to that poor pompous young doctor and apologize for the tongue lashing I gave him, or he will throw up the case. I would rather see him than that fool Ingoldsby whose shoddy genteelism always provokes me into being as ungenteel as I possibly can. Besides, I can get the truth from Savage, or whatever approximation of truth he settles on; and also I'm inclined to think he's a good doctor, under the manner. "The ancient Greeks used to slaughter the messenger who brought bad news," I'll write him, "and lately I've been feeling not only ancient, but also rather Greek. And so I lost my temper at you, the messenger——" Will he know what I'm talking about? Probably not, but then—does it matter? If I write at once, and at reasonable length, and with enough deprecating words, it will do, whether he know what I'm talking about or not. And I might as well write something that will amuse me! If I can't handle one more half-educated, egotistic, ambitious young man who suspects he's better at his profession than his chief is—well, then, I'd *better* give up!

No wonder men have always been uneasy about old women. No wonder we were often called witches. It's astonishing that so many of us have had our claws drawn now and settle down to live our lives out peacefully, like spayed cats. Well, there are always a few—enough —who will not give up, but go on messing in life even though our own physical title to do so is over. And men are afraid of us because we have no stake in the future, we are quite selfish, we do not have to think genetically of the race but can think for ourselves, of ourselves, make mischief and laugh behind our hands at male mythology, at God, and power, and hierarchies, and values. At everything except money and intrigue, our two last pleasures. (I wish they pleased me more!)

How interesting it is, how painful, how astringent, to look back from here across my whole life as a woman and see it begin. I date that beginning from the spring when I was sixteen. That would be in 1911, for my birthday falls early in the year, in February, under the sign of Aquarius as the year rolls up toward the sun. Two events marked the change: I put my hair up and became a young lady; and I met James Fennimore Greene.

I'm sorry to keep talking so much about hair, but it had a great symbolic value. As long as it hung down your back, you were a child. Or, to state the converse of this proposition, as long as you were a child, you could allow your hair to hang down your back. What it was a symbol of—naturally—was sex. Men got quite excited about it. In these days, when most women's hair looks like artificial fiber, it is hard to understand the emotion that was built up about it fifty years ago. I gather that this emotion is now applied almost exclusively to women's breasts. Fifty years ago it was spread around more over the entire body, with the hair as one focus of attention. It hung down your back while you were a child because your innocence then made you untouchable, and any little thrills of emotion that gentlemen got from little girls' hair were regarded as quite, quite unrelated to the large thrills they enjoyed when a woman let down her hair for them. This she would not do unless she were removing her clothes, and *this* she would not do unless—— Well, you see what I mean. So that putting up your hair turned you into a young lady because it meant it was taboo, and could no longer hang down your back innocently. If you let your hair down, it meant something. You were nubile. Your skirts came down, too, past your shoe-tops, and it was time you were chaperoned. For me, this last was more theory than fact. I was never very much chaperoned.

CHAPTER SEVEN

I put my hair up on my sixteenth birthday. It made my sister Mary absolutely furious. I don't blame her: her own had gone up only two Christmases before, and she felt that I was stealing almost two years from her, two years of being the only young lady in the family. On the other hand, as I pointed out to her, she could have put her own hair up earlier. She said it was unbecoming, and I was too young, and I didn't know how to behave anyway; I behaved like a savage and couldn't pour tea properly—— Dear Mary! It was all absolutely true.

"And now you'll tag along everywhere I go," she finished, "and you'll be bored and not talk to people nicely. You sat and *sang* to yourself last Thursday at the Church Guild tea, and crossed your knees and swung your leg!"

"I was singing a hymn," I said.

"That makes it worse," said she. "Swinging your leg to a hymn!"

"Well," I said, "I won't go to the Guild any more, if you want. I'll stay home and be a heathen."

"*That* won't take much effort," said Mary bitterly.

Ever since I can remember, Mary went through alternate bouts of trying to reform me and of giving me up. In spite of her good intentions and all her efforts, my mother was subject to fits of absent-mindedness, when she rather forgot about her children, and would go off into month-long brown studies during which she concentrated on Theosophy or New Thought or Christian Science and the meals got queerer and queerer as Pearl, the cook, fed us whatever came into her head. At such times Mary would nobly take over the housekeeping and see that our father did not suffer too much, that the laundry was counted, that Pearl didn't give us pork three nights running and did occasionally give us green vegetables; and she also provided an ironclad set of categorical imperatives for me.

She sounds horrid, as I read this over, but the proof that she wasn't is that in spite of everything there were times when I loved her dearly and did what she told me to. I would never, for instance, have got to that Church Guild tea at all if I hadn't gone with Mary. She embroidered beautifully. She had a young man at Yale.

So there I was with my hair up, as of February 25th, 1911. My mother was reading *Isis Unveiled* by Madam Blavatsky. My father had his usual February cold. It was up to Mary to discipline me, and she did the best she could, between bringing Pearl's menus into closer contact with the principles of diet and dosing my father with hot toddies, but it wasn't enough. "All right," she said finally, "put your hair up. But remember that from now on you're supposed to act like a lady. There will be no excuse for you if you don't. Don't let me catch you playing mumblety-peg with the Heffernan boys again!"

At that I retired in silent fury, for it was quite two years since I had played mumblety-peg with the Heffernan boys. I would, I vowed, show Mary that I could behave like a lady. I would not slouch or slump, but "stand tall" and practice walking about with a book on my head. I would even learn to pour tea. This came easier because I was at the moment in the throes of a passionate best-friendship for a very ladylike girl named Delia Anderson. She was a year older than I, her hair was up, and she poured tea like a dream and embroidered almost as well as Mary. She was new to our town, from the South, and she told me stories about the young men at the University of Virginia. She had actually been to dances there! She seemed wildly sophisticated to me, and her ladylikeness had little touches of Southern expertise about it that were very dashing. At the University of Virginia dances the young men sometimes got drunk. She told me how to deal with a drunk young man—or rather, with a drunk young Virginian, for I never found her technique useful with anyone else.

So all through March I was good as gold, following Delia about devotedly, and Mary relaxed a bit, and my father got over his cold, and Mother went on from Madam Blavatsky to the Bhagavad-Gita.

And then one day in April I woke up and smelled the earth yearning for spring. I looked out my window and saw that the willow at the end of the garden was yellow. There were starlings making a row in the apple tree. The buds on the maples were swollen and red, and behind them the sky was a million miles further away than it had been the day before—and I ached, I ached all over for I didn't know what; but it wasn't Delia Anderson.

I stood in the window, breathing in that air, and it came over me like a thunderclap that for weeks, for months, I had forgotten about escaping. It put me in a panic. I, Diana, had been learning how to pour tea! I was a young lady! My skirts were down and my hair was up, and you couldn't have told me from a hundred others in northern Westchester. I hung there in the window and felt the jaws of the trap about to close. I must get out, I must get out, I thought, and my heart pounding in my chest seemed to be saying the same thing, as if it would tear my ribs apart. If I'd been a boy I think I'd have climbed out the window and down the trellis, but since I couldn't do that in any kind of skirts, let alone long ones, I got dressed and went down the stairs. My father and Mary were eating oatmeal, and my mother was fussing over the plants she kept for the winter in the dining-room window. Whether it was Theosophy or Christian Science, she could grow things like no one else I've ever known.

I sat down at the table and ate my breakfast because it was the only possible thing to do, but I felt like a time bomb. There must have been conversation, but I didn't pay any attention to it.

At eight-fifteen my father took out his watch and looked at it and said, "Well," and I put my spoon down in my unfinished oatmeal and got up. It was time to leave for school. We always went together, he and I, and walked four blocks to where we took the Interurban, one of those vanished trolley lines that whooped and swayed from one town to another until the automobile and the bus line killed them. This morning, as on every morning, I put on my jacket and tam-o'-shanter, strapped up my books, and inspected the sandwiches Pearl had put up for my lunch. The week before she had made them with a filling of cold baked beans, and though I was ticking away and my fuse was shortening, I was not going off with any cold baked bean sandwiches. This time, however, they were no odder than usual, and my father and I set out.

I wonder if he still thought I might go to college? But the gap in my memory is complete. I have no idea at all.

I got off the Interurban first, leaving my father to continue to his office in Peekskill where he practiced the kind of law which is traditional in small towns and consists mostly of letting nature take its course because you know all about everybody and can predict their actions. He was much beloved and greatly respected and if, once in a while, he interfered with the course of nature, people were apt to do as he told them. He was everybody's trustee and executor and lived, I am happy to say, to be a judge before he died in 1920 in a backlash of the influenza epidemic.

But we are still in 1911. And on that April day I walked for just fifty yards in the direction of the high school and then, when I saw the trolley vanish around a curve, I came back and crossed the road and waited for one in the other direction. Some of my classmates got off as it arrived and not unnaturally asked me where I was going when I boarded it. I said I had suddenly felt unwell and asked them to let the school know that I had had to go home. Then, crash, whoop, off I went having neatly covered my retreat, but I didn't go home. I got off two stops short of mine and walked up into the hills.

I wanted to be alone. I wanted to think.

If I was going to escape it had now become perfectly clear that I had to do something about it.

Emotions were not enough. Tick, tick, said my heart. But it could blow up and burst for all anyone cared if I did not translate its demands into action. My heart could burst, and I would go right on turning into a young lady and behaving like Mary's sister and Delia's friend unless——

Unless what? That was what I had to think out.

I knew just where to go to do it: to the castle of James Fennimore Greene. I knew how to get in the back way so that the caretaker wouldn't see me. I'd gone there often before. In fact, for a year or so I'd probably spent more time there than James Fennimore Greene had himself. There was, back of the main house and cut off by a hedge, a high terrace with a wonderful view over to the Hudson, and a little pavilion that I had taken for my own.

I said castle, and it was one—one of the most hideous structures that I have ever laid eyes on. This Mr. Greene's father had built it in the 1880s when bad taste had run through every artistic possibility and was becoming sheer grotesquery. Old Mr. Greene had taken a modest fortune and turned it into a monstrous one and built this monstrosity to celebrate his achievement. His son did not often inhabit it, and who could blame him? He was a bachelor of forty of a sort that has almost vanished, cultivated, kind, worldly, traveled, knowledgeable, and the place must have been a nightmare to him. Nothing the old man had done, however, could spoil the view from the terrace, and it was there I went.

I knew all about James Fennimore Greene because my father had handled the purchase of some land for him a few years before, to protect the original property. First one bit of acreage and then another came on the market. Mr. Greene bought the first without question, but when it happened again, and his heavenly view was threatened by the opening of a quarry, and there was talk of an old right-of-way through his lawns, he began, behind his deceptively gentle and absent-minded manner, to feel that there was blackmail in the air. He was no fool, James Fennimore Greene, though he disliked having to prove it. He very sensibly went to my father instead of bringing in a lawyer from New York, and my father agreed with his estimate of the situation and undertook to look into it. He made one of his rare interferences with the workings of nature, and the threats stopped. So after that my father was Mr. Greene's lawyer for all local work, and I suppose that if I'd asked I could have come up the front way to the castle through the high tormented iron gates and sat legally on the terrace.

But I preferred to be on my own, an adventurer and intruder, as much entitled to the view as the swallows that swooped out of the pavilion when I appeared, and no more. I wanted no ownership because I wanted the whole world, and to be entitled to one spot in it would cut me off from all the rest. I sat down on the edge of the terrace in the sun and contemplated the hills to the west that dropped down to the river and the hills beyond that rose from it and after a while the ticking in my heart slowed down a little, and I could think.

If I did not want to become a young lady, what did I want to become? It was no good thinking that I could go on running off by myself to sit on James Fennimore Greene's terrace and read poetry. In another year I was to graduate from school and after that I could not even play truant, because there would be nothing to play truant from. One couldn't really play truant from pouring tea!

But what could I do, what could I become? Could I sing? No. Could I play the piano? No. Mary could, but Mary had practiced and I had not. Could I write? This was slightly more hopeful, but even I knew that I had been right to burn the poems I had written the year before. To say that I could write better than I could sing was hardly to guarantee myself a literary career! Could I draw? Here I paused. To be an artist! To study in Paris! How did I know, after all, that I couldn't? For some minutes I sat rapt in a dream of Paris studios right out of Trilby, of chimney pots against a hazy sky, of a clean, neat, and altogether delightful Bohemia which differed from ordinary life chiefly by being cosier—— But no. It was preposterous, and I knew it. It was, I saw reluctantly, the kind of sentimental daydream that would appeal to Mary's sister, Delia's friend, who was going to turn into a young lady. It wasn't going to get me anywhere.

The sun grew warmer. I moved to lean my back against one of the posts of the little pavilion. Somewhere, off to the right, someone was cutting down a tree, clearing brush. I could hear an ax chunking away.

How was I going to get out? Not by dreaming. Many women dreamed, I think, at one time or another, of getting out—perhaps not Mary nor Delia, but many. My mother certainly did. And none of it did any good—unless, I suppose, you were Madam Blavatsky or Mary Baker Eddy, whose dreams became so real that the dreamers couldn't contain them. But I couldn't do that, because I didn't have one unificd crazy dream to take command of me. All I wanted was a chance to grow into myself distorted neither by a dream of my own nor by the irrelevent rigid conventions of the time—and there wasn't any way.

I sat and I sat and after a while I faced the fact. There wasn't any way.

Oh, for a bit I thought about becoming an actress. I'd been to the theater five times in my life, twice in Poughkeepsie to see the stock company, but three times actually in New York. The first time I'd embarrassed my mother very much. She made a special expedition with Mary and me to see Maude Adams in *Peter Pan*—and then I wouldn't clap my hands. You remember that moment when Peter asks everyone who believes in fairies to clap? I wouldn't. Mary hissed at me in the dark, but she only made it worse, for I said out loud, "But I don't," and I wouldn't clap. And it was the same thing, the same principle, that day on Mr. Greene's terrace. Clap your hands, say you believe in fairies, say you believe you can run away and act.

No. I knew I couldn't. I didn't know how to begin.

Chunk, went the ax in the woods. A hawk was flying in circles very high in the sky. I wanted to run away and I was too old to pretend that I could and believe it. I wasn't going to get to Paris and paint. I wasn't even going to get to Poughkeepsie and play second leads in the stock company. I was going to sit at home——

No, no, no! cried everything inside me. One life, your only life, pouring tea and embroidering and going to church and growing up and marrying one of the boys at school or someone just like one of the boys at school—— No, no! Anything, anything, I'll do anything! I hunched up over my knees and rocked back and forth because there was such terror and agony and rage inside me that I didn't know how I was going to hold myself together, and I envied the hawk on the wing above me who soared and circled as his spirit told him to, and the man with the ax in the spring woods, and everyone, everything, who moved to his own tune in his own time, and the thought of never being able to do this was as bitter and obliterating as the thought of death.

"Are you in trouble?" asked a voice.

It went through me like an electric shock. All my walls were down. I was naked to the April air. Diana with her hounds, Gertrude wrapped in flannel—both of these masks had been dissolved in the acid of my despair. In trouble? Why, I *was* trouble—there was no me, no identity, only the emotion rocking itself and moaning, unaccepting, unreconciled. The question, the voice, the knowledge that someone had seen me, picked me right up on my feet and flung me back against the wall of the summerhouse.

I must have looked like Pearl White in *The Perils of Pauline* confronting an ogre, for I found myself with my fists pushing my cheeks up, and my eyes and mouth as round as saucers. And it was only James Fennimore Greene!

Poor man, I frightened him by my galvanic leap as much as he had me. He said afterwards that he almost looked over his shoulder to see what had sent me blithering. He couldn't believe that his own mild presence, in Norfolk jacket, knickerbockers and tweed cap, could produce such an effect. "I'm sorry!" he said. "I didn't mean to startle you."

"Oh my!" I gasped, catching at the first thought that went by. "I'm trespassing!"

He thought that was funny. I guess he'd taken in the schoolbooks and the package of sandwiches by then. "So you are," he said. "Have you done much damage? Shall I bring a suit?"

"Oh my!" I said again, but I was already over my terror. If it had been Mr. Greene's butler or chauffeur or caretaker who'd caught me, I'd have run, and run with my cheeks red with shame at having

been spied on in my agony. But Mr. Greene himself carried an air
of—— What can I say? Of universal mercy? Really, it was almost
that. I suppose it was partly due to his money. He didn't have to try
to frighten people, the money did that for him. And this bored him
terribly. The money was a burden which he carried dutifully and
with a sense of noblesse oblige, but he yearned not to frighten people,
and when he found anyone able to forget his money, or just to take it
for granted, he was delighted. People could be humiliated in Mr.
Greene's presence, but not because he humiliated them. Indeed, it
was only too easy for the brash to find themselves being a bit pert to
James Fennimore Greene. I know, because the first thing I said as
emotion drained out of me was pert: "You'd have to get my father
to sue me, if you did. I'm Diana Cummings, Mr. Greene. I apologize for being here."

In spite of my glib assumption that I'd explained myself, it took
him a minute to make the connection. I could see him doing it.
"Oh," he said finally, "you're Matthew Cummings's little girl?"

"Yes," I said, not liking that "little girl" at all.

"Did he say you could come here?" he asked suddenly, sharply. I
suppose people had tried so often to take advantage of him that, in
a bad moment, he could even imagine my father doing it.

"Oh my goodness," I said, losing my pertness with my poise, "I
hope you won't tell him I was here! Oh, could you possibly not? He'd
be furious."

Mr. Greene whistled softly. He did this, I discovered, when he
didn't want to say Yes or No. It made unwary people go on talking.

I went on talking. "I never go up to the house," I said. "I just
stay out here. Once it rained and I went in the little summerhouse."

"You come here a lot," said Mr. Greene. It wasn't a question, it was
a statement. Even though it was a gentle statement, it made me feel
ashamed of myself, the way Mary did sometimes. I blushed.

"Not an awful lot," I said. "I didn't know you were here. I'm sorry."

"Do you come alone?" asked Mr. Greene. I suppose even someone
as wildly innocent as I would have been suspicious of that question
if he had been another kind of man.

But he so obviously wasn't that I just said, "Of course!" and went
on to explain, "I come when I want to think. I come to *be* alone. I
thought you were—my father said you were—in Italy."

"I came back," he said absently. He turned away and looked out over the hills.

I decided it was time for me to go. If I could do it quickly and neatly, just fade out, Mr. Greene might forget to tell me not to come back. All the things I'd been feeling that day seemed to tell me that I never *would* come back, but even so, I didn't want it to be impossible. It was one thing for me to realize that there was no escape from the kind of life I was going to have to lead. It was another to have someone else cut off an avenue of freedom. I bent down very quietly for my books, and my sandwiches, and stood up all ready to say, "Well, good-by——"

"What were you thinking about today, Diana?" asked Mr. Greene abruptly. He must have been lonesome that day—as, I suppose, he was often lonesome. Had something, I wonder, gone wrong in Italy?

"I was wishing I could be in Italy," I said, for this seemed the easiest way to explain myself. I wanted to use his terms, anyone's terms, public terms. I did not want to approach again that terrible loss of self that I had experienced. "I was wishing I could be anywhere —anywhere but here. Oh, by here I don't mean *right* here, because this is where I run away to—well, not very often! But home—growing up—doing all the things I'm expected to do and saying all the things I'm expected to say— I don't want to! I don't mean them!" Did I even mean those words? I'm not sure. They weren't right—but they were not untrue, either.

"It's no easier to mean what you say in Italy," said James Fennimore Greene.

"But perhaps I would find other things, things I did mean," I said humbly.

Mr. Greene smiled. "Many people have thought that. I wouldn't say they were all wrong, in spite of the old tag about travelers changing only their skies. You must let me know how you find it, when you go to Italy."

"There seems remarkably little chance of my going to Italy to find out," I said.

"Why, now!" said Mr. Greene. "You mustn't say that! At your age it often seems as if nothing would ever happen, but things do."

I almost shook my head, I almost told him that he was wrong and that I had spent the morning realizing this—but I was afraid to. He would tell me that other people had felt the same way, and that would do me no good. Besides, some dawning social sense made me see that it would be rude to involve him in a discussion based so largely on my self-pity; so I asked him instead where he had been in Italy. He began to tell me, pacing back and forth along the terrace, and after a while I sat down in the sun again and tucked my feet up comfortably and listened. They were very ordinary traveler's tales, I'm sure, but they were new to me, and they were a blessed distraction from my own problem. I was, I suppose, as flattered as Desdemona to have a grown-up man telling me stories. Little by little I could feel myself becoming myself again, for the therapeutic value of flattery is immense.

I shut my eyes now and try to realize that this happened forty-five years ago—forty-five years ago almost to the day, and I suppose just about fifty miles due west of where I lie now trapped finally with all escape cut off. Grab, grab, grab! I want to tell that child. Breathe the air and feel the sun and remember, I need so to know what you felt! Lay up a store, fill up the trunks and barrels for me to pore over now, it is all that I have, you must live for me too. Grab at it!

As if she needed to be told!

Mr. Greene talked a long time. Like many reserved people, once he got started he found it hard to stop. In fact, he didn't stop until he was stopped. A manservant came around the end of the hedge and said, "I beg your pardon, sir, but Mrs. Davies wondered"—and then he caught sight of me and goggled for a minute before he managed to finish—"wondered if you would care to lunch."

Mr. Greene said, "Diana, may I invite you to lunch with me?"

This was not just flattering, it was unbelievable. "I must go," I said faintly. "I have—I have sandwiches."

"The packet looks a little battered by now. I should think you'd enjoy Mrs. Davies's lunch more."

"But you weren't expecting me." Then I blushed again. Mr. Greene's larder was not likely to be bare.

He said gravely, "If we run short, we can share your sandwiches," and he took them away from me and gave them to the manservant, who looked more startled than ever. "Lay another place, Davies," he said. "Miss Cummings and I will come up directly. Oh, and put some sherry in the library. You'll take a glass of sherry, won't you, Diana?"

"Thank you," I said grandly, for my self-esteem was boiling up until I felt that I would *rather* be hanged for a sheep than a lamb. We walked up to the house together, Mr. Greene indicated delicately where I could wash my hands (the faucets on the marble washstand were gold-plated), and when I came out Davies showed me into the library, and I drank the second glass of sherry that I had had in my life. And we lunched, and Mr. Greene talked——

But it's gone now, it's gone. I've lost it, that first lunch in the hideous dining room where a large bull moose looked down on me from over Mr. Greene's head. I know it happened, but I can't bring it back clearly. She must have felt, that little Diana, that the whole thing was so unlikely, and been so busy pinching herself, that she couldn't really take it in. Was it then or another time that James Fennimore Greene stood in a shaft of sunlight holding my chair for me and smiled and I saw—not just felt, but saw like a diagram in geometry—that he was my friend? I wish I knew!

I do remember the mixture of elation and terror with which I accepted his invitation to drive me home in his "motor" as we called them then. Perhaps "accepted" is the wrong word—I hadn't really much choice, and I knew it. By lunching with Mr. Greene I had put us both into some kind of recognizable social situation, and now I would have to abide by the usual social rules. Any illusion I might have had that my trespass and our lunch could be kept a secret had vanished. There was clearly no chance whatsoever that Mr. Greene would deceive my father about a clandestine meeting with his daughter. No, the balloon was going to go up when I got home, and my family was going to know all about my expeditions to the Greene castle, and my playing hooky, and my wandering about on my own and accepting invitations to lunch from strange men. The fact that the strange man was James Fennimore Greene might make things worse instead of better—my father's pride was as deep as it was deeply hidden and it was only too likely that *he* might feel I'd been taking advantage of his client, even if the client had dismissed the idea himself.

Mr. Greene's motor was nearly as big as a battleship, and winked with brass—headlamps and windshield and struts holding the wind-

CHAPTER SEVEN

shield, and heaven knows what. I climbed in feeling as if I were boarding a particularly elegant tumbril, but absolutely determined to squeeze the last drop of enjoyment out of the ride, since I was sure to meet an unpleasant fate at its end. Mr. Greene drove. His chauffeur sat in the back seat, for Mr. Greene was more sensitive to the demands of chaperonage than I.

How the motor roared! It was a monster car—expressing, perhaps, the only bit of inheritance (beside money) that James Fennimore Greene had received from his father. I think it was French. It had a right-hand drive. The gear lever was on the outside. I was so excited I nearly cried. "Oh my!" I said several times. We started, Mr. Greene shifting gears cautiously as we wound down the long graveled drive from the house to the iron entrance gates. He blew his horn here, and the gates were opened, and we went through and he said, "Do you like it, Diana?"

I said, "Oh yes!" He laughed, and shifted the gears, and we began to gather speed, and I cried out inarticulately with excitement, and my tam-o'-shanter blew off, and the chauffeur caught it—but he could not catch the two dozen hairpins that held up my hair—and yes indeed, there I was, tearing down the high road in the front seat of Mr. Greene's not inconspicuous car with a yard of hair (I could sit on it) whipping out behind me and every living soul we passed turning around to stare, and I laughing like a hyena and crying, "Oh! Oh! Go faster!" And something got into Mr. Greene, because he did.

So we got home very fast, but not ahead of the social rules. Someone who had seen the spectacle had had time to telephone and report. As Mr. Greene braked down and stopped the Juggernaut at my front gate, I saw, drawn up on the porch like the executioner and his helpers at the guillotine, Mary, and Pearl the cook, and the handy man, and even the part-time laundress. My hair stopped blowing and fell around my face. I tried to bundle it back, but I couldn't do this and take my tam-o'-shanter from the chauffeur, and my school-books from Mr. Greene, and be handed out of the car all at the same time, and there is no doubt that I looked like a perfect picture of disgrace as I came up the walk toward that stunned, incredulous group on the porch. What would you have to do today, I wonder, to shock anyone as much as I shocked them? I don't really think you could.

Dear, dear James Fennimore Greene marched staunchly behind my right shoulder.

Mary was opening her mouth when I forestalled her. "Hello!" I said with shaky vivacity. "What are you all doing here? Waiting for a parade?"

She changed color. She had begun, "Diana, where——" when my mother came out the door behind her. *Her* hair was not as neat as it might have been, and she was carrying a book with one finger marking the place. "My dear child," she said, "what have you been up to? Why—good afternoon, Mr. Greene. Was it you who brought Diana home? Pearl, what in the name of goodness are you doing out here? I can smell something scorching clear in the front room." Pearl, the handy man, and the laundress all disappeared as if she'd said scat.

Mr. Greene took his cap off, and the measure of his bad conscience was how stately his language became. "Good afternoon, Mrs. Cummings. Yes, I plead guilty to finding Diana meditating upon the view from the castle, and she turned out to be such delightful company that I really couldn't bear to return her at once. I hope that you and Mr. Cummings will forgive me. It's been quite a while since I was Diana's age, but I do remember how hungry it's possible to get, and I thought that Mrs. Davies, who looks after me, you know, would enjoy the chance to cater to a young appetite, so I persuaded Diana to share my lunch before I brought her home." We had now reached the steps and he came right up them and shook my mother's hand. This was to reassure her. If he had had, shall we say, anything with which to reproach himself, he supposedly should not have dared to shake her hand. I was struck, too, by the brilliant yet unobtrusive way in which he let her know that another female, even if only a superior servant, had been present.

"I'm sure you were very kind," said my mother. She looked me over from head to toe, and I suppose that what she saw convinced her that the outward and visible signs of disgrace which I bore were not matched by any like inward state. "I thought you were in school," she said to me.

"I didn't go today," I said. "I wanted— I had to think."

Mary snorted. "I see," said my mother. She considered me for a minute longer, and then I could feel her concentration turned off as if a searchlight had gone out. "Won't you come in, Mr. Greene?" she said.

"Thank you, no," he replied. "I shall have to get back." He cleared his throat and went on, "I'm anxious to see your husband while I'm here. I shall try to reach him this afternoon, but if I fail, perhaps you'd mention to him that I shall be telephoning him tomorrow, and hope that he'll have an hour free for me." This was not said to remind my mother that my father was, in a sense, in James Fennimore Greene's employ. It was intended to indicate that Mr. Greene was at my father's disposal, first, to assure him that no evil had overtaken me; and, second, to apologize for the appearance of evil, which had. My mother knew it, Mary knew it, even I had learned enough of the obliquenesses of social discourse to understand it. "Good-by, Mrs. Cummings," he finished. "Good-by, Diana. I enjoyed your visit enormously."

"Good-by," I said faintly. I couldn't even manage a thank you.

He bowed, swung around and went down the steps and out to the car. We all stood in silence. He climbed in, bowed again—cap off, of course—over the wheel, let in the clutch, and moved off past our privet hedge—deus ex machina, but going, alas, in the wrong direction. I shut my eyes and waited for the storm to descend. It did.

CHAPTER

8

April wore on, April the opener, chilly and warm by turns, undecided, transient. Lorraine knocked at a door which opened a crack: three afternoons and two mornings a week she was welcome at a shelter for temporarily homeless children, children whose parents were sick or dead or drunk or jailed or missing. Nothing heroic was demanded of her. Indeed, it was carefully explained that since she herself had two small children of an age to come down with infectious diseases, she must temper her charity with cold common sense and stay at home if Bobby or Jane had a runny nose.

"I see," she said humbly. "Yes, of course."

"And I imagine," said the assistant supervisor who was interviewing her, "that you take your children out of town for the summer?"

"Why—yes. We have a place on the Island. Perhaps I could get in one day a week——"

"Well, we'll see. We expect to be shorthanded in the summer. If you can get in, it will be a help. At any rate, I'm grateful to you for the time you can give us now. Let me know if you run into problems— when you run into them, I should say. Naturally there are bound to be disturbed children coming out of disturbed homes. Try not to let it disturb *you*."

Lorraine looked at her thinking, My dear woman, I'm disturbed to begin with—and suddenly the absurdity of it made her grin. The blind leading the blind, she thought. A busman's holiday. Who's loony now? Well, if I seem to be doing them actual harm, I'll quit. "Thank you," she said. "I'll do my best."

She told Herbert that night what she was doing; told him before he had time to ask. Her haste made her speak too abruptly, she heard uncertainty in her tone and knew from his considering gaze that he had heard it too. Nevertheless, her decision made him pause. He was waiting, in the silence between them, for her to be frightened.

But she had acted, not merely dreamed of acting. The faces of the children she had seen were real and clear. However tentatively, she was connected with them, and with the big bare room containing a battered piano, where she had spent an hour playing kindergarten games. Perhaps her activity was absurd, but it had happened and at ten o'clock tomorrow morning she was expected back. She had managed, she realized, to confront Herbert with a fait accompli.

The knowledge lifted her spirits and while he still hesitated (for the morning's scene had shaken him too), she went on, matter-of-factly, "I had only a little while there today with an old hand to help out and teach me what to do. It turns out she was at college with Alice Bellamy. Amy Burton's her name, Mrs. Russell Burton. Her husband's at the Guaranty. Do you know him?"

"I've met him," said Herbert looking startled and then wary.

"That's nice," said Lorraine. She was pleased at having been able to enlist respectability on her side, but was careful to keep her voice as calm and expressionless as possible. Perhaps, if she could establish her work as routine, Herbert would accept it.

"I hope it won't be too much of a strain for you," he said sharply.

"If it is, I'll stop," she told him cheerfully. "Why don't you make us a martini?" And though she felt Herbert's eyes on her from time to time, that was all that was said.

Doors opened elsewhere. Mrs. Belchamber was trundled through one in a wheel chair. She was so outraged that her eyes were shut tight.

"You've missed the morning sun all these months," said Nurse Tucker, "and I'm going to put you in the solarium for a little while. It's almost a prettier view than your own. Now then, here we are—— Oh, good morning, Admiral. You're out early."

"I thought I'd form a welcoming committee for our fellow patient on her first trip into the world," said a slightly breathless old voice, and Mrs. Belchamber, who wanted only to cry out: Take me back! was forced to open her eyes and undertake a crippled renewal of social life. She thought at first that it would send her mad for, immobile in the wheel chair until called for by Tucker, she had no retreat, and her previous invisibility had roused almost frantic curiosity among the other patients at Dr. Rushmore's. Little by little, however, she was able to turn their attention back to themselves: Ask a question for every one you answer, she told herself. And then bridge came to the rescue.

Admiral Bailey was a devotee of the game, and had been from the days when, serving under Admiral Dewey, he had taught whist to Spanish officers captured at Manila Bay. Old Mrs. Covington (the Senator's mother) was given to spectacular psychic bids which came off just often enough to unnerve her partners. She always smiled gently when she made her contract and told her fellow players what dear William James had explained to her about the workings of the unconscious mind. (Tucker claimed that her other great hobby was automatic writing and that via this medium she had heard quite recently from dear William, who assured her that his earthly statements on the subject had been, if anything, too mild.)

A certain amount of healthy acrimony was aired at such moments by the fourth player, Mr. Desseaux, a rationalist of the most acrid sort, who had no hesitation in greeting Mrs. Covington's remarks with such exclamations as "Poppycock! Balderdash!" or just "Ha!" He almost broke the game up completely once by referring to William James as "that Chatauqua lecturer with a predilection for hysterical women." Mrs. Covington threw three tricks at him (she had gone down seven on a bid of four spades), and it was several days before recrimination simmered down to a level where sketchy mutual apologies could be arranged.

"It's an interesting situation," Mrs. Belchamber said one afternoon to Dr. Savage, who had summoned her from the bridge table for her weekly examination. "What would the three of us do without the fourth? Together we are like some completely specialized ecological organism that can only exist in just the right grouping for just the right purpose—like the pilot fish and the shark, for instance. We are parasites on each other and if it weren't for bridge—— In a state of nature, we would wipe each other out, I'm sure. If I had to sit alone and listen to any of them—the Admiral on naval history (he's been refuting Mahan for fifty years), or Mrs. Covington on either of her subjects, William James or the great promise shown in boyhood by her distinguished idiot of a son, or Mr. Desseaux on the eighteenth century—he collects correspondence from, to, and about Horace Walpole—why I should reach for a bare bodkin either for myself or them. That hurts. Ah! Quite a lot. Yes, right there. Ah!" She shut her eyes as his fingers felt for the pain, opened them again on the white ceiling where sun flickered. "And you, Doctor," she asked through set lips. "Do you play bridge?"

"I don't have time," he said.

"Don't be a snob," she said, her words and tone as sharp as a cat's claws. "Age and retirement may come even to you one day."

He flushed. "I didn't——"

But she had recovered herself and was laughing at the outrageousness to which pain had reduced her. "How grateful you will be to me someday when you have finally learned never to lose your temper! I'll bring you to it, you'll see. I've nearly succeeded with Tucker already, haven't I?"

"Nearly, madam," said Tucker from the foot of the bed. The doctor stood up and went to wash his hands, and Tucker smoothed the covers back without, so far as could be seen, any sign of anger at all. "Shall I fix the pillows?" she asked.

"Not now. Perhaps I can sleep." But there was no repose in the face that Mrs. Belchamber turned to the doctor as he came back. "Run along, now, Tucker," she said, watching him, and the nurse went out.

He stood looking down at her with his hands in his pockets. Her eyes willed him to speak, intense, concentrated, waiting; but she would not condescend to question him. He looked away before he said, with elaborate unconcern, "Mrs. Belchamber, I think Dr. Ingoldsby should have another look at you, in the next few days. Suppose I phone tomorrow morning and let you know when he'll be able to get out?"

"What will he discover that you don't know already?" she asked. "No, don't bother to answer. Even I can see the logical fallacy in that."

"You're his patient," said Savage. "I've just been helping out."

"Of course. Quite clear. Protocol demands that it must be he who tells me that you have decided you have to operate."

"Mrs. Belchamber, I can't say what he'll decide, or what he'll tell you. You're his——"

"Who would operate? You or he?" He grimaced helplessly and she went on, "I'd rather you did, you know."

What Savage experienced at that moment had become only too

familiar—he felt it at least once every time he saw her. Equal and opposite impulses sprang up in his breast and pulled him with equal force in opposite directions. The only difference this time was that they were stronger than ever. Why didn't I give up the case? he asked himself. It's as if she was playing a game with me! I'm not a doctor, I'm an amusement! All that conversation, it isn't to say anything, it's to see if she can make me laugh, or give something away, and if I do, she scores a point. She's got enough energy to light up half New Haven, and nothing to use it on but me, no more society, no more husbands, just me and Tucker. My God, I'm scared of her! At the same time, pity for her and admiration for her courage touched him as deeply as his impulse to flee. It's as if my will power had stripped its gears, he thought, and angrily, self-protectingly, he grunted, "It isn't up to me!" He knew he sounded rude, and he knew that she knew exactly why he sounded that way. Dear God, he thought, can't I keep any secrets from her? Why in hell didn't I give up the case!

"Nonsense," she said now, enjoying his discomfort, he was sure. "You and I between us can manage Ingoldsby! Send him out to make the annunciation, if you must, but I want you to do the work on me. I'll tell him so. Well, then, all right, don't make faces at me, I won't—if you promise to arrange it."

Since he had every intention of doing just this, and since he certainly was not going to tell her so, he had again to remain silent, and she grew even more amused. "We'll talk about it later, shall we?" she asked with mock generosity. But then, as if she had enabled herself finally to face reality by her teasing of the doctor, she grew sober and went on, "Just one thing—do it as quickly as you can, won't you? Perhaps it seems strange to you that an old woman should still be impatient. I know that it's the problems of young people which are mainly discussed today—it seems sometimes as if their parents were as terrified of them as if they were a different species. And yet, in a quiet way, it's true for us too, you think of us as being different too, different from you, I mean. It isn't noticed as much, but I think that's just because young people enjoy flaunting their estrangements and dislocations, and we on the other hand want to hide them, just as we hide our foolish affections because the time for them has passed. And you don't like to think about it either, you people in the thirties and forties, you people in control, I suppose it reminds you that the sixties will come for you too, you will make this odd change and begin to be old, to collect and reminisce and play bridge.

"But you know, it's not as much of a change as you might think. We don't stop being human, and short-tempered, and impatient and greedy just because we turn sixty. I was beautiful once. I was expected to act like a beauty, to be imperious and demanding and capricious, that was the fashion then, and I was those things to quite a degree, to the degree that it was in me to be them. Well, I try not to be them now, but it's not easy to unlearn. And there are certain other qualities mixed up with those attitudes that I don't want to lose——" She broke off, looking up at the ceiling. She was not, he realized, talking to him at all, she had ceased to play her game of amusing and annoying him. He cleared his throat. She turned her gaze to him at once and went on, "Yes, well, that's of no importance, of course. If you talked a bit more, my dear man, I should talk less." She smiled and held out her hand to him.

"I'll let you know tomorrow when Dr. Ingoldsby will be coming," he said, and went out quickly, ignoring her cry, "You come too!" for he was afraid, increasingly afraid, that one day the enchantment would work, she would succeed, and he would begin to talk to her. Why the devil hadn't he got out, right away, that time when she'd fist infuriated him? He'd known he should. Why had he even acknowledged her letter of apology? She was like—like quicksand. It was terrifying. He knew what she was doing, and still he couldn't stop her. She had a kind of magic ability to create intimacy, to establish a relationship that would at once charm and astonish her partner in it until he became blind to everything else. He wanted no part of such intimacy. I can't afford it, he repeated as he had too often before. She could land me anywhere. How can I trust her? She's got no discretion, she's got no fear, she's never been up against it and had to learn to be careful. With all that money, all that energy, she must have run everyone around her for half a century, that's her hobby, not bridge, and when I'm around she concentrates on me. My God! What will she say to Ingoldsby? She's capable of anything! Sweating, swearing under his breath at the irresponsible rich, counting in his head what a thousand-dollar fee might do and what its absence would threaten, he unparked his car and drove off.

And found himself back, three days later, to meet Ingoldsby, who couldn't see any reason at all for his not coming. Just don't get involved, he told himself firmly. You don't have to, you know. Just stay out of it. She's a rich old woman, she amuses herself playing games with people, but it's nothing to do with you, unless you let it be. Unless you let her get your goat. You don't have to. Keep your distance, do your work, keep your mouth shut, and get the money. That's all there is to it. Once she's out of Rushmore's, once the work's done, she'll be too busy to bother you any more. They'll get her started learning to walk again, learning to use a crutch, she'll start hypnotizing some poor physiotherapist, and you'll find she's forgotten about you.

Mrs. Belchamber, indeed, seemed to have little time for him that afternoon. She was concentrating upon Dr. Ingoldsby, who bobbed and neighed happily, swimming as hard as he could through the deep waters of horticultural conversation—Mrs. Belchamber, it appeared, grew quite remarkable roses. In a corner sat the quiet niece, Mrs. de Something. Damn, thought Savage, I've forgotten her name. He smiled at her warmly to make up for it, and after a moment she smiled back. Why had she hesitated? he wondered with a touch of irritation; and then remembered that the last time he had seen her had been the day when they had all lost their tempers. No, she had not, poor thing. Everyone but the niece, then. It had upset her. He looked at her again, wondering if Ingoldsby had got her out on purpose to help her aunt receive the news of the operation, or whether she was there by coincidence. Would she, in any case, be useful if the old lady decided she didn't like the news she was going to get? She'd not been much use before. Well, handling Mrs. Belchamber on the rampage was not child's play for anyone. Today, at least, the girl seemed self-possessed enough. Perhaps she could be helpful. Or, more likely, the old lady would take everything in stride. She was certainly enjoying herself with Ingoldsby! How the hell could he get that much mileage out of roses? Savage wondered.

"Ninety-three varieties!" he was exclaiming now. "I don't know how you do it, my dear lady."

"Manure," said Mrs. Belchamber promptly. "Lots of manure. Roses are gross feeders. I always advise anyone who wants to go in for roses to plan on a stable too, it's a natural supplement. Though of course the roses don't do the horses any good. However, that's neither here nor there. What I am really anxious to know, Dr. Ingoldsby, is whether I am going to see my roses this year. Are you going to let me out of here? And when?"

"Ah!" said Ingoldsby, bobbing his crown of silver hair like a marionette. "That's the practical question, isn't it? That's the heart of the matter! Trust you women to bring us all back to earth. Well, now, Dr. Savage has been giving me the most complete and useful reports, but suppose I take a look myself? Your nurse, now, she's about? Savage, I wonder if you and Mrs. de Koning would send her in as you go out. Thank you, dear boy, thank you. I don't think the old head can add anything to what the young one has observed, but we mustn't leave any stone unturned if we are to get our patient home to her roses."

"Certainly not," said Mrs. Belchamber. "We might even ask Mrs. Covington if she can get an opinion out of William James. He was an M.D., wasn't he, Doctor? Or wasn't he? Well, never mind. Mrs. C. will know. If you see her, Lorraine, you won't have any difficulty bringing the subject up."

"All right, darling," said the dark girl whom Savage, in spite of relief at knowing her name, still found himself thinking of as The Niece. She kissed her aunt on the forehead, smiled at Savage, and they went out. Tucker, who had been hovering, raised her eyebrows in inquiry, and slipped in.

They walked slowly down the corridor together. Savage was conscious, with embarrassment, that it was not the first time. He sought rather feverishly for something to say. The weather? He could surely do better than that! Her aunt? No, that had to wait till Ingoldsby spoke. "Do you drive out——" he began.

At the same moment she said, "I hope you don't——" And they both stopped helplessly.

"Please," he said, in a moment.

She turned her head slowly, looking along the whole corridor before she met his eyes. She swallowed. Why, she's shy! he thought. She said, "What do you suppose we can have done in former lives to condemn us now to pace up and down this grisly place embarrassing each other every time we meet? Did William James believe in the transmigration of souls? Perhaps Mrs. Covington could find out for us. You can talk about what you're going to do, if you want—I mean, with Aunt Di. Dr. Ingoldsby told me yesterday when he called that you'd decided an operation was necessary."

"I see," he said, though he certainly didn't see what the transmigration of souls had to do with anything. "Well——"

"Or you can let Ingoldsby talk, if you want. I just meant—— Oh my soul, look. Those are the bridge players!"

Indeed they were. Within the sunroom, deprived for the second afternoon that week of their fourth player, sat Mrs. Covington, the Admiral, and Mr. Desseaux. As Lorraine and Savage looked in, they met three stares as hungry and resentful as those of a cageful of tigers. "Goodness!" said Lorraine and drew him past. "What—what's out there, through that door? A balcony? Can we go out? I don't think it's the moment to engage Mrs. Covington in conversation!"

Savage thrust the door open and they emerged on an upper porch where two or three chairs huddled in a corner. The lawns fell away before them and were succeeded by a wide view of fields crisscrossed by stone walls. In the distance woods climbed a long granite ridge. "How good the air is!" said Lorraine, and walked to the railing.

Savage, behind her, hung for a moment on dead center. He didn't, he desperately didn't, want to get involved even to the extent of a serious conversation with any connection of Mrs. Belchamber's. The old lady herself was all he could manage—if he could indeed manage her! And this girl whose sentences jumped all over the place, who was menacingly rich and disarmingly shy, whom he had (after all) been rude to, who must live in some distant and hazy whirl of society in New York, who humbly left him the choice of discussing her aunt's case or not discussing it—this girl was another confusion. The normal run of his patients were perfectly simple: either they crossexamined him out of a background of appalling ignorance and misinformation, or they left the whole business up to him, and assumed that of course they could not understand what had happened to them. Hedging uneasily, putting a decision off, he followed her to the railing and said, "It must have been pretty driving out today."

"It was," she said. "I haven't been out for a couple of weeks and things change so fast."

"I thought you came more often," he said stupidly. And then, realizing it, went on, "I'm sorry, I didn't mean—I hope there wasn't anything—you know, illness—to keep you away."

"I'm working," she said.

He looked at her, stunned. It was a plain suit she was wearing, all right, but he'd just assumed it was expensive—— "Working?"

She laughed. "Oh, not for money. I'm afraid I couldn't find anyone silly enough to pay me. I'm working about twenty hours a week at one of the children's shelters in New York. I told them I couldn't come more than three days a week because I have to look after my own two demons when the nursemaid's out on Wednesday, and I wanted one day to come out here. But last week the volunteer staff went down with grippe like a set of ninepins, so I thought I'd better stay and cope."

"Do you enjoy that?" he asked blankly.

"My God, no," she said. "They rub me raw. I hope I get over it. I suppose I'll have to toughen up in time. But they're lost, you know. Quite a lot of them are lost already. There are times I can't stand it."

"They're not all lost," he said. "They get saved—when you least expect it."

She looked up at him. "You must see them in your work," she said.

"I was one."

"You?" she said and went on looking at him. "Thank you."

"For what?"

"For telling me. I'll remember. It will be a comfort."

He rubbed the palms of his hands on the railing. They were sweaty. He grinned at her and said, "You mean if I made out all right, then anyone could?"

She made her mouth prim. "Now you're fishing," she said. "But I assure you you *seem* saved."

"And I assure you I was lost. The Waterbury slums thirty years ago were about as far from—from being your aunt's surgeon as it's convenient to get. You wouldn't want to go any further."

"I wouldn't want to go that far. I think you were great to get out."

"I didn't do it all myself. Not by a long shot."

"No?"

"No. Oh, I made a beginning. I took the first steps. I could play football, you see, and that got me through school all right, and then through college. But Medical School—that I didn't manage by myself."

"Why did you have to go there?" she asked.

He looked off across the fields. His mouth hardened and relaxed, hardened and relaxed. Old, unhappy, far-off things, she thought, watching him. "It was my father," he said harshly. "That is, not him. When I was nine, he—he had an accident. He worked in one of the brass mills, and his left hand and side and foot—— Well, it doesn't matter now. He didn't speak much English—I'm French Canadian by birth. There were supposed to be safety devices—— This was a new machine. I guess he just hadn't understood how to operate it. Well, and so, they put him in the hospital. Now naturally they wouldn't let a kid of nine in to see him. But eventually they brought him home, and after that he had to go once a week for a while, once a month after that, to the Clinic. I went with him. My mother couldn't get away, and I was the oldest."

He is seeing it all again, she thought. Smelling it, hearing it, too, I suppose, that hospital smell and the broken, foreign voices saying, "Doctor——" pleading, frightened. "And one of the doctors was kind to you?" she prompted him gently.

He snorted. It was a laugh. "They were too God damn busy—I beg your pardon."

"Nonsense. Go on."

"They didn't have time to pay attention to the patients, beyond what they had to do for them, let alone any dirty, Canuck kid who was always under foot. No. They weren't kind to me, or anyone else. But Je—— But boy, they sure were impressive. The orderlies ordered us, the nurses ordered the orderlies, and the doctors ordered everybody. There was one old son of a gun with a beard, he looked like he'd been left over from the eighties. He didn't even have to speak, just jerked his head, and the next one in line came up. He didn't ask any questions, he didn't want any information from the patient. My father tried to tell him something once—there'd been an abscess and some suppuration—but the old boy with the beard, his name was Hogben, Dr. Hogben, just said, 'Quiet, my man.' He cleaned the damn thing out so fast my father didn't scream till he was through. Well. That's why I wanted to be a doctor."

"Power," said Lorraine.

"That's right. Power."

Leaning against the railing she said, "And now that you have it, do you enjoy it?"

He looked at her and his expression slowly relaxed until he grinned again. "Now that I have it, Mrs. de Koning, I have your aunt too."

"So you do," she said. "It's too bad she never met Dr. Hogben."

"Yes." He continued to look at her. "I don't know why I told you all that. I'm sorry."

"You wanted to help me not to be upset by the children at the shelter."

"Yeah." He took a handkerchief out—not the neat one in his breast pocket—and rubbed his face. He said, "About your aunt. It's always a question with people in that age bracket. The break just hasn't knit right. She'll never stand on it the way it is."

She didn't say anything.

"You see?" he asked.

She nodded.

"So we've got to put some more stuff in there to patch everything together and take the weight so she can get around."

Her eyes had filled up with tears. "I'm so thankful," she said. "I—— It will mean so much to her. She's doubted it, you know. Well, of course you know. What I mean is, this last strain has been hard. Every time I came out, every time I've called her, I've been afraid she'd say, 'Sell the horses. Close up the house.' Now—I'm so relieved. You've been so kind. Thank you for telling me, and telling me ahead so I—so I wouldn't upset her."

But he was looking back at her unhappily. She stopped. She said, "No? It won't—help?"

"Help. Of course it'll help. Would we do it if we didn't think it will help?"

"Naturally—I'm sorry—I didn't mean——"

"It's no miracle. Yes, she'll get around—some. She won't get on a horse again. This place out here with the roses—she'll be better off in an apartment in the city, all on one floor. I—— We'll do all we can. A lot depends on treatment, and care, and recuperative power, and —oh, a lot of intangibles. I think she'll make a pretty good recovery, all around. But—you ought to know what the limits are. What just isn't possible."

She was crying.

He said, "I'm sorry."

She shook her head vehemently, she lifted it and stared fiercely in front of her for a moment. "I'm so stupid," she said. "I left everything inside. Could you—do you have a handkerchief you could lend me?" At once he produced the breast-pocket one for-show, and without looking at him she blew her nose and wiped her eyes. "You've nothing to be sorry for," she said. "You did right. You are right. I had to know. I'm not crying because you told me, I'm crying because it's true. And—I love her very much. I know she's a—a virago, sometimes. But she—in a way, she is alone, and I am alone—not literally, of course, neither of us. But she is all I have of a connection with the past, and I am all she has that is likely to give her a connection with the future. I hate so to think of her crippled!"

"I'm sure you do," he said tonelessly.

She looked at him. "But—— What—— You don't think I'm blaming you? Oh no, no! You've been—so nice to me. You mustn't misunderstand. I'm mourning her, not blaming you. I see this has to be."

He said, "I wouldn't tell her about it."

"Of course not!"

"There's a limit to what we can do, but there mustn't be a limit to what she tries to do. She'll accomplish a lot more if she works——"

"Yes, yes, I do see. I won't let on."

He said, "You can manage that?"

"Yes. I can."

"She may pry."

"Of course she'll pry. But you can just tell me what to say. You'll do the operation soon, won't you?"

"Next week, I imagine."

"In New Haven?"

"Yes."

"I'll come out. I'm glad I gave them extra time at the shelter last week. You'll let me know when?"

"We'll see what Ing—what Dr. Ingoldsby thinks."

"Yes." She looked at her watch. "Had we better go back?"

He nodded.

She dabbed at her eyes again. "Have I—does it show that I cried?"

He examined her face. This was the face of the woman he had told about his boyhood and his escape. Her eyes were gray. Why had he talked to her so? He had thought of her first as a girl, he had thought of her as The Niece, but he had been wrong. She was a woman in her own right. Though sad. Why had he talked to her? He hadn't wanted to get involved, and, unlike her aunt, she had not tried to charm anything out of him. He had just gone ahead and trusted her. It was odd. But he still did. He said, "You look fine," and smiled at her.

She said, "Thank you, that's reassuring," and smiled back. But as he followed her to the door he saw that she was blushing. His stare had affected her, and she was fighting it down. He was amused suddenly, for of course he'd meant nothing by it.

It was a good three weeks since he'd driven down to New Haven shouting doggerel about his intention of raping her——

He was a little hot himself as he held the door for her and she went in. She needed that bit of color in her face, perhaps, but with it—yes, she looked fine.

That's not for you, he told himself following her in. You stay away from that.

9

So I have three days now. They won't operate until Tuesday, but on Sunday evening they will carry me, flat as a fallen soufflé, to an ambulance, slide me into place, and drive me away. In the hospital I shall be reduced to being a body—a body to be got ready for the anesthesia and the knives, and I must welcome that. Tomorrow, Saturday, and Sunday are days of grace, days in which I can also be a mind; days in which I can face realistically the terrible danger of hope. I *must* not hope. I must not let myself look forward. I must commit *nothing* to a future that may be better or may be—— No. Even to define it is to let hope and commitment seep in. And I don't dare. I don't dare. I can't afford to hope—and to lose.

Three days. No, I must keep to the present or to the past. Perhaps I might spend them in the present, looking about for ends to be tied up which hang loose from these months of transitional existence—— But no, I don't think I shall. I suppose I hesitate because the obvious loose end is Lorraine, and I don't know how to help her. She is a dear girl and a good girl, and a very unhappy one. This nonsense of working with homeless children—I wanted to blow her up about it. It's the last thing she should be doing. It's a regression to Boston Puritanism! But what can I do? Of course she must find life with Herbert impossible, but really, homeless children! She ought to be learning how to enjoy herself! Only—I'm sure I don't know how to help her do that.

And then, to be fair, it is hard for me not to see Mary in her, or the effects of having Mary as a mother. *That* isn't Lorraine's fault, it's mine. I never in all our lives was fair to Mary. I should be ashamed, I suppose, but I'm not. People who are as close as we were are never, never, fair to each other. I suppose, on balance, Mary gained as much as she lost. She never would have married Spencer Forbes if not for me.

CHAPTER NINE

Well, you could make out a very good case for saying that I should never have married James Fennimore Greene if not for Mary. The very idea came to me—consciously, at least—because we had a quarrel at Christmastime, 1912.

There had been early snow that year. It seems to me, looking back, to have been so beautiful that I know I am idealizing and romanticizing my memories. I remind myself how protected, provincial, restricted we were, and how I hated the restrictions—and even these memories twist and play me false, for it seems to me that just because we were restricted, our occasional pleasures took us higher up, were infinitely more exciting than the excitements of today. Does everyone, growing old, think that life has grown flatter? I know we paid for our "ups," I know how I resented the payment, but we had them just the same.

Christmastime that year began as an "up." I was through school now, and I had been feeling all fall that I had worn out our little town. In fact, I had fretted so horribly, must have made everyone so miserable, that Mother had packed me off twice to visit relatives. This had been dull enough for me to be delighted to get home. In addition, Mary had been trying to teach me to cook (Pearl, the maid, threatened to leave, but Mary persisted), and I had been taking piano lessons; but the only thing that had really been interesting was working for my father. He'd arranged for me to come into his office, mornings, and I was trying to teach myself shorthand. My poor father! How he suffered over the letters I improvised for him when my pothooks failed! At least, though, something told me that his office had a connection with reality, that it was—however peripheral—part of a sensible world that I could understand and accept, where I could learn how things really worked. None of the rest of my life then had any such connection at all.

He let me off, pretty much, for the Christmas holidays. All the boys who went away to school were home, a beau of Mary's came to visit— I wish I could remember his name, I can see his face perfectly clearly—and there were lots of parties. Naturally, the parties came before any "job." My only important job was to find a satisfactory young man who would want to marry me.

Everything began well, I was properly gay, I danced at the parties, and went skating, and laughed with everyone and was invited to Dartmouth for the Carnival, it was just what a holiday time should be—until just after Christmas. Mary's young man, you see, had begun to get on my nerves. He was solemn enough to begin with but he was also trying to make a good impression, and the result was an excess of earnestness that made me, in the end, want to tease him.

I did. Embarrassed, he still tried to hold his own. The result was that we skirmished more every day. In the end, he was devoting less time to Mary than to me.

Now I suppose, in all honesty, that I must have intended this to happen. My greedy unconscious must have set itself to detach Mary's beau and either annex him myself, or make a fool of him, or both. I can see plainly how horrid I was, and can only wonder at Mary's patience—perhaps I'd knocked it into her. But, at the time when she finally broke down and laced into me, crying with rage, I felt absolutely innocent and stunned by her absurd jealousy—and God help me, I told her so, very condescendingly. "I don't want your silly——" (oh, what *was* his name!), I told her, "and if you've got yourself in such a state, I shall just go away for a while, you won't have to bother being jealous of me, I shan't be around." So I stalked out and went to stay overnight with my friend Jane Turrell. (Delia and I had decidedly grown apart.)

The next day my mother got hold of me and read me the riot act. She did it so seldom that, when she did, it was overwhelming. I was overwhelmed. Too overwhelmed even to apologize to Mary, or to dare show my face to her young man. So I ran off, for the first time in a long time. Not to Mr. Greene's, though. I didn't want solitude in which to think high thoughts and be superior, I didn't want to have to think at all. I wanted good jolly vulgar company. So I went sleighing with Mary's bêtes noires, the Heffernan boys. Oh, there were other young people along in the big hay-filled sledge, but they too were all pretty "ordinary," as the word was. We stopped at a road-house for supper on the way home, and to rest the horses, and the boys had some liquor, and I wouldn't say that all the girls didn't—and when they dropped me off at my house there was a bit of a disturbance. It was half past ten, too, and no one knew where I'd been. So there I was in disgrace again.

Don't think that because I speak of it lightly it was easy for me to endure. My mother was really upset. This was very unusual—one of the best things about her was the kind of warm inattention with

which she'd raised us. I see that it had its drawbacks, it had put more
of a weight on Mary's shoulders than she really should have had to
carry—and I suppose it had repercussions in the relationship between
my mother and father, and must have made it oddly tenuous at
times. Perhaps it was part of the background of that early memory
of mine of the queer scene between them. Perhaps he had got in the
habit of thinking that she wasn't always present; and he was right,
she wasn't. But, on the positive side—we were never nagged, and
though of course custom and convention ruled us, we were trusted to
see that this was sensible and reasonable, we were not terrorized.
Now, agonizedly, I could see that my mother was asking herself
whether she *could* trust me, whether she had not made a horrible
mistake and brought me up wrong. I could see her looking at me and
blaming herself for my misdemeanors. I wanted to reassure her, but
I didn't know how. I'd done two terrible things one on top of the
other, and telling her that I would be good in the future wouldn't
set them right. For a person who was a great reader, she had singularly
little use for words.

Mary's beau went off to spend New Year's with his family before
he went back to college, and she was very white and silent and cried
at night. I had to conclude that he had not proposed and that she
blamed me. Indeed, I blamed myself; only, stiff-necked, stiff-backed,
would not show it. I didn't want to be defiant, I didn't really feel
defiant. But Mary's tears and my mother's unceasing cogitation—I
would look up from what I was doing ten times a day and find her
gazing at me—combined to make me act defiantly. This finally roused
Mary, so perhaps it was just as well. "I don't know what's going to
become of you!" she burst out at me one day, when I hadn't done
anything but have a snowball thrown at me by the youngest Heffernan
which was not, as I said, my fault.

"Maybe I'll marry Mr. Greene," I said. He was staying at the
castle with a party for New Year's, and I had seen him drive by—in a
cutter, for the monstrous red car couldn't climb his hill in winter.
That was why he'd come into my head, for he had seen me too, and
bowed. I didn't mean anything by it at all when I said it—and Mary
didn't think I did, she didn't look scandalized, merely irritated by
my irresponsibility. And yet—as soon as I had said it, the words began
to get heavier and heavier in my head, I could feel them sink down

Carl A. Rudisill Library
LENOIR RHYNE COLLEGE

within me slowly, fatefully, heavier and heavier, until they reached my heart. There they stopped, with a little satisfied clanking sound, and the gates of my will swung shut around them, and I was left with a miracle accomplished. I knew what I was going to do. I had an intention, an aim. All the wild loose energy that had swept me around here and there and made such trouble for me and Mary and her beau and my mother and father, and even, I guess, the Heffernans— all this was channeled to one purpose. I was going to marry Mr. Greene.

How did I do it? Every possible way I could. How does anyone do anything? First, I told my father that I was bored at home and came back to work for him mornings. The second morning Mr. Greene called on the telephone. I heard my father make an appointment for four o'clock. Of course, I didn't know which afternoon, but I told him that I had decided that the old correspondence in his files had to be cleaned out—some of it was from people ten years dead—and that I had made a New Year's resolution to undertake it, and I set to work. I worked with a will, too. There's no use in doing a thing halfheartedly. So when Mr. Greene arrived I was truly surprised, and had to apologize for my grubby hands and put them behind my back and laughed instead of shaking hands, and ran out of my father's office, being careful to shut the door behind me.

Then I went and washed up and then I waited for twenty minutes, and then I said a small prayer and made tea.

I was at the door with a tray—a teapot, some cookies I'd brought earlier, and two cups—when I heard a chair pushed back, and I entered just as the conference was over.

"Well, Diana," said my father, "what's that?"

"A nice hot cuppa," I said cheerfully. "You both need it. It's going to snow again." And I set the tray down on the desk.

"A cuppa!" said Mr. Greene. "I haven't heard that since I was in London. Where did you pick that up?"

"From our laundress. Only I think she comes from closer to Cork. Is that too strong, Mr. Greene? Daddy likes it stewed. I have hot water in the kettle still."

"It's fine, Diana. But what about yourself, as they say in Cork? Aren't you going to join us?"

"Well, I don't want to interrupt——"

But they were finished, they assured me, they insisted I get another cup, and I sat down and drank stewed tea and beamed at them while they chatted about property assessments.

"It's nice to see you again, Diana," said Mr. Greene as he put his cup down. I could see he really meant it, and I could see that unless I did something, that was all he was ever going to mean. He was forty-one, and I was a charming child.

"It's nice to see you too," I said. "How are Davies and Mrs. Davies—oh, and the chauffeur?"

"Very well, thank you, as far as the Davies' are concerned, but I had to get rid of the chauffeur, the bills were being padded disgracefully. I'll get a new man in the spring. Will you come motoring again with me, Diana?"

"On one condition," I said. "If the chauffeur will teach me to drive."

I could see my father beginning to frown, but Mr. Greene laughed heartily. "I'll wager you could learn, too," he said.

"A little more tea?" I offered, and poured him another cup, and passed him the cookies. Then I poured my father a cup quickly, to distract him, for I could feel that an idea was slowly being born within Mr. Greene's head.

"That rather depends too much on the chauffeur, though," he said. "And it's quite a time till spring. You'd better come visit the Davies' and me first. Mr. Cummings, won't you bring Diana to lunch?"

"I never," said my father, "have the time to lunch very far from my office." Then he added, "I'm afraid," for politeness, but it wasn't convincing. His face was getting quite rigid. He was about to feel that I was taking advantage of Mr. Greene. So I was, so I was. I could only pray that my father wouldn't embarrass me by saying so right out loud. I acted quickly.

"Oh Daddy," I said, "you're too mean! And I just know Mary would love to see the inside of the castle. Mr. Greene—could my sister and I come to tea instead one afternoon, if we wouldn't be in the way—your guests and all, I mean?" Oh Lord, I added under my breath, please let Daddy not explode!

"Now, Diana——" he did indeed begin, but I could hear that it was merely a minatory rumbling, not absolute crashing denial.

"I would be delighted!" said Mr. Greene, and then of course Daddy couldn't say a thing. "My guests would be very happy to meet you both, I'm sure." At this point he told Daddy their names, to make clear that we would be well and truly chaperoned, and offered to send down for us any day I cared to name.

I was blushing. It was relief. But I hope my father thought it was because I was ashamed of myself for being so forward. I murmured that the Church Guild Meeting was tomorrow, but perhaps the day after that—— And so it was arranged, and Mr. Greene left.

I could feel my father being uneasy as we walked together to the Interurban stop, and so I began at once, with never a qualm, the career of lying to my nearest and dearest which got me married to Mr. Greene. "I'm sorry, Daddy," I said. "I know I shouldn't have. But Mary's been so upset since"—oh, *what* was his name!—"since Whoever-it-was went home, that I thought this might—you know— give her something else to think about. I hope I wasn't too awful, but I wanted her to see the house, and the ladies' dresses—— It'll take her mind off things."

My father sighed. "That's all right, Puss," he said, and I knew I was forgiven, and even that didn't make me ashamed of myself.

So we went up to the castle. We hired a rig instead of having Mr. Greene send down, because it made my father feel that we were less of an imposition. How lovely it was! The drive was planted with an evergreen screen behind the dogwood and other flowering shrubs that made it beautiful differently in spring, and late sunlight splintered off the snow that lay on the evergreen boughs. I could feel Mary beside me being excited, rising to the occasion. I can't do that and never could. Either I can manage or not. But I was relieved that Mary was looking forward to it. It was a sop to—not my guilt. Or was it? To my uneasiness, my intellectual uneasiness, it's impossible to give it a more exact name. I was using her, but at least I could feel that she was going to get something out of it—if only the chance to exercise the social abilities she was so proud of.

We drove into the porte-cochere—this was on the east of the house and enormously gloomy in the late afternoon—the driver threw back the robe we'd had over us and helped us down—and then we looked for a way to announce ourselves. We couldn't find a bell, and the bronze knocker on the door looked as if no one had dared tamper with it since it had left the hands of its maker (whom I tentatively named Cellini Jenkins). Finally, feeling the gaze of both driver and horse, I lifted it in both hands and banged it down, expecting the house to shake. It didn't—in those years it couldn't—but Davies finally appeared. We greeted each other with reserve, he took our outdoor things, and ushered us into the drawing room.

My goodness, it was hideous! Carved dark wood, red brocade, an emphatic Persian rug as big as a skating rink, a mantel that looked like a Gothic cathedral—and as far as we could see, no one at all. This didn't nonplus Davies, however. He announced us loudly and went out. Mary and I stood staring about the room and wondering what to do next.

"Well," I said, "at least there's a fire. Let's go and get warm."

"There's no one here," said Mary, faintly.

"Then think of all we'll have for tea," I said, "just for the two of us." I took her hand and pulled her toward the fire. We came around the end of a polished refectory table and there, lying flat on her back on a sofa, was a girl about our age in a shirtwaist and skirt.

We all three stared. She was a nice-looking girl, with chestnut hair. "Hello," she said.

"Hello," we replied.

She yawned. "I'm sorry! I just waked up. We went skating this morning and then I ate an enormous lunch. You must be—no, don't tell me, Uncle Fenn said you were coming, I'll remember—you must be the Cummingses. How do you do. I'm Louise Ford. It's so nice to see someone young, I wish you'd come up before, why didn't you?"

"We just got invited," I said, but I grinned at her and sat down as I said it, so that she'd know we didn't resent it.

She swung her legs around and sat up and stretched. "Honestly," she said. "Uncle Fenn! He's a love, but he doesn't think! Here I am cooped up for the holidays with no one under forty and it's almost time to go back to college before he produces anyone my age."

"Oh," I said. "Do you go to college? Where?"

She began to tell us about it, but I didn't listen. I was too elated. It *was* almost the end of the holidays, I had almost no time left, but for what there was, Louise was the perfect liaison with the castle. And it all pointed away from me, it was so natural, so simple! All I had to do was to get her included in one or two of the local festivities, and then we'd have to be asked back and—yes! Mary was going to do it for me! Of course she was—she knew my social sense was lacking, and she wasn't sure, I suppose, that I wouldn't introduce Louise to the Heffernans. But there was a perfectly proper party that very night, and Mary invited Louise to come with us! I wanted to stand up and sing.

"You're angels!" said Louise, and got to her feet and shouted, "Mamma, Uncle Fenn, everybody! Where are you! We have guests!"

Mamma, who was Mr. Greene's sister, gave me a qualm or two when she appeared, for she had all Mr. Greene's rectitude and none of his kindness. Louise told her about Mary's invitation, and there was a little pause while Mamma inspected us. I tried to look like a rice pudding—one without raisins; but it was Mary who carried the day. She blushed and said, "Mrs. Ford, you must think me very forward, but the party is at my best friend's, Dorothy Dewey's—Mr. Greene, her father's president of the bank?"—("Oh yes, of course," said Mr. Greene.) "—and she'd *expect* me to ask Louise to join us, if you'll let her. Her brother's home from Dartmouth with two friends who live in the West, and Mrs. Dewey's been doing her level best to keep everyone entertained and busy all vacation. Oh, we've all had lots of fun together. But it would be even more fun if we could bring someone new—I mean, Mrs. Dewey would be delighted——"

Louise, who had pricked up her ears at hearing about three Dartmouth men, joined in, and Mamma finally agreed. I'd have given a great deal, sometimes, to have been able to command Mary's air of complete trustworthiness and utter respectability. But never quite enough. I wouldn't have been willing to be Mary.

I don't think she ever knew how much she helped me. She came really to like Louise. They corresponded, and Mary scolded her about not having a serious purpose in life, and about leading boys on, which was one of Louise's problems, and why she'd been at the castle in the first place. She'd got herself engaged to not one but *two* unsuitable young men, and Mamma had snatched her out of New York to the wilds of Westchester as punishment. Louise eventually inherited eight million dollars. She was attractive, too, I don't mean she wasn't; but somehow there's a particular scent to eight million dollars that unsuitable young men can smell through reinforced concrete. I saw her four years ago. She was a Baroness then. I didn't meet the Baron, but it looked to me as if she still had all her millions.

But that's all gossip. For me, the great, the important, thing was that now our connection with the castle was established. We could visit back and forth, and though Mary would not have done so unless Louise was staying there, I saw that we did. I told her that it would be cruel to Mr. Greene to give him the impression that we cared only for Louise and came to see him only when she was there—— What a liar I was! Butter wouldn't melt in my mouth, those days.

Oddly enough once all this had happened, once the visits became an accepted thing, and baskets of fruit and vegetables arrived from the castle, and Mr. Greene asked Mary and me to come to lunch early enough to make sure the flowers were done right—once this was all set in motion and not to be stopped, my father liked it better than my mother did. With all her absent-mindedness and inattention, my mother was capable of feeling things through any number of layers of disguise. Social propriety meant very little to her. She would never have felt, as my father almost did, that there was a barrier of class between Mr. Greene and ourselves. She was sorry for people who had bad manners, and she felt that wealth and position carried obligations and responsibilities, but that was about the limit of her class consciousness. So she was neither pleased nor distressed by her daughters' sudden intimacy with the rich and great. But I think she felt, alone in the family, that I was up to something. She felt that there was a kind of disproportion in my interest in the castle. She would not have expected it of me, and it worried her. She gave me a long talk, in her usual rambling style, on the evils of snobbery, and how easily one could become spoiled and sophisticated, which was then a horrid word, and lose the life-giving ability to take pleasure in simple things. I'm not really sure that she thought my too great concentration on the castle to be due to snobbery, though. My feeling is that she thought a lecture would be good for me somehow, whether it was exactly pertinent or not, and that this was about as pertinent as she could get. "Think," she said, "of poor tragic Marie Antoinette, so stupid, so spoiled! Only someone who had forgotten the good simple taste of bread would have offered cake to the starving."

"Mummy darling," I said, "she didn't offer——"

"No, I know," she agreed, "but what I say is true anyway. Morally true. The most terrible thing a person can do is to cut himself off from life. You mustn't ever let yourself be tempted by false values——"

"I won't," I said, not too patiently.

She sighed and said, "Well, I've tried to tell you. I know I don't speak very well. But remember what I say, Diana. It may all seem useful someday." One day it did, but at the time I was gently contemptuous.

And summer came, and I reminded Mr. Greene of how he had promised—which he hadn't, but could not contradict—to teach me to drive. Naturally the new chauffeur accompanied us, and once in a while Mary came too. But the focus of action, the center of what was going on, lay between Mr. Greene and me in the front seat, no matter who else was there. I was very careful at first not to learn too fast. Aside from the mere element of time, time together, I wanted Mr. Greene to feel very manly about his ability to do well something that I did badly, and also to have a sense of accomplishment about having taught me, finally. But then I got interested, I felt the challenge of learning to drive well, which was a very different thing then from what it is now. It took strength and finesse and a sense of timing just to coax that car into top gear, and when I could do it without horrible clashings and grindings and slowing downs, I felt really proud of myself. You know, I don't think I would have done it, if I hadn't.

I suppose I mean really that I wouldn't have undertaken the whole thing and I could never have carried it through if I hadn't been truly fond of Mr. Greene. And more, if I hadn't truly respected him. I did. He knew such a lot, he moved in the Great World, the world I knew existed somewhere though I'd never seen it, and he wasn't stuffy about it, not making a show of it, but not concealing his knowledge either, and never talking down to me. Men did then, to women, but never Mr. Greene to me, he wasn't amused by ladylike ignorance, and we'd been over architecture and philosophy and politics and poetry that summer. I was out to get him and all that he had (not money, but a chance at life, life, life!), and later I deceived him for I told him that I loved him—but I liked him so much, we got on so well together, that it did not seem to me then to be a fatal deception at all.

I called him Mr. Greene, right through the summer. He called me Diana as he had from the beginning when I was a child. Nothing seemed to happen, nothing seemed to change, except that we grew very slowly to have enough experiences in common so that we once in a while talked privately to each other in public. But—— But I knew something had really happened because once, when Mr. Greene laid his hand over mine on the brake and helped to pull it back, his hand shook. And in the early fall, when Louise was staying at the castle before she went back to college, she gave me, once, a long speculative look. I sat perfectly still and smiled back at her, making myself go relaxed and comfortable. She didn't say anything. Afterwards my heart pounded.

And then in October he told me suddenly that he was going abroad. We weren't driving that day, we were walking through the woods. Not alone, of course. There were people staying for the week-end and Mary and I had come to the castle for lunch. Six or eight of us went out afterwards and walked down to where some deer had been seen. We didn't see them, but the tracks were there. When Mr. Greene told me he was going away, we were on the way back up the hill. The two of us were a little behind the others because Mr. Greene was thinking about thinning out some of the timber, and kept pausing to shake his head over patches of brush.

When he told me I stopped walking altogether. It is now or never, something said inside my head. Faint. Scream. Immediately I answered, Then it will be never, you will spoil everything if you get into a panic. Be quiet. Be still. Out loud I said, "How lovely, how I envy you! Will you go to Spain this time, as you planned?"

"Not until spring," he said heavily. "I am anxious to see the Easter ceremonies, they are said to be remarkable. I plan to go first to the Near East, and perhaps into Egypt. I should like to see Greece again, but there is trouble in the Balkans."

"There is always trouble in the Balkans," I said, not knowing what I was saying. He was planning to be away for six months! I felt as if I had sustained a secret wound, I felt as if I were bleeding.

"Yes," he agreed, as distrait as I. Ordinarily he'd have liked nothing better than to instruct me on Balkan nationalism and the history of Turkey in Europe, but now he was silent and did not look at me. In a moment I became able to begin walking slowly uphill again, toward the laughter of his friends.

"I hope," I said, "that you will remember to send postcards to Mary and me from everywhere that you stop. Though I suppose postcards are not a matter of course in the Near East. Well, perhaps you will write us descriptions of—will you see the Cedars of Lebanon? Or Damascus? You may skip the Sphinx and the Pyramids, I've been tired of them for years."

He didn't say anything for a minute, and I stole a glance under my eyelashes and saw that his jaw was set and the tension of his muscles pushed his lower lip out angrily. I looked away at once. He was running away from me. How, how, how could I stop him? He said, "Yes, Diana. I'll write."

"Do, please," I told him, quickening my pace, "for I shall miss you." Then we caught up with the rest of the group and were not alone again all day.

I didn't sleep that night. I sat up in bed with the blankets huddled around me and watched the stars move across the sky through the window next to my bed. I have always hated to sleep where I cannot look out. At first I tried to think how to stop him, and I couldn't. I would have been willing to trap him if I could have thought of a way. Cleopatra, I remembered, had herself delivered to Caesar rolled up in a rug. I'd have rolled myself up in a dozen if I'd thought Mr. Greene would have accepted me when I arrived—but I knew that he would just ship me home to my mother. He thought he was too old for me. He thought I didn't love him. He thought it would be difficult for both of us to adjust to marriage across almost a generation of time between us—— I knew all the things he thought, and I knew something else, too, something that was the most important hindrance of all, and perhaps a fatal one. He was afraid of me. Not that he was a coward, I don't mean that. Neither his irony nor his kindness ever stopped him from doing what his duty told him should be done. But he didn't like violence (I suppose because of that fire-breathing old monster, his father), and he sensed violence in me. *He* knew I wasn't a rice pudding without any raisins, and he wanted me and was afraid of what having me might mean all at the same time. He was a man who was very private about his emotions too, and I think he must have wondered whether people wouldn't laugh if he married a girl of no family, from Nowhere, New York, who was less than half his age.

He had said he would write, there was that. Perhaps if I were patient he would come back and marry me, I told myself. Alone in

Spain, alone in the Near East, fleeing from me, would my presence not haunt him? He was going to try to forget me, and though I did not know much about myself then, I did know that this kind of well-laid plan might often "gang agley." If I were patient—— But of course that was the trouble. A kind of fury shook me at the thought. For how many years would I have to sit and knit and practice the piano and type my father's letters while Mr. Greene fought himself to a standstill in order to marry me? And when he had finally won, or lost, whichever it was, and had come back to lay his heart at my feet—would I be there? For I really was not patient.

Sometime during the night I indulged in an elaborate daydream of getting him to take me driving, losing the chauffeur somehow, arranging a breakdown in a lonely spot where there was no transportation, and so managing to compromise us into marriage. But I knew perfectly well that it was a daydream and not a plan, and I told myself (not too successfully) to stop it. I knew it made no sense. It was not the *kind* of thing that would happen to me and Mr. Greene. It was the kind of thing that happened to stupid people who didn't trust each other because they didn't understand each other, and the problem between Mr. Greene and me was quite different. He *didn't* trust me, but to go in for schemes and traps would only make everything worse. After all, he'd been a "catch" on two continents for twenty years. If he could have been caught by calculation, he would have been caught long ago. What I needed, I saw finally, was a way to make him trust me and not be afraid. I could not think what this might be.

Finally, at about four o'clock, I gave up my efforts and lay down on my back in my bed. I relaxed. I said—probably blasphemously— "Oh, Lord, please help me. I can't do this myself. Please help me. Oh, Lord, into Thy hands I resign my spirit." I lay for a moment listening, but nothing answered me except the wind in the trees outside and the long silence of the night and I thought of Mr. Greene sleeping in *his* bed in the castle, and I projected myself at him, all my spirit, all my intention, all my will, and said, "James, dear James, don't be afraid of me. Don't be afraid. Dear, dear James." And then I fell a thousand miles into sleep.

The next day was Sunday. I slept late and when I opened my eyes the sun was pouring into the room and I lay in a great dazzling pool of it. I felt as if I'd waked into another world, a world in which there was no strain or fear or hurry, a world of warmth, and I got up and got dressed and went down to the kitchen and ate a bowl of oatmeal out there, and said "Good morning" to my family, and asked Mary if she was coming to church with me.

"Well," said Mary, "I'm certainly going to church! I didn't know you were."

"I'm going to church every Sunday," I said, in a sort of radiant calm, and I pinned on my hat, and we set out——

And Mr. Greene was there.

Had I known he was going to be? Well—I knew that he did go on occasion, and more often when Mrs. Ford was staying at the castle as she was that weekend. But I hadn't really known in so many words.

I felt my heart hesitate and give a great thump when I saw him across the aisle between Louise's mother and another lady. Then I knew it was all right, everything was all right, for though Mary and I came in very quietly and sat behind him, he turned around as we went into our pew. I smiled at him. It was different from any way I had ever smiled at him before. I smiled and said, in my head, Dear, dear James, it's all right, everything is all right, you need not be afraid of me, you may run away if you want, but you needn't, I shan't harm you, dear James. He blushed. He smiled back, his mouth opened a little with joy. It was all quite different from any way it had been before. Then Mary tugged at my sleeve and I knelt down and bent my head and prayed, "Thank You, thank You, dear Lord. Please, oh, please let me know how to make him happy. Thank You and please, thank You and please."

When we met afterwards coming out I found myself next to Mrs. Ford and I talked to her enthusiastically about Louise for quite five minutes, while Mr. Greene teased Mary gently—I think about the stained glass in the church: it really was dreadful. He always pretended to her that she could do anything she wanted with the Church Guild, and the Guild anything it wanted with the Rector, and he wanted her to get rid of that awful glass. Then we turned toward each other at exactly the same moment. I didn't smile again. I didn't dare. I was afraid he'd fall down at my feet if I did, and that would have caused a commotion.

"Diana," he said, "I have an idea. Why don't we rescue Louise from college next weekend, you and Mary and I, and take her on an expedition?"

"Why don't we," I said, and the words came out of my mouth without my knowing any more what they were going to be than if they were in Chinese, "why don't we all drive to New Haven to the football game? Mary, you said Douglas White had written you about it. Mr. Greene, could the wonderful chariot do it?"

"Upon my soul!" said Mr. Greene. "What a good idea! Why—we'd have to start early, young ladies. Are you good at early rising? Louise must come down Friday night—— Hm, hm. Lucy, what do you think?"

Mrs. Ford did not think much of it, it was clear—but she could hardly tell her brother not to offer her daughter a treat just because the treat was going to include me—though she would have liked to, for she was afraid of me too, and there were no arguments on the other side in *her* mind. But she wasn't enough afraid of me to be willing to seem mean, so she hemmed and hawed, and wondered about Louise leaving her work, but Mr. Greene swept her before him, and everything was arranged——

Ah yes, ah yes indeed. Everything, everything was arranged, including my life, outside the church on that sunny morning, and I've never really understood how it came about. Was it God's will? Was it magic? Was it because I had suffered a change of heart and it showed? Was it my middle-of-the-night message? Or my prayer, resigning myself to God? Or the fact that I *did* smile at Mr. Greene in a new way, a different way, wanting not to frighten him, wanting not to be violent, wanting to throw away everything about me that might separate us? I shall never know. I only know he proposed to me in the crush between the halves at the football game the next week.

Such a preposterous time and place! And yet I'd known it was coming—well, part of the time I knew it was coming—as well as if we'd made an appointment. I won't pretend that the rest of the time I wasn't frightened and panicky, when I didn't see him during the week and pictured him in New York, in a new panic of his own, buying steamer tickets, and cabling Cairo for reservations at Shepheard's Hotel. But on Friday afternoon he came by himself to say that Louise was arriving that evening, and to remind Mary and me to be ready to leave at eight the next morning. I gave him some tea. It always amused me and made me feel good to give him tea because of that first time I had at my father's office. He didn't want to look at me, and talked stiffly to my mother, but it was out of embarrassment, because he knew what he was going to do. I did not let myself become frightened or greedy, but spoke to him in my head quietly by his name, and out loud quietly too. I didn't sleep much that night either, though.

And then, absurdly, it happened as we left our seats to get coffee between the halves. Mary and Douglas White and Louise and the young man whom Douglas had provided for her were cut off from us by a twisting line of people, Mr. Greene and I were pushed together almost under the stands, and he put his arms on either side of me—not around me—to protect me. He was standing behind me. Then there was another push and we were jammed together even more tightly and he said, over my shoulder and into my ear, "Diana, you said you envied me going away. Will you come with me?"

I said, "I will go anywhere with you."

He said hoarsely, "What?"

I turned my head so that my cheek was against his mouth—we were close to the same height—and said again, "I will go anywhere with you."

He said, "Oh, God," and his arms closed against my sides like a vise—and then suddenly the crush was gone, and Mary and Louise were pushing through to us, and it had happened, and I was trembling so I could hardly stand up.

I said very quickly, "Oh, that was scary, look at me, I'm shaking. Douglas, your classmates are very rough boys. Where is the coffee?" And I walked over to the man selling coffee without looking at my dear James, because I was afraid, now, that I would fall!

He didn't speak again during the game. I don't mean to me, I mean to anyone. He sat next to me looking straight ahead. He opened his mouth and moistened his lips once or twice. His arm touched mine, and we both shook, and he pulled it away. Louise got quite worried about him, and asked him as we came away if he wanted to start home at once. "No, no," he said. "No, no, I'm quite all right. Quite all right." But he so obviously wasn't that in the end we started home earlier than we had planned.

Driving helped him. He loved to drive, always. He loved to maneuver the powerful car. As we spun west out of New Haven, he began to come to himself and to talk, and finally remembered a good restaurant somewhere before we got to Danbury, and we stopped there for dinner.

Mary and Louise went upstairs to wash their hands and fix their hair. Mr. Greene wanted to see to the garaging of the car. I went into a little parlor where there was a wood fire and waited till I heard him come in. Then I went and met him in the hall. There was a good smell of dinner and no one around. He stopped dead when he saw me and for a moment we just stood like two dummies looking into each other's eyes and my heart slowed down with terror and almost stopped because I thought that perhaps the emotion of the afternoon had upset him again.

Then he reached out his hands very carefully and took both of mine and said, "Diana, did you really say what I thought you said?"

I said, "James dear, if you asked me what I think you asked me, then I said what you think I said."

He moistened his lips and said, almost roughly, "I ask you to marry me, Diana."

"I will," I said, nearly in a whisper.

"I am older—more than twice your age."

"Yes. It doesn't matter."

"I have—— There have been women—— You must understand, Diana, that there was someone I cared for and couldn't marry and—others that—that——"

"That you couldn't marry either. I know, James, I'm not that young. But—don't tell me about them, if you don't mind. That was before. Now—there is just you and me. Or—is there?"

That was mean of me, wasn't it, to ask him that and make him say it? But I didn't want to hear about his arrangements, or whoever it was he'd loved and not been able to marry. And his hands hurt mine, they were crushing them. So—I hurt him. A little.

"Oh, God," he said. "Yes. Oh, God. I want to kiss you. I want so badly to kiss you." He dropped one of my hands and made a gesture at the door. "Someone will come in."

"It doesn't matter in the least," I said. Then he kissed me. It was rather awkward. My hat slid a bit. I felt as if I had run a long, long race and wanted to faint. His mustache was bristly. Dear James, dear

James, I said in my head, I will make you happy. When he released me I said out loud, "I love you," for it seemed to me time for someone to say it. Then I heard Mary and Louise moving about upstairs, and I turned away from him and ran up to them, straightening my hat as I went.

That is the moment I remember best, the moment of achievement, although I cannot remember what I felt, if I felt anything. I remember it better than my wedding day, or any of the months in between. We were not married until February, just before Lent and my nineteenth birthday, for both families were turned upside down and inside out by the news of our intentions. Louise's mamma was in a condition. She charged, and charged again, at the citadel of our engagement like the leader of a forlorn hope so obsessed with how disastrous failure would be that she couldn't stop, couldn't admit she had failed. My own mother was terribly shaken too, at first, for I *had* been up to something, and it might very well be just what she had feared. By and by she came round and was pleased, but it was a long time before she could stop thinking first, when she thought of me, and denying the thought but still thinking it first, that I had married Mr. Greene for his money.

In all this Mr. Greene was never for one moment shaken, and so I was not either, and was happy and calm and fulfilled, and this helped my mother to begin denying to herself her fear of my motives, and defeated Mrs. Ford. And so we were married in February 1914 in the church with the horrible stained glass, Mary as my maid of honor, looking lovely, Louise, her mother's forces scattered and broken, as one of the bridesmaids, and we went to Italy on our honeymoon——

Dear, dear James. He has been dead for almost twenty-seven years, more than a quarter of a century, but there are times still when I feel how his arms pressed against my sides as we stood in the crowd behind the stands at the Yale game, times when his face comes before me saying, "I want so badly to kiss you," and I see, not remember but see, how pale he was and his muscles working in tension to hold flesh and bone together. My dear, dear James.

10

When Herbert de Koning came home Monday evening he couldn't find his wife. She wasn't waiting for him in the library reading a novel, she wasn't in the bedroom sitting at her dressing table filing her nails, she wasn't even still in the bathroom under the shower as she had been (inconveniently) several times recently when she had come home late from her days spent looking after other people's dirty and degenerate children. He looked in all these places and, finding them empty, stood angrily and uncertainly poised in the hall, wondering whether to ask the maid if she had telephoned. Had something gone wrong, her dreary work at the shelter tried her too hard, perhaps? Had there been another bout of hysterics—this time before strangers? Through the empty rooms the question blew like a cold little breeze.

Then he heard her laugh. She laughed and the children laughed and shouted something from the nursery rooms at the end of the corridor. Lorraine cried, "Read it again? But I've read it three times! Three times is all! Three times is magic! I'll read it another night. No, not tomorrow, because tomorrow I'll be up with poor Aunt Di. But Hilda will read it——"

Herbert stood in the doorway and looked in. Bobby, his face shiny with soap and excitement, had climbed up the back of Lorraine's chair and was balanced at a precarious angle, leaning over her shoulder. Jane, in her lap, was bouncing up and down and crying, "Read! Read! Read!" They were both in their pajamas and both, obviously, much too excited to settle down in bed.

"Well! Good evening!" said Herbert.

A silence as deep as it was brief held them all for a second. Jane spoke first. "Hi, Daddy!" she said. "Hi Daddy! Hi Daddy!"

"Low Daddy!" cried Bobby at once. "Low Daddy! Hi Daddy! Low Daddy!" This was such a successful joke that he let go of the back of the chair, waved his arms hilariously, and fell to the floor where he sat looking astonished.

"My goodness!" Lorraine said, twisting to see him. "That was a bump! What a good thing you landed on your sit-me-down! Can you——"

But Herbert had reached the child and jerked him up. Bobby roared. Herbert said, "Lorraine, the child may be hurt. He could injure his spine that way," and Bobby roared again.

"I know he could," said Lorraine, "but there's no reason to scare him to death, besides! Now, Jane, let go, let me see if your brother— Jane, let go! Bob, darling, come to Mum. Herbert, please—— Oh, Hilda, take Jane will you? Where did you land, lovey? Bump on the bumpsie part? There? Stand up, angel, don't hang on me. Now take a walk and tell me if it hurts."

"It hurts, it hurts," roared Bobby, and Herbert's eyes flashed.

"Of course it does," said Lorraine. "You landed bingo-bango. But you walk beautifully, kind sir. Will you walk in the other room with me and get a peppermint for you and a peppermint for Jane?" She leaned down and whispered, "And an extra peppermint for a brave boy who stops crying? Come on, that's the boy."

Subsiding slightly, Bobby took her hand and they went out. Jane, bouncing in Hilda's arms, began to shout, "Hi Daddy! Low Daddy! Bobby fell down!"

"Now you just quiet down, miss," said Hilda firmly. "I'm afraid she's a little excited, Mr. de Koning."

"Much too excited," said Herbert, as Jane threw her head back and her arms open, laughing.

"Now, Jane, settle down! You're all in a perspiration. Excuse me, Mr. de Koning, I'll see whether a damp cloth to the face mayn't help."

"By all means. I can see she needs quieting." When Lorraine came back, he said, "Let the child go to Hilda, Lorraine. He's been too excited. Good night, Bobby."

Bobby opened his mouth to howl again, but Lorraine hugged him quickly and said, "Good night, love. I'll see you in the morning. Trot in to Hilda now." And she walked out quickly, ahead of Herbert.

As they reached the bedroom he said, "Was there any reason for that?"

Lorraine said, "All children get excited. I'm sorry you hit one of the high spots. Usually they're very good."

"Usually they're with Hilda. I hope your discipline with the tenement brats is a little better."

Lorraine stood frozen for a moment. Then she said, "Oh, much. You must come and see one day."

"Thanks. I'll take a shower now. Tell Norah I'll want an old-fashioned in fifteen minutes."

"Yes, Herbert." She walked on to the library.

In exactly fifteen minutes he reappeared, Lorraine touched the buzzer, and Norah carried in two cocktails on a silver tray. The tray shone, Norah's black uniform and white apron were crisp, the cut crystal glasses and muddlers glinted in the lamplight, and Lorraine was sitting quietly with her hands in her lap, waiting. Herbert said, "Well, that looks very good. Thank you, Norah." Norah smiled and went out, Herbert sipped his drink and said, "Ah!"

The telephone rang.

Lorraine started to get up.

Herbert said, "Norah will answer it, won't she?"

"Of course. But I called Aunt Di—— The doctor was there, and she was going to call back."

"Well, if it's she, Norah will tell you."

Lorraine said, "Naturally she will, darling. But I *am* anxious about her."

"Please don't think I'm not," said Herbert, and Norah came in to say that New Haven was calling.

The long skirt of Lorraine's housecoat swished as she went to the phone. "Aunt Di? Oh—Tucker. Is she there? How is she?"

Herbert unfurled the evening paper with deliberation and began going through the stock tables. Lorraine seemed to be having a little difficulty with her aunt. "But you're all right, darling, and comfortable?" she was repeating. "Well, I'll be there tomorrow, angel. The children are fine. Slightly rambunctious, but fine."

"Please remember me to her," said Herbert.

"And Herbert sends love. I'll see you tomorrow then. Good night, darling." She hung up reluctantly and walked back to her chair rubbing her hands as if they were cold. "She sounded so far away," she said. "As if—I don't know. As if she'd retreated into being just a body, waiting for—for the knife and didn't want to have to be a person."

"They've probably drugged her," said Herbert.

"Oh—do you think so?"

"Certainly. They always put them under sedation the night before an operation. Much less strain. Are you sure you should go out tomorrow? She mayn't even be aware you're there, you know."

Lorraine said (and heard her tone as too abrupt, too defensive), "I thought I'd stay over a day or two. You told me you and Mr. Miller had to see those men from Chicago tomorrow evening, and the Abbotts' party is the next night, and I can bear to miss that. It's the usual enormous buffet she always has in the spring to pay off all the dinners she owes. You go, if you feel like it. I told her I wasn't sure I could make it, and she couldn't have cared less. Hilda will stay in Wednesday gladly if I give her Saturday off, so the children will be all right. And Dr. Ingoldsby's nurse has got me a room at the Taft."

From behind the paper Herbert said, "Very efficiently arranged."

"You don't mind, do you? With Faith out in Arizona, there's no one but me——"

"Of course I don't mind. You've forgotten something, though, haven't you? What about your slum children?"

"I was there all day today and I'll go all day Friday." She meant to stop there, she had every intention in the world of stopping there, but her tongue got ahead of her and went on, "Herbert, why should you hate them so? They're pathetic and lost, why——"

"Hate them?" His breath came in sharply, he sat up in astonishment, throwing out his chest and squaring his shoulders. "I don't hate them! What an idea! Why should you imagine such nonsense?"

"You sound as if you did," said Lorraine. Her head was bowed and she appeared to be staring at her hands, loose in her lap. "You are quite—mistaken."

They had never been one of her beauties, her hands. They were oddly square and capable-looking against the velvet of her housecoat. She said, "You speak of the children so unkindly."

"Nonsense. How could I? I know nothing about them."

"Then you must mean the unkindness for me."

"Lorraine——" He stopped, the paper across his lap, his hands gripping it too tightly, his pleasant drink only half finished beside him but now growing watery. "No good can come of this conversation," he said decisively.

"No," said Lorraine. "I don't suppose it can." She got up and wandered over to the window and pulled the curtain aside. Below on Park Avenue cars swept by and stopped, swept by and stopped, to the pulse of the traffic lights. Two couples came out of the apartment house across the street and stood laughing together while the doorman whistled for a taxi.

Herbert said, "I'm a practical man, a money man. I can't help it. That's not only my vocation, it's my avocation. I think in practical terms, terms of results, terms of return on investment. I can't help it. In those terms, what you are doing seems to me to be the most utterly frivolous undertaking I have ever heard of. You and dozens of women like you, I suppose, around this city and other cities, are filling up your time by lavishing attention on youngsters who—to put it mildly—will never be worth one one-thousandth of the effort you're putting into it. In fact, most of them will end up on the debit side of the ledger. As you say yourself, they're lost. You said it then, and I've heard you say it before. In other words, you're engaged in what the Army would call Operation Time-Waste. And worse. Worse, because you're spoiling them. You're actually contributing to the delinquency they're heading for. You're softening them, giving them the idea there's more for them than life is going to give them. Later, that kind of indulgence always backfires. It did in the Roman Empire and it's going to today. Every time the Social Security rate goes up, the crime rate follows. Those people don't need pampering, they need discipline.

"Gratitude is a pretty word but——"

Lorraine forced herself to say, "Herbert——"

"Let me finish, please. Since I've begun. I'll say it once, and that's all, but now that I've begun, let me finish. You went into this without consulting me at a time when—when I knew that you were under psychological strain. There are people who would say that it was my duty to stop you. Well, I didn't stop you. I was derelict in my duty, if those people are right. I don't happen to think they're right. I think, on the contrary, that it's a man's duty to treat his wife as an independent, responsible adult who can plan her own life. I've let you do that, this last month, and I think I'm right in saying that no

122
CHAPTER TEN

matter how worried I may have been, I haven't interfered. That's
true, isn't it?"

Lorraine had been standing before the window with her hands
clutched together at her waist. Herbert's words were like a gale. It
was at first all she could do to bend into them and stand against
them. Then, within her, some spark leapt, as if the gale had blown it
awake from smoldering ash. It grew, it burned brighter, she stood
straight. For this was different from last time. This, oh, this was
different! When, weeks ago, he had said "analyst" to her she had
run from him in terror, terror of him, terror of his ally within her.

But now! But now! That ally strengthened her, not him! Awaken-
ing anger mounted like a column of smoke, like a djinn from a bottle.
Her eyes gleamed, she took a deep breath, I hate you, I hate you,
shrieked the Murderee within her. Do you think you can forever
bind me down and jail me, order me about, speak to me with contempt? You want to kill me with your orders and strangle me with
your bonds, but you won't! I hate you! I could kill you, kill you,
kill you! cried the demon Murderee-Murderer; and in her grip Lorraine
took a step forward and another breath of joyous rage, her hands
locked on the back of the chair before her, the words only just
unspoken trembled already, eagerly, on her lips. Herbert's face, taking
in the mask of fury before him, began to change. He put down the
paper, one hand tightened on the chair arm, she saw exultantly that
he was frightened——

And Norah appeared in the doorway, the goddess of all convention,
holding her tray before her like a sacred object. Lorraine caught
herself by the very last trailing end of her control and the words "Not
Before the Servants" appeared in the air before her as if shining
from a neon sign. She could not stop one quick burst of nervous
laughter as she turned away, but she thrust the knuckles of her left
hand into her mouth and bit on them until she felt the terrible wave
begin to ebb.

When she could hear, Herbert was saying, incredibly, "—Jack
Daniels. It comes in a square bottle with a black label. This is an
excellent cocktail, Norah, but the Daniels is very good too."

"I see, sir."

"I'll order some and you might try it when you make old-fashioneds
again. Does your drink need freshening, Lorraine?"

"Yes please," she said, though she didn't want any more, but anything that would keep Norah in the room long enough to give her a chance to get hold of herself was a help. Norah came and got the glass, Lorraine went and sat down helplessly, and Herbert continued to chat firmly to the maid on the question of cocktails. Norah brought her drink over from the barstand in the corner and gave Herbert his. Oh, God, thought Lorraine, now she's going! Herbert——

But as Norah left Herbert picked up his newspaper again and said, with the firmness of a professor delivering the opening sentence of a lecture, "This market is too high."

Lorraine looked at him in astonishment. Except for a spot of red in each of his cheeks, he had himself completely under control. How does he do it! she thought. Devastated and humble, she said, "Is it?" Then, because the conversation must at all costs be kept going, she asked, "Do you expect it to go down?" She trembled a little, wondering if that was really as stupid a thing to say as it sounded.

Herbert, however, said, "A good question. No. Not at once. But my feeling is very distinctly that we're bumping into a ceiling. The Eisenhower Administration can't permit spending to climb any more, not and hold onto its self-respect. Oh, you may say that it's an election year"—here Lorraine nodded wisely as if she were indeed about to make this observation—"but corrupted by politics though some of them may be, there must still be some vestige of respect for their past pledges left in Washington. A man like George Humphrey, now," said Herbert, "is a man who can talk back to the politicians. Inflation has got to be stopped and I believe we'll begin to see a change——" he continued, and Lorraine let go of the thread and just nodded from time to time and sipped her drink carefully, not worrying about what she was going to see, as long as he was well launched. He was saving them from the very ugly scene that she had almost made and she was numbly grateful to him, for she could not have done it herself.

Only later, standing in the darkened hall between the children's rooms listening to their quiet breathing before she herself went early to bed, did something move within her, and she found herself thinking, I can't live this way. What am I going to do?

I knew from the beginning, she acknowledged, that he was going to fight me, but I forgot it somehow, I thought things could be all right. I should have known better! I should have seen it was only a truce, that he was just waiting and giving me time to make mistakes or get discouraged and give up. Now he will fight me, it will begin again. How can I stand it? If I frightened him tonight, I frightened myself worse! I don't want to lose control, I don't want to scream at Herbert over cocktails any more than I wanted to cry into my coffee at breakfast. But what can I do? How can I change things? Must I fight him? Is there no way out? I don't want to end things!

It was a freezing thought. She did not want to pursue it.

She had seen marriages break. Her own sister, lovely, fragile-looking, stubborn Faith, had firmly married two impossible men, divorced them, and was now living in Arizona with a third husband whose only advantage over the others seemed to be that he did not beat her when he got drunk. Faith's stories, in the years before she disappeared into the West with Julian, to play at running a ranch, had seemed to come from a world that Lorraine had never penetrated and could hardly believe in, a world of sordid, distasteful violence and distrust. Faith in hysterics, Faith pulling the dress off her shoulder to show a bruise, Faith drinking herself to sleep, Faith opening a dark red alligator handbag and taking out some letters, smiling triumphantly, saying, "I got them. I had to pay her five hundred dollars but I got them. I knew she couldn't resist seeing the money——" All these things Lorraine remembered as messages from that horrible, lost world. She had shrunk from it, clutching the children to her, thankful again and again for Herbert's rectitude and probity and the order and decency of their lives. She had chosen this life of hers over and over, again and again, struggling only not to be too angry at Faith, too hurt and contemptuous. And now——

It will pass, she tried to tell herself. It will pass. You can watch and be careful. This was a warning, and luckily nothing happened. You're tired, you don't have to decide anything now. Put it off. Put it off till Aunt Di's all right. Summer is coming and things will be easier then, they always are. You'll be out on the Island with the children, Herbert will only get out on weekends so there will be less time for conflict, for this kind of thing to happen. There's that trip of his too. If he goes it will be for six weeks at least. Any way you look at it you need time, and you will have time, time to relax, time to swim and ride and enjoy the children and catch hold of yourself.

You can manage this next month in the city, that's all it is, if you're careful and don't panic.

But somehow the promise of the summer wore an air of falseness. She conjured up memories of sun, of beaches, of surf, of the browned children laughing, racing toward her. The pictures flickered palely, like an old movie film. They had lost the power to convince. She could not believe that she would see this again, live it again, wake early to blue mornings, sleep in the afternoon with the sun swaying on the wall, glinting off the water, collect shells with Bobby, run a booth at the annual fair, worry about the lawns turning brown in the August dry spell. The woman whom this simplicity had healed last year and the year before was not the same one who stood here now. That one had lived in a closed and almost two-dimensional world.

And I can't go back, she thought, moving on down the hall. In the library Herbert, on the telephone, talked to Chicago. Behind her the children slept. What am I going to do? I can't even talk to Aunt Di, now—if I dared talk to her. To break up my life and live like Faith, or to hang on and on and on getting more frayed and less useful all the time—either is terrible. Either is impossible. And yet I have no choice but to choose, to go on living somehow, doing something.

She stopped in the bedroom door and leaned against the jamb. Move me, she said to God. Move me. Show me. Anything. Any way. Please, please, please. I don't ask to be happy. I ask a direction. Which way? How? Move me, move me! Asking flowed up through her, fountained out in the darkness, praying and searching, searching and praying. But nothing happened at all. And in a few minutes, hearing Herbert moving about in the library, she went into the dark room and began to get ready for bed.

11

Things being what they were, Lorraine found the waiting difficult the next day. She got to the hospital during the morning, after her aunt had gone up to the operating room, and they sat her down first in a wicker-furnished cul-de-sac on the seventh floor with a sprawl of dog-eared and coverless magazines on the table. Tucker found her there, however, on one of her patrols up the corridor, and arranged to let her wait in the big, bright, room—the best as always—that was her aunt's. There were flowers from the Admiral and Mrs. Covington, flowers from Mrs. Belchamber's lawyer and her man of business at the bank, books from Mr. Desseaux, and a long exclamatory wire from Faith. Lorraine read it and imagined her aunt making a face at Faith's too emphatic style, but was pleased that her sister had at least thought to send it, for Faith on a ranch was hard to visualize, and Lorraine felt sometimes that they had got not just out of touch but almost literally beyond communication. Now she put the yellow sheets (three of them, Faith's exuberant anxiety was elaborate) on the bedside table with a feeling of thankfulness, and looked around for something to do.

There was nothing. Tucker, who had insisted on coming down from Dr. Rushmore's, had done it all. Mrs. Belchamber's lotions and creams and colognes were neatly arrayed on the bureau, books and magazines were just so, even the stiff arrangements of the flowers repulsed the visitor. Lorraine was useless. I should have brought knitting or found some socks to darn, she thought, staring out the window. I should think of someone to call up. I should go for a long walk—it was a bright, blustery day, a March day that had somehow slipped back almost into May. But she did not know how long the surgery would take, and she could not bring herself to go out into the windy streets below. She picked up a book and put it down and disarranged the magazines. When Tucker popped in and asked about the children,

CHAPTER ELEVEN

it was a relief, but ten minutes of making conversation was all she could stand, and it was equally a relief when Tucker took herself off again. Then there was nothing at all but the passage of time—slower, and slower, and slower.

She had slept very badly, plagued by dreams: scenes of violence and escape, of searching for one of the children through the rambling house at East Hampton on the Island while voices muttered behind her and the train that she *must* catch drew out of the station, South Station in Boston. Was it Bobby or Faith she had been looking for? It was all still very close, just below the surface of her mind, in a wild mélange of red and black and sharp blue, painful, painful. I will have to get away from this, she thought, it is really too difficult. And yet, how can I go far from Aunt Di now? There is no one else to be with her. Why can't I think? Why can't I plan? It's absurd not to be able to see the problem clearly. There must be a logical solution! There is no reason for this dreadful confusion that has fallen upon me. What has changed in my life? What?

Only, she thought, the passage of time. She looked at her watch. It was an hour and ten minutes since she had come. She took it off and dropped it in her pocketbook.

Eight years with Herbert. Two children. She could not remember at all clearly what it had been like married to Herbert before the children were born. Only the memory of his courtship remained. He had pursued her with a kind of impersonal passionate intensity: had sent her flowers every day for weeks, gone to a great deal of trouble (for a New Yorker in Boston an almost impossible mountain of trouble) to find out where she would be every day. Whenever possible, he had appeared there and looked at her and done nothing. It was like being laid siege to by flying saucers that never landed. It had confused her and then—well, it had gone on confusing her, she supposed. That kind of thing didn't happen in Boston. And everyone had known about it. "Who is that young man?" her father had asked her, very early. Quite soon after that he had checked Herbert's college and clubs and business standing. It was all quite unexceptionable; though not what the Boston aunts had expected for her. Confused, eager, looking forward to the adventure of New York and an unknown husband, she had got married.

I don't know any more now than I did then, she thought, and

CHAPTER ELEVEN

looked at her wedding ring. Since she had taken her watch off it was the only piece of jewelry she wore, for Herbert's diamond to celebrate their engagement, the ruby for the fifth wedding anniversary, were much too much to wear every day. She pulled it off her finger. It would be quite easy to drop that in her pocketbook too. But that was absurd, dramatic, false. She put it back on.

And yet, she could not stay where she was. Confusion was worse confounded. Dreams, emotions, time and space whirled about her, shutting out reality, whose voices penetrated as if through a fog. Who was Herbert? Why had he ever wanted her? In what image had she appeared to him, those years ago, an image radiant, desirable, and now so changed? For Herbert, she saw, must suffer too. Obsessed with a dream, he had caught a woman who did not understand him or his work, would not try (it must seem) to enter his world, a Galatea only half awakened from the marble, and the living part a pursuer of futilities: charities, books, music, and the kind of personal relationship that never brought a return. She could not reproach Herbert. She had failed him. She was neither clever hostess, nor intelligent businesswoman, nor sympathetic responsive female. The Fury within, the Boston rigidity without, its virginal gestures almost unchanged from the day they were married: that was what Herbert had got instead of the bright dream he had pursued. She knew it, and knew it without shame for she was past shame, and did not know what to do to change it.

Go down, she said to herself now. Go down, go deeper, do not ask, but wait. The desert. The Murderee. The river. These are the symbols. Go down and down, wait. Something must tell you if you do not even ask. There must be a direction. What do you know for sure, for true, down in the dark? What do you want, under everything? Something must know, must want to live, something must push you.

Aunt Di, dear Aunt Di, she thought, be my sacrifice. You wanted so much, and had so much, and want it still and after today will never again have all you want, not even for a moment. Let me reach you through my dead mother, your sister, who loved my sister best, and through your dead mother who loved you best. We are still bound together, bone to bone, flesh to flesh. Aunt Di, I want to live, to not be afraid, to act and respond and feel. Now let me live for you. Be my sacrifice and I will be yours as children must be to parents and parents to children. Let me inherit and carry on, the pain as well as the joy, the joy as well as the pain, and all the contrivance and compromise in between, day after day, with Herbert or without him, loving him or not loving him, going or staying, but living and not lying. Teach me to choose, to be willing to do wrong, to abide by what I do. I want to want, I want to be greedy, to eat too much and laugh too loud. Oh, touch me, touch me! she thought.

The words swirled and rose and died away. Were they only words, like everything else? Desolation waited, the bright day blew outside. Then the door opened and the doctor came in.

He stood in the doorway and said, "You were asleep."

She was so far away that she could not open her lips to deny this before he spoke again. "It's all right. It went very well. She's got a heart like a trooper's," and he came in and sat down on the arm of another chair and smiled at her.

"I'm so glad," she said, and began to cry. The tears streamed down. "This is absurd," she gasped. "I'm so glad!"

"It's the relief," he said calmly, and she saw that he was holding out a box of Kleenex.

She took it and mopped at her eyes. "I still have your handkerchief. Every time I see you, in fact, I burst into tears. There really is nothing personal about it. Please tell me, where is she?"

"We'll keep her upstairs with special nurses till the anesthetic wears off. It'll be a couple of hours, anyway. I wanted to let you know."

"And it's all right?"

"It's all right."

"I feel as if I'd waked up from a nightmare." She wiped her eyes again and shook her head. "I don't know. Waiting——"

"Go get yourself some lunch," he said. "Take a walk. Have a good stiff drink. You're staying up here for a couple of days, Ingoldsby says. That right?"

"Yes, till Thursday."

"That's fine. I'm glad." He smiled at her and she smiled foolishly back, welcoming the careless warmth that he gave out as he sat resting, relaxed, pleased at a job done and done well. That's what I must learn, she thought but thought without urgency, to be just that simple. Here is natural man, angry and stubborn and pleased with himself, but kind too, to come now and tell me this. I push and strain and do things the hard way, but though this man has had a hard life, everything about him says, there is a way to live easily, to breathe and smile——

"Where are you staying?" he asked.

"At the Taft. It's quite near. I left my car there this morning and took a cab, but I could have walked, it seems. Can I see her later?"

"Sure. I'll be in myself around five. Tucker's taking the first shift, and there are other nurses laid on for night and morning. You can kind of drop in and out for a few minutes at a time."

"Yes." She rolled her head against the back of the chair and shut her eyes. "I was so tired," she said. "This feels good. Perhaps I can sleep."

"Sure you can. Look, I'm due at my office. I'll run you to the hotel, you take that drink, and sleep till five o'clock or so."

"All right." She looked at her wrist but there was no watch on it. Of course, she had taken it off. What a silly gesture! But for a moment it was pleasant to be disoriented and adrift. She took her bag. Her hat was on the bureau. She stood up, took a step——

And at once blacked out. Why do I have to have this nonsense now? she thought, and the thought trailed off in the blackness. She went down and down, came back, it was all perfectly familiar, it happened when she hadn't been sleeping well and wasn't serious, merely a nuisance—— He had her elbow. He was saying, "—damn fool! Did you eat any breakfast?" His voice grew louder. Her eyes cleared. She was, in a moment, going to be able to stand alone. But his arm——

Burned like fire around her shoulders, holding her body. She thought, My God, I want that man. My whole body wants him. My God!

Stop it! Stop it! Her hands came up to push him away. They wouldn't stop. They reached the back of his neck and pulled his head down—they did not have to pull hard. She felt like a fountain spilling over, end and beginning, forever renewed.

Then she was sitting back in the chair she had left only a moment ago and he was standing looking out the window. You are crazy! she said to herself looking at his back in the white coat. You are behaving like a crazy woman. How could you! How could you!

CHAPTER ELEVEN

Doctors—neurotic women—— You wanted to want something, to be greedy, and this is how you get your wish! My God! My God!

He said in a voice as heavy as stone, "If you didn't mean that you had better say so now."

Mean it? she thought. What does he mean?

He turned and looked at her. "I don't have time to play games. So if you didn't mean it, say so."

The puzzlement within her held for a minute more and then it cracked all over, like an old pavement broken by surging grass. Why, she thought, he wants me! He wants me too!

She wanted to burst out laughing, but in the towering light of the revelation that she had just received, she saw in time that he would think she was laughing at him. First thing to remember, she told herself laughing inside, never laugh out loud! It did not, at the moment, seem like a rule of conduct which might become wearisome, but rather like a discovery with all of the delight that goes with discovery. She smiled instead, therefore, and said with infinite joy, "I didn't know I meant it but it seems I must."

12

Three days since they operated. I am propped up in bed. The radio, at last, is mercifully silent. I must finally have made it clear to the day nurse that I do not care for it. Dear Tucker, who has worked at this hospital before, comes from four to midnight and says she will come home with me. Yes, they are going to let me go home from here, they say it has been a success and that I may say farewell to Dr. Rushmore and his elegant establishment. I feel as if I should send condolences to my bridge partners.

A week. They are going to teach me to walk again. A buxom female patient named Harrison appeared in my doorway this afternoon attired in a perfectly hideous garment made out of a cerise candlewick bedspread. She was caught up in something resembling a tubular chrome version of the Iron Maiden. It is called The Walker. I am to begin, in a few weeks, perambulating within the embrace of this affair.

May 11th. Bad night. I must not hope. I must not plan.

Tuesday—the fifteenth, I think. Lorraine drove out today. She has offered to go to Woodbury with the children and make sure that the house is running properly and ready to receive me. Herbert is going to Europe next month and she says that she would rather be with me while he is away than out on Long Island at their own place. I'm touched, and I told her so. Besides, it's a practical idea. I shan't be able to manage the stairs for—well, they don't say. It depends. But it will be some little time, at any rate. Lorraine suggests turning the small sitting room into a downstairs bedroom. She thinks she can get a shower stall put into the lavatory. I gave her the names of architect and plumber—and my blessing for her enthusiasm, for she seems delighted to set to work on this nagging little job. At any rate, this plan will get her away from that unhealthy preoccupation with living for others that got her into welfare work—she'll have to drop that for a bit, anyway. I told her to hire a chambermaid, we'll need more than Charles and Marie if she and the children and their nursemaid and Tucker are going to be added to the household. I hope she can find one. She seemed undeterred, which pleased me, for I've always felt she disliked having to deal with people and preferred the simpler relationship with things—or, to give her credit for she is not a stupid girl, with ideas. I suppose that is how she made the awful mistake of marrying Herbert.

May 22nd. I shouldn't use this book for writing these dull day-to-day notes. But I've got in the habit of writing in it. And I've finished writing about Diana. She's married off. She's become Mrs. Greene. Doesn't "They lived happily ever after" follow automatically? Bad night again. They're cutting down on the sleeping pills. Well, they have to, I suppose. But I don't understand what makes them think that the thrilling activity of being pushed up and down the hall in a wheel chair will be a sufficient climax to my day so that eleven o'clock will see me drop off to a dreamless sleep. I wish I knew a new kind of solitaire. I might teach Tucker to play chess, I suppose—she can certainly beat me at canasta. That would still leave the day, though. Little Miss Bunce is sweet and obliging, but her head is filled with fungus or thistledown, or anything you choose but brains. It amazes me that she is able to read a thermometer. "What a lot of books!" she said, on looking at the modest dozen I'd brought with me, which Lorraine kindly changes on her visits. Miss Bunce has decided that I am an author, having seen me scribbling, and this has more or less reconciled her to my library by establishing an official—or do I mean a commercial?—reason for its existence. To tell the truth, I've read so much that all reading is beginning to seem repetitive, and I can almost sympathize with Miss Bunce. Not quite enough, though, to try to collect more bridge players.

It will be June in three days, a month that I've been here. I slept four hours last night. I think I will ask Lorraine to get me the Greek grammar I laughed at once. Then I could wake at two-thirty and work at my Greek until I go off at five or so. There is remarkably little of the world's literature that is readable from two-thirty to five in the morning.

June 1st. I told Savage, finally, about the sleeping difficulty, and he has given me something new to take. I slept last night and feel wonderfully well today. I needed to, for they brought in The Walker after lunch and hoisted me into it. It was perfectly horrible, a physical experience of weakness and manipulation and dependence—— Ugh! I know now how a horse feels while it is being broken. And yet it has to be done, if all the rest of my life is not to involve even worse things, even greater dependence and compromise. This is what I pay for dangerous hope, for the chance of a future.

Yet how ungrateful I am! Six weeks ago I was still at Rushmore's, still Mrs. Covington's crony and confidante. It only goes to show that hope is a poison. I wrote somewhere in these pages (which I will never re-read) a condemnation of despair. Well, let me say here that hope is as bad. They are poles of the same emotional attitude, and I wish never to find myself again in that attitude, which is one of refusal to accept fact. Having slept eight hours for the first time in a week, I find myself newly acquainted with, newly favorable to, facts.

June 2nd. The Walker again. Lorraine, who moved to Woodbury last week, reports that the plumber has gone into action. I am so tired of thinking about my body!

June 6th. I have begun to dream. Told Savage. He says he will find something else for me. Thank God for that rude young man! If I had been left in Ingoldsby's hands, I might well have killed him by now. They measured me, or fitted me, or whatever the proper term is, for crutches today. Thus do we make progress—both the thing itself, and the definition of it.

June 13th. Very bad night. I shall have to stop the new sleeping stuff or have a nurse in the room from midnight on. I started to get out of bed. Fortunately, before I had set foot on the floor and ruined everything, I knocked over the lamp and the water pitcher and the glass and everything else on the bed table and a passing nurse heard it and got to me. It was a miracle she was there. I can't remember anything about it at all—not even whether I was after something, or trying to get away. Poor Savage! He blames himself for trying whatever the dose was on me. I told him I wouldn't tell Ingoldsby; and he pointed out coldly that everything that is given me is of course entered on my chart for Dr. Ingoldsby's perusal. I'm sorry. It's absurd that I should be having this trouble when I am getting better, when I am going home, when I can see an end to these black months. In the nursing home, when I had resigned myself, I slept and slept.

CHAPTER TWELVE

June 18th. Two-thirty. No dreams, thank God, but here I am, wide awake as can be. I haven't tried writing at night. Is it possible it could help? I've always hated giving in to wakefulness enough to try it. But why not? I *am* awake.

Sixty-one. Twenty years ahead? My parents were relatively young when they died, but it was the influenza that took my father, and Mother never looked after herself—particularly after that. Mother's mother lived into her eighties, blighting everything around her, and so did two of my aunts. Everything considered, twenty years is a perfectly possible span.

At night, somehow, it is impossible to think of one's life in terms of time. I remember once having a flash in which I felt that I had understood eternity: that is, experienced it, connected with it, been there. I think it must have been a moment when I really experienced being, and the two things are the same thing. To be is to be eternal. When it ends, everything ends.

I re-read that and realize that it means nothing at all. No wonder the mystics are incomprehensible! Words are public, not meant for private experience.

I suppose that is why it helps me to write. The mere act of putting things into words makes them public (though I shall burn this book when I am well). I mean, it makes the feeling a public, a potentially shared, a conventional thing. Without it—here, when my life can begin again, *will* begin again—I lie in that queer numb agony that I remember from childbirth. It wasn't exactly pain, it was bigger, more nebulous, vaguer than pain. What am I trying to bring to birth? Not the twenty years ahead, they couldn't be simpler to foresee. I can plan them in toto with no trouble at all, beginning with the day, not too far off, when I go home. No. I am afraid it is the past that is trying to be born.

It's too much! I lived it. Must I relive it? What possible good could it do?

It was a mistake to write out my youth. I wish I hadn't.

I must ask Lorraine to get a list from Benson of the annuals he has put in. And to ask whether we can hope for any apples after these late frosts. And whether the delphiniums——

A mistake at any rate to end where I did, when I did. The happy

ending! Well, any ending is just an artistic convention. There aren't
any endings. Only changes, transformations, metamorphoses.

So many for me; too many. I said seven years ago, I will have no
more. I am finished. I am past the years of being a woman, nothing
can touch me now. Then, like a bad joke, this happened to prove
how blind I was. I thought I could control my mind and that, since
I was too old for physical pleasure, I was safe. I never thought of
physical pain. And though I knew (how could I not know!) what it
could do to the spirit, it never occurred to me that I could suffer this
way myself. What vanity! It had seemed to me that courage was a
kind of exemption, but it is not so.

It is growing light. I think perhaps I can sleep.

June 20th. I mean 21st, it's two-thirty again. And I pick up my
book. Poor book! I have made you, but I give you no autonomy. I
look to you for salvation, make you an instrument. Of course, a real
writer can't do that. *His* book must stand alone. But since, in spite
of Miss Bunce's convictions, I'm not a writer, I'm spared cutting the
cord, I can use this stored emotion, pretend that my creation is both
part of me and not part of me. Does God pretend this? If so, it would
explain the Problem of Evil. I'm not at all sure that I believe in
God but, like Voltaire, I have had to invent Him.

Last night I slept right through, they must have given me something
without telling me. But I suppose they can't every night. If they
would only let me go home I would be better, I'm sure. It's nearly
six months since I've seen my house. I didn't realize that I'd put down
roots there, but I miss it. I look forward to seeing it again, the garden
particularly, and to good long satisfying disagreements with Benson
over mulches and fertilizers. I'll spend the summer and finish my
lessons in walking, and when I've graduated to a cane I'll have people
to stay. Old friends.

Or shall I? Old friends, unfortunately, are so often old. Some of
them get about with canes themselves. Oh dear! I have no intention
of enlisting for permanent service in the stick brigade, but I can hardly
tell this to members of it. Or to those old enough to fear it for
themselves, who may only too easily find a bit of pleasure in imagining
that I am more than a temporary recruit. No. I think, on the whole,
not old friends, I was right to refuse to have visitors at the nursing
home, I know only too well who would have come: all the old

vultures who would have sat about my bed hooding their eyes and waiting for the end. Let the old friends wait. I'll make new ones.

It's a pity that Lorraine is so little use that way. It's partly that confounded Boston upbringing—everybody already knew everybody and had for three generations. I asked her if she'd called on any of my neighbors in Woodbury, and of course she hadn't. I made her write down a list of a dozen families and promise to do something about them. She's met at least half of them already, when she's stayed weekends with me. There's no reason for her to be shy with them even if Herbert's away and she's temporarily an unattached woman. That kind of thing doesn't matter any more! I can't believe that she's missing him; she's at least as absent-minded as usual, but apparently happy enough even though she has no one but Benson and the plumber and the carpenters to talk to. As a matter of fact, when I asked her what she heard from Herbert, she politely produced three postcards. Really, Lorraine, I started to say, doesn't he write any letters? Surely postcards are an odd medium of communication between husband and wife! But I stopped myself in time. I am not, I never have been, an interfering woman, but there are times when I feel an irresistible desire to lead Lorraine's life for her. I could do it so much better!

June 23rd. Two-thirty again. I am so *tired* of this horrible hour! Is anyone else in New Haven awake? I suppose a few carousing Yale students—— No, of course not, it's vacation time, they're all carousing at home. In Paris it's eight-thirty, eight-thirty of a June morning. I am afraid that if I think about it I'll cry. And I haven't done *that* for a thousand years.

Well, for seven.

Ah, God, write it down, write it down! It'll be better said, finally. Why do you think you haven't been able to sleep?

I cried last seven years ago when John died. I tried to see Claire and they would not let me, but I did not cry then. Then I came back here.

One, two—— Those three sentences have just two words in them with more than one syllable. Would you believe you could write such desolation in words of one syllable?

There are times like this when Catholicism becomes a temptation so enormous, in spite of Claire, that I don't know how I manage to resist it. To be forgiven! What it would mean to me to be forgiven! But then my mind asks, How could forgiveness alter events? How could it change what happened? And I see it for what it is, a comfortable lie. It is very hard to be born a rational being in a world that has decided that feelings are more important than facts. My Catholic friends would tell me that I am vastly confused about their faith, I know, they have told me so before. Never mind. They seem to understand *my* faith no better than I understand theirs.

I caused irremediable pain. I set in motion a chain of events that condemned other human beings to—— Well. To what was certainly great unhappiness and deprivation and what seems to me to have been evil—sin, if you like the word. It happened. It can *never* be cured. So how can I be forgiven?

Other people's psyches apparently see some connection between suffering and forgiveness. Mine does not. Apparently they believe that if you suffer enough you will pay for what you did wrong. But that's sheer nonsense. If something was wrong once it will always be wrong, and when you think of it, you will always suffer. I really don't see how there's any escape from that.

Well, they might say, you haven't suffered *enough* yet, that's all. Perhaps they are right. But then, enough is always too much, at least by my moral arithmetic. How can you weigh suffering? All they can mean is that it will finally fray you and numb you until you are ready to forget, and thus forgive yourself. If I live twenty years, perhaps I'll have time to find out. By the time I am really old, part of the stick brigade, mumbling with senility, I may forgive myself.

This helps. This helps, to write. To use the public symbols for the private pain. To name it, for things with names become less intimate, by being defined, than those inward agonies one can only feel. Perhaps writing will do for me what turning Catholic has done for so many people, and legitimize my grief. Really, it's not Catholicism itself that keeps me from conversion so much as my friends who are converts. They were all scared into it. I don't know one who hungered and thirsted after righteousness. They were all grabbing, they were all terrified, this great gift of life had given them nothing of pleasure or joy or wisdom or capability. It seems so unmannerly to bring God nothing but a bottomless well of need and terror, surely He deserves better than that from His creatures. And besides—I'll be damned if I'll be terrified into any intellectual conviction.

A joke. A poor one, but still a joke, which is an achievement at this hour. For my Catholic friends would tell me that I'll be damned if I don't.

My God, if I am ever to be damned, I am damned now, and will be till the window pales with dawn and I can sleep again. And wake up in a world where there is a sequence, where the doctor looks in in the morning, and the physiotherapist follows, and The Walker appears after lunch, and Lorraine arrives at four to report on the plumber's progress and on Benson's intransigeance about the delphiniums——

Where is that world? Where is that world? The sequence has broken. Events roll about my feet like beads from a broken string. Seven years since John died, thirty-eight since I first saw Gerald, thirty-five since I left Claire, fourteen since they came to tell me about Jimmy—— What a litany!

Will it never be light?

I'll have to cut out these pages or I'll be afraid to open this book.

Tucker told me I fought the anesthesia. I was afraid to go under. Why should it have happened now? When I was in the hospital last January, I howled to go out whenever I came to the surface. Well, I'd lain in the cold for five hours before they found me, and then the fools didn't know how to move me. They picked me up and put me in the back of a car—— I went out then, thank God! But I was awash in an ocean of pain and pneumonia for days, and anxious only to be unconscious.

This time I had to choose to go under and be mutilated in order to be healed. It was harder than I had thought, when the time came. I was afraid.

Yes, and I know what I was afraid of, and why I can't sleep. I shouldn't have written Diana's story. I should not have remembered it all and then stopped, for memory is treacherous. Memory doesn't stop at a happy ending. Even under the changes and transformations, it persists. I was afraid then, I am afraid now, of seeing Gerald.

Forgive myself? Why, it is as if it happened yesterday. I can see his face.

No wonder I fought the anesthesia. I was afraid I'd see his face and feel his arms and his lips and speak his name again, the name I haven't spoken——

Did I? I wish I knew! Could just the fear of it do this to me? Or did I, somewhere between sleep and waking and hurt and healing, brush past him just now, just the other day? Who was I looking for the night I tried to get up?

I wonder if he is dead. He wasn't seven years ago. Why should it make any difference? Yet, I wonder. I don't believe in ghosts. I don't really think he would haunt me more closely if he were dead and free of his body——

Diana, you know very well that it is not Gerald who haunts you, but the emotion you felt for Gerald. Don't pretend. Don't elaborate.

I started to write to amuse myself, to pass the time in limbo. Now see what I have done! There is nothing amusing about this. Can I stop? Must I go on? If I do, it will be an attempt at exorcism. A hopeless attempt. For I know it is not a ghost that torments me, but I—I—I—— What I was. What I did. What has not died within me whether Gerald's bones are buried or burned or sunk in the sea and will not die till I do—nor even then.

Nor even then.

It is beginning to be light. Thank God, thank God.

June 24th. They are going to let me go home tomorrow.

13

"Well," said Lorraine, "for once Dr. Ingoldsby was as good as his word. He said he'd try to get you home to see the roses, and here you are." They were at the entrance to the rose garden on Mrs. Belchamber's home-coming tour. Along the dry stone walls, on trellises, staked and propped in beds raked to perfection, the roses bloomed violently, making with final conviction the statement of every formal garden: that the cultivation of nature by art is a major virtue.

"Hmph," said Mrs. Belchamber. She put her hands on the arms of her wheel chair and shifted herself in it. "Tucker, push me up the path. Ingoldsby had nothing to do with letting me out, or getting me out. I got out myself. Savage would have kept me caged there all summer if I hadn't fought."

"Oh now!" said Lorraine. "He was only trying to do what was best for you. He wouldn't have let anyone else out so soon."

"Oh now, indeed!" rejoined her aunt acerbly. "Don't try to apologize for him. What does anyone else's case have to do with me? He's too stubborn, and I told him so. 'You won't get on,' I said, 'if you don't learn to be more flexible. It isn't as if I couldn't have care at home.' He thanked me. In the end."

"Anyway it's over now," said Lorraine diplomatically, "and you're here. I've never seen the roses lovelier."

"He hasn't done a bad job, Benson," Mrs. Belchamber agreed grudgingly. "Here, at least. Though why he thought he had to prune the heart out of the shrubbery around the house, I will never know. That man simply cannot be trusted when it comes to pruning, he gets carried away. Lorraine, cut some of the Charlotte Armstrongs, my dear. Those. No, you silly girl, those right in front of you. Tucker, push me closer. Begin with this bed. Then take some of the Frau

Karl Druschkis—all right, some of the white ones. I realize you don't know their names."

"If they only looked like their names," said Lorraine mildly, "I'd do better. Charlotte Armstrong may be a lovely girl to those who know her, but these heavenly things ought to be named for someone more exotic or dramatic, Marilyn Monroe or Eva Gabor, or Porfirio Rubirosa for those dark red ones, why not?"

"I'm sorry to tell you that the red ones are Chrysler Imperials."

"Well, there you are," said Lorraine, disentangling herself from a determined Charlotte Armstrong. "I do call that unimaginative. Why not——"

"My dear, when rose breeders grow imaginative—and they have been lately—you get varieties named Jiminy Cricket or Fashion or Peace or Circus. I'd rather have Ulrich Brenners and Dr. Van Fleets, at least you don't feel like a fool discussing them. Benson wants to try a new hybrid tea called Love Song. Can you imagine a conversation beginning, 'Benson, how are your Love Songs?' I think I shall order Dr. Debats instead, he's pink but he isn't embarrassing."

"It's the wrong approach," said Lorraine, beginning on the Frau Karl Druschkis. "They should be named after events and crises, Sevastopol, Shiloh or Austerlitz. The South Sea Bubble. The Siege of Lucknow. The Relief of Mafeking."

"My dear child, how bloodthirsty you are! And if Charlotte Armstrong is inexpressive, the names of plenty of crises and battles are downright silly. You'd find yourself with varieties named The Battle of the Bulge and The War of Jenkins' Ear. That one's too open. Take buds, take buds. I have enough trouble trying to name our colts without taking on roses too."

"I don't know," said Lorraine, moving up the path. "It might be fun to name everything over. And see if the world changed."

"Nonsense. That's been discredited for centuries. It's nominalism or sympathetic magic or somethingly equally illogical."

"Then why do people change their names?" Lorraine leaned down and put her cuttings in the flat basket at her feet. Her aunt did not answer. Surprised, she looked up.

Mrs. Belchamber was staring at her. "Why do you ask me that?" she said abruptly.

Lorraine said, "Why—I don't know. I was just talking. I—— There's no reason! I used to hate being called Lorraine, but I could never settle on anything else."

"Then you deserve to be called Lorraine."

Lorraine stared. "Tchk!" said Tucker, and pushed the chair slightly. Above Mrs. Belchamber's head she mouthed silently, "Over-tired."

"Well, and so I am called that," said Lorraine.

Mrs. Belchamber turned her head to the side. "I beg your pardon," she said. "That was unpardonably rude of me. Lorraine is a very pretty name. Move over to that bed now and take a few yellow ones, and then we'll go in before Tucker decides I'm behaving too badly and must be put to bed without my supper."

The flat basket filled slowly. The wheel chair left narrow, snakelike tracks on the gravel path. Lorraine's left forearm received a long scratch from the old-fashioned Silver Moon climber on the wall. At last they had circled the garden and came out by the twin cedars at the gate. "Let me hold the basket," said Mrs. Belchamber. Lorraine, who had walked a step or two ahead, turned and put it on her aunt's lap. Across the lawn, toward the house, built first in 1757 and altered by every generation since, they proceeded at a slow processional pace. Under an apple tree, by the swing and seesaw which Mrs. Belchamber had ordered installed, Bobby, Jane and Hilda the nurse-maid drank lemonade. The garden held its breath at its June height, the year stood at a peak of glory. The declining sun reached toward the northernmost moment when it would set behind a ridge that one could never, in January, imagine it approaching.

"Look," said Mrs. Belchamber, "there are still a few iris along the river!" Tucker stopped pushing and Lorraine shaded her eyes against the sun glinting off the stream which ran through Mrs. Belchamber's land.

"Yes," she said. "Well, everything came at once this year, I guess, spring was so late. Shall I cut them?"

"No. They won't last. But push me down there for a minute. Unless Tucker's too tired."

"I'm quite all right, thank you, my lady," said Tucker, who had lately adopted this form of address; as a satiric reaction, Lorraine suspected, to the absence of "Miss" before her own name. "I'm not tired, though I can't say others won't be. But there are some people who can't be argued with, so I don't waste time arguing." She turned the chair toward the river and the three women moved slowly toward the water through the golden light. The great pile of roses riding on Mrs. Belchamber's lap seemed to give the group both a focus and a purpose. The year, at the solstice, rested a moment. It had achieved the roses. The women went with them—the one who served, the old one, and the one in love. They are mine, thought Mrs. Belchamber, They are beautiful, thought Lorraine, and Tucker pushed the wheel chair. They reached the planting by the edge of the river.

Lorraine picked up the basket of roses. As her aunt looked up, startled, she said, "We should offer them up, I think. Why is there no shrine, Aunt Di? You should have a worn stone goddess who would like these, an uncertainly anonymous one, plowed up some-where in Italy, not of the best period, but expecting roses at mid-summer. I would like to give her a votive offering. Why didn't you bring a goddess home from one of your trips?"

"It didn't occur to me," said Mrs. Belchamber. "And if I had, I'm afraid she would be lonesome here. In Connecticut we plow up nothing but flint arrowheads, and grow our roses to please ourselves. Why do you want to make an offering?"

Lorraine lifted the basket and looked at its burden, and then smiled at her aunt. "In honor of your return," she said.

"Thank you." Mrs. Belchamber bowed ironically. "I should think you might offer them to me then, since they are mine."

"Yours? Are they really? I don't think they can be anyone's."

"A possible point. Or perhaps they are mostly Benson's, if you want to take account of the labor theory of value. But if none of us is entitled to anything, and mine and thine mean nothing, I can't see that your ambiguous goddess should have them either."

"Only as a gift."

"Then grow your own roses, my dear, don't give away mine. These iris need thinning. I'm sure I wrote Benson to do it. Of course things are always neglected if one isn't there to see to them oneself. Tucker, have you a pencil? I want to make a list of things to go over with that man. I'm not at all sure he sprayed the euonymus."

"I'm sorry, my lady, I haven't a pencil."

"Then remember what I say. You too, Lorraine. Iris, euonymus. Wasn't there something else?"

"My goddess," said Lorraine.

"Nonsense. I'll put up a sundial if you want. Give me back my roses before you spill them."

"You're very unkind," said Lorraine, handing back the basket. "I ask for eternity and you offer me time."

"And you're very whimsical today, I must say," said her aunt. "What have you been reading? You should get out more. When is the Appletons' dinner? What you need is some good, dull, table talk. All right, Tucker, we'll go back. I want my tea."

Tucker turned the chair at once. Across the lawn they went, their shadows gliding ahead of them on the cropped grass, toward the west entrance where Lorraine had had the carpenters build a ramp for the wheel chair over the steps before the door. Two huge maples shaded it, planted nearly two hundred years before, when the old road had run by here and this had been the front door. It was all gone now, as if the stagecoach route, when the house had been an inn, had never run past here, as far away as the time of the flint arrowheads. Whimsical, thought Lorraine. Sentimental. Moralizing. Time and eternity. And she smiled lazily, for her thoughts didn't matter. They had ceased to be important: bright images floating on the surface of her mind, like the birches and the clouds that swam on the surface of the river, and as superficial, for everything important happened in the depths.

A man came out of the shade of the maples into the sun. "Why, there's the doctor," said Tucker, and Lorraine missed a step and fell back. Was her face under control? But Mrs. Belchamber was not looking at her.

"So it is," she said irritably. "What a time to get here. Well, he'll just have to have tea too, even if it makes him late home. If he can't come when he says he will, I shan't hurry for him. What time is it, Lorraine?"

"Quarter to five. Perhaps he couldn't get away before."

"Obviously he couldn't get away before. I haven't lost my mind, you know, merely broken my hip. Good afternoon!" she called.

Savage waved and started toward them.

"Why does he always need a haircut?" said Mrs. Belchamber, none too sotto voce. "And he buys his shirts a size too small."

I won't speak! thought Lorraine, but thought just too late. "What a snob you are, Aunt Di!" she heard herself say, and tried to lighten the words to jest since she could not stop them.

But some resentment must have come through, for her aunt raised her eyebrows and looked interested. "I?" she asked. "Good heavens, Lorraine, I'm nothing of the kind. But he looks so uncomfortable, poor man, and I can't think of a way to tell him what to do about it. You can try it, if you want to. Just say, 'Why don't you buy size sixteen and a half next time?' Don't hurry," she called again. "It's too hot."

"Thank you, I don't care to," said Lorraine. "I don't see what difference it makes, either, or why it needs comment."

"Hoity-toity!" said Mrs. Belchamber. "It's been many years since my manners were corrected. Well, all things come to those who wait."

Lorraine bit her lip. "I'm sorry, Aunt Di. I didn't mean it that way at all. I just—judging by the way he worked on you, he's too busy to care what he looks like."

"Then his wife should. All right, Lorraine, I'm not ungrateful and I'll hush." She raised her voice. "You're just in time for tea, Doctor. Was it hot in New Haven?"

"Hot enough," said Savage arriving, panting. "How are you?"

"Very well I think, but you must ask my niece and Tucker too, they won't agree. They've been telling me I'm rude, bad-tempered and—what else was it, Lorraine? Oh yes, unkind."

"Is that so?" said Savage. "How are you, Mrs. de Koning, Miss Tucker. Has she been acting up, then?"

"Nothing unusual," said Tucker promptly.

"Oh well, then, we don't need to worry. Hey, are those your roses? No wonder you wanted to see them."

"You like them?" Mrs. Belchamber held up the basket and cocked her head on one side to look at it with a judicious eye.

"I'll say. They really are something."

She held out the basket. "Take them back to your wife."

He swallowed. "Well, I—I have a long drive. I'm afraid they'd die."

"Nonsense. Lorraine will put them in water for you. We must have some kind of old pail or bucket they can travel in. If there's nothing in the flower room, Lorraine, ask Benson to see what he has. They won't die, they've just been cut. Come now and have some tea, and

I'll perform on my crutches for you. Here, dear." She handed the basket to Lorraine, Tucker gave the chair a shove to get it started and then picked up her pace to match the doctor's stride. Off they went across the lawn. Lorraine's hand tightened on the basket's handle. Here, dear, she repeated to herself. Lorraine will put them in water for you. Ask Benson to see what he has—— Rude. Bad-tempered. Unkind. Aunt Di, I am going to take these roses back to the river and *throw them in!*

Don't be a fool! she told herself. She's just teasing you, she doesn't know anything! Don't let yourself get mad and show something! Come now, stop! Tucker, the wheel chair and the doctor had now reached the door. He opened it, held it wide, and looked back at her. She made herself move. It was necessary that this minor episode be made even more minor—to him, as well as to Aunt Di. She forced herself to smile, nod, wave, and walk slowly around the corner of the house to the room off the kitchen where the flowers were always arranged.

An overgrown lilac shaded the door. She stopped under it to carry the roses in, set them down on the table where a collection of vases and bowls stood. It was dark there after the light outside, she felt oddly reduced by the twilight, and bent to look under the table for a pail as if this submission to her aunt's whim were a duty laid on her by Fate to be scrupulously fulfilled. She found an old aluminum pot with one handle, filled it with water at the sink, and plunged the roses in.

And now to go to tea—— But she could not. An old bench stood under the table. She pulled it out and sank down. Her eyes were growing accustomed to the dimness, the roses glowed brighter and brighter. They were for his wife.

How absurd! she said to herself. As if I resented her! Of course I don't! I accept it as it is, I do, I always have!

It was true. But there had never been roses to be sent to her before.

There had been at first only amazement. Like a tree in the wind, Lorraine had swung back and forth between the old and the new. It was terrifying. He had been nothing, and suddenly he was there, closer than anyone ever, the one to be put first, the one to be lied for. It was terrifying and wonderful, first one and then the other, as the wind of strangeness beat against her, but it was always one or the other, always new. "It seems I must mean it," she had said and had never looked back. But what *that* had meant was still not clear. Complete commitment? Yes, certainly. She had lied without hesitation and, since she had never lied before, very successfully. She had walked into a dream and given it her total allegiance, and pulled it around her to shut out any of the rest of the world. In those weeks in New York before Herbert left, she had worn it like an impenetrable cloak. He had, she supposed, felt something between them—but something had been there already, he had already been frightened and wary. His announcement of his European trip was a relief to both of them, that was quite clear; Herbert must have been as ready as she to turn away, to wait and see what the summer might resolve or change.

Still, it was pleasant, when she came to Woodbury, not to lie. Even before she moved out she had found a place where she and Savage could meet. It was very simple—she merely rented a cottage for the summer. It was off by itself, the road petered out in the woods behind it, no one ever drove by. She paid for everything in advance and spent a day cleaning and airing, a day when they thought in New York that she was in Woodbury and thought in Woodbury that she was in New York. Savage came out, late in the afternoon. They had been together in the hotel before, but this was like nothing else, ever.

He left her around ten. She did not mind, she knew he had to. "Get up and lock the door behind me," he said as he left.

"I'm not frightened," she said sleepily, smiling.

"Do as I say," he told her. "I can't afford to worry about you." So she got up and trailed after him, naked and sleepy and grumbling. "You're a caution," he said, laughing, and kissed her by the door. "Lock it now, do you hear me? I've got to go." But she stood in the doorway until the lights of the car came on. "God damn it, get in there!" he said, and she laughed and shut the door and forgot to lock it, and had to get up again to do so.

How quiet it was that night! Sleep rose gently around her and she let go, let go, let go of laughter and amazement and lying, of danger and desire and wonder. Whatever there is to do, she thought, it's done.

I can't do any more. Whatever will happen now, will happen. And slept.

And slept. What a sleep! We don't sleep like that often, not once we've grown up, but must all have done so once or twice. Have slept so, and waked, and not known where we are, except that we are safe. So Lorraine slept in the house in the woods and waked and knew when she did that she had come past a barrier. There were the birds outside, clamorous around a house that had been empty for months, there was green light through the trees and fresh morning and somewhere the knowledge of a journey taken below the level of dream, a long journey completed, to a strange place that she knew all about. It was as if she had been out of herself, rid for a night of that troublesome person, herself, with whom she was usually so deeply involved; had been over and past and through the human limit. It had ceased to exist, had been cast like a snake's skin, it had melted, could melt; and this being so, this limit called "Lorraine" having been proved an illusion, she was no longer bound by it, and need never again suffer its wants or fears.

She waked, her eyes opened, the white ceiling floated above her like a blessing, even the cobweb in the corner that she had not seen the day before; ceiling, roof, house, shelter, seemed a brand-new miracle. For everything was new-made each minute and at the same time, each minute, made new. All that was strange, all that she had so perilously, unthinkingly embraced, was also old, the fulfillment of a promise made a thousand years ago and forgotten by everything except the marrow of her bones.

What was the promise? Not love. She stretched lazily, she laughed at the thought, all alone in the green morning. Oh no, not love. Love was unimportant. It was another illusion, another mask that could vanish. Savage was unimportant. He and love mattered, his arms and his mouth and his body, only because they were a means to this knowledge, a passport for the journey she had made. And I to him, she thought, not important; except together. Each of us as a person is only a symbol. When the symbol grows thin between us and melts away, when we touch each other, that is important, for then life touches itself and this is renewal. Each of us is a means, we are not ends. If I never see him again, it would hurt but it would not matter to this, it could not change where I have been. What has happened has happened and can never not happen, for time is irreversible and I have been outside it and am free. She opened her arms to sleep and waking, to dream and reality, she smiled at all the flickering, shadowy, lovely world maintained only by change, at all matter that is only speed and position and evanescence constantly renewed——

And reached her hand out now to the roses, smiling. For she had wanted to give them, she remembered, to an anonymous goddess. In so far as this could be done—and it could not quite be done, for she knew his wife's name was Norma—it would be done. You are going to Norma, she said to the roses. I was angry, but that was only foolish. I'm not angry now. Go to Norma without anger, or jealousy. Go as what you are from me as what I am. I hope she is pleased and thinks you are beautiful. She picked up the clumsy pot (she had to clasp it with both arms), and went out, carried it around the house, and set it down by the door where Savage would come out. Then she went in to tea.

"Well!" said Mrs. Belchamber. "We gave you up. The tea is stewed." But Lorraine only smiled and said she didn't mind.

What she had not allowed for was that Savage might not want to take the roses. She walked out with him when he left, and he looked down at them and said, "Oh Jesus!"

"I'm sorry," she said.

"Do I have to?"

"Well, they have to go somewhere. You can dump them out in a mile or so if you want to."

He nudged the pot with his toe. "What set her off anyway? I thought she'd be like a cat with two tails, to get home."

"Tucker thinks she gets tired and won't let on. Then I called her a snob."

"What did you do that for, for heaven's sake? And why did it set her off at me?"

"I'm sure I don't know," she said, turning away.

He bent to pick up the pot. "Well, damn it, you should have better sense. Oh, for God's sake, this thing has only one handle!"

"I'll take it!" she said angrily. "I got it this far. Give it to me." She held out her hands.

"Oh shut up," he said amiably, regaining his temper. "I'm sorry,

Laurie. It was ninety-three in town and the air conditioning went off in the operating room. We had a picnic. Don't be mad."

"I'm not mad, silly. Were you operating? What happened?"

"I sweated, what do you think happened? I was picking bits of bicycle chain out of a small boy who rode his bicycle into a garbage truck so I went on till I was through, and then I put his damn left tibia back together. Then I went home and took a shower. Which I am now about to do again. When will I see you? Tomorrow?"

She walked in silence beside him, toward his shabby car. "It's not going to be so easy now she's home, you know," she said finally.

It was his turn to be silent for a moment. "Don't blame me for sending her home, Laurie," he said. "I thought about all this. She was going to tear the place apart and hurt herself——"

"Oh, darling, I know that. I'd have been shattered if you'd let this interfere with that. I was speaking factually, that's all. Tomorrow, as a matter of fact, there's a dinner party at some people's called Appleton that I have to go to."

"To hell with people called Appleton. Meet me instead."

"How can I? She knows all about it. I've got to go places, Peter. I can't sit home with her and then vanish unexplained if you call. It would look rather odd."

"Oh hell," he said. "Look odd. What do you care?"

"Well, as a matter of fact, I care quite a lot. Partly for you." They had reached the car and she opened the door for him. "Put the roses down on the floor there. I don't think they'll spill."

"I'm sorry," he said straightening up. He took a rag out of the glove compartment and wiped his hands on it. "I swear at you and you worry about me. You're nice, Laurie. I don't mean to be mad. I want you. I don't like being in a box."

"It's a nice box, inside."

"No box at all would be nicer."

"There's nothing we can do about that." She was looking at the roses as she spoke.

He began to swear again. Sweat came out and glistened on his forehead. She looked up at him once and then away, until he stopped. They stood together, one on each side of the open car door, in the late afternoon. The garage and stables lay behind them. Someone was whistling softly back there and they could do nothing but stand still and not touch each other.

"You have no right to be resigned," he said at last.

"I won't spoil what we have for what we don't have."

"Then at least I want what we have. Can't you get away from that place early tomorrow? It's been nearly a week."

"Yes, I suppose so. I'll do my best."

"Ten? Ten-thirty?"

"More like eleven, probably."

He put his big hand on her forearm as it lay on the edge of the car window and shook it gently, just enough for her to feel how much strength was held back. "Be there," he said. "You hear me."

She smiled at him. His black curly hair was going thin in one place, but it was crisp around his forehead. Yes, his shirt collar was too tight. She must be careful to do nothing about that. His eyes were gray—or hazel? She was never sure. He'd shaved again when he showered, before he drove out. She could draw his face with her eyes shut. "You're awfully bossy today," she said.

"You bet your sweet life I am," he said. "If you're late I'll tan your hide." Then he got in, shut the door and turned the car while she watched. He stopped, between her and the garage, and said, "Kiss me quick while no one can see," and she stooped and did so through the window of the car. "You're my good girl," he said, releasing her, and drove quickly away.

She began to walk back to the house, saying to the joy within her: Be quiet, be secret. No one must know. Be quiet, lie hidden, be still.

CHAPTER

14

How good, how good it is to be home! I knew I was right. Here at home, after that torture in the hospital, I can feel myself growing better every day. Oh, perhaps it will take a week or two longer before I am completely mobile, for of course the physiotherapist can't see me every day as could be done in the hospital, but she drives out three times a week and Tucker has got quite clever under her training. And as far as peace of mind goes, why I'm a different creature! Lorraine and I have actually entertained company a couple of times, and she is very good about reporting on the people she sees, both here and during her occasional trips to New York. Then there are the children. With all the space we have here, they're not a bother, for they have room to run during the day and after tea are content to settle down with Lorraine and me and be read to, or play quiet games until bedtime. I was a little worried about having them here at first, but they are quite individual children, they remind me of no one.

I hope, in fact, that I can keep them here all summer. I'm sure it is good for Lorraine, she looks rested and well. Herbert, it seems, has gone on to Germany and may continue to Sweden. We learn this still via postcards, but it would be no use, in any case, to expect Lorraine to know just what he is planning, she has a really invincible ignorance of business—so like Mary! But of course German recartelization is obviously only a matter of time, whatever bans may have been placed upon it ten years ago, and Herbert is certainly not the only American who has decided that Düsseldorf is worth a visit. They're able, the Germans, though I can't say I've ever liked them very much—I mean, even personally. Which is absurd. There must be plenty of likable Germans. Unfortunately I seem mainly to have met the other variety. And I began, of course, by falling in love with England and the English in 1914.

How long ago that was! What a vanished world! Would it be

absurd for me to write about it—to write a proper book, I mean, proper memoirs to be properly published? I met so many people and saw such a lot. I don't see why I shouldn't put it all down during these next few months while I'm getting well. After all, beside Lady This and the Duchess of That, I knew some of the really great figures, Yeats and Augustus John and D. H. Lawrence and Churchill and Lloyd George. I saw them come and go, Churchill down, after the Dardanelles, commanding a brigade in the trenches, Lloyd George up, conducting the war as if it were a Welsh chorus when he'd winkled poor Mr. Asquith out, and then everything reversed.

I was in London when the First War began, and in Paris when it ended. If I've caught the scribbling habit—and people do, at my age, even when they haven't been bedridden for six months—if I'm going to build a shelter out of the past against the present—well, why shouldn't I really make something of it? All the personal history that I've been rehearsing to myself I'll throw away, of course, and just begin with something about being in London for the season in 1914——

Let me see.

My first husband, James Fennimore Greene, had many friends and business connections in London. So it was that when I came, as a young bride, to what was then the capital of the world—what then seemed the capital of the world—of a united and peaceful world——

Humph. Surely I can do better than that!

The London season before the First World War! There are many who still remember its gaiety, of course; but perhaps few who remember it quite as vividly as I, for I knew but one—for I, a young American—a young bride from the wilds of America, knew but one, and that one was ended—shattered—broken by the war. By the first terrible barrage of war——

Oh dear. It does seem rather stilted. Perhaps if I just make notes, just put down what I remember all helter-skelter, the way I have been doing, a real writer could straighten it out. And then, if I didn't like what he did, I could change it around myself a little once it had been organized. I wonder if that's the way people write? I'll drop the Knopfs a note, I think, or better still, ask them to come up from

Purchase for lunch one Sunday when I can get around a bit better and have something to show.

In the meantime—London. In June. We came up from Italy slowly through France. We spent three weeks in Paris. My mouth was open most of the time—partly to eat and drink, of course, but mainly in astonishment. It was there, all there. I was seeing it. But London— in London I wasn't just looking, I was being. James knew masses of people; I must make a list, Balfour, Asquith, Lady Elcho, George Moore, Lady Cunard—that was where I met Yeats, which I would never have expected—Lord Curzon, Eddy Marsh, Reginald McKenna —oh dear, I can't put them all down here, I'll carry a pad around with me and write down names as they come. Well, everyone was fond of my dear James, how could they not be? And he explained to me carefully that the English were apt to be stiff, that they either knew you well or not at all, and sometimes a stranger couldn't tell the difference, and I wasn't to mind if people were not introduced formally to each other all the time, but just to sit and smile and wait. And then it was all right! They looked me up and they looked me down, and I thanked God for those three weeks in Paris and the clothes I'd got, but they loved James, he made them laugh, he was their tame American, and so they took me in.

Gay? Yes, it was gay. The dances lasted all night. Lorraine told me about this musical comedy they've done in New York out of Shaw's *Pygmalion*, about the scene at Ascot where everyone is so bored. Well, I don't remember it that way. I don't remember that we danced as if Swiss clockwork moved us about. Quite the contrary! I've danced my shoes right through, in one night. Try a fast waltz, sometime, with a partner who likes to reverse. Try a galop when the sun is already up, and coming through the cracks around the curtains in the ballroom, and the band is kept from collapse by champagne and the promise of a larger cheque, but half is bone-white with fatigue and half bright red—— On one such occasion a friend of mine, a perfectly proper young lady, the granddaughter of an earl, was picked up by her partner, a perfectly proper young man, and swung in the air so high and so hard that the heel of her shoe sent flying the tiara of one of the last lone chaperones. Bored indeed!

Sometimes we walked home through the sunny morning, a group of us laughing together, while the streets which still smelled more of horses than of gasoline were being washed; and I'd fall into bed at the hotel and sleep the day away. Sometimes I'd wander around London while James talked to people about business, and do bits of sight-seeing that my English friends had fits over. They wanted to come with me but after one try I wouldn't let them. I was *intensely* romantic, I promise you, and they howled at me because I burst into tears over Anne Boleyn at the Tower, and so I never would go with anyone again, but said quite firmly, "No thank you, I'm going sight-seeing, this is one of my days for being an American tourist," and went off by myself, free to weep in sheer excitement at Wren churches, and the Abbey, and all the obvious places.

On weekends we weekended. James, naturally, had acquired an automobile. Out of deference to English sensibilities and taste this one was not red, it was, instead, a curious tawny yellow and it had, heaven be praised, a top. I was rejoiced to see it—but it turned out that, although the top could be raised in bad weather by the combined exertions of a squad of trained men, James liked it down. He liked, he said, to see where he was going. So when we drove down to spend Saturday to Monday with friends, I still wore goggles and a veil, and tied my hat on.

And when we got where we were going, I may say, and I faced the problem of washing off the dust I had acquired en route, I still found myself doing so in a bowl on a stand in my bedroom more often than in a bathroom. Not that you couldn't have a bath. You could. Maids carried in a tub with a large can of hot water in it and dumped the water in, they really did. Actually you *had* to bathe by an open fire in the winter—you'd have turned purple and died of the ice age if you hadn't. I met, in one aristocratic house, a sweet little Austrian governess who had chilblains on her hands that didn't even heal entirely in summer! As for electric light, well, it was an open question. Some people had it. Some didn't. There was apt to be a telephone strategically placed in the hall at a point where a draft blew down your neck on the warmest day.

And I loved it all. I adored it. I was absolutely swept away when one of my new friends said, as a compliment, of course, "Oh, I don't mean *you* when I say 'Americans are provincial,' you're hardly like an American at all." I smiled sweetly, for I knew better than to cry out, in the wild, provincial, American way, "Oh, thank you!" But I cried it inside.

Well, do remember that I was just nineteen, that I had just burst out of my chrysalis, that when I said "America" I thought of those Church Guild teas and the unendurable boredom of my youth which I had nonetheless endured while denying every waking minute that I was really a part of it, and that I had been proved right: I *was* no longer a part of it, the world *was* enormous (oh, that huge world of youth!), and anything could happen, even happiness, even wishes-come-true. Think of me thinking this on an English Sunday, having tea on the lawn, with a young man with a blond mustache to bring me cakes and an enormous dog at my feet pretending to sleep but hoping for a bit of cake himself. This is just past the longest day of the year. The sun is still high. People have been playing tennis and are beginning to discuss playing it again. A neighbor, a retired General, is beating with his hands on the arm of his wicker chair—the spoon jumps in his cup—and describing the state of the Army, which distresses him. One by one we all fall victim to this tirade, because it is impossible not to, but everyone is thinking him a great bore about the Army, and wishing he were a retired Admiral, for Admirals are much less apt to go on that way about the Navy. Though what some of them have to say about Winston Churchill sets them to beating the arms of their chairs on occasion. No one will tell the General what we are all thinking: that his army is an anachronism, that war is over and done with except for outbursts in odd little corners of the world like the Balkans, or among excitable Latin types in Mexico and South America who "take" a revolution every now and then as other people take pills. Courtesy preserves an uneasy silence—and then, too, there is the Irish problem, which has gone from its chronic condition to a state of acute inflammation at the moment and is, probably, why the General is finally not interrupted, but allowed to go on until he runs down into occasional huffings and puffings.

What none of us knew, and what, for nearly a month, meant nothing to us after we knew it, was that a man named Princip had stood in the street of a provincial Balkan town that afternoon, about the time our tennis began, and had fired two shots into a passing automobile. He killed the Archduke Franz Ferdinand who was the heir to the Austrian throne and his morganatic wife, Sophie Chotek, but he did a good deal more than that. The impact of his bullets started the world turning upside down, very slowly at first—as I say, no one noticed for weeks—and then faster and faster. Five weeks later I didn't feel like laughing at that foolish, angry old General, and two months later the boy who had brought me cakes was dead. He was in the Guards and he died at Mons.

I *cannot* tell you what it was like. You, all of you who are younger than I (and some days that feels like the whole world), all of you have inherited a world that you know is already cracked, broken, chipped—what's the word I want?—flawed, somehow. We had a whole world, a whole round solid world given us, and we saw it crack, right across, the flaw running and spreading before our startled eyes. It was unbelievable.

James suspected long before I did. Well, naturally. He knew the world, he knew the actors and agents. He asked me, latish in July, if I wanted him to arrange passage home for us. We hadn't planned to go till September.

I stared at him. Then I was very, very clever. My brain worked hard. I said, "Do you think—— You mean—there really is a chance of war?"

"I don't know," he said. "I think there's a chance, yes, though I don't know how big a one. But I don't believe Austria can permit Servia——"

"Servia!" I said. "Austria! What have Austria and Servia got to do with it?"

Then it appeared that we were talking about two different wars. Sometimes I feel that I have gone slightly mad, or at any rate that I remember things differently from other people, for everyone else has completely forgotten about the other war, my war. And yet I assure you that it was what we meant, in July of 1914, when we said we were worried about the possibility of war. It was what the newspapers gave their leading articles to, what Parliament was debating, what Mr. Asquith's government almost came to grief on—it was the imminent, important danger, and it had absolutely nothing to do with the Archduke Franz Ferdinand. It was, in fact, the reason that none of us had quite dared argue with the furious General about the Army: the Irish question. Ulster had been included in the bill that would give

Home Rule to Ireland, and Ulster did not like it. The threat of war was civil war across the Irish Channel.

I knew all about *that* war—about the anger in the northern countries at the idea of submitting to rule from Dublin ("Home Rule is Rome Rule," they said in Belfast), and about Sir Edward Carson's encouragement to the rebels in defiance of Mr. Asquith, his chief, and I had great opinions on the position of the Ulster officers at the Curragh base who had refused to agree to help put down a revolt of their friends and relatives—— Oh, I could talk for hours about it all, it was over this that I received the compliment about not being like a provincial American. But I didn't know anything about James's war, the one that Austria and Servia were mixed up in, the one that seemed so unlikely. Very well, a fanatic had shot an Austrian Archduke in the Balkans: this seemed to me so exactly what an Austrian Archduke might well expect if he traveled indiscriminately about the Balkans that I couldn't understand why he hadn't stayed home. But as you know, James was right and I was wrong.

However I did not, at the time, believe him. A nasty intellectual pride strengthened me in the belief that James's war was not likely to come to much. That foolish old General, he couldn't—James couldn't —be right, not in our round, solid world. How stupid I was! James was right so often, and it always surprised me. The result was that we were caught in England. Two days after James asked me about going home Austria sent an ultimatum to Servia. The world tipped a little faster. We were still talking about Ireland that weekend, there'd been a conference at Buckingham Palace and it had come to nothing —but there was a new undertone beginning, a new uneasiness. Of course it was impossible and yet, and yet—— And then Crack! The flaw, the crack spreading! Between one Sunday and the next, Servia, Austria, Russia, France and Germany mobilized their armies. I *cannot* tell you. How I wish I could really write, could make you see! It was unbelievable, impossible, like a nightmare—and then, all of a sudden, enormously exciting. I felt as if I were drunk.

James asked me again about going home. By that time there were stories in the papers about panicky Americans storming the offices of the Cunard Line, President Wilson was sending a battleship to evacuate travelers, and I said, No, I certainly did not want to run away, nor travel eight to a stateroom, nor swing in a navy hammock, nor miss all the fun. Did I really say fun? It seems to me that I did. At any rate we stayed. James cabled and cabled to his brokers and other men of business, but I think he was glad himself to stay. He was as fond of England and the English as they were of him and he felt, I think, that it was good to show our friends that there were at least two Americans who would not desert them and dash off to bucolic Boeotian safety.

All my dancing partners disappeared. A few held commissions in crack regiments. These died almost at once, for they were flung into France immediately and met the first shock of the German thrust that nearly took Paris. Some were in Territorial regiments, reserve sort of affairs. These lived longer, for often they were held at home to train volunteers. But most of them *were* volunteers, and *they* died in droves, incessantly, all the time, for four years. I remember the casualty figures. Do you know that on a quiet day on the western front the expected, normal standard loss was five thousand men? That is, five thousand Allies; the Germans lost another five thousand. Do you know that the attempt on Gallipoli cost a quarter of a million casualties before Ian Hamilton's troops pulled out and left everything as it had been? Do you know that to gain from five to ten miles on a twenty-mile front, in the Somme offensive of 1916, cost the Allies six hundred thousand men? The Germans lost about that many too, the French lost another three hundred thousand or so before Verdun, and the Russians lost over a million that summer. Yes, I know men died in the Second War, but they didn't die in quite the same way. The advances and the losses in the west between the two Battles of the Marne, one in 1914, one in 1918, were measured in fractions of an inch for each dead man, or crippled man, or blinded man, or man who suffered progressive amputations as gas gangrene spread through a limb——

I must stop. I am unreconciled to that slaughter still, I will never be reconciled. Our world cracked, and this was what the crack revealed —absolute, nightmare hell, so much worse than one could have imagined in advance that we were subjected again and again to new shocks of surprise that this could be, even when we thought we were numb. I know the last war was bad, I have talked to people who were in Japanese prison camps, and about Belsen and Dachau and the rest I came to know a great deal, perhaps too much. But there is a difference, and the difference is partly this: in 1914 we were innocent as no one on earth could ever be innocent again. And another difference is this: it was possible to hate Hitler and what he stood for and what he did, so that even if many people felt that it was not quite worth dying for that hate, still they hated honestly. In the First War there was no one to hate like that. My friends were killed by decent and honorable men out of ignorance and stupidity. They came very soon not to hate the men in the other trenches whom they killed, and who killed them, and the Kaiser was a joke. Their hate turned on their situation, and it was a terrible situation and worthy of hate. They hated the crass, brute inefficiency and ineptitude of the men who sent them to die, and came to feel that these men were killing them. So they were. And they were good men, Mr. Asquith, Sir Edward Grey, Churchill, that old monolith Kitchener, and the rest. Well, it is a hard and bitter thing to be taught in your youth to hate good men. It calls a great deal into question, old truths, old definitions, old beliefs, and for many the foundations of the world are always a little askew afterwards. No wonder the Russians, who were the worst off of all, made a revolution. No wonder that the logical French refused to go through it again in 1940. All right, the English did—but first of all, the English hadn't fought on their own soil in the First War (neither had the Germans), and secondly, the English are crazy.

Well, now I am writing history or something—though I don't know why I shouldn't, really, for I was there, I experienced it, it was not just history for me, rumbling along somewhere, but private experience too. You see, I got myself mixed up in it. I worked as a volunteer in a big hospital in England in 1916 and 1917, and later, when James had to be in Paris, after we had come into the war, I got him to pull strings and managed to go over with him, and got myself attached to the American hospital in Neuilly.

Why? I've spent years trying to assign values to the different motives that led me—married to a very rich man with, one would think, other duties—to do any such thing. The scale of values I give my motives has changed often, depending on how charmed I am with myself at the time. But even when I was most complacently smug, I've never been able to eliminate the factor of curiosity; and of a rather unpleasant desire for excitement.

CHAPTER FOURTEEN

We went back to America in the fall of '14, when the first Battle of the Marne had finally halted the German advance. That was when the Paris taxicabs went into action, you may remember. And I must tell you that I was very, very bored. I did all the things that wives were supposed to do, I entertained, I spent quite a bit of time buying perfectly lovely clothes, and James let me do over the town house in East 63rd Street and even attack the problem of redecorating the castle—and I was bored. So I did something wives were not supposed to do, I joined the suffragettes, though in a vague kind of way, and marched in a parade or two, and shouted "Votes for Women" once or twice in places where I shouldn't have (one of my English friends shouted this when she was being presented at court, which really raised a brouhaha); but I didn't want to embarrass James, so I did not fling myself into the movement and do everything that Mrs. Catt and Mrs. Whitehouse wanted me to. I would have been delighted to embarrass Mrs. Ford, James's sister, who changed color to bright red and then to pale green while she talked to me about my activities, but I couldn't do that without hurting my husband so—for me—I was quite restrained.

Actually it was Mary, my sister Mary, who succeeded in putting Mrs. Ford's nose out of joint, which shows, doesn't it, that truth is stranger than fiction, and that there are more things in heaven and earth, Horatio, and so forth. Mary did this very simply. She married Spencer Forbes. And I think they were happy together.

But, you see, Spencer Forbes had been engaged to Louise Ford. That was how Mary met him, for she and Louise went on being friends after James and I were married. Now, I don't mean that Mary—Good heavens! Mary!—went and snaffled Spencer out from under Louise's nose. Nothing of the kind. First, Louise broke the engagement. Well, she was always doing that. It was her idea of fun. She didn't mean that she was really giving Spencer up, nothing of the kind there either. She was just bringing a little variety into life and in her mind Spencer went right on belonging to her.

Well, Spencer didn't know this. In Boston, apparently, when you get engaged, you are engaged, and if you get unengaged, then the young lady has jilted you and you may be hurt and angry and have powerful emotions about her, but you are no longer her property. Now here was where Mary was devious. She didn't tell Spencer that

CHAPTER FOURTEEN

Louise was not through with him, and might very well be willing to get engaged to him again in a couple of months. She *knew* it perfectly well, but she didn't tell, not even when Spencer turned to her for comfort and to have someone to tell about how disappointed he was in Louise and how badly she had behaved. Mary didn't say a word about the fact that Louise would very soon be willing to have him back. Instead, she sympathized.

How do I know? Because I was their chaperone. Spencer was working in New York that winter, very broad-minded indeed for a Bostonian, almost heterodox, but he happened to have an uncle in New York and he was going, in rather a gingerly manner, into a study of how New Yorkers ran a private bank. And Mary came in to me for two or three weeks at a time. We had a box at the opera Mondays. Spencer usually made a fourth. When James wanted a quiet evening of bridge, Spencer was handy. Spencer liked to walk. So did Mary. They tramped around Central Park together and then I'd meet them for tea somewhere. In short, Mary proved herself to be the proper kind of bride for a Bostonian, and in the spring he asked her to go up to New London for the Yale-Harvard—I'm sorry, Spencer, the Harvard-Yale—boat race in June, and then on to spend a few days with his family at Pride's Crossing.

"Shall I?" Mary asked me.

"Do you want to?" I said.

"There'll be quite a number of people there," she said. "From Boston."

"I didn't think it was a private rendezvous," I replied.

"Don't tease me!" said my sister. I looked at her and saw that she really was confused, she really didn't know what to do about the interest shown in her by this extremely eligible young man.

"Mary," I said, "it's up to you. Do you want to go?"

She started arguing with herself. It was queer to hear her. She wanted to go, and she was scared—partly of Boston, and partly of what she called a "commitment"—a commitment, she meant, to get married and live with a man. I concluded that she must really be very much in love with Spencer if he could upset her so; and also that she must have a considerably more passionate nature than I had ever given her credit for if her emotions about him were strong enough to frighten her to the extent that she was frightened.

It made me stop and think. I wasn't by any means as sure as I had been, ten minutes before, that she ought to pop off to Pride's Crossing, purpose matrimony. Was old Spencer the right man to respond to all the turmoil that Mary's demure exterior was concealing? As far as I was concerned, he looked like something that a Gloucester fishing smack had hauled up in a net off the Grand Banks on a particularly foggy day. Since my taste was not Mary's, however, this could be ignored. But could I leave it to Mary's taste? It ceased to be sensible to tell her to do what she wanted to do; because she wanted to do it, all right, but she wasn't in any condition to know whether it was a good idea or not. The argument circled and circled, but it seemed on the whole that it was up to me to decide.

I sat and thought. I thought of my youth, and Mary's. I thought of the young man whose courtship of her I'd ruined. I thought of my father. He would miss Mary in a very different way from the way he missed me, and he wouldn't know it until it happened. He'd always known I was going to leave home. I thought of my mother. She had always been a bit like a captive balloon, with Mary providing the string that kept her connected to reality. Without Mary, she might very well drift off by herself into the blue. But Mary, I told myself, when I had thought this, can't stay unmarried in order to keep contact between our parents! That's absurd. Mary must have her chance. And everyone everywhere would say that Spencer is a very good chance for her.

But I was still uneasy. You see, I was just realizing that I really loved Mary very much. No, love isn't exactly the right word. What I mean is in the Bible somewhere, isn't it, the thing about being "bone of my bone and flesh of my flesh"? Mary and I were part of each other, and I had to do the very best for her I could. All other considerations could be, must be, ignored—though I must say the thought of Mrs. Ford's face when she came to hear of an engagement between Mary and Spencer Forbes was one it was hard for me to ignore. So I sat and I thought, and Mary walked over to the window and looked out at 63rd Street, a dull view, and came back and looked at me and finally plumped down on the sofa and said, "Don't you think I should go, Diana?"

I said, "Yes, I think you should." I hadn't known I was going to say it, and there were times later when I wished I hadn't, times when I wondered whether I hadn't taken pride in my own power to push Mary one way or another, and been afraid that not to push her, to leave her alone and let her decide, would be to misuse this power—which was surely even more arrogant of me than usual. And besides, Spencer was the smuggest man in the entire world about some things. But there were more times when I thought I had been right, whatever my motives, and on the whole I still think it was a good thing I did that day. In many ways they were made for each other, and certainly Spencer appreciated Mary—not the things about her that I liked best, but things that were there. I think he made her happy—oh, how do I know, really? But happier than many men would have made her, she was used to order, she liked routine—I don't know what happened to all the passion I felt in her that day. Can it be ordered, fitted into routine? But I don't know what would have happened to it if she hadn't married Spencer, for Mary was not, on the surface at any rate, the type to attract a passionate man. It seemed to me then—and yes, it still seems to me—that she had best do the thing that was prudent, that she wanted to do, and that would please everyone except the Fords; but I agree that I thought this because I couldn't see her doing anything that would serve her better.

I never really knew how it turned out. Way inside, I mean. They were a fine, typical Boston couple on the surface. I wondered sometimes. Mary always looked quite young, but I don't know whether that's a good sign or not. Some people look young because nothing has happened to them. As for the girls, Lorraine and Faith—it's not fair to judge. Mary died when they were both in their teens, a very impressionable age. Each of them is emotionally immature, but——

Heavens, how I wander! What I started to write about was how I came to do hospital work during the war. Well, after Mary and Spencer were married in the spring of 1916, and after I'd fussed around doing over the 63rd Street house and made a feeble beginning on the castle, I got more bored than ever. You may well ask why I didn't have children. I don't know the answer. I didn't think I was unwilling; and I still don't know whether the kind of psychic, unconscious unpreparedness (and therefore, I suppose, unwillingness) that I must have had within me—I don't know whether this could really keep a woman from conceiving. All I know is that I didn't, and I got very restless. In these years I started to ride, James bought me a beautiful little five-gaited mare, a chestnut, I named her Jezebel, and when we were at the castle I could ride myself tired.

Then there was a great deal of activity going on about America and the war. With all his English friends, James was naturally very much interested in this—well, all right, in this propaganda. Visiting Englishmen of all varieties descended upon us on the way to explain their country's idealistic war aims to the American barbarians in the Middle West. They were fascinating, many of them. I gave a lot of dinners for them. In between times, life was dull. And the propaganda worked on me, whatever it may have done for the Middle West.

Well, and so, in June of 1916 James and I went back to England again. He had letters to our Ambassador, Mr. Page, and to Reginald McKenna, who was Chancellor of the Exchequer, and he had people to see in Paris too. What about? I'm not sure, but this was the time of the big loans, the big private loans made through Morgan's and so on to the Allied governments. James did not talk about his business to me—I think he thought I was too young and might be bored—but I remember that two gentlemen who were partners in Morgan's dined with us the week before we left. So did Gilbert Murray, by the way, he was to lecture at Columbia that summer. A perfectly charming man, so delightful that I paid very little attention to the other gentlemen. Anyway, I was awfully excited to be leaving for England. As it happened, it was a safe time to sail. The U-boat attacks were being suppressed by the German Foreign Office for political reasons that summer, and we had a lovely smooth crossing.

But oh, London was sad! I'd remembered it as it was, at peace, and then in the first excitement of the war. Everything I'd heard since then had been—here I think propaganda is too strong a word. What I heard had been true, but only part of the truth. I'd heard about nobility and sacrifice and quiet suffering, and they were there. But there were other things too. There were the ambulances that met the hospital trains at Charing Cross. There were the boys who were too young and the men who were too old in uniform, the women bus drivers, the infirm old gentlemen acting as chorus boys in the revues, meatless days and, later, heatless days. But worst of all there was the feeling that these things merely symbolized, merely pointed to: the feeling that something had taken possession of the human race, and that this Invader, this Strangeness, could not be controlled by reason

CHAPTER FOURTEEN

any longer, that it had gone mad and was devouring us. A young man once told me that, after some months in Flanders, he had not dared look over his shoulder. He was afraid that the clouds in the sky and the rubble of the town that lay just behind the line and a blasted tree would one day form into a meaningful, comprehensible signal (a large, laughing face was what he feared most); and then he would know that everything that he was going through was intended. He thought he could stand everything except that.

All of this was a terrible shock to me, to my intellectual pride. I had always been extremely proud of my realism and my preference for facing facts. Now it seemed that for two years I had been seeing the war through the most idealistically naïve eyes. Illogically I grew quite angry at James because he did not seem shocked—he had, of course, understood things better from the beginning. But because he did not quiver with horror every time I quivered with horror, I decided that he was callous. When I told him that I, somehow, wanted to help, he replied that of course we all did.

So I asked a friend how to go about volunteering for hospital work, and I went and signed up for the proper training course, and tied and untied and retied red tape (though the whole affair was still very amateur compared with the Second War, volunteers cropped up in the strangest places, particularly volunteers who knew The Right People), and there I was with a hospital assignment before James knew anything about it. I was very pleased with myself.

When I told him, he sat down and looked at me. He started to speak twice, and stopped, and then he said, "But, Diana, we're going to Paris next week."

I said, "No, James. You're going to Paris. It will give me a chance to do the first aid extra fast while you're away."

Then for the first time in our whole marriage I saw him angry. His face was very quiet, it wasn't until you looked close that you saw this was because it was rigid. He said, "Why did you do this?"

"They need me, they need me," I said.

He said, "Nonsense. If it were a question of need——" I never knew how that sentence was supposed to end, for he broke off and got up and went over to the window and stood looking out and pushing one fist into the other hand with a little, recurrent smack.

Do you know something? I was afraid. I lifted my head and squared my shoulders and said, "I told you that I wanted to help, and you didn't say——"

"Be quiet," he said, and I was, for over a minute.

Then I said steadily, "I told you I wanted to help, James, and I am going to help. It's arranged, they are glad to have me, and I am going to do it."

"How old are you, Diana?" he asked.

"Why——" I began, for I had thought that of course he knew, he must remember the pearls that he gave me for my birthday. "Why, I'm twenty-one!"

"Yes," he said. "I'm still more than twice as old as you. Why did you marry me?"

It took him an appreciable time to turn and look at me after he'd asked that question, but my face was still expressing appalled shock. He came and took me in his arms at once. "I'm sorry," he said, "I didn't mean it, Diana. It was stupid of me, I know you want to help, I'm sorry."

I pushed him away and said, "I don't understand, James. Don't you think I—I love you? Because I feel I should do something? How can I sit with my hands folded in all this suffering? I'm young, yes, but just *because* I'm young and strong and good with my hands, I can really be a help. I know there is horror and pain and things that are terrible to see, and that I'll have to cope with bedpans and dressings, but surely that's little enough to bear compared with what the men themselves bear— I'm not afraid, James, I'm not soft."

"No, of course you're not," he said. "But there are other women who can do it."

"Why yes, but they need everyone they can get, just the same. It's no excuse for me *because* there are others!"

"Diana——" He put my head down on his shoulder and held it there with one hand. I couldn't see his face. "I need you, you know. I need you too."

"Why, James, why, darling!" I cried, enlightened at last. "You don't think I'm doing this because I want to be away from you! But suppose we were at war, the United States, and you had to go— I would understand that you didn't want to, but had to!"

"I shan't have to," said James quietly. "I'm too old."

That made me afraid in a different way. I realized that I had hurt him, that I had been thoughtless and not put our marriage first, and I had always intended, whatever my feelings, to do that. It was the least I could do. I went a little cold inside, for it was true, I had never thought of James or weighed his need for me, I had seen only myself and the bleeding world, myself in a fixed posture of mercy, as if I were on a poster. I began to babble along the line of reasoning suggested by the poet who told his mistress that he loved honor more.

"It's all right," he said at last. "I understand why you want to do it, Diana. I understand."

"Do you," I asked, "do you really?" I felt that I would rather like to know myself.

"Yes," he said, and smiled. "You have been very bored—no, dear, don't look like that. Why shouldn't you have been bored? You're young and energetic and you haven't had enough to do. I don't mean that you've been bored with me, I understand——"

"Oh, James," I managed to say, "please, you mustn't——"

"I understand that you feel that you have resources that are not being used, and that you want to offer them where you think they're needed. Isn't that so?"

I almost said yes, because it was so. Then I thought about those "resources that are not being used," and I knew that if I said yes, James would live with that answer for the rest of his life. Since I hadn't answered at once, I waited a little while longer, and then shook my head in a puzzled sort of way and said, "I don't know, James. You're cleverer than I am. Perhaps what you say is true, even if it doesn't seem so to me. What I feel is just that I want to help, that I ought to help. I—it doesn't seem wrong to me that I have to make a sacrifice to help, and stay here and work while you're in Paris—— Because there are so many, many sacrifices being made. I realize —I should have realized before—that I'm asking you to make a sacrifice too, that you'd like to have me in Paris with you—but is it so awfully much? Compared to—all the other sacrifices?"

His eyes came right into me then, probing me. I felt their force, I felt his mind searching my words just the way the searchlights over London probed and searched for the Zeppelins or the Gothas. And I knew, consciously, that I was lying to him, consciously, for the first important time in our married life. I was not sacrificing anything. I had been bored to tears. I was fleeing into nobility and hospital work

170

CHAPTER FOURTEEN

as if I were fleeing from jail to the great, gay world—as I had fled from my youth and home to marry James in the first place.

I tried to cover the knowledge and hide it from him. I don't think I succeeded; because I was so surprised myself. For three years I had been telling myself I loved James, even though a little, little part of me, a pair of crossed fingers, knew better. But to be flooded with the knowledge was a shock, and I am afraid that James realized—something. Something that a part of him, another pair of crossed fingers, knew too.

He said, "Diana, please remember one thing."

"Of course I will," I said. "I will be careful. I will take care of myself. I'll remember how I love you and you love me——"

"No," said James, "not quite that. Remember that I am a very jealous man."

People I knew:

The Waldorf Astors, Lady Charles Beresford, the Aga Khan, Mrs. Duggan who married Lord Curzon, the Duchess of Sutherland, Evan Charteris, J. M. Barrie, Lord Haldane, F. E. Smith who became Lord Birkenhead, Sir Thomas Beecham, Lady Diana Manners, Maxine Elliott, Forbes Robertson, H. G. Wells, and Sir Oliver Lodge.

15

"Lorraine," said Mrs. Belchamber one hot afternoon, "how well you look." They were sitting on the terrace back of the house.

Her niece glanced up from her book. "Thank you," she said.

But Mrs. Belchamber continued to regard her. "I think," she added, "that you've gained a little weight."

Since Lorraine was stretched out on a chaise longue directly in front of her aunt, and dressed for hot weather, there was little she could do to dispute this. "You feed me too well," she said. "It's Marie's sauces."

Mrs. Belchamber fanned herself with a magazine. "I thought perhaps it had something to do with your liking it here," she said. "You seem to me much less tense than you were—oh, last winter."

"I'm loving it here," said Lorraine firmly, and smiled. But——
What are you up to, Aunt Di? she wondered behind the smile. A bee was circling the half-empty pitcher of iced tea that stood on the table between them, and her aunt, she thought, was circling too.

"I was afraid you'd find it dull," said Mrs. Belchamber.

Aha! thought Lorraine, and said politely, "Not at all."

"Don't you have more going on at East Hampton, though? More excitement?"

"I like this better."

Mrs. Belchamber pursed her lips. Lorraine waited, not quite daring to go back to her book. The silence stretched——

"It's charming of you to be contented with an old woman, my dear, but I don't really understand why you should be. And as far as I can see, the only thing you do is go in to New York and look after your orphans every week. Why——"

"Now, Aunt Di, that's not so! I've been out to dinner once or twice every week, and you've had people here too. You mustn't worry about me."

172

"Well, I do," said her aunt. "I keep thinking you could be in Europe——"

"Darling, the last thing in the world I want to do at the moment is tour the Saar and discuss the future of the European Steel Community. I'm lazy. I'm happy. Do believe me!"

"It's very odd," said Mrs. Belchamber discontentedly. "I should think——"

But at this point the bee plunged into the iced tea. "Oh dear," said Lorraine, "I'd better get rid of that. It's the sugar that attracts them." She stood up and picked up the tray with pitcher and glasses. Negotiating the screened door she called back, "I promise to tell you if I get bored and we'll organize a water carnival on the river for everybody for miles around." The door slammed, she was inside and safe for the moment, but putting down the tray in the pantry she thought, Confound it, I'll have to be careful! She can see through a brick wall if she puts her mind to it.

Peter darling, Peter darling, Peter darling. The trouble is, I'm too happy, it makes her suspicious. I always thought people in love were up and down, but I'm just plain up.

She sighed, turning on the water in the sink, running the sticky glasses full. But it was a false sigh, and she knew it. How could she regret being happy? How could she pretend not to be? Everything was so peaceful here, the big house resting around her, and she so at peace—— Only her aunt was dissatisfied and curious. What shall I do? thought Lorraine. How can I distract her? I don't suppose anyone's ever managed to do it if she's really set her mind on something! I'll just have to be careful and defend myself. She went into the living room and picked up the portable radio so that, returning to the terrace, she could offer the five o'clock news as an alternate subject of conversation.

And that time Mrs. Belchamber had apparently thought better of prying into her niece's state of mind, for she entered with vivacity into a discussion of whether or not Stevenson would, or should, be renominated at the Democratic Convention.

Two days later, however, there was another prickly moment when Lorraine was ready to leave on her weekly trip to New York to work at the children's shelter—with a detour en route to her rented cottage, and Savage. Mrs. Belchamber looked up from a complicated game of patience to remark that she could understand why Lorraine wanted to get away from an old invalid, but not why the place she chose to get to was an orphanage.

Lorraine drew breath and plunged without hesitation into lying-by-telling-the-truth. "Ah," she said, "but you don't know what I'm planning to do tonight. Suppose I told you that right here in my suitcase" (and she waggled it at her aunt) "I had my best pale green Dior sheath? And a date to go dancing at the St. Regis roof with an old beau who's in New York on business? What would you say then?"

"I'd say, 'God bless you,'" said Mrs. Belchamber promptly, "and tell Tucker to go look in your closet to see if you'd taken the Dior."

"Well, as a matter of fact, I haven't," said her niece, kissing her cheek. "That was just a for-instance. But I might, you know, one day." Exit laughing, she said to herself, doing so quickly. She's perfectly capable of having Tucker rummage through my things, I must remember that! She put the suitcase in the car (the only dress it contained was a gray cotton, suitable for looking after children), and drove off to wait, drowsing happily in the twilight, for Savage whenever he might come, however long he might stay. When he did, she had so completely forgotten her aunt's touch of temper that it never occurred to her to mention it. They were together and they were happy, as if the cottage were in another universe where the lonely compulsions of this one could not reach. That night Savage managed to stay with her (she never asked him in advance whether he could), and when she left in the wavering, watery early morning light, she sang with the disc jockeys' records all down the parkway, awake to enjoyment and unsuspicious of it.

For her divided self had healed. She had come together now not in fury, but in joy as well. She and Savage didn't talk of love. They talked of what they had been doing, they compared experiences right back to their far-apart childhoods, the well-brought-up little girl and the grim boy fighting his way out of the dirt, who could neither of them have imagined they would ever meet. "Tell me a story," Lorraine would say, and Savage would think for a while and begin anywhere from "Well, did I ever tell you about the radioman who went crazy? That was when I was in the Sara——" to "Well, did I ever tell you about Miss Tumulty at the relief office?" Then she told him stories of boarding school and Boston, and he said, "But, my

God, why did she do *that?*" Both of them were trying to give the other as much of their lives as they could.

Happiness didn't end with Savage, though. Lorraine found herself enjoying everything else too. Waking, sleeping, breathing, eating, exercising one of the horses, taking Marie, the French cook, to market and listening to her attack the butcher on the subject of American veal, blueberrying on the hill behind the house with the children—it was as if Time had accommodatingly slowed itself down, so that every experience came at just the right speed to be perceived wholly, spreading its meaning right down to her toes and out to her fingertips. At the beginning she'd felt as if she were dreaming, but now it was as if she'd been asleep all her life and had finally waked up.

She enjoyed people, too, and perhaps most of all those she had always enjoyed, the children. They had been, in a way, a refuge. Now she needed no refuge, she loved them simply, from a full heart: solemn, determined Jane who was still in bud, and Bobby, beginning to be aware of the world and watching it in utter absorption. That summer he had taken to waking early. From the children's wing whose door, close to her own, Lorraine always set ajar when she came to bed, Bobby's morning song would often begin to escape long before anyone else had thought of rising. "I don't know what's got into him!" said Hilda in despair, and Lorraine supplied books and crayons and plasticine and toy automobiles and toy boats (*that* morning the bathtub ran over), but nothing worked for very long. Sooner or later Bobby's sagas began again, quietly at first and then louder as he grew absorbed. Sometimes he just sang his name over and over, "Bobby, Bobby, Bobby-oh! Hm, hm-hm, hm-haw! Bobby, Bobby, Bobby-oh!——" But other days he composed long ballads about nameless heroes, full of delightful violence. "And then the lions came down and the tigers came down and the camels came down, and they ate him all up, they ate off his shirt, and they ate off his pants, and they ate off his socks, and they ate off his shoes——"

Here Lorraine, who had been about to arise and put a stop to this dreadful tale, found herself bemused by the problem of how the camels managed to eat off his socks before removing his shoes.

"And they ate off his wonderwear," Bobby continued, kicking the wall by his bed now in time to the slow beat of his chant, "every bit,

bit by bit, and they licked off his hair, every bit, bit by bit, till he was bald, all bald all over——"

Before she had to hear what happened next Lorraine got quickly out of bed, pulled on her robe, and stuck her head round the door. "S-s-s-t!" she hissed. "Shhh! Good morning."

Bobby's song stopped and the big house lay very still for a minute.

"You can come in here," said Lorraine in a stage whisper, and retreated to bed. In half a minute there was a little noise at her door, and Bobby came round it with his blond hair in his eyes and a very shabby stuffed monkey tucked under his arm.

"Come snuggle," said Lorraine.

Bobby flew across the room and hit the bed with an impact that any respectable tiger would have envied. "Shhh," said his mother, "you'll wake everyone up. Let's pretend we're asleep. Let's see who can go to sleep first. I bet I can."

Bobby burrowed his head in her neck. Why do little boys' heads smell so extraordinary? she wondered. I'm sure Hilda washes his hair! "You need a haircut," she said. "You tickle."

"Huh," he said, "you tickle too. You need a haircut too."

"Well, we'll drive to town today and see if the barber will cut both our hairs. I don't know if he cuts ladies' hair, but you can ask him when he's done yours. Now sh-h-h. Hug me. Hmm. That's nice. Now I'll race you to sleep. No breakfast for an hour." And she would shut her eyes and breathe deeply, hoping she could hypnotize Bobby into doing the same. Sometimes for as much as ten whole minutes she could.

They were lovely minutes, lying there in the early morning, with the sun creeping across the wall and the garden scents coming and a talkative bird or two still chatting, while her son's warm hard little body lay close to her. Dear little dumpling, she thought, my funny B. You will grow and grow and be tall and strong and all this will be forgotten, but it doesn't matter because it's true now. My duck, my darling, she thought, drifting toward sleep where tangled time is tied in a knot.

Then from across the valley came the whine of a big truck, New Haven-bound, changing gears on the hill, and Bobby stirred and wriggled and said, "Come on, Mom, let's get up. It must be an hour. Come on."

They got up and had another race, dressing, and since Bobby was allowed to go barefoot on nice days, Lorraine never won unless it was raining. Then open the door, peep out, listen up the hall, is that a noise from Jane's room? No—just Hilda having a morning dream. Tiptoe down the stairs and out the side door so that Aunt Di won't be disturbed, hand in hand, both of them in shirts and khaki shorts, and so into the freshness of the morning because there is no sound in the kitchen and everyone knows perfectly well that it's still almost an hour to breakfast. The lawns are sopping with dew, the mist not off the river, and the light not yet sure of itself, pale and tentative. Smells come clear over the wet grass, the stables announce themselves by more than a whinny. Some mornings they go to see the horses and the fat pony who has been imported for Bobby, and the cats who live in the barn, special cats, white and with seven toes. Sometimes Lorraine takes a basket and cuts flowers and Bobby gets into the raspberry bushes and eats a pre-breakfast there.

One day they took a canoe out on the river and Bobby behaved beautifully, sitting very still, with his eyes black and enormous, as Lorraine paddled softly down to the pond where the river was dammed, past the gardens and boathouses of neighbors, and coming back they smelled coffee as they went past the Rivingtons' cottage, which was rented to an old college friend of Mr. Rivington's who had recently retired from the practice of law, though he was not at all old, and taken up painting. One rumor was that his heart had acted up, but there was another to the effect that it had something to do with the departure of his wife to Reno: either he was too heartbroken to work, or else he wanted to cut his income down to where very little alimony could be exacted. Which story you heard rather depended on how many drinks Mrs. Rivington had had when she began explaining him. This morning he came out on the porch over the water as they went by, with a bath towel around his waist, and when he saw them he called, "Hey there!" though normally he was the most silent of men. The smug clubmanship of those who find themselves early awake in a sleeping world seemed to have infected him.

"Hey yourself!" said Lorraine, and Bobby bent over in a neat little Japanese kind of movement which made allowance for being in a canoe but also for having to laugh at grownups talking like babies. "Isn't it a lovely day!" Lorraine went on, rummaging through her memory for the name of Mr. Rivington's friend. "Your coffee smells good."

"Won't you have a cup?"

Burnett! Lorraine remembered. Thank goodness. "Why I'd love one," she said.

"Just a sec, then!" cried Mr. Burnett excitedly, and vanished. Lorraine turned the canoe and drove it toward the landing platform under the balcony.

"Catch hold of that cleat, honey," she said, and put her paddle in the canoe. The morning sun was brightening, it was going to be another hot day, a blue day, a gold day. Lorraine shut her eyes and lifted her face to the sun's warmth.

"Coffee for me too?" whispered Bobby.

"Maybe milk with coffee," his mother whispered back. "We'll see."

"He's a nice man," said Bobby, clutching his cleat, but determined to make his judgment known.

"Very," agreed Lorraine, who did not much like Mrs. Rivington.

"You know I like coffee in my milk."

"I do know that."

"Well, won't you come in, or up, or whatever?" said Mr. Burnett, appearing now in trousers and plaid shirt. He carried a tray which held two cups of coffee, a glass of milk, and a plate of sweet buns, and Bobby sucked in his breath quite audibly at the sight. So they climbed out and Mr. Burnett pulled the canoe up on the bank, and they sat all in a row on the landing stage dabbling with bare feet in the river and eating buns, and Bobby had three spoonfuls of coffee and a lump of sugar in his milk and Mr. Burnett told them about how people in Shanghai lived in houseboats on the river there and ate all their meals like this and never came ashore: he had been there to see some twenty-odd years ago when he was just out of college and had got himself round the world one way and another before entering the law and meeting Mrs. Burnett.

"How lovely," said Lorraine drowsily, for the sun was warm and slightly hypnotic. She shifted around and leaned against a pillar. "Where else did you go? What else did you see? Did you ever paint any of it?"

"Well, do you know," said Mr. Burnett, who had certainly had the stopper drawn on his conversation, "I've been thinking about it all lately, and I have an idea it's percolating through. For instance, New Guinea—— The colors—— There's a lot of woodcarving—— It's a little hard to explain without showing you—— I don't think you've seen any of my work?"

"I'm afraid not."

"Well, it's non-representational," he said defiantly and Lorraine, nodding encouragingly, wondered if Mrs. Burnett had objected to this, for the poor man sounded as if he were accustomed to defending his muse against attack. "I feel there are influences—— Of course they mayn't be apparent to anyone else—— But that Melanesian stuff is very—— Would you like to see some things?"

"Very much, but I'd better warn you that I'm stupid about painting."

"I doubt that, I doubt it very much. You may be uneducated, but that doesn't mean you're stupid. Now just stay there a minute—— Do you want a cigarette?"

"Please," said Lorraine. Non-representational art at seven-thirty in the morning was more than she had bargained for, but she couldn't let Mr. Burnett down. He was nice, Bobby was quite right. Besides—it will make a funny story for Peter, she thought, and smiled, because this was a very likely day for him to come out to see her aunt. Mr. Burnett, emerging with a large canvas done in streaks of dark red and gray, took the smile to himself and flushed happily, and Lorraine giggled internally. How funny, but it always worked! If one man found you attractive, others always would too! It was silly, but pleasant, and she was very nice to Mr. Burnett in gratitude for his obvious admiration, while Bobby ate buns and the dew dried on the grass. Besides, she thought, with pride in her deviousness, I'll introduce him to Aunt Di. He'll be a fine distraction. She won't have to go snooping after Peter if I produce Mr. Burnett.

At last, stretching, smiling, she said, "We must go, we must go! Thank you——"

"Oh, have another cigarette, have some more coffee, won't you?"

"Best have my own coffee at home, I'm afraid, or they'll think we're lost. But this was so interesting. I enjoyed it."

"Won't you come back one day? There are some other things I'd like to show you."

"Why, thank you."

"And Bob, here, too. My own boy's at camp now. He's older, of course, nine. Do you like the pictures, Bob?"

"Mmhm," said Bobby through the last of the buns. "I like the owl best."

"Ah," said Mr. Burnett, "do you? Which is the owl?"

"That one," said Bobby without hesitation, pointing to a rust and black swirl in which Lorraine could distinguish no trace of any fowl whatsoever.

"Is it?" she asked blankly.

"Why not?" said Mr. Burnett and tousled Bobby's hair. "Why do you think it's an owl, Bob?"

He looked back and forth at the grownups. "The color?" he asked. "I think—I think it's an owl?"

Oh dear, thought Lorraine, now what do I say? For a second the old terrible inadequacy moved quakingly within her. How embarrassing of Bobby! Then she thought, Darn it, it isn't! This silly man shouldn't have asked him, just because he's lonesome for his own son! And then, coming even further out of herself, remembered that this man hadn't seemed silly. He was lonesome, yes, but just because he had a son, might very well know how to talk to children about painting. Let him handle it. Let Bobby speak for himself. Why, she thought, how much trouble I've made for myself all my life, bursting in where I'm not needed! She leaned back against her pillar and smiled at them both.

"I wasn't thinking exactly of owls," said Mr. Burnett, "but I had what might very well be an owl-feeling about it. Something a little frightening and sudden and silent? Something watching? Yes, it might very well be an owl. That's interesting, Mrs. de Koning. That's one of the ones where I was working from some of the Melanesian carving —no owls, but the ancestors return, if you follow me, and must be propitiated—I'm complimented. It sounds as if he'd felt some of that. Tell your mother to bring you over again, Bob, and you can paint too, if you'd like."

Lorraine had a spasm of absolutely pure maternal pride. But Bobby, blinking solemnly up at Mr. Burnett, said cagily, "Can I use a brush?"

"Yes, of course. Or your fingers. Or your nose and your toes too."

"A brush." Bobby ignored the joke part, this was too serious. "At school I have to use my fingers. Two brushes, maybe? A little, little one, even?"

"As many as you like."

"Okay!"

"That's wonderful," said Lorraine, getting up. "How nice of you. He means 'Thank you,' by the way."

"I know. He means 'Okay!' too. I think I like it better. Will you come soon?"

"We certainly will, we'll plan on it. And you must come and meet my aunt, she's quite decently educated about painting, not like me. Thank you again." She held out her hand, he took it, beamed at her, beamed at Bobby, helped them into the canoe, and stood watching till they passed up the river out of sight.

"The day we went in the canoe," Bobby called it, "the day we ate breakfast at Shanghai."

But for Lorraine it became another day later. She duly took Bobby for his haircut and stopped at the market on the way home, so that the mail had come and her letters were waiting for her on the table in the hall when she got back at noon. There was one from Herbert. For a moment it was impossible to pick up the stack. Then she made her hand reach out and take them all, bills and notices and advertisements forwarded from New York and on top—Herbert's first letter since he had left six weeks before.

"Run and get your lunch," she said to Bobby. "Hilda will be waiting for you," and she went past the living room and out the side door, as they had that morning, for it seemed to her that she could not read Herbert's letter inside.

There was a bench that someone, Benson perhaps, should have had painted and had not, between the cutting garden and the vegetables. There twined the despised Dorothy Perkins ramblers that Mrs. Belchamber would not admit to the rose garden. Between the delphiniums and the gladioli on one side and the asparagus gone-to-seed on the other, it was very private. Lorraine sat down to read her letter. The sky was high and pale blue with sun at the zenith. Dried dark green paint flecked under her fingers. What time is it in Germany? she wondered. Six o'clock, too late for business, too early for cocktails, Herbert would be in the shower or shaving (he had a blue-black beard), or changing his shirt, in an anonymous hotel room.

CHAPTER FIFTEEN

Or, just possibly, driving with someone out into the country for dinner, down one of the autobahnen (his last postcard had shown one), in a Mercedes, with three or four men and perhaps a neatly groomed, silent, blonde girl or two. The picture of him, the reality of him—the tuneless hum that he emitted from time to time under the shower, the smell of his shaving lotion, the memory of his newly, only momentarily, smooth cheek against hers, for it used to be his habit to kiss her always when he finished shaving—all came back with a pounce. The garden, the present, here and now, rocked and swayed about her. Who was Peter but a man she knew?

Open the letter, open the letter, she gabbled at herself. Yes, she must open the letter without stopping for one instant. She ripped it across and took out the sheets—four of them. His handwriting was as neat and legible as a copying clerk's.

"Dear Lorraine," said Herbert. "I am sorry that this interesting and fruitful trip has not left me time, before, to write at length. I have thought of you every day, and have wished often that I might be pointing out sights of interest to you as well as observing them myself, or discussing new acquaintances with you. But just because I have found so much to absorb here, I have hesitated to attempt to sum it up prematurely. Let me say briefly that this has been not only an educational, but a profitable time, and that I am inclined to believe that in the future I should return fairly regularly. There are a number of extremely interesting business opportunities here and I become, each day, more amused at the stupid American attitude that Poor Old Europe is finished. Your aunt, I imagine, shares my views!

"And now, how is she progressing? Very well, I hope. You must remember that convalescence, in a woman of that age, is always a slow process. I hope you are satisfied with the doctors and the care she is receiving. I was, frankly, distressed to learn that she had been discharged so soon from the hospital. A distinguished Swiss surgeon, with whom I chatted one evening, could not understand it. If you have any doubts or questions, Lorraine, may I suggest that you talk to Dr. Edison, Wilbur F. Edison, I believe, at the Medical Center? Gerard Miller has just gone on the board there, and I'm sure that if you mention his name, you'll get a straight answer. You know how these doctors are, unless they know you they will always cover up for each other. Please, in any case, give my regards and good wishes to your aunt. Tell her that she would not recognize this part of the world: it is booming. You might say that I look forward to giving her a full report on it when I return.

"But that, I'm afraid, will not be for another month. There'll be no sense made in the States until after these political conventions, with all their shenanigans and half-baked promises, are out of the way and I shall, under the circumstances, extend my trip to include Hamburg, Copenhagen and Oslo before going to London. This brings me to a suggestion: why don't you fly over and meet me? We could easily have a month here. You have not, if I remember correctly, ever seen Scandinavia, and so while I worked you could have a new region to play in and explore. Not that I intend to work all the time! If your aunt is progressing satisfactorily and if you think the children could be left (with the nurse, of course), under her supervision, won't you come?

"Lorraine, I don't write this lightly. I am not, as you know very well, particularly clever with words, and it's very likely that this letter sounds to you distant, formal, cold, businesslike. My dear—that's my bad luck, my awkwardness. It isn't written like that, out of such feelings. I know (and this isn't easy for me to write, but I do write it) that when I left things were not right between us. Here let me say that I know I must shoulder part of the blame for this—my awkwardness again, no doubt. You were tense, you were under a strain, you were depressed. You were looking for an outlet. And though the one you found was not very useful or sensible, still at bottom you were right. I have come to understand all this a great deal better than I did, and to sympathize. Lorraine, you are not the only one who has been lonely or under a strain. I have thought about all this—somehow traveling and the break in one's routine makes you think—and I begin to see how much I was at fault. Believe me, I blame myself more than you. If you have found me sometimes dull and uninteresting, if my work has seemed foreign to you—that is my fault, not yours. I cannot expect you to share my life and interests unless I am able to make you feel an interest, a responsibility of your own.

"All this is not for a letter, and no doubt I have explained myself badly—those words again. I shall just have to trust to your understanding. I can see a way toward a shared and mutual life for us, that is all I mean to say now. No doubt there are areas in which *you* can instruct *me.* No doubt I tend to grow narrow, it is the common fate of busy men. But that can't be planned, it can only be worked out little by little, if there is a mutual desire to work it out. All I can say now is— won't you fly over to me and let us try? I know how you would laugh if I used a phrase like 'second honeymoon.' But I do think that we might find a new beginning easier in the privacy of a strange land. There is a way of life here, too, in which marriage is seen as a give-and-take, a partnership of mutual respect, that is rather different from the American emphasis on aggressive individualism.

"Tonight I go to dine with a remnant of the old nobility, now adapted to modern times. The von Schwarzenbachs live in a real storybook castle which is, he tells me, a proper white elephant, capable of eating thousands of marks in one bite—releading the roofs, for instance. So much for romance! you may say. But I reply, He spends them! (He is high in the Siemens-Halske organization and has them to spend.) That is, he finds his romance worth what it costs, although he is also a modern business executive. Are money and romance, then, so far apart? I wish you were here to debate the point with me!

"A cable will reach me here for the next week. Then I go to the Atlantic in Hamburg. Miss Winters at the office will make all arrangements for you. The flights east now are not as crowded as last month and I am sure you'll have no trouble finding space on a convenient one. Copenhagen, they tell me, is beautiful.

"My love goes to you with this.

Herbert

"P.S. Please hug the children for me. I have sent several packages off to them in the last few days—the mechanical toys here are fascinating even for grown-ups!

"H."

The sun is too bright, she thought, I shouldn't have read this right in the glare; and shivered. Her hands, oddly detached from her will, smoothed the pages and folded them and put them neatly back in the envelope. "Mrs. Herbert de Koning," said Herbert's writing, labeling her, and she shivered again. The empty garden around her was frightening. All the strong green life leaped toward the sun. Mindless drive, she remembered from somewhere. Its ferocity was terrifying. It ate the light.

You don't have to do what he asks! she told herself. And found herself floundering in a wave of memory: the first time she had slept with Herbert. It was three days before the wedding. How had she held him off that long? she wondered, and then realized that she hadn't. He had done the holding off. When his restraint broke, hers vanished. She did what he asked her as if she were a sleepwalker, or hypnotized. At two o'clock in the afternoon. In his suite at the Ritz. "How will I ever come in here again?" she had said afterwards. "When you do, you will be my wife," said Herbert. As a matter of fact, she had never been upstairs in the Ritz again to this day——

You don't have to do what he asks! Are you crazy? Because he writes you a letter——

His eyes had devoured her, sucking out her assurance, her identity. "Now," he had said, watching her face. "Now, now——" What had he seen? Mindless drive—— She put her hand to her mouth and bit the back.

And Peter? said her mind. Is it any different with Peter? Isn't one body like another body? Isn't there compulsion there too? Aren't you fooling yourself, pretending that "love" makes a difference? Isn't passion and greed always passion and greed—Herbert's, Peter's, your own?

These are very queer things to be thinking!

All I have to do is lie to Herbert. I lied to him in New York. I must just write him a lying letter.

I lie to Aunt Di every day. To everyone. Why should I mind suddenly lying to Herbert? Why isn't it simple?

But she knew. She was still afraid of him.

It was terrible! She collapsed forward, her elbows on her knees, her head in her hands. The new person with her new pattern of confidence and courage—where was she? Dissolved, melted, gone as if she had never been. Laurie, waked up, enjoying life, in love, Laurie was gone. Mrs. Herbert de Koning who was afraid of her husband had taken her place. He could order her and she would obey, she belonged to him. No, no, no! she thought. I will not! But her will had nothing to do with it. Shivering, sweating, staring at the ground, at the grass edging of the path, she knew that what she felt was beyond the reach of her will or of her reason, or any conscious intention. It was like an infection: she reacted to Herbert's desire like the poor, mindless flesh to an invasion of bacteria. It was uncontrollable.

But then to go to him is to choose to be sick! I will not go to him! Then what will he do?

Nauseous, dizzy, she lifted her head and looked around the garden. How still it was! There was no defense here. She could not imagine what Herbert would do if she did not go to meet him. His brain, his reasoned actions (and this letter was one, surely, weighed and pondered for weeks), remained a labyrinthine puzzle. Think, she told herself, think! How can you not know what your husband will do? But always, always, he had commanded her, she had been afraid—— When she tried to think of Herbert, she saw her fear, it stood between them like a screen.

Before they were married he had wanted her beyond the reach of reason—and that had been frightening, puzzling. He put his reason to work to get her, he succeeded. And something went wrong. She had been puzzled still—what did he want of her? Her friends were married, their lives seemed open, she understood the relationship they had with their husbands, but hers with Herbert was always different, he wanted something else. He never said what. How was she to know? After the birth of the children the years of marriage sifted down between them, hardened, solidified into a wall. It had seemed easier so. But she to him (as he to her) had become—— What? A stranger? Oh no, more than that. Alien, alien all through, each to the other a symbol of distance and of what could not be assimilated. Industriously, busily, day by day, she and Herbert together had built the desert around her. Then one morning he had said "analyst" to her, and some last little bit of herself, not quite paralyzed, had managed to see beyond fright to what he meant. He meant "not normal, not human." He meant "without rights." He meant "dependent, a slave, mine to do what I want with——"

Now he said, "Come." But why? But why? He was lonely—— She considered this monstrous image. Herbert, lonely. But he was always lonely, she saw. He was insatiable. He wanted unattainable things, because the wrong things. He would never get them from anyone. He was lonely, Herbert, a lonely monster. There he was—she saw him now quite clearly—Herbert on the bank of the Rhine in a storybook castle. His clever mind, his excellent reason, his perception, shrewd as it was narrow, met other minds, he was interested—and then uneasy, unsatisfied, something was missing. Why, he was lonely! Turn, therefore, to the familiar antidote: herself; forgetting that the antidote failed, always failed, ended in the passionate exasperation that cried "Not normal, not human!" What a terrible need it must be that drove him to forget this and to set out so determinedly, so cleverly, to try again to turn her into the companion he had never had who would slake his loneliness; poor pathetic monster looking for its mate! Poor Martian landed on earth, poor pterodactyl surviving the ice age, poor, poor Herbert!

She lifted her face to the sun, through her closed eyelids its light came like a weight. Must I do that? she whispered. Must I try again? Peter, happiness, myself—sacrifice them all? For compared to the old, the intense, current of Herbert's demands, what were Peter, happiness, herself? New, thin, hardly born. She was in love with Peter? But it was an impossible, a summer, love. Where would Peter and happiness be in November? Herbert was the prevailing wind, the tree grew as it blew. How could a summer breeze change it? If she wrote to Herbert that she would not come, and broke their marriage, she would not in any case have Peter and happiness for long. What she destroyed had stood for eight years. Live in the present, don't clutch, she had told herself. But how capricious to throw away past and future for such a little, little present! She would get nothing for it, it would be almost pure destruction.

And now she opened her eyes and saw the shape of the world and herself in relation to it. Nothing, she was nothing, less than a speck of dust. Whatever she thought or did or planned or wanted, however she rebelled, the world would still pour on, gaudy, rich, argumentative, blind. Will and desire moved it, they *were* its motion. Who was she, therefore, to sit on a bench and disobey their urges? Herbert wanted her: the vacuum of his want, the drain of his desire, pulled her forward. She felt herself stumbling, falling, toward that emptiness. No one would say she was wrong, no one would think to stop her if she went to Herbert, there was no help in anyone else, for no one would interfere. Aunt Di would let her go. Peter? But if she were to tell Peter that she was going to her husband because he'd written and told her to, Peter would no longer want her, she would not be the person he had loved. There would be no one called Laurie left, she would have died, right now, at noon, in the cutting garden.

Suddenly from behind the clematis vine along the wall a cat emerged, one of the barn cats, white, seven-toed, who had found his way up to the garden. He stretched, he blinked his yellow eyes in the sun and then, tail aloft and waving gently, purring machine at full throttle, snowshoe feet stepping neatly along the path, he came toward her. She sat very still. Come to me, come to me, she thought. Answer my desire, come to me, I have nothing to give you but come to me of your own free will and for no reason, come to me. The cat sat down on the path and licked his right forepaw, working carefully over the tufts of fur between his toes. Come, come, thought Lorraine, be my luck. A butterfly flew by. The cat stopped licking, followed the movement of flight with his eyes. The butterfly vanished behind the asparagus. Then the cat got up, walked straight to Lorraine, and butted his jowly, fighter's head against her shin.

With a sigh she bent and picked him up. He grunted and settled in her lap, his purr was throttled back to a murmur of content. His overgrown paws sheathed and unsheathed their claws against her thigh in a ritual of pleasure. "Oh, you safe, solid, contented thing," said Lorraine. "You know what you want, it's all right here and now." He blinked his golden eyes at her, dense and drenched with life, he put his big foot out and touched Herbert's letter where it lay on the bench, curled his claws into a corner, and then withdrew them and shut his eyes. His weight was warmth.

Up from this center, Lorraine felt herself begin to return. A cat was a cat, not an oracle. And a woman was a woman, responsible for her life. I can go, she thought, or I can not go, but what I decide I must decide. Even Peter was not a decision, I shut my eyes and was pushed. Since then—— Yes, I decided a little how it should be, but very little. Now I must begin. But for a moment she sat on, feeling rather than thinking. She had come through another door and finished another stage on her journey. First there had been only Herbert, Herbert and terror. Then there had been only Peter, Peter and joy, larger than life. Now there were the two of them and she between, and something waiting to be done. Something she had to do. Was she strong enough? Wise enough? Could she act? It was time and past

CHAPTER FIFTEEN

time for her to take her life in her own hands. Until she did and unless she did, muddle and fear and make-believe would dominate it.

She hugged the big cat and put him down. What shall I do? she thought, standing up, and then thought, No, it's too soon to know. Let me get used to knowing I have to do it, first, whatever it is, and that no one can do it for me.

She walked quickly toward the house, reminding herself to see that the dubonnet she had brought was opened and ice ready, it was too hot for sherry.

16

My God, how undignified the human situation is! What was it Yeats wrote? "Tied to a sick and aging animal I know not what I am. But gather me into the artifice of eternity——" That's not right. But the poems are upstairs and I—undignified—am down. However, it's reasonably close, close enough to take as text. I don't know what good the artifice of eternity would do me, though he obviously got a great satisfaction from it, but tied I am, for sure, to a sick and aging animal. A deceived one, too, it's very likely—or is this also deception? This morning, waking early, I was ready to take my oath that they are all fooling me and that I will not be well again. I counted the reasons for being certain of this, the slips they seemed to have made (and there were plenty), I weighed the emotional atmosphere about me since I came home last month; and lying there in the dawn, unable to turn myself, feeling my body unwilling and resentful, I drank the very bitter draught of belief in deception. They were lying to me, at six o'clock this morning.

And now, having come to this reasoned conclusion—I don't believe it. I was just exactly as certain, a week or two ago, that I was on the mend. Just exactly. For the sick and aging animal (not right, not right! "the dying animal"?) can depress my mind into believing that I will never be healed, and a momentary contentment can convince me just as easily that I am all but well. What remains? That I can't trust my judgment. This mind, this instrument of reason and logic, jumps, wavers, wobbles about—I know it, better than anyone. And the useless, blunt, inaccurate thing is still all I have to know with.

Why should Lorraine come back from a perfectly ordinary trip to market looking as if she'd seen a ghost? Why should she retreat into silence and awkwardness of a kind that she's been free from all summer? I thought she'd been happy here.

Then, why should Savage turn brusque and short, and speak to me with the kind of profound inattention that can only mean his mind is somewhere else? Surely I have taught him to enjoy my company!

This morning it seemed perfectly convincing to me that these changes in attitude meant that my condition had somehow changed. Now, I see that it is just as likely to be coincidence, that Savage may be worried about a thousand things beside the one that naturally seems the center of the universe to me—namely, myself. And I remember that Lorraine has had spells of awkward, shy withdrawal all her life. How egocentric to imagine that these perfectly ordinary emotional changes mean that they are conspiring, she and Savage, to keep something from me! I'm ashamed of myself.

It's so hard to do nothing, to accept that there's nothing to do. I'm sure that fatalists must lead an easier life than the stubborn idiots like myself who have made their own lives (or think they have), and imagine that this ability will always be with them. All I can do is scribble away industriously, invoking the illusion that I am reliving those moments when I was able to change myself and others, when I was free.

"What are you writing?" Savage said to me the other day. He'd caught me unawares. I don't like questions. But Lorraine had deserted me to call on the painter at the Rivingtons', and I'd had little to do all afternoon but write.

"An historical romance," I said. I'm old enough to enjoy a joke alone.

But it didn't even interest him. "Is that so?" he said, slipping into that bedside manner, that professional not-listening, with which doctors defend themselves from the dull or the whimsical or the querulous. Men used to listen to me.

How reluctant one always is to realize that there are no certainties in the world. I thank my lucky stars that at least I was not brought up rich, not brought up a beauty. I became those things, but was not in my earliest days, and so my habits were formed before I became them. Surely, then, I can unlearn the reactions I grew into when I was someone men listened to! If I can't stop the habit of becoming, if I can't sit still and just be, why can't I use the habit and become— oh, something appropriate. Humble. Old. Tied by the leg to a wheel chair, crutches, a nurse, and resigned.

Are they lying to me? Would that Swedish physiotherapist make me work so hard, if there were no hope? No, that's no use, you can't ever tell with Swedes, that mask of grim health hides everything. Tied to a sick and aging animal——

I could ask Savage outright. And he would lie to me. Inattentively. Damn him! Damn him!

Why is it suddenly so hard to live these summer days? The air has got heavy, I can feel its weight. There's expectancy about somewhere, something is waiting. I move with dread toward evening, I wake and turn my face from the light. There are times when Tucker's care, Lorraine's affection, change like an optical illusion into mocking opposites. I see myself then as an irritable, arrogant old woman, someone to be humored, I who was——

Stop it. What was I going to write— "I who was rich and a beauty"? Stop it. There were other times. Remember those too. There were other times. There was 1920. You were not rich then and no one turned to look at you——

In 1920 I had no money, none at all. You think that's a joke? Try it sometime. In 1920, after Gerald left me when I was five months pregnant, I stole. In order to eat. That was the worst thing that ever happened to me.

I think.

Was it?

Or was it, to be logical, running off with him in the first place? That was sheer unadulterated absolute madness. I fell in love with him.

I used to wonder, sometimes, how many women had. Hundreds, I'm sure. Hundreds, before he was through. That was what he was for. He should have been stuck up in a temple as a cult god. We'd have come and worshipped him in droves, but at least we'd have known what we were doing. The mistake I made—and all those hundreds of others, too—was to behave as if he was an ordinary human being, instead of a perambulating sexual fetich.

Like Valentino, I suppose. If Gerald had ever made contact with Hollywood, he would have found his niche.

As it was, he just walked around unlabeled like anyone else. I met him in Paris in 1918. We were all crazy then. I was doing dirty work at the Neuilly hospital. I was an old hand by then and shouldn't have minded, but after the German breakthrough at the end of March (they broke the British Fifth Army, under Gough, and the French never forgot it, Pétain rubbed Churchill's nose in it in 1940), after that we came closer and closer to being a front-line hospital, and the dirty work was dirty. By the end of May the Germans were back on the Marne, and many of my dearest acquaintances had found it suddenly necessary to leave Paris, and I was very much—not alone. But by myself.

James had had to go to London during the spring. The first American troops were beginning to come over, and there was a great official welcome for them, and then—trouble. It might have been expected. The British picked that moment to arrest a new batch of Fenians, which was not exactly popular with our Irish-Americans. Nor were the English enchanted with our attitude, which was that we had come over to win the war for them; though myself, I think it was largely true. Then, again, the caste system in the England of those days was rather surprising to a number of simple American souls. Well, at any rate, there was a good deal of tension, and somebody felt that James, an old friend of the English with enough money to patch up things that only money could fix, might be extremely useful. I never was told, officially, who felt this, but of course Colonel House was a great believer in the efficacy of amateurs, being one himself. So James went.

He wanted me to go with him, and I planned to. I was tired. I'd worked very hard in England in '16 and '17, and that February, in Paris, I was just coasting, involved in some nonsense, the forerunner of occupational therapy, teaching men who'd lost their legs to weave mats. They were very polite to me. And two days a week I made dressings, and since I'd taught myself to type for my father, those thousands of years ago at home, I did clerical work, typing medical reports by the million.

What kept me in Paris was that the woman who was going to take over the mat weaving with the legless poilus never appeared. So I said to James, "Go on. I'll follow in a day or two, as soon as they find someone. Just be sure everything's airtight and in order with my papers." And of course he did, and went off at the beginning of March.

CHAPTER SIXTEEN

He wrote me frantically in the middle of the month to come over at once, the German offensive was due to begin.

He was dead right.

I wonder why I didn't go? Laziness? Inertia? I *was* tired, and a cross-Channel trip in wartime, by yourself, was no fun. But it was more my besetting sin, curiosity. And pride. I was ashamed to run away, another sin. The need to take a dare, the need to feel superior— it's always plagued me. Anyway, once the offensive began, once I'd seen the crowds in the railroad stations fighting to get out of Paris, I couldn't go.

After that everything gets mixed up. I'm not sure exactly when things happened, or what was rumors and what was true. I've never read a history of the time, so I probably remember things all in the wrong order. But Big Bertha was true, Krupp's gun, named for his daughter. She threw a shell into Paris from seventy miles away every fifteen minutes like clockwork. Seventy miles away was too far for our planes then. Was it true that untrained troops were sent into the line—drafted and sent up? They said so, but I don't know. I know that men over fifty were because I saw them in the hospital and had to deal with their papers. Though not everyone who looked over fifty was. Some of them were in their thirties.

Of course the air raids were nothing compared to the Blitz, but they shook us then. I remember two in particular. I took shelter in a Métro station one night, on my way home from the hospital. I never knew what people meant by "crowd sickness" before, but, oh, I knew that night. The crush, and the smell—yes, of course. But more, but worse—humanity, just like me, but strange, not me, not mine, not my people. I knew that if I fell they'd trample me to death. There were stories that the Apaches got into crowds like that and stole; and if anyone noticed, they cut throats. Then there were reply stories that this couldn't be so because all the Apaches had been sent to the front to fight for their country. I wonder what kind of soldiers they made. I could never go into the Métro again, which was often inconvenient, I assure you. Though as the German drive went on, cabs grew more plentiful; or rather, riders grew fewer.

The other raid that I remember took place when I was at dinner with a charming young Englishman. Someone had the remarkable, and rare, sense to discover, after he'd been wounded in the line, that he spoke excellent French and was most intelligent, and he'd been posted to liaison duty in Paris. He had quite a good-sized party that night in what we'd call a penthouse now. Well, the Gothas came over and everyone fled except he and I, and the English Ambassador, a dear old boy, Lord Bertie. I would have fled too if the Métro hadn't put me off taking shelter, and our host naturally stayed out of courtesy, but what kept Lord Bertie there was sheer rage. When the guns began he took a tray and a spoon off the sideboard and went out on the roof and banged away at the enemy overhead for all he was worth. "It relieves my feelings," he explained.

Let me see. What else? The barrage balloons were bright yellow. They had little bags—ballast, I suppose—hanging down from them. These looked exactly like feet, and transformed the balloons from sausages into fat yellow caterpillars. People were shabby and so was Paris. The sandbags that had been piled around the Arc de Triomphe and the other precious monuments rotted in the rain and burst and the sand spilled out—— What a mess. I went to Versailles one day when the grass was so long that it needed a scythe. There were signs on shut shops, "*Fermé momentanément,*" and the addition, in another hand, "*A cause de frousse,*" or "*Frousse et Cie.,*" which means Panic and Company. I remember a night on Montmartre where we could not only hear the guns, but see the flicker of the fire, and bribed the restaurateur to stay open past the curfew.

Well, that was with Gerald. There I am back again.

I met him at a luncheon party. Not a big one. We all felt like survivors. I'd had two nights at the hospital in the operating room. I was only supposed to deal with papers (each man had his documents and I had to enter on them what the doctors did as they did it), for the Sisters were terribly huffy to us amateurs. But we were shorthanded and I did—other things. The men lay on stretchers in the corridors for hours waiting to be taken into the operating room, and died there. And the operating rooms themselves—well, they were literally like slaughterhouses, except that they smelled worse. We were blacked out so the windows couldn't be opened and of course there wasn't any other ventilation and wounds that have gas gangrene in them smell like—— Never mind. A luncheon party on a late spring day in Paris was like a dream.

We had a wonderful flowery chablis, I remember, and Gerald was

there. Dear, dear, dear. I took against him. Well, I thought, he *is*
satisfied with himself! How I dislike too handsome men! Ordinarily
I didn't blame anyone for getting out of the line and into Paris
whenever they could, I'd seen enough to have no feelings left about
other people's duty, but I held it against Gerald right away. He was
flirting with our hostess, giving her good value, I suppose, and I
looked at him and thought, Oh, you pretty, pretty boy! How long
would you have lasted at Chemin des Dames? We were across the
table from each other, a round table, in a restaurant. He made everyone near him laugh. *I* had a fat American Colonel to amuse. He
drank too much wine and got sleepy, and I was sleepy to start with,
after the night I'd had.

I left early. I knew it would annoy my hostess, for young, personable
women were not easy to come by in May 1918, but I couldn't keep
my eyes open, and I had three thousand or so forms still to fill out
back at the hospital. So I fled; left the Colonel, smiled at my hostess
and got a grimace in return, and then I was out in the street, in the
Paris spring, and it was so lovely that I had to walk a little, tired as I
was, before I took a cab.

Footsteps behind me, uneven and hurrying. I didn't look back, I'd
been followed by experts. A voice, "I say, could you slow down just
a bit?" English, but that had happened before. I didn't slow down,
I didn't hurry, I ignored the whole thing. "If it's an intrusion, I'll
vanish on the spot, but I really had to ask you if you had any sisters,
unmarried sisters, and if they look like you. I've never fallen——
Sorry to pant so, it's this damned gimp of mine, I'm not used to it
yet. I said, I've never fallen for anyone without speaking a word to
them before, Mrs. Greene, but it took about three seconds for me to
decide that you——"

I took two steps after I heard my name (people do after they're
shot sometimes, I understand), and then I swung around and faced
him. Gerald. He blushed. You wouldn't believe it, but he did. His
voice tailed off and he finished, "—that you're the loveliest woman
in the world. I've offended you. I'm so terribly sorry! It was one of
those idiotic impulses. I made a resolution a couple of months ago
to obey that impulse. It was when I woke up and found they'd left
my leg on. But I suppose there have to be exceptions to every rule.
Really, I'm truly sorry. I won't do it again."

I said, "I'm afraid you're going too fast for me. The whole thing is a bit of a blur. At this speed I can't tell whether you've offended me or not. Could you go a little slower?" I shouldn't have, I should have suppressed him, I know it, but remember where I'd been and where I was going.

"Nothing I'd like better," he said. "Look, there's a cab. Why don't I take you wherever you're bound? The leg's all right for standing purposes, but a stroll isn't its idea of fun as yet. Hi! Here! *Ici!* Doesn't have to be asked twice, does he? Hey there, *mon vieux.*" In execrable French he went on, "Quite a conveyance, did it assist at the Battle of the Marne?"

"And expects to assist at the next one," replied the cab driver.

"No," said Gerald, "no, no. *Ça suffit.* Drop the war, old man. Not today. Mrs. Greene, I await your pleasure. Where can I take you?"

"I'm going to my hotel," I said, and told him which one.

"On an afternoon like this you're going to your hotel? Is someone waiting for you? Mr. Greene, perhaps?"

"A comparative stranger named Morpheus is waiting for me," I said. "I finished at the hospital in Neuilly at five-thirty this morning."

"I see. And you must go back there tonight?"

"If I don't get there before seven I'll have three days' worth of red tape to unwind instead of only two."

"I see. How dull. How noble. Do you work every night?"

"Every night that they need me."

"And how do you find out whether they need you? *Un petit coup de téléphone,* perhaps?"

"Often they don't know themselves. It depends on—how the trains come in."

"Ah, yes. I see. Well, why don't *I* telephone, as your medical adviser? You look a little peaked to me. I prescribe a change of air. I prescribe a spell of irresponsible and frivolous company, namely, me."

"So kind of you to be interested. Perhaps another day."

"You mean it. Hmm. A woman of conscience. A will of iron. Terrifying. Naturally the casualties need you more than I. And you need to be needed, I expect? It's a common attribute of women with consciences."

Up to that moment, I had felt I could handle him with one hand tied behind me. It had been fun to fence, to flirt, and I felt I deserved this tiny opportunity for fun. But I didn't want to be analyzed, and particularly did I not want to be analyzed correctly. I blushed. Gerald had not only got under my skin, he'd reminded me of how ruthless I had been toward James's need for me. He, of course, was enchanted to see me redden. He grinned. I felt myself grow wary. Better get rid of him, I thought. This might be more than a joke.

"Whatever my emotional state," I said, and I couldn't not sound angry, "I am now going to my hotel, and then out to the hospital as soon as I've changed."

"Rather mean of you not to go that way. They'd like that hat, I should think."

"I'm afraid a uniform is required."

"Well, it's probably charming on you. I became quite a connoisseur of uniforms in my immobilized state, and look forward to adding you to my souvenirs."

"I am going to the hospital alone," I said.

"Really, that *is* mean. I can see the reason for the uniform, but why in the name of heaven can't I drive you to Neuilly? We were properly introduced, after all."

"I'm afraid I didn't catch your name."

"Fitzherbert. Gerald Fitzherbert. Flashy, isn't it? I've often thought of changing it. Strangers eye me with an odd lack of confidence, and when I babble that Fitzherberts have been living for some seven centuries in a particularly inconvenient castle in Ireland, now absolutely ruinous and still infested by litters of my cousins, they grow even more suspicious. John Smith or Tom Robinson are what I favor. They carry the solid touch so conspicuously lacking in my ancient cognomen."

"I shouldn't change it," I said. "It suits you."

"*Mrs.* Greene! That was unkind! By the way, where is Mr. Greene?"

"Waiting at the hotel," I said. "This hotel. Right here. Thank you so much."

"It won't take you long to change, will it?" he asked. "You look an efficient type. Very well, I'll keep the cab on and sit out here remembering you and the wine, and waiting. Just look for me when you come out, and wake me if I've dropped into a light doze—you and the wine are rather hypnotic. But I wake easily, you'll find. By the way, our hostess mentioned that Mr. Greene was in London."

"He came back today," I said.

Gerald got out of the cab and helped me down. He said, "And you still plan to spend the night at the Neuilly ambulance? What a heartless creature! No, I can't believe it of you, you're just a remarkably poor liar. Run along now and climb into that fetching uniform. I shall be here on your doorstep." He nodded and smiled.

Dear, dear. He *was* an expert. I told them at the desk to send him off, I told the operator that I could take no telephone calls, I slid neatly out the service entrance and got to Neuilly alone——

And when I dragged myself out of the hospital next morning, he was waiting for me. I even think it was the same cab.

I burst into tears.

That did frighten him! I'm sure it really did. And move him—or come as close to moving him as anything could.

"I'm so tired, I'm so tired," I said desperately, turning away, the tears streaming down my cheeks. "Why do I have to fight you now? I'm so terribly tired!"

"But you don't, you don't! My poor darling, of course you don't have to fight me! Just get in the cab, dear, and I'll take you back to the hotel and deliver you to the concierge. Climb in, cry all you want, don't fight. Lean back, I shan't touch you of course. My poor darling, you're exhausted. You've got to take a night or two off. Your lovely face looks thirty instead of twenty-three."

That upset me horribly. "How do you know how old I am?" I gasped.

"I know all I need to," said Gerald. And he did.

There were times when he didn't have to touch me, just look at me. But the touching was nice.

What an absurd word. Nice! Do you think I don't remember what it was like?

We had six weeks then. Gerald was expert at wangling all kinds of things, not only women, and when his leave ran out, he wangled some kind of temporary duty attached to Staff in Paris. The English weren't popular with the French in '18. Pétain had sent twenty divisions to back the British Fifth that spring, and there were nasty stories about some of the French arriving to find that the British had pulled out without waiting for them to take over. When they did meet, greetings often began "A *bas les Anglais*," and continued in the same vein. What we call "public relations" now was certainly needed. I don't know how much Gerald purveyed to the Staff itself, but heaven knows he was effective with their wives. The wives had been ordered to stay in Paris, and most of them were both furious and terrified, so I suppose Gerald was really a very good choice.

Not that I cared whether he was good or bad, or how he managed to stay. I was mad about him.

It could have been the end of the world. The Germans were right outside the city all through June and into July. Everyone we knew had elaborate plans for getting out and getting away. I was supposed to go with the hospital, and once they cleaned it out, and we all thought we were moving. But it turned out they just filled us up again. I remember one woman talking all through a dinner party about how clever she'd been: she'd pawned all her silver and valuables so the French government (which operates the pawnshops) would be responsible for their storage and safekeeping, and she'd have someone to sue if they got lost. I wonder if she lived till '40? The only people who had no plans were Gerald and I. Our love affair tasted of blood, it sounded of guns, we didn't call it love, we tore at each other and at each day to get all we could out of it before the world ended. I can recognize the flavor of those days even now, in dreams— quite unrelated dreams usually. Usually warning dreams, dreams that say, Don't do it.

My God, my God.

In July it ended. In July the noise of the guns began to fade and dim. In July, finally, Gerald's orders to report to his regiment again came through. The Allied offensive was beginning, the war was going to be won and over.

Gerald said, "You know I will find you again as soon as this is all finished."

I said, "Don't! Don't say it! It's bad luck to say it. Just say good-by."

"Good-by, my darling," he said. "Don't forget me."

"I'll try to forget you as hard as I can," I said.

He said, "Diana, Diana——"

Thank God the hospital was full. Full! We had six hundred beds and there were days when sixteen hundred men came in. I worked and worked and worked, usually at night, because I could sleep better when I knew the sun was up and life going on somewhere around me. I lost weight. One of the doctors was very worried about me. Well—he was in love with me. He kept trying to make me eat. But the night I did, I was sick all over the floor during an amputation. They burned the arms and legs in the cellar furnace, if you've ever wondered about it. There were beginning to be lots of Americans. Of course that was largely due to inexperience. The percentages of casualties dropped during the summer from the horrible figures of June—sixty per cent of the officers and forty per cent of the men lost at Cantigny, for instance. One day I bought all the toothbrushes and all the razors and blades I could find, and when I handed them out to the men I felt like Florence Nightingale.

And when I read this over I feel a thousand years old, I feel like the Ancient Mariner, I feel like that bore, Old Kaspar, who kept telling his poor grandchildren about the Famous Victory. I don't know. Is it possible for one generation to convince another that youth and passion were just the same forty years ago? How I cried! There were days when I walked around just sobbing over everything. Not at the hospital, I was all right there. But I went into a shop to buy a blouse, once, and cried because they didn't have what I wanted in the right size. I cried in the hotel dining room. I cried in the streets——

I've never been positive whether anyone wrote to James about this or not. Gerald and I had been very circumspect, because he always was. I would have been entirely open about the whole thing, but he had been trained—or had trained himself—to be always, always careful. It was after he'd gone that I became conspicuous, for when you sit at someone's dinner table with tears running down your cheeks through two courses, it becomes noticeable that you are having some kind of a breakdown. It's quite likely that a well-meaning soul wrote James that I was overworking myself and must be made to stop. Indeed, I had written him myself about how hard I was working —as an excuse for not writing other things.

In August he came over. I took one look at his dear, kind, worried face and broke into the sort of crying that needs a doctor and a hypodermic needle to stop it. I got both of them. I was put to bed and kept there for two days. James, I learned later, went out to the

hospital and administered a tongue-lashing that must have made his
father's ghost jump for joy, about letting volunteers work themselves
into states where they need hospitalization more than the patients.
Then he took me to the country, to a sleepy village southwest of
Paris. It had been full of refugees in June, but it was emptying now
as the armies moved east, and James was the only man older than
sixteen and younger than fifty there except for the curé and three or
four *grands blessés* hobbling about on crutches. He stayed a week. I
was able to eat by the end of it. Then he went up to Paris, still on his
job of pouring-oil-on-troubled-Allies, and came down weekends and
I ate and got quite fat and stopped crying.

I didn't hear anything from Gerald, which was a great blessing.
After a while it all began to fade. No, that's not the right word. It
didn't fade. When I was back there, I was there. But it began to move
further away, to occupy me less. Everything was still perfectly clear
and vivid and all the emotions had their full value, but I frequented
those memories less often. It came to seem to me that they were a
part—the peak of, but still a part too—of those June days when Paris
shook to the cannons, when everything stood still at climax and the
Germans made their last, too expensive effort with troops from the
crumbled Russian front just too late, just as the Americans arrived.
What had happened between Gerald and me was a crisis too, ex-
travagant and doomed, but complete and part of those days.

One doesn't live like that, I told myself. It happens once or twice
in a lifetime, but ordinarily one lives quietly and sensibly with one's
kind husband and builds a pattern of life for the future.

Ah, yes. And if I'd done it, built a pattern, all might have been
well. But James did not know I needed to, and I could hardly tell
him. What he remembered was my urge to get out of the pattern of
his life, my need to leave him and to adventure, and he was con-
sequently afraid that too much quiet would be bad for me. So I
went back to Paris in the fall when everyone knew we were finally
winning. That was rather shocking—the deep, bitter joy in people's
faces and voices when they spoke of the German retreat, the exultation
with which they awaited our armies' entrance into Germany, and the
fury they felt when the Germans "cheated" them by surrendering
before we crossed the Rhine. I listened to women who wanted, apparently, to bayonet German babies themselves.

We were in Paris when the Armistice was signed. I won't write about it. Everyone else already has. The only important thing is that it felt like waking from a nightmare. It seems to me now that something within me *must* have known that this was untrue, that the world could never be put back together again, round and solid and whole as it had been in 1914. But that is my reason speaking. When I close my eyes and sink back and back until I become that young woman who cried with joy in the street in front of the Radio Agency watching three men unroll a big scroll that read *"L'Armistice est signé—"* then I know that I did believe just that. That Peace had Come. That we had wakened to morning and joy.

I think now that this was not just stupidity. I think that Gerald had corrupted me, cracked me and flawed me like the world, so that I could no longer judge what was whole and what was not. I rang reality against myself and heard a tone that seemed true. But we were both of us in-valid.

About a month after the Armistice I got a postcard from him, from Gerald. It was a photograph of the cathedral at Cologne and it said, "Hope you are still in Paris and all well. Having interesting time here. Look forward to seeing you again and thanking you for all you did for me. Best wishes. Tom Robinson." I told James that it must be from someone I'd nursed but that there'd been so many of them that I couldn't remember them all. Which was certainly true, for perfect strangers turned up again and again, to whom I'd given a toothbrush or a bedpan, whose feet or faces I'd washed.

I prayed Gerald wouldn't write again. He didn't. But it was a relief when we went home, which we did at Christmas. I felt safer with an ocean between us.

James was in Washington a lot for the next few months, until we went back to Paris during the Peace Conference. I went out to the castle when he was away, if the weather made it at all possible, for New York was not my town and never has been. I was at the castle in April, just before we sailed. It was a day—oh, a day exactly like the beginning one, the melting opening day when I met James. Cold spring, early spring in northern Westchester, but you know something is to happen, and you remember that it will be summer, but anything else seems more possible than the heat and fertility of summer. April deceives us because it promises, but promises what does not happen, something colder, stranger, wilder, than July—— I walked on the terrace and down through the woods that were now mine, where someone again swung an ax, trimming brush. I tried to understand all that had happened to me in the eight years since I had huddled on the terrace envying that sound, and could not. But terribly, the envy returned.

For the memory of Gerald came back and my body stirred and I forgot eight years ago, and heard myself saying, "Spring. It is nearly spring again. Last spring in Paris——" I ran inside and changed and rode all afternoon until, out of shape as I was, I could hardly stand that evening, and it didn't help, every now and then I would see him or hear him or feel him.

My father had been made a judge. It was lovely to see how proud he was, and my mother too. He didn't talk about it at all, but though he'd aged, when someone said, "Judge Cummings," he stood an inch taller. My mother acted as if her life had been justified and her judgment vindicated. It annoyed him a little, but not enough to matter or to spoil anything. He asked me one evening, late, when I'd had dinner at home with them and Mother had gone to bed, to look after her "if I go first." I told him that of course I would. When he went, a year later, I was—on my way to stealing food.

Indeed, I may have killed him. I've thought about that. James and he conspired to lie to my mother, but my father knew I had eloped with Gerald. A broken heart never helped anyone fight influenza.

It's night and late. I'm alone. I've written till my fingers are cramped and sore and my brain wanders back and forth between then and now. That bad time, this bad time. That pain and this. That trouble, those years that ache the way a once broken bone aches in wet weather, and this confusion within me now of lying hope or lying despair—it is all different and yet it all echoes as memory moves and touches that time and now; my father drowning in mucus; my hunger and my nonchalance as I looked arrogantly about the shop on the Rue Neuve in Brussels; my acceptance, my acquiescence in the fact that I was at the end of my rope and that absolutely anything could happen, but that nothing could be worse. I did more than surrender to fate, I threw myself upon it. I can see my hand taking a package of chocolate, a package of figs. Another shop, and my hand taking three silk ties and putting back two; and I not caring in the least whether I was caught, ready to turn with a smile of welcome at a hand on my shoulder since it would at least end the vacuum where I had been living and restore me to a predictable, governed world. And, since I did not care if I was caught, I wasn't, for the secret of successful thieves, I think, is that they don't feel guilty. I felt I was merely taking what was owed me. I was right outside of society and had very little interest in it—except that I was hungry. One of the people I have been was a criminal.

Tired. I must ring my little bell for Tucker and shut my poor book away. And know that as the light goes out I will see Gerald again, as I saw him across a restaurant in London in the summer of 1919. He came toward me at once. I am still vain about that. It had been a year, and he left the people he was with without a word and came to me.

CHAPTER

17

July turned to August, and the heat stood like a giant over the countryside. Mrs. Belchamber was restless, she looked Mr. Burnett up and down when he came to tea and then ate him, as a cat would eat a mouse, hardly even licking her lips afterward. Lorraine, escaping to Savage the next afternoon, did it at top speed, afraid that if she hesitated she would never get away. Driving through the heavy air (there was a storm coming), she was angry at herself. It was careless to be abrupt with her aunt, it invited notice and remark. If she was merely driving to New York in order to spend the next day at the shelter, why did she have to leave so early? "I want to get in before the storm," she had said, but now as she repeated it, it didn't seem very convincing!

Damn, oh damn! she repeated, seeing as clearly as if it were there that letter from Herbert, her name on the envelope. It had to be answered by more than a cable saying No. I must decide! she thought, as she had been thinking all week, but the urgency only deepened her indecision. How could she, by a mere act of will, settle what her life should be? If you could choose freely between right and wrong, didn't wrong almost equal right? How could you tell them apart? Damn, she thought again, can't I forget this for this evening at least? I'm so tired of thinking about it!

But even after Savage had come, she was tense. He arrived as she was sweeping the living room, attacking the week's dust as if it were her dilemma. He dropped his jacket and tie on a chair, he took off his shoes, and groaning with relief spread out on the sofa. "Give me a drink, Baby," he said. "I'm dying."

"If you took off twenty pounds you'd be more comfortable," she told him shrewishly, but she went to the kitchen for ice and glasses.

"You're absolutely right," he said. "Don't nag. God, it was hot driving out. How are you, Pet?"

"I'm—just—fine," she answered, wrestling an ice tray out. "Damn this thing, why don't I ever remember to defrost it?"

"Because you're a rich bitch who expects a maid to do it for her," said Savage cheerfully. "How's Mrs. B.?"

"Impossible." Lorraine turned on the water to loosen the ice cubes, effectively stopping the conversation. When she came back with the drink mixings, Savage blinked at her but was cannily silent. She's feeling the heat, he thought, she'll relax when she has a drink.

But Lorraine, having fixed them both gin and tonics, put her glass on the mantel and picked up the broom again. "Drink your drink," said Savage. "Let that wait."

"Not having a maid to do it for me," said Lorraine, "I prefer to finish it up. It will blow all over if I don't."

"Sweep it under the rug."

"Is that what you did in Waterbury?"

"Didn't have a rug. Boy, you're bitchy today."

She went on sweeping for a minute. Then she leaned the broom against the wall and sat down. "I know I am," she said. "I'm sorry."

He got up and handed her her drink and kissed the top of her head. "Go right ahead," he said. "What's the matter?"

She chewed her lip, looking up at him. Herbert. Peter. How could she talk to Peter about Herbert? How could she say, Shall I leave my husband? Wouldn't he think she was saying, Shall I leave him for you? Will you take me, break up your life, and remake it with me? And she didn't intend ever to say that because she didn't see how he could.

"Come on, Baby," he said, standing over her. "Tell about it. Is the old lady acting up? Did I do something wrong?"

She shook her head. "No. I—— Oh, it's everything and nothing. I'm an idiot and it annoys me. What's the use of talking about it?"

"More use than sweeping the floor, I should think."

She laughed abruptly. "That makes me feel better, though. As if I were accomplishing something. Do you want a shower? I put clean towels out."

"Yeah," he said. "That's what I drove out for. I forgot about it till now. I wanted a shower and some clean towels and all the dust I could eat. How'd you guess?"

"Oh honey, I'm sorry," she began. But he was already strolling out of the room, unbuttoning his shirt, and in a few minutes she heard the shower come on.

She stood up wearily to finish her sweeping. The air was heavier than ever and the sky, as she went out to dump her dustpan in the refuse bin, was gray-blue and ominous. It would storm soon. She stood looking up, thinking—Herbert. Herbert. Herbert. Why is it I can't decide? Is it because I can't see him clearly? She had been trying for days to picture a life without Herbert, but in order to eliminate him she had to draw an outline around him and that was so difficult! He had dominated her life for the past eight years, and when she tried to remove his influence, there was very little left. She stood still, thinking, It would be a life to be lived alone at my own tempo, but adjusted to the children. A small house near good schools. Nantucket in the summer because the Boston cousins still go there and the children could get to know the rest of the clan—— But what will I do all day? No Herbert. No Peter. How empty it will be!

It's your life, she argued with herself. You can do whatever you want, why should it be empty? You've always known that this, with Peter, can't last. You told yourself that from the beginning. Can't you keep separate things separate? Being in love isn't an occupation! And you certainly aren't going to "start over" with Herbert because you're afraid of being bored and lonely!

She went slowly back into the house. Savage was out of the shower, she could hear him whistling down the hall, and she went out to the kitchen to put away the broom and wash her hands. She wanted to be ready for him when he came back, bitchy no longer but clean, pleasant, sweet, adaptable, like a wife in a magazine story. We don't have much time left, she thought, I mustn't spoil it.

At once her heart contracted with pain. The easy words were true! She was going to lose him, they would have to part!

Stop it, stop it, she told herself, but it wasn't easy to stop. He would go back to the anonymous goddess, Norma—— Or quite possibly he had had girls outside before and would again. She might very well be one of a series—— Stop it! Now she really had frightened herself. Jealous! She was jealous! How mean and squalid! How disgusting! The water ran cold over her hands and she thought, I've never been jealous in my life! How can I! But it seemed that she could. I won't, I won't, she resolved, drying her hands, and went back to the living room in tight-lipped determination to be easy and happy and to enjoy herself. As Savage came in she smiled at him cheerfully.

"Hi," he said, and went and turned on the radio. Someone was reporting the baseball scores. He stood with his back to her looking out the window and finishing his drink. The announcer began on the weather forecast and Savage said, "The Sox play tonight, I guess," and turned off the set. "You want another drink?"

"Perhaps I'd better fix dinner," she said coldly. She was certainly going to suppress her emotions and not spoil things, but there really was no reason why she should suppress them in favor of the baseball scores!

"Whatever you say. We got any more gin?"

"There ought to be a bottle in the cupboard."

He opened it and looked. Rummaged. "I don't see it."

"Well——" She went over reluctantly. The gin was in plain sight, but on a higher shelf. She took it down and gave it to him.

He set it on the table and put his arms around her. After a moment she felt herself let go. A bear, she thought. He's a big bear. She could feel his heart thumping softly, steadily. It seemed at once tragic and all-important that his heart, her heart, would beat on and on and on for all the years after they parted. Her mind, her emotions, her life, would all go elsewhere, into the empty landscape she could not imagine, but never with anyone else could her body forget him. She shivered in his arms.

"What is it?" he said into her hair.

"I'll never get over you," she said; and then would have given anything except the immediate moment to call the words back.

"Is that what this is all about?" he asked after a minute.

"That. Other things."

"What things?"

"Things I should manage and can't. Or haven't. Oh, what's the good of talking?"

"What's the good of eating yourself out?"

"None, of course. How do you stop?"

"How can I tell, if I don't know what's eating you?"

"Well——" She moved away from him, got her half-empty glass, put ice in, poured the end of the bottle of gin. I don't want to do this, she thought, and so did it badly, saying flippantly, "What shall I do with the rest of my life? It's something I certainly ought to be able to figure out, you'd think. But I can't seem to. The more I think, the more I get muddled. That's my problem, Doctor."

Her brittle tone was no defense, she could not look at him. She had posed the question she meant never to ask. Quickly she put the top on the old bottle, opened the new one, and poured him a drink as if this scurry of activity on his behalf would cover her asking.

"Thanks," he said calmly. "Why do you have to come up with an answer today?"

She sat down in the armchair by the fireplace. Now that she had started she would have to go right through. At least she could try to match his noncommittal calm! "I had a letter from my husband last week."

Savage dropped back on the sofa and waited. Finally he said, "So?"

"You don't really want to hear all this."

"Why not?"

"Well—you don't talk to me about her."

"About who?"

"Norma. Your wife." Lorraine was cursing herself for having got into this. How had she ever done it!

"What in hell is there to tell you about my wife?"

"I don't know. Nothing, I suppose. I meant—it would be a kind of betrayal, wouldn't it? To talk about them?" She raised her head and looked at him defiantly.

He was laughing. She felt herself begin to blush. It crept up and up, painfully. He said, "I was brought up to think committing adultery was a pretty fair betrayal all by itself. Do you think it makes it all right to go to bed with me if you keep your mouth shut?"

Blushing, she nonetheless said stubbornly, "I think there are things that—that—that I wouldn't want to say, or to hear, or—to have said about me. I think—— Yes! I think there are all kinds of betrayals."

"Laurie, I don't give a hoot in hell about your husband unless he writes you a letter that gets you so upset you'd rather sweep the floor than make love to me. And when you kiss me, you make like you'll never do it again. He's all your business unless he interferes with you and me. Then he's my business. The same with Norma. What did he write you?"

Lorraine said flatly, "To come over and meet him and patch things up."

He looked at her curiously. "And?"

"I cabled him I couldn't get away. But I've got to write him a letter. I've got to write something that makes sense. And I don't know what to write. I don't know what makes sense." I was going to be cheerful and gay, she remembered. What a *fool* I am!

Dusk was creeping into the room. Far away the thunder grumbled. The swallows from the nest under the porch roof were swooping low past the door. The evening held its breath.

"He must be quite a letter writer," said Savage. "The creep. He's certainly thrown you into a spin."

"Well!" Lorraine caught her breath and thought, Fool! again. After a moment she went on, "I told you you wouldn't want to hear about it."

"Want to! What difference does it make if I want to! Look, you're all mixed up, somehow. What's happened? Just a letter, is that all? I thought things were fine with us. I thought—hell!—I was as good for you as the other way. Then one letter, and you get in a state. What does he do to you, for God's sake?"

"Oh, Peter—I know I'm taking it out on you when I——"

"Will you for Christ's sake stop worrying about me, and tell me what the trouble is with you? Come on over here. Come on. That's a good girl. Now sit down and tell me about this jerk."

"Don't call him names! I've been married eight years, you know. I don't like you to call him names."

"All right, Baby, I won't. Go on."

"What can I tell you? I don't know what to tell you."

"Anything you want. It's not eight years, but I know a fair amount about you myself. Tell me what's bothering you. You were bothered last spring."

She took a deep breath. "That—yes. Last spring and—— I don't know when it began. Does anybody ever? We had a couple of—— blowups, last spring, but I suppose it's been years since we—since we had a good marriage—— Peter, why should you laugh at that!"

"I'm sorry, honey. I'm not laughing really. It's just that you sound so solemn, as if everybody else in the world had a good marriage and you were a leper or something because you didn't. You're sweet, the way you try so hard, and worry, and won't quit. Look. It's not your fault if you didn't have a good marriage."

"How can you possibly know that?"

"Hell, I'm the one guy who has to know. At least, I think I am. You haven't been sleeping around, have you? Who was that painter you were——"

"Peter! Oh, damn it, why can't you be serious!"

"I'm serious. If you've been worrying about its being your fault, you can quit." He stroked her arm gently.

She said in a voice that choked a little, "Herbert isn't—— You're different."

"You mean he's different. Anyway I think you do."

In the fading light she studied his big commonplace face. Compared to her ugly, distinguished, Bostonian father he looked like an oaf. Compared to Herbert's nervous, precise awareness he looked like a bull in a china shop. "Do I?" she asked.

"Uh-huh."

Herbert, she thought, trying to think from the outside. Of course he's *different*, he's lonely, inarticulate, wanting he doesn't know what, but——

"Is he a fag?" asked Savage.

It took her a minute to comprehend. He saw shock on her face as she began to shake her head.

"You sure?" he went on. Maybe she needed a shock. "No, I mean it. I've seen it. You could tell better, probably, about anyone else in the world. Just because he married you, you'd be bound to think he wanted you. And he would want you, in a way. Think now, and tell the doctor."

But she went on shaking her head.

He wasn't convinced but he let it go. "What's the matter with him, then?"

"Does something have to be the matter?"

"Yes. Because there's nothing the matter with you. Now don't try to tell me there is, because I trust the evidence of my senses."

"There was last spring," she said stubbornly.

"Yes, and you're upset today. He upset you. Can't you see that, honey? Jesus, I never knew a woman before who was so slow to blame a man! Every God damn wife that I meet or treat wants to blame her husband for her troubles. Except you. What does he do to you?"

"He scares me," said Lorraine faintly. "He scares me to death." In the silence the thunder muttered. "I'm ashamed!" she added loudly.

"Why, Baby?"

"It is, it is a betrayal. I shouldn't talk about it! I shouldn't even feel it, but that's a different thing. I'm past caring about that, I'm a coward and that's all there is to it. But I shouldn't, I shouldn't talk about it. That's dreadful. Dishonorable."

She had half turned from him and he looked up at the curve of her cheek as she stared toward the door. "Look, Laurie," he said. "This is me you're talking to. I'm on your side, even when you want to beat yourself up. You'll have to beat me too." She sat rigid staring past him. "Do you think I'm dishonorable?" he asked.

"No." She barely breathed the word.

"Are you afraid of me?"

"No."

"Do you think I'll use what you tell me, somehow?" He waited. "To hurt you?"

She turned her head and met his eyes.

"That's what he does to you, isn't it?"

Even now she wouldn't answer.

He said, "You didn't tell me. You didn't tell me a God damn thing. How long has it been going on?"

"Ever since I can remember," she said in a whisper.

"Some coward," he said. "Eight years."

"I'm so sorry for him," she said quickly. She was shaking a little now as if she were cold. He took her hands. "He doesn't get anything he wants. Oh, money, yes, but it isn't exactly money he wants, it's what money stands for—power, influence, people looking up to him, and he doesn't have that. He's so lonesome, so terribly lonesome. He's not close to anyone or anything. He's like the whooping cranes."

"He's what?"

"There are only twenty-seven whooping cranes left in the whole world. Imagine being the last, the only one of your kind. He's like that. It must be so terrible for him! Why, if he *were* a fairy, it would be better! And I don't do him any good."

"Baby, I bet you tried."

"But it didn't work, I didn't know how. And to be so scared—it was shameful, shameful! You say, 'Not my fault.' I say, 'I failed.' And I did, I did. Peter, he's awfully clever, he's awfully able, there *ought* to be a way to help him. If I were brighter, or better, or—if I'd just loved him with some imagination, I might have found it. Don't tell me it's not my fault. He needed—he needs—help terribly. Why shouldn't he ask his wife for it? And I let him down. I have, you know. That letter——" She stopped.

"Laurie, I know all about it now. Go on."

"I'm sorry. I'm silly. The letter. It's so clever! It's brilliant. And so unutterably pathetic. It's just clumsy enough. Why, he must have been writing it for weeks, it's a work of art, just made for me. The people he's met, European marriage, the toys he's sent the children. And even the implication that when I joined him I would be having fun while he was working. To make me feel just guilty enough, do you see, because he knows I feel guilty about him, and this way he gives me the exact peg to hang my guilt on, he controls it. Think of the mind that can contrive all that! It ought to be saved! It ought to be—I don't know—humanized."

"Did he ask you to save him?"

"He asked me to try again. He's serious."

"What about you?"

"Well—there you are. The rest of my life. What shall I do with it? I'd like to do something useful with it."

"Jesus God, there's useful work——" He stopped.

"I know." She went on quickly because, of course, he couldn't say, Come to me. "I don't think I have any talents, but I'm strong as a horse and I have plenty of money. Not from Herbert, from my father's estate. I can work at the shelter. There are children to be helped. One of them might be you. I have Bobby and Jane. I tell myself all this, I have been all week. There are two difficulties. In the first place, it just doesn't seem as if it would be a life. You—— This summer—— I'm spoiled, I guess. In the second place, maybe I can't help him. But if I can't no one else can. It—sometimes it seems like an obligation. Do you see?"

He said, "I never heard so much crap in my life. An obligation, for God's sake! What are you, the Red Cross? Does being useful mean being a martyr? Don't give me that bull!"

CHAPTER SEVENTEEN

"He wants me," she said stubbornly. "I don't know how much it means, but it means something."

"And I don't?" asked Savage. The dusk drifted in, thickened. "Laurie——"

"Don't, don't, don't!" she said quickly. "Don't say it. You don't have to say it."

But he said it. "I love you. I want you."

"Don't," she said again.

"Because you don't believe me? You know."

"I believe you. *Because* I believe you. Because there's nothing we can do about it."

"We can do this," he said and pulled her down to where he could kiss her.

18

What I was trying to remember of Yeats's comes in the middle of *Sailing to Byzantium*—"Consume my heart way; sick with desire and fastened to a dying animal It knows not what it is; and gather me Into the artifice of eternity."

He meant art. It's odd how much it helps. Not that you can call this art, my scribbling. But it works in rather the same way, it folds life over and gives me the illusion of standing outside, of having come round another way in another dimension and being judge, not actor. Or observer, rather than judge. Perhaps I had better not judge. Indeed, I don't know how one does judge, in cold blood. What kind of a measure can one weigh agony in? Or joy?

But to observe—yes. That helps. It helps to know that I will never have to live it over again, for one thing. It's not much of a pleasure, perhaps, to become reconciled to being old because one no longer has the strength and flexibility to be young. But the pleasures of age are few. It's best to make the most of those we have.

I say it helps me to write, and then do I do it? No, I dither and quote and philosophize, fitting myself out in bits of hand-me-down Yeats. Am I afraid to go on?

Yes, I am.

But I must. No one can help me but myself. Lorraine came in half an hour ago, kissed me, and announced that she's going to New York. I had a moment of real irritation—there's a thunderstorm brewing, she was oddly abrupt, and so on. Then I remembered what she has done for me—given up her summer and a European tour, made herself a companion to a cross old woman, lent me her children and stopped them from being a nuisance, and kept for herself no more than a day or two a week. And I was resenting it! I caught myself (I hope she noticed nothing) and told her to have a pleasant time in the city. But it was a warning. Greedy, demanding, insensitive, headlong—forgivable at fifteen, disguisable at twenty-five, they are not qualities which make one endearing in one's sixties. Even to oneself. She's gone, now, and I've picked up my book and my pen, resolved to face myself if I have to write all night.

A thousand years ago, then, on a summer day, being demanding, greedy, insensitive and headlong, I left my husband in London and went with my lover to France. It was a bright day, warm for England. We had a smooth crossing.

I can see us still. Two minute figures stand at the rail watching France approach. Gerald and I. I am very smartly dressed in a taupe suit and a small feather toque with a veil. Gerald looks tired. This has been a strain for him. He has never run away with anyone in quite my circumstances, with a husband so rich, that is, so everywhere acquainted with the powerful and the established, the people who do not forget. Or rather, whose servants—the police, the bureaucrats—do not forget. He is putting himself in great jeopardy for me, being very rash. This is out of character for Gerald. It is I who am headlong, not he. He is worried. I am a great gamble. I may very well ruin him. And I don't seem to understand this, quite, being conventionally more attentive to my own chances of ruin.

Yes, 1919 is really that long ago. There had certainly been non-ruinous elopements before, but the one I was undertaking was the kind that asks for ruin.

It is, in fact, a considerable tribute to what I was in 1919 that Gerald ran off with me. All his experience and reason must have argued against it. But he came.

And I—I was frightened not to go. Because of James. I had seen, the night before, that he was about to believe the stories about Gerald and me that people must have been telling him for weeks. He was watching me in a kind of open, astonished wonder which of course could only change to conviction the minute he began to doubt me. And therefore I did not wait.

We got away all right, no scene with James because we went so quickly. And we had shared enough time already to manage ourselves quite decently in public. We could travel alone or together and no one looking at us would have guessed anything. But the war had unfortunately left behind several light-years of red tape which kept curling up around the feet of travelers crossing frontiers or registering in hotels. And we had passports with different names, and we had to keep showing them.

In other words, no privacy. We could not disappear and turn up somewhere else as a honeymoon couple named Smith. I don't mean that the French were censorious to us, just that room clerks and chiefs of police and customs officials and conductors knew all about us. There is, I suppose, a special temperament that enjoys sinning in public, making an exhibition of oneself, startling the bourgeois— I don't share it.

We tried Spain where there hadn't been any war. Things seemed easier. Then I decided to rent a house and I had to get out my passport and it wasn't made out in the name I had been using— Well, it's a detail. We had apparently picked a village with a rabidly anti-Protestant priest and—and so we left, after the children spat at us.

And, you might say, gave up and went to the obvious place, Capri. Where naturally they knew all about us too, but didn't care. Capri was riddled with people that other people knew all about. I daresay it still is. We took a house with a view and a patio and a grapevine. That is, I did. It was my money.

Is that one reason Gerald came with me? I suppose it had some influence, though he must have known that the real money was all James's. He told me quite frankly that he didn't have any himself. There'd been a small income out of Ireland before the war, but Irish rents didn't get paid to absentee owners in 1919. And yet—he didn't come with me for money. It was my money that made it possible for us to go, that's all. I mean the three thousand or so in my personal bank account, and my jewelry. It was Gerald's idea, or so he said at any rate, that he would set up an agency somewhere, in Rome perhaps, to sell British motorcars. Every now and then he would go off to Rome for several days to talk about this to people and to sell some more of my jewelry. That is what we lived on through the winter and into the spring of 1920.

It was that February that my father died, but of course I didn't know it. I must have got pregnant about the same time, but I didn't know that either. You see, I never had before and it didn't occur to me to worry about it.

Would you believe it? It's true. What did I call myself—greedy, demanding, headlong, insensitive? Insensitive is hardly the word. I must add stupid. It was as if my brain were waterlogged and my reasoning power simply cut off at the source. My passion for Gerald and the life of the flesh occupied all my time and energy and attention. This was where my greed sucked its fill, where my demands beat and were answered. It was a revelation. I had never lost myself before, I had always been conscious, alert, present. Even the time in Paris was not like this. *There* our passion had seemed a part of the bloody climax of the war, there was something outside, bigger, containing it, of which it was a reflection. But in Capri that winter and spring, it was everything, all experience, and I was unfolded like a napkin and laid out on its surface, absorbed into it, I *was* my experience— sun in the morning, light on the sea, bougainvillea and lilies, a cart creaking by on the road to Anacapri—I was completely passive at the heart of action. It moved through me, and I lived it.

Every now and then before I realize what I'm doing and stop, I find that I have read a bit of an argument that seems to be bothering people today about women's role in the world: one side of it says that everyone would be happier and better off if women became totally passive, members of a harem without walls who left initiating action to men. I always think of Capri when I read that—or to be explicit, I feel a sensation at the back of my head that *means* Capri. It's a sort of numb tingling, and it's enough to stop me reading or thinking along the lines that awaken it.

Well. As I say, I hadn't bothered to think about becoming pregnant. It was Gerald who figured it out one morning. He waked me to make love and afterward must have lain beside me counting. I wanted to sleep a little again, but he was restless, I could feel it. Finally he asked me.

I said it was nonsense, stretching and yawning luxuriously.

He got up out of bed and went and looked out the window. There was a view down to the sea there. He must have been thinking about getting away already. Then he came back to bed and caressed me and asked me to see a doctor.

I said again that it was nonsense.

Do I have to put all this down? I can't, really. It is *only* nauseating. If it were more, if there were a lesson or a moral—— But surely the moral is already clear. If you are stupid, you do stupid things.

Very quickly, then, this is what happened. I refused to see any doctor on the island, so Gerald took me up to Rome. The doctor there told me I was three months pregnant. Gerald's face became very smooth, smooth all over. I was stunned, I remember that. Then I was simply ablaze with joy. This reaction came so quickly and was so triumphant that Gerald never even had a chance to ask me whether I would have an abortion. Before he could begin to hint that a child might be a slight inconvenience, I had started a speech about the miracles performed by love, about the child who would be both of us, and was not that in all truth a miracle even though it happened every day, and about how I had been afraid of time but now we had set our mark upon it, Life did conquer Death, and Order Chaos—— I really talked like that.

What could he do but take me back to the island, settle me down, cosset me and plan his escape? Nothing at all. So that is what he did.

He stayed two months. I thought he loved me more than ever. It's possible I was right, as one can love the last gleam of light before the sun sets, knowing that it must set. He knew he must leave me. I don't doubt that he regretted it. If he had wanted to, he could have gone any time, any time at all, but he stayed two months. For those two months we loved each other with a passion that devoured time. Summer came on. I was not able to generalize enough to notice it. I lived in Gerald, in his looks and presence and touch. It seemed to me that we two were as much one as the child and I. We did not have to speak to each other, even.

Though we did speak. He said to me once, "You are me and I am you, now. Nothing can ever change it. It's like a dye that won't ever come out. There are old dyes like that, that people now have forgotten how to make. All except us."

And he said, "You have given me an American accent, do you know that? All the rest of my life, people will think I am lying when I say I have never seen America."

That was a mistake on his part. It put America in my mind. I can't say that I thought about going home, because I wasn't yet able to think. I was still toxic with love—or lust—or passion—or whatever name you prefer. They are all the same thing, all. But the child within me was beginning to stir and at the same time—because of it, maybe—I myself began to stir a little. My brain cells experienced a first faint revival. The child was becoming real as it moved within

CHAPTER EIGHTEEN

me, instead of just a symbol of the union between Gerald and me. It was going to exist. I was going to have to be responsible for it. The maternal instinct, wakening, brought with it dim stirrings of rationality.

I "thought," then, in the preposterous, dreamlike fashion that I thought in those days, that I would like to have the child born at home, in clean, antiseptic America.

The moment I thought anything, I said it—to Gerald.

This was the signal to him that time had run out and he must leave me. Naturally he was not going to go to America with me, and get himself a job, and meet James to arrange a divorce, and take me to an American hospital for the birth of the child, and wait in humiliating anguish while I was in labor. It was just as likely that the Apollo Belvedere would do these things.

But he was not going to not do them, either—lie about it, I mean, or argue with me, or persuade me to stay in Italy through the summer. He was going to leave me. I was in for a tragedy—through my fault, through my fault, through my most grievous fault: my own stupidity. Gerald was completely aware that I was in for tragedy. He was sorry, but he did not intend to take part in it. He did not want to, he did not have to, he did not intend to. Yes, he was sorry. If an animal is hurt and must be killed, its owner is sorry. But the owner does not stay to watch the veterinary perform the foreknown act of death. That is the way Gerald felt.

My pregnancy was beginning to show, too. I expect it embarrassed him. No, that sounds too bitter. After almost forty years, what is there to be bitter about? It made him uncomfortable and unhappy, that is closer to the truth. He had found an extraordinary pleasure in my body, my ease of movement. I was very strong and lithe and able to run and swim well at a time when most women who did these things were hairy amazons. It was hard for him to see me clumsy, or wait with me while I paused on a flight of steps which I had always flown up in an instant. He winced.

Everything, everything, said that he should go.

I did too. I gave him all the jewelry I had left—my pearls were there—and sent him to Rome with it. We would have to have money to travel home. I was beginning to notice things, to plan. I got hold of a paper that listed some sailings for America and instructed

CHAPTER EIGHTEEN

him about taking passage. I reminded him to see about a visa. I was becoming myself again, headlong and demanding, in touch with the real world, the woman who had picked him up one morning a year before and dumped him in France before night fell. That must be the ultimate reason why Gerald came away with me, after all. I took him. Now I seemed to be about to do it again.

But he wasn't going to let me. He had seen me open my hands and drop all my power, all my command, hand over all my strength. And now, without so much as a "Please," I was taking it back. He couldn't have liked that a bit.

You must see this: he was afraid of me. He knew that I loved him more than he loved me, in spite of the fact that—I believe now and have always believed—that he loved me with every possible bit of himself that was capable of love, to the fullest extent of his power. Since I loved him more, my power was greater.

The thing about Gerald was this: he was afraid of power, disinclined for it. He was perfectly honest about it. It meant responsibility. Responsibility meant that you had to act. If you acted you did not know what would come of it, you could never see the end, and thus you put yourself in jeopardy. I had forced him to it once, and now his fears were proven right. Over and over and over again his actions had made this clear, but I did not see it.

For I enjoyed—enjoy—power and responsibility, I have never been in the least afraid to act, and so though I thought I knew all about Gerald, I didn't.

You see what I am doing, all these years later? I am excusing him. In fairness, I must say this too: when he left me, taking my pearls, vanishing into Rome, he honestly and truly did not think that any harm would come to me. Any physical harm, I mean. My strength and power and the fact that he associated me with the world of the rich persuaded him that materially I could look after myself. I don't know what he thought I would do. I do know he thought I would do something.

As for the rest of it—you know the kind of person who says, "I couldn't stand to see her suffer"? He couldn't. He left.

He didn't leave me a note; I suppose because he wanted time to vanish. He didn't write me from Naples or Rome; I suppose because then I would have known at least one place he had stopped at. But

I got the news about his going a couple of days after he'd left, long before I'd begun to expect him back from all the errands I'd given him to do in Rome. It was really very simple. He took a little English girl with him, a sweet, round, cozy little thing, like a kitten. She and her family were staying in a ramshackle villa that an aunt had left them. Her father, God help us, was a clergyman. *She* wrote, once they were on the mainland, that she had eloped with him and that they would marry as soon as they got out of Italy, because she naturally could not marry in a Roman Catholic church, they would go to France and be married in a civil ceremony there.

Her father came up to see me. He was speechless. He held the letter out to me. Tears ran down his cheeks——

I was sitting in the patio under the grapevine. What I could not understand was how Gerald had got to know her at all, for it seemed to me we had not been apart for a minute, for months. I found myself saying, "She must be mad. She has made this up. I'm so terribly sorry for you. My husband has an attraction for young girls, I'm afraid. There is an age, you know, where they imagine things——"

He had found two photographs of them together. He showed them to me.

I got rid of him somehow. I suppose it was easy because he could see my condition, and he was a kind man, even in his distress. And I left. At once. In a complete daze. I shook, I couldn't pack. I dropped things. Julia, the Italian maid we'd had, packed for me; and robbed me, I found out later. *She* didn't seem very surprised at Gerald's defection. It came to me sometime, I don't really remember when, that he must have made love to her too.

I didn't know where I was going. I hadn't money to get home—to get to America, that is, where my father was dead and my mother had been told that I was ill, recovering in a nursing home from a breakdown brought on by too much war work. I had to get out of Italy, that was all I knew. I went north, traveling "hard" to save money. People could see I was pregnant and were kind. I had one nightmare fear—that somewhere along the way I would overtake Gerald and the little girl he had brought along in his pocket to comfort him for the hurt of having to leave his love. When we stopped at a station, I cowered. I always got out last, after peering around. Everyone thought I was hiding from some man's pursuit, instead of desperately attempting not to overtake him. He must be a beast, they felt, seeing me pregnant. So they helped me and hid me and I vanished.

I mention this because it turned out to be why I ended starving and stealing. James had known where I was. In a sense, Gerald was right in thinking that, because I had been rich, I could not come to physical harm after he left me. James had had a detective agency track me. It couldn't have been simpler, as I say everyone knew we were sinning, and who we were, though at Capri they were polite enough to call me by Gerald's name. But at any rate, James knew I had gone, alone, within a week after I left. He even knew the name of the girl Gerald went with. Only he couldn't find me.

I wanted to die, I guess. Not that I tried. It didn't seem necessary. It was painful to breathe. It was painful to have anything touch my skin. Light hurt my eyes. Noise hurt my ears. I wanted to go somewhere dark and not be bothered, nor touched, nor spoken to.

I went right through Paris. I had met Gerald in Paris. I couldn't stop there. I went to the Gare du Nord, planning—if a lemming plans—to go on to England. But I saw two people I knew, the Maudsleys. They didn't see me, they were quarreling with a porter, for they were always stingy, but the sight of someone I knew was like a blow in the face and I walked past them trembling and found a place to sit and thought, Where can I go? Where does no one know me? Where have I never been? And I realized that Belgium, in another world during the war, was now quite close, and that my French would do there as well as here, and so I went to Brussels. I found a hotel near the station that advertised rooms for twenty francs —it was called The Splendid and Swiss and wasn't either—and for as long as I had any money I didn't go out of my room but lay in bed, hurting.

James looked all over France for me and northern Italy and Switzerland, but he didn't think of Belgium. I don't know why. Probably because we'd never been there. I don't know whether he ever would have found me but, as it happened, the police found him. I wasn't arrested for stealing, though I'd been living on what I could pick up for over three weeks. I don't know that I was technically arrested at all. But I tried to spend the night in one of the parks, and I was found and escorted to a police station. I'd been locked

out of my room, my bill unpaid, and I had no money. No money
at all—not a centime. I didn't make any trouble. It was September
by then and the nights were growing chilly. The police were quite
polite. I was seven months pregnant now, and my clothes were the
clothes of a rich person, though wrinkled and stretched out of shape
by my pregnancy, and I had an American passport. There hadn't
been enough crazy American tourists around, in 1920, drunk and
penniless, for the police to have become hardened to them. They
were very kind to me, very correct, though I didn't give them a bit of
help. They kept asking me where my husband was. I said I didn't
know. Finally I turned my head away and said I definitely had no
idea, and began to cry. I could see them all thinking, like the people
I'd traveled with, He must be a beast!

"Do you think he is in Belgium, madame?" one of them asked me.
I just shook my head.

"In France, perhaps? Where—where were you with him last,
madame?"

I was so beaten and tired and sick and hungry that I sobbed out
"London!" though I had not meant to say a word. Then I started
to say that that was over a year ago, and then I didn't say it because
I was distinctly too tired to explain how the devil I was, in that case,
seven months pregnant.

"In London," they said thoughtfully, repeating it to each other
until it sounded like a long roll of drums, "A Londres, Londres,
Londres," and I fainted while I listened.

That simplified everything. They put me right in the hospital. The
roll of drums reached across the Channel and of course the American Embassy had James's address, and of course the hotel knew
where he was—looking for me in Lausanne.

I knew he was coming even before he got to Brussels because in
the afternoon two nurses came into the ward where I was lying.
They had a wheel chair and instructions to move me into the most
comfortable private room in the hospital. I laughed so hard I lost
my breath and they gave me a sedative because they thought I was
hysterical. I think it was the wheel chair that set me off. I had been
so tired, so horribly tired, the day before, dragging myself through
that park. I didn't dare sit too long anywhere and each time I got
up the muscles of my poor big swollen self hurt more. It came to me

that I could sit quietly in a church and so I went out of the park and found one and sat in front of a statue of the Virgin and had all kinds of blasphemous sleepy troubled thoughts about whether she, on the road to Bethlehem, had got as tired as I was now. Then a priest came in to hear confessions and I got up and went back to the park—and the whirligig began, the police, the police station, my fainting, the half-dreamlike trip to the hospital and the bed in the ward which had been heaven enough for me all night long, but where I could not be allowed to stay because my rich husband was coming, and then I laughed some more—— Oh, I suppose I was hysterical. When they got me into the big sunny private room and put me to bed there they shot me full of something that knocked me right out. So James saw me before I saw him. He hadn't known I was pregnant. Don't ask me why. Maybe the detectives were too delicate to tell him.

I suppose most men would have walked right out and never come back. James walked out. He walked around Brussels all night, but he came back in the morning.

He looked like death. He looked as if he were the one who'd fled across half Europe, who'd starved and slept in his clothes. I, on the contrary, had slept about twenty hours out of the last thirty-six. I said, "Well, James. I'm sorry they bothered you."

He stood looking down at me and I looked back, but I couldn't see into him any more. It reminded me of the time when I was a girl and he was Mr. Greene, all-powerful. "You're alone," he said.

"Yes." It was ungracious of me, that monosyllabic reply, but I had gone back to being a pauper before him, and it exacerbated my pride. I hadn't put myself in the best room at the hospital at his expense, he had. Very well, then. Let him arrange our relationship! I wasn't asking for anything.

"I shan't ask you any questions," he said.

I almost said I wouldn't answer them if he did, but it seemed really too rude, so I said, "Thank you," in a rather sullen tone.

He said, "They say the—birth——" He brought it out finally, and I realized he couldn't say "child" "—will be in two months or so. Where—what are your plans?"

Fortunately seeing him had got me over my silly hysterics or I'd have laughed again at the idea of having plans. "I haven't any," I said.

He went over to the window and looked out at the tower of the Hôtel de Ville, where St. Michael floated in the morning sky. St. Michael is engaged in killing a dragon. I thought, looking at James's back, that he was trying to do the same thing: Gerald; Gerald and I; Gerald and I and the child. This idea seemed to me like a very real dragon for James. Looking at his back I began to realize what I had done to him.

I said, "I had a funny idea I'd like to have the baby at home. That is, I mean, in America. If—you could possibly help me to do that, I would appreciate it. If you would lend me the money to do that, I'd —pay you back afterwards. After I got a job."

He didn't turn around. He just hunched up a little. "A job," he said after a while.

I didn't say anything. What could I say? We both knew the only job I'd ever held was the war work I'd done. Alone in Paris, doing it, I'd met Gerald. Finally I said, "Maybe I couldn't pay you back. I don't know. I'd try."

"You can't go back to America," he said. His shoulders were still hunched up, his hands in his pockets. I realized he was telling me, by this negative, that he would be responsible for me. It should have been a great relief. It would have, I'm sure, if I'd ever thought ahead. I thought it would be polite of me to make some demonstration of gratitude, cry perhaps, but I couldn't.

So I just said, "Thank you very much." I was sorry for him, in a remote kind of way. There he was, in agony, and I had done it. What a sad, sad story, I thought. How tragic life is. Poor James.

Poor James said thoughtfully, "I don't need to be thanked."

"James," I said, "you don't *need* anything. You don't *need* to help me. There isn't any obligation from you to me."

"I wish I could believe that," he said. "I think there is. I married you. I knew it was wrong but I did it anyway. I've been telling myself that it was your fault, you could have stopped me. But it wasn't. You were a child. I knew you were a child."

"I wanted to marry you!"

"You don't give a child what it wants just because it wants it. A child can be greedy. Or misled. Older people owe it an obligation. I did you a bad turn."

Well, now I wasn't remote at all. I stared, appalled, at those hunched shoulders. Greedy! Misled! A child!

I choked out, "You—I did it——"

"Yes, you did, Diana. But I let you. What do you think I was afraid of? This. This. When I saw you with him——" He stopped. He turned around, he said, looking at me, "When I saw you with that vulgar cheap male whore I could have killed you. I saw it, I foresaw it. I warned you. I warned myself. None of it did any good. You insisted on humiliation—mine, yours. You wanted your roll in the dirt with him just the way you wanted me and money and position. You had to have it. Do you think you're a mystery to me? Do you think I don't know greed and desire and obsession when I see them? I know all about you. I've always known."

I was a long way beyond crying then.

He said, "I hope you're taking this all in. I hope what you learned in Capri will not go entirely over your head. I had him detained, by the way, and got the pearls back. The girl's gone home to her family."

I said, "Perhaps I can do that too."

His face changed. Of course I did not know my father had died. James stood looking at me and I looked back at him. We were both seeing each other without any deceptions—maybe for the first time. I found myself thinking, How interesting that he should have cared about the pearls and got them back! That is what being born rich does for you, you are trained to think of such things. It seemed to me quite admirable, more sensible and realistic than I would have expected of James.

He said, "Naturally you don't have to go anywhere now. Until this is over. That is—do you want to stay in Brussels? Did you come here for some reason?"

"Only because it wasn't England. I wanted to go where no one knew me."

He winced a little at that.

I saw it. It cheered me. I said, "I appreciate your helping me, James. If there were any way on earth I could manage without it, I would."

"Ah," he said, and smiled. "I hurt you then, didn't I, Diana? Good. Good. Bite on the bullet, my dear. You have a long life ahead of you in which to realize the value of stoicism." He came over to the bed looking down at me and almost laughing. He was not like himself at all. But then, he'd had a year to think of things he wanted to say to me.

I looked up at him as expressionlessly as I could and said, "Whatever I am, it isn't a coward."

"Quite right. I know that too. Well, now you will have a chance to prove your courage. I have been proving mine for a year. Good-by. I'll be back this evening and we can decide where you will spend the next two months." He nodded and started to go.

I let him get to the door before I said, "Oh, James."

"Yes?"

"If Gerald is still in jail, could you arrange to have him let out? Now that you have the pearls back?" I lifted my head and met his eyes with an expression of bright interest as I asked this. He had hurt me, had he! I thought. Well, we would see who bit on the bullet!

It hit him. He had to bow before he could speak. "I'll wire at once," he said, and went.

CHAPTER

19

What a morning, oh Lord, what a morning! thought Lorraine, riding, gliding, into New York, with the sun climbing behind her into the freshest, palest sky. Night mist when she started and the shadows faint, but now on the edge of the city, where the sedge and the cattails bowed in the breeze over the marshland, now—what a morning! Traffic was picking up, but only enough to make it fun to drive, to calculate where to pass, pull out, pull around, leave the slowpokes behind, feel the wind in her face and the car's smooth speed as extensions of her own bodily senses. Oh, what a morning, after last night's storm, after the dull heat and aching discomfort of yesterday! Today she could handle things, today she could ride her life, control it, drive it—— Where? Well, that she still didn't know; but she knew that she would know when she had to, when it mattered. Rest and relax and act from there, from the center. Don't plan, don't worry it out ahead of time, you can never know ahead what to do, no one knows enough to see ahead. I'm happy, she thought. Why mince words? I'm happy. What more can you be than that? Everything changes and flows, no one can stop and build a fortress and be safe inside. Safety is in riding, driving, changing, flowing—the sun climbs, it will be hot today, and every moment is different. But what a morning!

Seven-thirty as she turned off the parkway and started down through the Bronx. The city was waking. Trucks cluttered Bruckner Boulevard and the East River Drive was beginning to fill up with car-pooled commuters. She turned off in the seventies, heading for the apartment. Park Avenue at not quite eight o'clock was never very wide awake, and in summer, with its tenants away, it hardly stirred in its sleep. She parked in front of the house and the night elevator man, yawning, took her upstairs.

The apartment was hideously stuffy and she went through it quickly opening windows. A cleaning woman came in twice a week, kept the dust down and tidied anything that Lorraine left, for she almost always ran in once or twice when she came in to the city. Now she put some coffee on the stove, rooted in the icebox for the end of a loaf of bread, set it by the toaster, and then decided to shower while the coffee got ready to percolate. Oh yes—and find a bathing suit and cap, for this was the day on which some of the older children at the shelter were to be taken on an expedition to the beach. She whistled cheerfully as she moved around, she put the radio on for the news, she dropped on the bed that the cleaning woman kept made up for her and drank her coffee there, she changed and left soiled clothes in the hamper and finally, when she went out at quarter to nine, she had given the apartment a quite thoroughly lived-in look.

Which was as well, for ten minutes after the day elevator man took her down, the phone began to ring. The SAS flight from Copenhagen had found a favoring wind high over the Atlantic and come in early. No answer, of course. But when Herbert climbed out of a taxi in front of the apartment building, the doorman assured him that he had just missed Mrs. de Koning, she'd gone out for the day only forty minutes before. Was she coming back? Why yes, she was. "She was laughing, sir, and saying she was going to the beach, she and another lady taking some of those poor kids for a treat. She said she'd leave the car here and come back for it around five or six, because she could never make the drive to Connecticut without a bit of rest and one good stiff drink. 'A lay-me-down and pick-me-up,' I says and she laughs again at that, the words struck her funny. 'That's just right,' she says, 'A lay-me-down and pick-me-up.' I don't think she knew you was coming, sir."

"It was unexpected," said Herbert in a tone intended to repress any further intimacies of expression between members of the de Koning family and Charlie Broderick from County Mayo. "Just bring the bags in, please." He gave Charlie a dollar for this service, but it was pocketed resentfully. Charlie preferred Mrs. de Koning's laughter at his sallies to tips from her husband, and he resolved to be sure that she was warned about the arrival of one whom he and the rest of the staff referred to as Old Fishface.

Like so many good intentions, however, this one went unfulfilled. But who, in the first place, would have expected Mrs. de Koning to arrive in a rattletrap of an old station wagon? It pulled up in front of the apartment at the end of the afternoon and Charlie's sole purpose, as he started toward it, was to tell the driver not to block the entrance. But out of it climbed Mrs. de Koning, with her hair tied back and her nose sunburned red and—here was the second difficulty—not alone. "Oh, Charlie," she was saying, "will you look after Mrs. Donahue's car? She's coming up with me for a few minutes. He'll park it, Molly."

And another lady followed, saying, "All right, I left the keys, but my goodness, Laurie, it's certainly the least chic conveyance this elegant apartment house has ever seen! I should have put it around the corner."

Charlie agreed wholeheartedly, but Mrs. de Koning said, "Now, Molly, don't run down that wonderful wagon! Charlie, we hauled nine children out to Jones Beach and back, what do you think of that?" I think you're crazy, Charlie didn't say—she was a good woman, and he liked her. He didn't get a chance to say anything else, either, for Mrs. de Koning swept gaily on: "None of them drowned, either, though I must say I thought about throwing Ricky Toreno to the sharks myself after he ducked Honey Smith for the fourth time. Have you got the limes, Molly? That's the secret of gin and tonic, you must never make it without fresh limes——" And she and the other lady were in the lobby, in the elevator (it was waiting of course, with no one home), and Lenny was shutting the door on them before Charlie had a chance to utter a sound. He stood looking after them and kicking himself for not thinking quickly enough to say, "May I have just a word with you, ma'am?"—for of course he had the sense and the manners not to let on, in front of anyone else, that Mrs. de Koning wouldn't have known when her husband was coming back. Well, it was too late now. Unless Lenny managed to drop a hint as he ran them upstairs—but he wouldn't, the loon. Charlie got gloomily into the ancient station wagon, which he had every intention of parking out of sight around the corner, wondering whether he should ring up to her on the house phone. No, better not. Mind your own business was a rule he'd learned long ago. Anyway, he decided, the man will have left his suitcases, she'll see them. Or even a note, likely.

But the man had not. Lorraine, cheerfully ushering Molly Donahue in, had no suspicion that Herbert had returned, shaved, showered, called his office, disposed of his dirty clothes and put his emptied suitcases in the hall closet. His toothbrush in the holder, his razor on the shelf above the washstand in her bathroom would have caught her eye, she would have stopped with her hand on her heart, but she sent Molly Donahue through her bedroom and into the big bath to freshen up and, snatching a towel from the linen closet in the hall, dived into the children's bathroom herself. And what was a razor or a toothbrush to say to Molly Donahue?

So, when half an hour later the front door shut, Lorraine, filling Molly's glass again with quinine water at the bar in the library, stopped talking when she heard it, in the middle of a word. She swung around, frowned at Molly and said, "What the dickens?" and stepped out into the hall. And then she neither screamed nor dropped the glass she held, though afterward she couldn't think why not. For Herbert was standing by the hall table putting his briefcase and the evening paper down with the immemorial fussy neat gesture that she had watched night after night after night for eight years and never noticed till now. She said, "Herbert," quite quietly.

He looked at her carefully. He said, "That's right. Herbert." And so they stood for a second without saying a word. Who was going to say something first? Who was going to define the situation? Lorraine— riding her life, in command, happy? No. Herbert, it seemed; for he went on (really he'd only paused for a moment), "How are you, my dear? You look well. I was surprised to find you in town."

"I came in last night," said Lorraine, lying unconsciously.

"Yes, I just missed you this morning, but the doorman said you'd be back." He now walked up the hall to her and, Molly Donahue being in full sight of the door and all eyes, Lorraine accepted his embrace and kissed him on the cheek.

"This is Mrs. Donahue," she said firmly, turning Herbert so that he could see they had an observer. "Molly, this is my husband. I did that the wrong way round, didn't I? I always do, it's like telling right from left. But at any rate, Herbert, Molly works at the shelter too, and we've had a passel of young'uns out at the beach today. Oddly enough, we decided we needed a little peace and quiet and gin after it. Will you have a gin and tonic, or what would you like? What—— You flew in, of course. Was it comfortable?"

"As comfortable as it ever is. We had tail winds and didn't have to put down at Gander, so we were ahead of schedule. I'll have a gin and tonic, thank you."

"My goodness," cried Molly Donahue, "you mean you just came in today? From Europe? Laurie, you didn't say a word!"

"I didn't know just what day he was coming," said Lorraine steadily, squeezing lime.

"They phoned me yesterday at the hotel that they had a seat for me, and since my *work* was done, I thought it best to take it. It's been a very busy season most places. I don't think I've been on an air liner that wasn't full anywhere in Europe. Very interesting situation there." He took his glass and sat down. As he began to give Molly Donahue his views on European conditions, Lorraine felt herself swept by a violent urge. She was by the door. She could put down her glass, snatch her pocketbook from the desk by the telephone, slide out, run down the hall, run—run—run—— You know it always takes Lenny five full minutes to get up here with the elevator, she told herself. You'd never get out without being caught. And imagining herself facing an icily furious Herbert and an astonished Molly Donahue, with her back to the elevator door waiting for Lenny to rescue her, she managed to reduce the impulse to a joke. Something to tell Peter: "I almost ran——" No. Not Peter. That was what not to think about if this was going to be manageable at all. And she mixed herself another drink (very light, this one), and sat down to be a hostess.

Herbert, she became aware, was being neutral. His manner was almost ceramic in its glazed and noncommittal objectivity. He described the rebuilt steel plants of the Ruhr. He related a conversation held with an ex-Premier of France, with a Governor of the Bank of England, with a General at SHAPE: all of them had spoken entirely in clichés. He remarked upon a helicopter flight to Brussels, the incidence of Algerians in Paris, and the unfortunate manners of Americans abroad. Politics, economics and hotel accommodations were accorded the same measured treatment, as if an observant IBM machine were reporting on its travels. Lorraine sat quietly and concentrated on her breathing: if she breathed slowly and relaxed her shoulder and neck muscles, the physical attributes of panic could be held at bay.

But Molly Donahue, though she smiled and nodded and encouraged Herbert as if he were a very Othello among travel raconteurs, had at last to go home to her family in Pelham. "It's been *so* interesting," she beamed, shaking Herbert's hand warmly. "Mark—that's my husband—will just eat this up. I do wish he could have heard you! Perhaps you'll come up to Pelham one evening, won't you? It's only a step, you know, with the parkways, and it would be a treat for us. Laurie, dear, thank you so much! I'll see you next week, won't I? And we can plan a dinner, if you wouldn't mind coming out. We'd just love it."

"Of course," said Lorraine. "So would we. We'll do that." And she walked Molly out to the elevator. It did indeed take Lenny some time to arrive—not five minutes, but nearly three. Lorraine looked at him and Molly and the lighted cage of the elevator, but she had got over the impulse to run. Better to get it over with now. She waved to Molly, shut the door and went back to Herbert.

"Where are the servants?" he asked as she came into the library.

Whatever he says, thought Lorraine, I will answer quietly and sensibly. "Hilda's in the country with the children. I let the others go. They weren't anything spectacular. Oh, I have a woman twice a week to clean, just to keep the place in shape."

"Can you get someone tomorrow? I've got rather tired of hotels."

So this is how we do it, thought Lorraine. Am I going back to Herbert? Do we try again? Or do I chop my life in half at six-thirty in the afternoon of August 8th? We beg all those questions and talk about the servants. Unless I am rude and forthright and altogether unpleasant and bring the big thing up myself.

"I can find someone, I should think," she said. And then heard herself go on in the most matter-of-fact way out of some deep unknown place where a decision had been made, "—someone to look after you. But I shan't be here myself." She took a deep breath, she felt a mad, dizzy, ridiculous sense of achievement. It was done, done, done! "Perhaps a sort of butler-valet would be the thing."

Herbert said in his deepest tone, "What does that mean?"

"It means that I'm not going to be married to you any more." Yes, it did. She knew it as she said it. It was done and over and irreversible, as irreversible as a river. You could as soon turn the river around and pump it back uphill. "I'm very, very sorry to tell you this on the day you get home. You deserve a better welcome. But there just mustn't be any misunderstanding about it. Very much through my fault, I'm sure, our marriage is over."

"It is, is it?" said Herbert and sat down on the edge of a chair. With a sense of complete astonishment, she saw that he was trembling and had gone white. Why he's shocked! she thought. He didn't expect it!

"My dear," she said impulsively, "I'm so sorry! I am so sorry, Herbert. Truly, truly, it's best for both of us! I've thought and thought—— My dear, there are so *many* women who can make you so much happier than I ever did! Women who can understand your work and help you and participate! I've been a drag on you, I know I have, it's been a mistake for years. Herbert, really it's best. If you think, I'm sure you'll see it, too."

She stood in front of him, her hands knotted together. There was sweat on his forehead and he was breathing through his mouth. "Over," he repeated. "No, it's not over." And he looked up at her with a concentration so intense that it turned his face into someone else's: every line was sharpened, his mouth turned down into the classic mask of tragedy, his eyes shone wetly under down-drawn brows. "Not over," he said.

"Yes, it is," said Lorraine gently. "I'm sorry. I realize this is a terrible thing to do with no warning, but it has to be done. It will only make it worse to delay it or pretend. We did that long enough."

"No," he said and reached out and took her hand. He held it in his palm as if it were a stone, encircling her wrist with his thumb and forefinger. "No." And he shook her hand a little.

Why this is terrible! thought Lorraine, and a first faint touch of fear moved within her. She turned her head, looking out the window at the drawn shades of the deserted apartments up and down the avenue. They are all gone away, she thought. Park Avenue in August, a series of empty rooms, like a beehive when the swarm has flown. And lost in one of those echoing uninhabited honeycombs was she, was Herbert, acting out some compulsive phantasm of behavior.

"My dear," she said, still reaching for sanity and reason, "my dear, think. You don't want me. I've never given you what you want. You must try again, you must start over. Herbert, you only have one life! You must live it, dear." Now who's talking entirely in clichés, she thought, no wonder he doesn't listen! But what can I say? What else can I say? "You must find someone who will make you happy," she went on, longing for and not finding any fresh words. "It isn't me. You know that, deep down. You've told me so often that I didn't do things right, that you were disappointed——"

Clutching her hand, he was shaking it. "Be quiet," he said. "Will you be quiet? How can I think when you chatter so?" And he leaned his head forward against her arm. After a minute he turned so that his face lay against her forearm. She felt his lips move on her skin. "Lorraine," he said, and kissed the inside of her wrist. "Oh Lorraine, Lorraine!" His mouth moved up and down her arm.

She endured it for one icy immobile moment while the skin prickled along her spine and then she found she had leapt back and was standing by the door, yards away from him. "Don't do that!" she said and the harsh voice she heard didn't sound in the least like hers.

"And why shouldn't I do it?" he said in a voice as loud, as harsh. "Aren't you my wife? Or have you found someone else already?"

She was so rigid that she neither started nor spoke at his words, nor changed expression.

Nevertheless, "Ha!" he said, leaning back. "That's it, isn't it? All your concern for me! It's you who want to start over."

"When I start over," she said steadily, "it will be alone. Whether I might ever remarry, I haven't even thought. It has nothing to do with the case. The case is you and me. We shouldn't ever have got married. All we do is hurt each other. We must stop."

"You're a child," he said. "And you talk like a child. How dare you dictate to me what I may or may not do? I shall do what I want."

"Yes," she said, "of course." Now she was frightened, now she had almost lied, now she *must* get out. She picked up her pocketbook. "I'm going back to Connecticut," she said, "there's no sense in talking now. Shall I call you at the office tomorrow?"

"You will not call me at the office," said Herbert, "nor will you go back to Connecticut. Sit down. You're going to hear a few things from me, right now."

"No, Herbert, I'm not going to hear anything. I——"

"I said, 'Sit down.'" He stood up and came toward her. "Now do it." He took the hand that held her bag, led her to a chair, sat her down, took the bag and opened it.

"What *are* you doing!" she said.

"I'm looking through your pocketbook." His voice was level and unemotional. "I've been gone quite a while, after all. And during my absence a great change has come over my wife. She tells me our marriage is over and talks about starting again. Is it so remarkable that I wonder whether something besides absence has caused this change? Ah—whose telephone number is New Haven 8–7937?"

"Aunt Di's doctor," said Lorraine, thinking Yes, now I lie, now I begin to lie, and making her voice angry—righteously angry—to cover it. "I probably have the physiotherapist's too, and a nurses' registry." And, she thought, panic rising, I have the key to the cottage. Oh God. Oh dear God!

But Herbert had unfolded another slip of paper. He smiled at it gently. "Or is this relevant, perhaps? Stewart Burnett. Who is Mr. Burnett, my dear, who telephoned at two-thirty one day?"

"A neighbor. A painter. Herbert, for heaven's sake, if I had a lover would I carry his telephone number around with me? Wouldn't I be likely to remember it?"

"I'm afraid I've had no experience." But he shut the bag and put it down. She almost closed her eyes in relief. No, she thought. Show nothing, show nothing. "Evidence," he said, standing over her. "Why do I need any evidence? I don't, of course. I have it." He stroked his finger down her cheek and left it there for a moment on the line of her jaw. "You can't bear my touch," he said. "That's evidence, isn't it?"

"It's evidence that I won't live with you again." I shouldn't have said that, she thought, but she could feel anger rising within her, real, solid, massive anger pushing out the fear. It's stupid to provoke him, she thought, but her anger couldn't really be sorry.

"Oh, I think it's a little more than that," he said. "It might be evidence that there is evidence. For a court, you know. A New York court where the grounds for divorce must be adultery——"

"Herbert, this is no way to talk about things. I'm tired. You must be terribly tired. Let me go, please. People—lawyers—can settle things. I don't want to hurt you——"

"Ha!"

"Yes, I know it sounds silly. I mean, hurt you any more than I have. I know I have, I am. It hurts me too. I'm not giving up eight years lightly or easily. You lived with me eight years, you ought to know that—that I wouldn't hurt you if I could help it. Well, I can't help it. But let's not make things worse."

"I suppose," said Herbert, "that in a world of moral idiocy, that is intended to be a generous speech. As well as a self-serving one. What a hypocrite you are, Lorraine! And how stupid, stupid, stupid!" He swung away from her and went to the bar.

"Then you can't want me," said Lorraine.

He went on pouring gin into his glass. "Perhaps I don't," he said finally and came and sat down across from her. "Perhaps your announcement tonight—your typically abrupt and tactless, graceless, announcement—has only injured my pride. That's what you think, isn't it? Isn't it?"

"I don't know, Herbert."

"You don't know what you think. Another Lorrainism, if I may coin a phrase."

"I meant that I didn't know what your feelings are."

"Ah, that's a little more accurate, I should imagine. And not too surprising, after all. It's quite possible that you have no inkling, after eight years, as you say, what my feelings are. Nor, I suppose, could you imagine them."

"I don't want to."

"Thank you. Thank you. My absence has at least given you a certain forthrightness."

"What good would it do for me to imagine your feelings? And what business is it of mine? I know my own feelings."

Herbert drank off half the liquid in his glass. My God, it's pure gin! thought Lorraine. He put the glass on the coffee table and leaned forward. "Lorraine, I would have said I loved you more than my life. What do you think of that?"

"I think you're wrong. That's what I think. I—— Herbert, I am not going to say one more word tonight. You can call me anything you want—cold, hypocritical, stupid, I don't care. I feel what you say, but it won't change me. We are not going to have any scenes or any hysterics, because I'm leaving. I'm going back to Connecticut now, and if you want to talk to me, you know Aunt Di's number. I apologize for what I'm doing to you, but I will not talk about it. Good night." She stood up. She took her pocketbook. A tag end of memory from a sensible life reminded her that she had intended to bring back some extra sweaters for the children. Well, the children would get on without extra sweaters. She started to the door.

"If you go through that door," said Herbert, "you can never come back. Your life as my wife ceases at the moment you go through that door." Lorraine walked through it. Herbert's voice followed her. "But don't think you can walk out of marriage that easily. I'm not one of your sister's drunken playboys. You won't find me agreeing to any Nevada hugger-mugger. Just try it and see. You'll get something you don't expect. You'll get a countersuit——"

Here Lorraine reached the outer door of the apartment, went through, shut it behind her and rang for the elevator. Three minutes, she thought. Lenny, hurry please, for once. Hurry, please. She reached to the bell again and pushed it twice, three times, as a desperate signal. How could she know that Lenny, glancing at the indicator, would assume that only Old Fishface would ring so rudely, and, in retaliation, decide to let him wait? Hurry, thought Lorraine, but Lenny did not hurry.

Instead, the door behind her opened and Herbert stood there. His face was waxy yellow. He said, "What am I to do?"

"Please, Herbert," said Lorraine. "Please. Don't do this to me or to yourself. Please."

"Hostages to fortune," he said. "My wife. My children. Taken from me in one hour. No one has the right to do this, Lorraine. Look at me. Can't you see that? No one. You are shattering my life."

"Herbert, I'm not. I want you to have a better life and a happier one with someone who'll love you better, and be kinder and more understanding than me. You don't want me really, Herbert. You don't. Believe me."

But he just stared at her. Lorraine turned and rang the bell again, a long peal. Lenny laughed, and shrugged and looked at his watch. I'll give the old bastard another minute, he thought.

"You can't wait to get away," said Herbert. "To leave me like this in a public hall. And I have no words. How I wish I had words! There must be a way to make you feel what you are doing." He stopped, peering at her. "No, there isn't any way. She doesn't feel it. She doesn't know. She's forgotten everything. This is a stranger. Lorraine!"

Lorraine began to beat on the elevator door with her fist. At last, far down, the whine of the ascending car began.

"Your heart has turned to stone," said Herbert. "Your eyes are blind, your ears are shut. All the old saws are true. There are no words. How I loved you."

Turned from him, Lorraine leaned on the door. Lenny, Lenny, for God's sake, faster! The light flickered under the door. The car arrived. Lorraine turned and said, "Herbert, I'll call——"

"No," he said. In the light from the opening elevator she saw him strike himself preposterously in the chest and thought, What is he doing? This melodrama—— And saw a red stain spread across his shirt and he hit himself again and only then did she see that he had the knife she'd used at the bar to slice the limes. He was stabbing himself.

Her mind said, This isn't happening, it isn't so, but her body knew better, it screamed. Behind her Lenny cried, "Jesus Christ!" She hurled herself at Herbert's hand, grabbing for the wrist. Lenny shoved her aside and she hit her hip painfully on the table that stood under the mirror in the hall, to find the bruise only days later and puzzle over how she could have hurt herself without knowing. Lenny's hand, Herbert's hand, strained up together struggling rigidly for the knife. Just like the movies, thought Lorraine. Just like the movies, Herbert's fingers opened reluctantly, the knife was pried loose and dropped. She swooped on it. Herbert leaned against the doorjamb. His shirt was ripped. She could see the impossible gaping lips of the wound. He began to slide to the floor.

Lenny caught him and held him. He'll get blood all over his uniform, thought Lorraine. "Shall I get him inside, Mrs. de Koning?" he asked.

"Yes. Where? The couch in the library, it's closest. And a doctor. Oh God, a doctor in August, they're all out of town!"

"The hospital," said Lenny. "It's just up the street." He bent. He strained. He wasn't a big man at all, nor young. He had Herbert in his arms and carried him through the hall to the library with an odd staggering walk, but he got him there and half dropped him on the sofa. Herbert's eyes had rolled up and his mouth was open. "Jesus, he's dead," said Lenny, panting.

Lorraine dropped on her knees and frantically felt for the pulse.

Where—— Where—— How could she have forgotten all that first-aid business they went through at college during the war! Where—— Yes. She felt it, faint but there.

"Get the doctor, get the doctor," she cried. Lenny turned, still panting, and ran for his elevator. She heard the door slam and almost cried out. Why couldn't he have called from here, she thought, why ever not? But of course, if he had any brains he wouldn't be running an elevator; never dreaming that poor Lenny, seeing his hands red with blood, had felt he must not smear it all over Mrs. de Koning's desk and phone. She had enough to bear, spare her that.

Herbert's breath began to grate in his throat. The bloodstain was spreading, soaking. Oh God, thought Lorraine, here I sit as if I were outside it all, and do nothing! She scrambled up, almost lost her balance, and ran to the linen closet. Clean towels. Her best clean towels to stanch Herbert's wound, a tag from the first-aid course told her to take linen ones, ironing would have sterilized them. She ripped the rent in his shirt wider, trying not to look at what was underneath, covered the bloody, mangled flesh with the sweet lavender-scented linen, and tightened another towel across the pad to bring what pressure she could on the severed blood vessels. Then she knelt, holding the bandage in place.

Near her right hand, on the coffee table, was the half-finished drink that Herbert had made himself—what?—ten minutes before. She fixed her eyes on it. Waited. Waited. Waited. She did not dare to look to see how soon the blood would seep through the towels.

"You see," said a voice, the ghost of a voice, Herbert's voice, "you were wrong. More than my life."

Lorraine began to cry. The tears ran down her cheeks, a drop collected on the tip of her nose, and she could not let go of the towel to wipe her face.

CHAPTER

20

I spent the weeks until my child was born in Bruges, a town with an imposing past and a non-existent present. How appropriate to my state! I thought the moment I saw it. James had taken a small, solid old house for me, and hired the woman who owned it to stay and look after me. She was a widow who claimed that her husband had died defending his homeland from the Boche, but a neighbor kindly intimated that he had really met his end falling drunk into one of Bruges's numerous canals. Living with his widow, I found this quite possible to believe. She was as mean, grasping and hard as any Balzacian bourgeoise. It was a good thing. I don't know how I'd have passed the time there without our daily battle, she to cheat me and I to prevent it. It gave me a good healthy interest in life, and I got my exercise walking out every day to check on prices at the markets.

Otherwise I was alone. Bruges is full of tourists in the season, but October and November are not the season. The wind comes off the North Sea like a handmaiden of the Goddess Pneumonia and when the Goddess is really feeling at the top of her form she sends a fine drenching rain too. In between, Bruges enjoys fog. James drove me there, and established me, and introduced me to my landlady, a doctor, and the gentleman who would handle my account at the bank. It was a lovely fall day—the Goddess Pneumonia had not yet waked from her estivation—and I stood by the door of my house and watched him get into the car he had hired and reverse it to drive off. He stopped by me and said, "Good-by, Diana."

"Good-by," I said politely.

"You can let me know at Claridges if you need anything. They'll know where I am."

"I shan't need anything."

"Dr. Frenet will arrange everything at the hospital."

"And nature no doubt will arrange everything else."

He looked at me thoughtfully. I couldn't have said anything nice or sweet or kind to him, in gratitude for what he was doing for me, if I'd been threatened with the rack. Well, I suppose I could under those circumstances, but under no others. "Would you like some books?" he asked.

"Thank you, I would," I said. "I've been planning to learn to make lace, but reading will give me a pleasant variety."

"I'll send you some from London."

"You're very kind."

He knew all about me, James. He'd told me so himself. He sat looking at me, held up by pride and pride alone. I knew he knew why I couldn't really thank him. You can't humble yourself if there's nothing left to hold you together but pride. He said, "You'll be all right, you know."

I was completely astonished. "What did you say?" I asked.

"You," he said. "You'll manage." And he drove off. It broke me up. I went into the house sobbing. James had tried to give me back to myself and comfort me and I couldn't stand it.

For two months I saw no one but my horrible landlady, Mme. Jordaens, and the doctor, and M. van Balen at the bank. James sent me a huge case of books, but no letters. I didn't know where he was. I read some, but mostly I thought.

What, I tried to find out, were the lessons to be learned from my life? I sat beside the fire in that overstuffed, poky, Flemish house, a house that breathed every maxim of prudence and greed, and tried to reconcile the two. God knows the latter came easily to me, but now I must practice the former. Mme. Jordaens and the house managed both attributes. Why shouldn't I? Indeed, I must. For now I was to have a child for whom I would be responsible, solely responsible. A child without a father. What kind of a raft of beliefs could I weave together beneath the child's feet and mine? Or were beliefs, like generosity, a luxury? Be practical, be prudent, I told myself, and I would sit reading, and whenever I came to a general principle, or an allusion to an ideal, I would put the book down and think off into the past, testing the point I had come on, and trying to decide whether it could have any use for me at all. We couldn't carry much on that raft, my child and I. We had no room for luxuries. Honor and honesty and kindness and care; loyalty; independence; what were these things worth to me? Had I not left James, the repository of so many of these virtues, for Gerald who had none, only charm? And I had been quite wrong. Now charm made me sick at my stomach. Stony, grasping, Mme. Jordaens and I judged it more or less the same: when we saw anyone charming coming, we were inclined to cross the street. I didn't think about Gerald at all—as a person, that is, or wonder where he was, or what had happened to him—any more than someone getting over the measles thinks about the character of his disease. I thought about the child, trying to penetrate the future. But not trying too hard, because that would invite bad luck. And I thought about James.

Because James was not who I had thought he was. He claimed to have been the one who supervised and controlled our relationship when I had been quite, quite sure it was I who did this. Perhaps he was wrong. Still—the James I had imagined myself living with would never even have made the claim. He would never have believed there was such a claim to be made. If the new James were real—then I had lived for five years with a man who deceived me about himself every minute. He was a man who saw much more than I had thought possible; but even more upsetting was the fact that he could see and judge and—not act. Hold himself in control. Let me run about his feet like a puppy, yapping and playing, and never knowing it was on a lead. There were people who saw and did not act because they were afraid. But the more I thought, the more I knew that James was not like that. If I wasn't a coward, neither was he. It was strength, not weakness, which made him hold his hand, not jerk the lead, let me run and play. For someone like me who acted instinctively, the stoic strength of refraining seemed—still seems—much greater, frighteningly greater, than my own impulsive energy.

So I thought about James. Without having to force myself to, either, for he had become more interesting than ever he'd been before—except, perhaps, for the time before he'd noticed me, when I made up stories about him and the great world. Now I'd had both. And though I'm sure I'd have bitterly regretted the great world if I'd had to settle down in a small American town and live without it, what I regretted, in Bruges, was James. It became clear to me that he was really a more interesting man than Gerald. More decisive. More able. Except for the one thing, more virile. In a way—intellectually—he was actually more attractive than Gerald. That is, he gave you something to chew on, whereas Gerald just appeared and disappeared like Jove in a shower of gold.

Did I think about winning James back? Yes, I certainly did. I acted out the scene where he asked me to return to him over and over again, whenever I needed to comfort myself. I always refused him. Disdainfully. My God, how I wanted to beat him, and hurt him! For the letters that never came, and the fog and rain and wind that did, and the things he'd said to me, and the answers I'd thought of later! For helping me when I needed it and going off and leaving me alone—— It used to be a standard, if unscientific, theory that pregnant women were a little crazy, and from my own experience I think it's so.

Then I reached my time, one afternoon in early December. It was a sunny day, and Mme. Jordaens went and got the doctor and he came in a horse-drawn vehicle of a shape strange to me and took me to a hospital run by a nursing order of nuns. My room was small and whitewashed and bare, like a cell, and there was a crucifix on the wall.

I had a hard labor. It was the evening of the next day before the child was delivered.

On the morning after that they brought James in. My throat was very sore from the anesthetic they'd given me and I didn't speak, just licked my dry lips as he came toward me. He didn't say anything either. I was glad he had come. I hadn't expected it. He took my hand and I—I don't know why—I pulled his hand to my face and rested it against my cheek. I think I must have been lonely, very lonely. We stayed that way for a moment and then he said to the nun at the door, "I would like to see my wife alone." She told him it was against the rules, but he said he would make it all right and finally, unwillingly, she went off.

He's come, he's come, he's come—was all I could think. After all the daydreams and the long imaginary conversations, he is really here. Instead of the angry joy I had expected, I felt tears run out of my eyes and over my temples—I was lying flat on my back. They wet James's hand. This is reality, I was discovering—yourself torn and aching and crying and vulnerable, not yourself witty and disdainful and furious. This is what the world is like. The pain had revealed it to me. I had never felt pain before. I knew now I could be a coward.

CHAPTER TWENTY

"Was it so bad?" asked James in a strained voice.

"No," I said with a gasp. "It wasn't really. It wasn't bad at all. They've all been good to me."

"I would have been here last night except for the snow."

"Is it snowing?" I asked.

"Yes. Quite a lot."

"How funny. It was sunny yesterday—day before—whenever I came here." Here, since we'd finished with the weather, the conversation ran down.

But at this point the nun came back, with the Mother Superior in tow, and James had to go out in the hall and have a good thorough argument about being left alone with me. They went off finally, he must have promised to buy the hospital something, I wonder what. Anyway he came back and pulled a chair out and sat down facing me. I turned my head and managed a smile.

He said, "Di, I had a story all fixed up for you. I thought I'd tell it to you until the minute I walked in here. Dr. Frenet would have backed me up. So would the old girls. I had it all taken care of. You'd have believed it, too."

I must still have been misty from dope because I just blinked at him.

"A story," he said, and nodded his head. "A lie."

"What for?" I asked.

"To get rid of the baby. You had a little girl, Di. I was going to tell you it was dead. Frenet has a family that will adopt it—for a certain amount, of course. Enough to pay its keep."

I was still staring. "But why?"

"Because I can't—have the child. I'm sorry. It can't be done."

"Why should you?" I said. "I don't see——" Then I stopped. He was sitting and looking at me and waiting for me to understand. He was strong and patient and he didn't move at all. Not even to blink. I turned my head on the pillow. The window was small and the wall was thick, I could barely see that it was indeed snowing hard. He was asking me now if I wanted to come back, and I didn't have any answer.

I could go back to James, or I could keep my child.

"A girl," I said. "I was going to call a girl Claire."

"She's quite healthy," said James. He cleared his throat. "The doctor says she's—you know—fine. Nothing to worry about. She's perfect."

The tears began to run out of my eyes again.

"What would you do with her, Di?" said James. "How would you live? This is a good solid family, cousins of Frenet's, not here but south, he's a Walloon, not a Fleming. I didn't ask him where, even. He comes from Liége, some place around there. They want the money to buy another farm. They'd get enough income out of it to raise her decently and then give her the farm as her dowry. She'd—have a family, and roots, and all that. Wouldn't she be better off than—the way you'd have to live?"

I remembered then how he'd left me in the fall, by my door. "You said I could manage," I whispered.

"And you did. You managed all this without—without any fuss or trouble or being sorry for yourself. You did fine."

"Why shouldn't I—go on, then?"

James said, "Because I won't give you a penny, Di. Not a penny."

I turned back and looked at him instead of the snow.

"Oh hell, I don't mean I won't pay Frenet and the nuns and everything till you're well and out of here. I'll give you enough to get home, too. After that—not a penny."

I stared at him.

"Look, Di," he said, "I can't. Not because I'm a monster, not because of anything I feel or don't feel, for you or anyone else. The law says that any child born to my wife while I still acknowledge her as my wife is legally my child and the heir to my property."

"But I don't——" I began. "But I would never——"

"I don't think you would. On the other hand, I didn't think you'd— leave me as you did in London. I had thought of the possibility, I had seen there was a danger, but I didn't honestly think you would. So I can't take a chance. Besides, whatever *you* might swear you would never do, you can't tell what she might do."

"She?"

"The child."

"The child! But——"

"Look, Diana, have you never heard of a contested will? Nothing you say or swear to now could take from her the right to contest any will of mine if you are my wife and acknowledged by me to be so when she's born."

"But—but I am! You're here! I mean——"

"No, dear, it's no good. I have divorce papers drawn, Di. I don't acknowledge you if you keep the child. I can't. I'm sorry."

After a while I asked, "And if I don't keep her?"

"Why, then it's up to you. There's no obligation."

"But you'd take me back."

"I'd be willing to try." He was sitting on that hard little nun's chair—neat, spare, wiry, his eyes alert and alive. In that bare room, that house of women all dressed alike, soft-footed, indistinguishable, his personality reached me like a strong, sharp odor. How long it was since I had seen anyone so intelligent, curious and aware as James was. So extremely, humanly, civilized-ly able! So different, I'm afraid, from Gerald.

"And the divorce?" I asked.

"It could be stopped. I'd be taking a chance, of course. If I take you back I can't sue you again over——" He jerked his head to indicate Gerald.

"Oh, couldn't you?"

"No. If I take you back I condone it."

"I see."

"You'll have to think about it pretty carefully. I'll take the risk, but not unless you feel fairly sure you want to."

I was beginning to get misty again, and James's preposterous calm gave the scene a dreamlike quality. I felt as if I were negotiating, in a nightmare, some very complicated contract, on which the fate of heaven and earth hinged, with some powerful supernatural figure. I opened my eyes wide, but James's dark figure against the white wall seemed to float, ominous, portentous, not larger but more intense than life. "It isn't right," I said.

He blinked. "What isn't?" he asked warily.

"To sacrifice the baby. You're trying to make me forget it. You have everything on your side, but it wouldn't be right."

He sat taking in, I suppose, that I was tiring and not in control, for he spoke quite gently. "I won't press you, Di. I told you how things are and have to be with me. Keep her if you can manage. But consider whether *you* wouldn't be sacrificing her, in that case, sacrificing her to your pride. I think my plan is best. But rest a bit, and think, and I'll come back tomorrow." He stood up and came over to the bed and touched my hair. I watched his face dumbly. There was kindness in it, and tolerance, and patience, but no hope. I watched him out and I knew I would have to give her up. A nun came in to me, after a while, but she didn't bring the baby and I didn't ask for her.

Later—oh, later I got so I could forget all about that time, for months and months. It was because the whole thing was so far outside the rest of my life that it was like a tuck in time—eighteen months stitched up out of the way, and the fabric stretching strong, in the same pattern, on both sides of the seam. For years the only thing that reminded me that the tuck was there at all was when Mary or my mother spoke of my father's death. And they didn't do that often because they believed that I didn't like to be reminded of a time when I had been suffering from a nervous breakdown.

And yet underneath I never forgot. I went back to James and was his wife and two years after Claire was born we had a son. But if you've been at the end of your rope, you never forget it. That room in the hospital is as clear before my eyes today as if I'd been in it ten minutes ago, and James sitting there invested with my guilt until his quiet neat human person grew numinous and frightening with it. I gave up my child. No doubt I had no real choice and James was right. To keep her with me would have meant that he had to ruin me, and what could a ruined woman do for her daughter? And no doubt I brought it on myself, and Gerald was right about risks and jeopardy. That day in the hospital in Bruges was the necessary end of the action that began in Paris the day Gerald and I met. No choice. So I gave her up. But part of me went numb then, and wooden—crippled, I suppose. And crippled now, nodding across the years, I realize that ever since I have dragged a foot, needed a crutch, covered a deformity.

CHAPTER

21

A kaleidoscope, thought Lorraine. That's the name of the thing. You shake it and it changes, and you shake it and it changes. I had one when I was little, and when I took it to pieces, there were just a lot of little bits of broken glass inside. I must get up and go back to the room where they left me, or I may miss the doctor.

But she sat on in the phone booth leaning her head against the door. She had called Woodbury, spoken to Tucker, said only that she had been delayed and would not be out that night. Nine-fifteen the clock had said when she went in. And the doctor's name—what was the doctor's name? But she could not remember.

Would her aunt wonder, worry, guess something wrong? It was possible. Nine-fifteen. But there was nothing to tell, nothing yet to tell. Her skirt was still wet, under her hand, where she and the nurse had together, distractedly, sponged at the stains on it. How could everything take so long? Stone, that was his name. Dr. Stone.

If I could call Peter—but I can't. Just to hear his voice? No. No. Get up. Go back. Suppose the doctor comes looking?

Just to call, to ask for a moment of comfort? I wouldn't ask for *help*.

An orderly rolling a stretcher came down the hall. Lorraine had the door open, was out of the booth, was over—— On it lay an old woman with white hair. A startled nurse had come out of a room, she plucked at Lorraine's arm, she turned her around and away, another nurse appeared—up through the floor, as far as Lorraine could see— and led her back to the waiting room.

Then there was no time for a long time, and then someone shook the kaleidoscope again and Dr. Bryan (his name wasn't Stone at all) was telling her to go home.

"Where is my husband?" said Lorraine, leaning, craning, getting up stiffly.

CHAPTER TWENTY-ONE

"You can't see him tonight, Mrs. de Koning. If you come back in the morning——"

"Is he dead?"

"No, of course not!"

Lorraine sat—fell—back in the chair. The doctor's voice was a thin wire of sound above her head. He sounded annoyed: how absurd of her to imagine Herbert dead! What a foolish, emotional woman she must be to conceive such an improbability! But I saw him, she wanted to say. I saw him. And again, in the light from the elevator, appeared Herbert's confusingly over-dramatic gesture, he thumped himself on the chest, the little knife hidden in his hand until the blood betrayed it and the gesture became something else, and yet kept its confusion, its aura of melodrama. I always liked that knife, thought Lorraine, it takes such a good edge. I hunted for it especially, in the kitchen table drawer.

She looked up wonderingly at the doctor, he was talking still, she must attend. "Pierced the pleural cavity," he was saying, and she tried to understand, but it was hard, a jungle of medical terms surrounding his meaning. Does he use them as a shield with everyone? she wondered. Or is it that he dislikes me? But she must try to understand! Herbert would live. Herbert would be very uncomfortable for a while. His condition was serious, but not critical. Transfusions——

"What time shall I come tomorrow?" she asked.

He told her and she told herself to listen, but the words flicked through her head like a flight of birds. Not dead. Not to die, said her thoughts, looming under the doctor's speech like rocks in the ocean's floor. Her hand on the knife, taking it from the drawer. His hand on the knife, driving it home. What a weird chance! said her thoughts, and Never! said her thoughts. Chance is Destiny, the opposites are the same.

The doctor had asked her a question. She searched back hastily for the words—— Oh yes. Had she anyone to stay with her?

She shook her head.

"No family?"

"In Connecticut. They're all in Connecticut."

"Isn't there someone you could call? You've had rather a shock, you know. It would be a good idea——"

This time she stopped listening because he was being so silly. Yes, it was rather a shock, she could agree, but if she did she would laugh. "I'll be all right," she said. "Can he talk?"

"Talk? Your husband? My dear Mrs. de Koning——" She had been absurd again. She listened in pulses: the operative technique, the anesthetic, the injury to the lung, the nurses needed——

"I see," she said. "Yes, of course. In the morning, then." And now it was time to go but she couldn't get up. There must be more, she thought, something more to explain it all. The operative technique, yes, and the loss of blood, and the pressure in the pleural cavity—— But what has happened to Herbert? One minute he was there, furious, hating, reaching; himself and not himself, doing some things more intensely than ever and doing some things he'd never done before, but still Herbert. Herbert shaken like a kaleidoscope and changed. But then, change became transformation and he was not Herbert at all, just a hurt body, embraced by Lenny (how he would have hated that!) and lugged up the hall. How did that happen? It was too much, too much to believe. She shook her head at it, unbelievingly. The motion was somehow comforting and she went on shaking it.

"What you need now is a good sleep," said the doctor abruptly. "Do you have a sedative? Any sleeping pills?"

"Some of the red ones," she said obediently.

"Take two with a glass of warm milk. But I wish you'd call someone to stay with you."

"I haven't anyone to call." The doctor looked at once impassive and unbelieving, and Lorraine felt herself again being difficult. "Everyone's away," she said, trying to help him. But can he believe, she thought, that people just call people up casually and say, "Oh, by the way, my husband tried to kill himself this evening. Could you drop over and spend the night?" If he did, they would have trouble communicating. Still, it was only polite to try.

"You live just down the Avenue?"

She nodded.

"They'll get you a cab downstairs."

He wanted her to go. She said quickly, wheedlingly, "Can't I see him for a minute, just a minute, just as he goes by to the room? I won't say a word. Can't I wait?"

"It'll be some time still. You go and get some sleep. It's half past ten, you know."

"It is?" She was astounded. But he was right, the clock said so. He stood up. She stood up. He walked beside her to the elevator, pressed the bell. He was going to see her out, send her home, like a bad child from a party, a child who was over-excited, "beside herself" her nurse used to say. She was ashamed. I must be good, she thought.

But there she was waiting for an elevator once more. It was coming, it was all coming back, the waiting, Herbert's voice. She could hear the whine of the rising car, it seemed to squeeze the words out of her in spite of herself—— "It was unbelievable. I had no idea. Lenny had no idea. We couldn't believe it. That's how it happened. Lenny stopped him as soon as he saw. I haven't even thanked him. But it's hard to believe, you know. People say it so often without thinking, but it's true. 'I couldn't believe my eyes.' He never——"

"Here we are," said the doctor as the elevator doors clanged back. Lorraine bit her lip and got in. The back of the elevator attendant was ready to listen. She bowed her head and rode down in silence. "I'll get you a cab," said the doctor. I've forgotten his name again, thought Lorraine.

But a man loomed up in front of her. It's someone I know perfectly well, she thought. Who is it? And heard herself saying, "Why, Charlie! I didn't know you without your—your hat." That sounded politer than "without your uniform." It was the doorman, mopping his forehead, in shirt sleeves, with his jacket over his arm.

"How is he?" asked Charlie.

"The doctor——" said Lorraine.

The doctor said, "Mr. de Koning is in fairly serious shape, but there's every reason to suppose he'll recover perfectly."

"Thank God," said Charlie. He means it, thought Lorraine, and yet it sounds—too used. All the tips he's had because he's so nice have got into his voice, somehow. And yet how nice he is to come! "That's great news," Charlie was saying. "A great relief. Lenny's been nearly wild, thinking if he'd got up faster with the car he might have prevented him entirely. He'll be a new man, to hear this."

"He didn't do it at all till Lenny came," said Lorraine, "he'd have done it whenever Lenny came. Lenny mustn't think—— Why, he was wonderful. Charlie, what are you doing here? You haven't been waiting for me, have you? All this time?"

"No indeed," said Charlie smoothly, in his rich Irish liar's voice.

"I just dropped by to inquire. Me room's just over east, in the sixties, and on a hot night like this I often take a stroll before I sleep. Tonight I thought I'd stroll here. Are you ready to leave?"

"They won't let me see him till the morning."

"And why would they, the way they've been working these hours on the poor man? He'll need the sleep, no doubt. Is that so, Doctor?"

"Ah—yes. Yes, exactly. You're—ah—a friend of Mrs. de Koning's?"

"Indeed he is," said Lorraine. Tips and all, it was as true as anything was.

"I'm on the door at the building," said Charlie, " 'twas I called the hospital." His brogue swelled a little with sentiment at being Mrs. de Koning's "friend." He's a snob, thought Lorraine; and how mean it would be of me to say, Don't be a snob, Charlie, to deny him the pleasure of hearing me say he's my friend! "I've known Mrs. de Koning these six years, since they bought the apartment," said Charlie. "And him too, of course. And the children."

"I wish she had someone with her tonight," the doctor recurred to his worry.

"She has only to ring the house phone, sir. I'll pass the word to the night men. They'll be up in two shakes. We'll see she's looked after."

"Please," said Lorraine, "really, I'm all right. What could happen to me now? It's all happened, you know. No one else is going to——" She broke off. She swallowed. "Good night, then. I'll come in the morning."

"I'll just see you home, ma'am," said Charlie. "It's on my way." He took her elbow and piloted her gently out into the soft, hot night.

A little group of people stood at the foot of the steps outside the entrance to the Private Pavilion. As Lorraine emerged they shifted in the light from the street lamp. "Is that her?" asked a voice and another called, "Oh, Mrs. de Koning?"

"Yes?" said Lorraine turning, startled. Charlie tugged suddenly at her arm and at once a light flashed in her face.

Charlie was pulling her back. She heard him say, "Mother of God, those damned photograph-ers!" Another light went off. "Vultures!" said Charlie. Then he had her back inside the hospital lobby.

"Oh, Mrs. de Koning, I just want to ask——" a woman was calling, but Charlie ran her around the desk out of sight of the door. The doctor was still there, staring with his mouth open. The girl at the cashier's window was leaning out, trying to see what was going on. "It's them damn yellow rags, them tabloids!" said Charlie, who read them every day. "Damn them, damn them all! Someone must have seen the ambulance, and telephoned a tip. We had a call to the house, and we thought we got rid of them. How they got your name I *don't* know. Not from us, ma'am." He glared at the doctor.

"They got no information here, I assure you," said the doctor coldly. "Of course there has to be a police report on every——"

"Police!" said Lorraine. She looked back and forth at the two men. The doctor looked embarrassed and sorry, but Charlie knew something.

He said, "They're at the house now, ma'am, a detective from the precinct. I was going to tell you on the way home."

"Police!" said Lorraine again.

The doctor said unhappily, "It's routine, the hospital has to report on all injuries from acts of violence that are treated here——"

"Herbert, Herbert!" cried Lorraine and beat her hands together. "Oh no, no!" She drew in her breath to scream, to sob——

The doctor caught her hands and held them. "Mrs. de Koning!" he said. "Listen to me! Get hold of yourself! They can't see him tonight. They can't see him tomorrow. I won't let them in. Get hold of yourself. It won't help if you go to pieces!"

"No, it won't at all," she said. But she was shaking so she could hardly stand. It was like falling downstairs—first the impossible, startling plunge, the terror, the disbelief; then a battering blow as you fell, and then another, and another, pain mixing with fright; and all become grotesque, farcical, so that onlookers must laugh, in spite of their horror and sympathy, at the ridiculous figure you cut. Reports, pictures, her astonished face in the *Daily News* tomorrow, and now this final touch of ludicrous horror, the police!

"Sit down," the doctor was saying, "wait here, I'll get you something——" Charlie took her over to a bench against the wall and settled her as you settle a child. She leaned back. Time passed. She thought, I'm not going to be sick, that's lucky. And thought, I should tell Charlie I'm all right. But it could wait a minute.

Squeak of rubber shoes, rustle of starched skirt. A nurse appeared. "Mrs. de Koning? Dr. Bryan sent me down with this for you." She had a glass in her hand. "You just drink that, now, and sit quiet for a

few minutes, and you'll feel better. Can you take it? Any faintness?"
She turned to Charlie. "Was she faint?"

"I'm all right," Lorraine whispered.

"Well, of course you're all right. That's fine, you just drink it right off. That's a good girl. Finished? Oh, go on, finish it up. Fine, that's fine. Now you sit back and rest for a few minutes. Dr. Bryan's gone to see if he can't get you out the back way through the delivery entrance on the other street. By the time he gets it arranged you'll be feeling much better. Lean back, that's the girl, shut your eyes——"

Go away, be quiet, go away, Lorraine wanted to say, but it would be useless now. They wouldn't leave her alone. They were very kind, they wanted to help, and they wouldn't leave her alone. Charlie, the nurse, the doctor, they were her defenders. She felt her face jerk into a sickly smile for the nurse, her defender, who was proving the horror real.

"That's better," said the nurse. "Lean back."

Lorraine leaned back.

Deep in her private world she had reached a decision—that day? The day before? A month ago? She didn't know herself. From deep in his world Herbert had responded: emotion hidden since their marriage, grief that he had never thought to feel, had burst out. Blood had bloomed under his hand. Who could have imagined it? Not he, not she, had foreseen this strange flowering. Now, their private agony was to be dragged into the street by that waiting group outside, was to be tasted, tested, handled, trampled over by anonymous millions, avid for experience, who called murderers and movie stars by their first names. To be alone, to be clean, to be private, was over for both of them. As swiftly and finally as if he were casting a spell, Herbert's action had changed the world. Now a nurse sat by his bed listening to every difficult breath. Now the reporters waited outside, at the apartment were the police. She and Herbert were public property.

How unkind I was to Faith, she thought. Columns and pictures in all the papers after the last divorce. And I did nothing but behave as if it were her fault. It *was* her fault. But why couldn't I have forgotten it? She didn't need me to tell her it was her fault. And she has never been east since. How smug I was, how righteous, how respectable!

If the reporters find out about Peter it will make Faith's divorce look pale, and the scandal would be worse for him even than for me. At that, she almost groaned aloud. But the draught the doctor had given her was beginning to take effect. She could feel her mind losing its edge of realization, her emotions beginning to grow numb. It was as if herself and her situation had been thrust apart: it was as sordid as ever but not so close. Within it, a figure bearing her name walked through experiences, left her lover's arms, drove to New York—— Would the police want to know what time she had arrived? Where she had spent last night? Would Charlie, her defender, lie for her in the voice that had said "Thank you" so often for a dollar or ten dollars? Would he suborn Lenny and Floyd, the night man, to lie too? What would he expect, after that? For how much, then, would he say "Thank you"? And Lenny who had carried Herbert's bleeding body down the hall? And Floyd? Adultery, bribery, perjury, acts of violence—— She wanted to lift her hands and cover her ears as if the gesture would shut out the catalogue of what she had done and, worse, had still to do. For somehow, tonight, she must speak to Charlie, arrange the necessary lie that she had spent last night in New York, smear herself with still another guilt, and open herself to another jeopardy. There was no reason to imagine Charlie, her friend, a blackmailer. But in this strange world, there was no reason to imagine him not.

"I think the doctor's ready now," said the nurse. Lorraine stood up. "There! You're much better now!" She took one arm, Charlie the other. Between them Lorraine moved unresisting down the hall, through a door, into a yard with a fence and a gate where a silent rank of garbage cans waited. Beside her walked her defenders and her guards. They were her torturers too, instruments of the greedy, waiting world who would read about her tomorrow. She moved between them like a prisoner, away from the event that, unforeseen, had set familiar ritual in motion. The kaleidoscope shook again, wiping out the truth of that phantasm who had cried No!, hidden the knife and, in defiance of all sense and reason and decorum, his own and hers, done what he could not have done; but did. Other events waited, the doctor waited, with a taxi.

"I'm coming with you," he said. How odd! thought Lorraine, accepting it. "You can't talk to the police tonight. Don't worry, it's on my way home. If there's anything they have to ask you, they can

do it tomorrow. You're going to sleep, and that's doctor's orders."
"You're too kind," said Lorraine, and meant it. But nothing, she
saw, could stop him. He and Charlie were going to rescue her. If she
said she didn't want to be rescued, they would nod to each other and
send for a nurse. Don't you see, she wanted to tell them, that I must
face it? This is all pretense, you know. You can't rescue me from
what has already happened, and from what has to follow it. You've
saved me from more photographs, but they have two already. The
reporters can't talk to me tonight, but their files are full of Faith's
story, they'll just run that over again. You're very kind, you're pleased
with yourselves for being masterful and clever, but you're not accomplishing anything. Can't you see?

There was no use in saying it. Charlie had begun to reminisce, as the
taxi ran south, of days in the IRA—"before you were born, ma'am, that
was"—and wanted men smuggled out of the country under the
very noses of the Black and Tans. The doctor (Charlie, at any rate,
had remembered his name was Bryan) contributed the exploits of an
uncle who had been right-hand man to Ernie O'Malley himself.
From very far away Lorraine perceived that they were enjoying themselves.

Even that began to seem unimportant.

22

For all the years of agony, there were kind years; or years that seemed so at the time. James took me back as his wife, but he did not—could not—act to me as a husband, at first. We both tried to ignore it. I know he didn't do it to hurt me. It was fastidiousness. He could not touch what Gerald had touched. My body had borne Gerald's child. There were times, I know, when James desired me and then literally could not force his flesh to satisfy itself where Gerald's had. It was hard for me not to try and help him, for headlong and greedy and impulsive I was still. But not foolhardy enough to forget James telling me he had let me arrange our marriage. If James could not easily come into my bed, I could not easily undertake again to "manage" things. I must have thought of it a hundred times, for my subconscious impulses would start toward a solution over and over again, and sometimes I was almost sick with sorrow and humiliation and the sheer physical need to lie in a man's arms and be comforted and healed. I would lie alone in my room at the castle or in the New York house and stuff my fist into my mouth not to cry, and often and often I didn't succeed, I cried.

He came into my room finally one night when I was like that and said, "Diana, Diana, don't. Don't, dear."

"It isn't any use," I said, all garbled. "I didn't know you could hear me. I didn't mean you to. There's no sense to this. I had better go. Let me go, James. This is foolish."

"It's I who am foolish," he said, and sat down on my bed. It was still the wide bed we'd both slept in, though I'd wanted often enough to change it for a single one, but how could I? "Please, Di, dear. You must stop." He stroked my hair.

"I'd stop if I could," I said, paying no attention to his hand, refusing it as a caress. He went on stroking my head.

"You know I love you," he said finally.

"If you say so," I said.

"No, Di, you know it. You must know it!"

"You've been very kind to me," I said, and at the thought of his kindness and how eagerly I would have exchanged it for blows and anger and his arms around me, I turned my head under his hand and cried again.

"Oh God," said James, "what am I to do?"

"Let me go," I said.

His hand stopped on my hair. "Really, Di? Is that what you want?"

"Yes," I said. It was a lie, but I had to say it. It was a lie because when I had chosen to go back to James and relinquish my child I had chosen once and for all. I had shut away that never-seen little ghost into a world that could not exist, just as surely as if James had told me his "story" that she had died. What would I do, then, if my choice proved wrong, if I lost James? I was committed to him, I had bought that commitment dearly. I did not want to go, I wanted to stay, I wanted as much as James ever had to make a marriage between us. But the sad doldrums where we drifted then—that was not a marriage, and I lied.

There was a long silence. He was relinquishing me, giving it up. And I—I don't know. Perhaps I was just waiting. I thought (but it was only the top of my mind that thought it), I can reproach him now and in a way it will be managing, but it will be true, and it might work. I can tell him how I admired him when he came to me in Brussels and taunted me, how I waited in Bruges and thought of him and began to understand him and his strength. It would all be true. And it might work.

But I waited. Was there a deeper truth? Was it on my side? I lay still and receptive like a medium waiting for a trance—as, all those years ago, I had lain in my bed at home, waited, thought of him, given up my greed for once, and my managing and my desire, and simply tried to be. What could help me? I thought. Unless everything helps me? For if there is nothing except contrivance, I had better go. I can contrive with anyone. With James it seems there will have to be something else. Perhaps it can only work between James and me if there is no "my side" or "his side." Perhaps the truth will not help me, but only help *us*. Or hurt us. But both together.

And before I knew it I said, "Dear heart, why did you want me again?"

"You are my life," said James. "Without you——"

I sat up and threw my arms around him and there we were, clinging together like the two last people in the world, crying and clinging, so much to be forgiven and all of it forgotten then, just dropped and kicked aside out of our way. Our separation ended that night, and I thought I could never be unhappy again.

But of course I was. There were times when it all came back on James and I could see him remembering, measuring me with his eye as if he were trying to value this creature he couldn't rid himself of; wanting, longing, to get over the disease of his need for me, searching and searching to find the secret within me so that he could release himself from me, as if he might someday find a spring, and press it, and snap! I would let go and he would be free. He would be angry at me. I never knew what would bring it on. A mention of Lausanne where he had had news of me was as difficult as a mention of Capri itself, and when he talked of going to London he shut his eyes in pain and I found we were to stay in a different hotel from before. And when I knew I was pregnant I didn't know how to tell him and put it off and put it off. He didn't know how to take it either, but swung back and forth between joy and pride on the one hand, and rage that it had never happened until after I had been with Gerald. Those were difficult months. I encouraged him to get away from me and he traveled a great deal, looking at the plants and the mines and the timber stands where his fortune was invested. Actually, he was an excellent businessman, not a moneymaker in the first place perhaps, but one who could not only conserve but go on. He had a better head for finance, certainly, than his roaring lucky old father had ever had, and the things he began to do then ended by doubling—no, more than doubling—the value of his holdings.

Then the baby was born, in enormous elegance in New York, I had three doctors but no easier time than before, and they shook their heads at me, but thank God, it was a boy. Ah, that meant everything. "My son," said James, "my son——"

"He looks just like his daddy," said the nurses, and Jimmy roared at them.

"He looks like an angry baby," said James, pretending not to be proud. But things were easier between us after Jimmy's birth and little by little we managed to begin covering over the horrors, or even turning them into jokes.

Dear, dear James! When people say "The Twenties" now they think of flappers and the Charleston and Scott Fitzgerald and prohibition and Flaming Youth. Certainly all those things were true. But the Twenties were still very formal in many ways, and James, who had been a young man in the Nineties, took formality naturally. When we had the castle open and running full swing, in the late spring or in the fall, we had an inside staff of fifteen—butler and chef and three footmen, upstairs maids, kitchen maids, my maid, Jimmy's nurse, James's valet, beside the outside people, two or three chauffeurs, the gardeners and the grooms. I had a social secretary in New York to keep my lists straight and write invitations (by hand, of course); she skittered around corners with her mouth tucked in and the butler hated her. Miss Dyer, her name was. She was the last of an old family and much more entitled, by birth, to a place in society than I was. As far as Prohibition went, James rather ignored it. He'd given orders to lay down wine and whisky in the cellars of the castle, and there was plenty of it still there when I sold the place finally, in 1934, to the Benedictines. He had to get gin from a bootlegger, though. It had never occurred to him that he might entertain people who drank gin.

People say the Fifties are like the Twenties, a boom time again, a postwar decade. They may be, for young people, I don't know. But the Twenties I knew haven't left an echo behind. All that way of life has vanished, and what they call "society" today is hardly even a caricature of it. Oh, I don't miss it. I wouldn't (I don't think I would) want to live it again, though there are satisfactions in order and ritual and formal obligation for people of my age. But in any case, it all died for me when James did. That was in the spring of '29. He knew he was dying and told me, at last, when he had to tell me. Oh God.

I surely don't need to write down that he died with the utmost courage—and courtesy. He wanted to go into a hospital because he thought it must be very difficult for me to see him in pain; but I wouldn't let him. He arranged with the doctors and the nurses so that the best half hour he had each day was saved for the time when Jimmy came home from the park at the end of the afternoon and he got through that time without showing any pain until three days before he died. Jimmy would sit and tell him about school, or about a game he and his friends had played under the watchful eyes of the young man who took a group of them out every afternoon, or about a party he'd been to, and James would laugh and chat and talk nonsense with him and try to keep his eyes from devouring the child whose seventh birthday he would never see. I always left them alone for that time. Then, about six, I'd come in and shoo Jimmy upstairs for his bath and a nursery supper. James was wet with sweat sometimes, barely able to speak. But Jimmy never knew. Then the nurse and the valet took over and I'd go and dress for dinner with him in something soft and pretty and come back and drink a cocktail while James pretended to sip a glass of sherry and then we'd have dinner. That got harder and harder for him. Finally we had it served in his sitting room. Finally I ate alone. He couldn't eat and it distressed him to think of me having to watch him while I dined.

He wanted me to go out. I did, once in a while. In fact, there were times when it felt like getting out of prison, times when I'd come out of the house bursting for laughter and conversation and gaiety, when I wanted to dismiss the car and *run*, not even walk—— It never lasted long. I saw more first acts of plays and excused myself and went home in the middle than anyone except a drama critic. Music was more satisfactory. I found out the little I know about it then. To be fair, the credit must go to James's sister, Mrs. Ford, who thought the spring series at Carnegie Hall would be "appropriate" or something for me to attend. I made a face, but I went, and the music spoke to me as it never had before. How pleased James was when I told him that I'd found something new! So I went back for him as well as for myself. He wanted me to go to dinners, too—"You mustn't lose your friends, my dear," he said to me very seriously, but I avoided it whenever I could. I was just too selfish and not well bred enough to be able to make conversation with people I didn't care for when my heart was breaking. I had no comfort but him. My mother came down and stayed with me at the end. I was grateful, but she had drifted so far in such an odd direction by then—she was a devout Theosophist—that it was rather like entertaining a sweet but slightly mad ghost. Jimmy loved her though, so that was all right.

And then James died and at the time—he hadn't slept for days or eaten for weeks—it was only a blessing. I knew that, but I went all to pieces, screaming and shouting and walking the corridors like Lady Macbeth, appearing and disappearing, frightening the maids into fits. Mrs. Ford was absolutely livid with rage at me—Couldn't I at least have *tried* to behave like a lady?—but my mother made contact with reality as she always did when it was necessary and made them leave me alone. She sent Jimmy to Mary's in Boston after the funeral and took me off to Hot Springs and made me learn to play golf. She walked around the course with me, gently explaining the tenets of Theosophy. That was when she cast back to my youth, too, and astounded me so about my abortive college career. After a bit I felt well enough to ride and she sat on the verandah and rocked and chatted with people, usually managing to work in a good word for Mrs. Besant or Krishnamurti, and after a month when she took me home I had stopped screaming and crying myself to sleep every night.

But I couldn't stand the house and I couldn't stand the castle. Mary suggested I come to Nantucket with them, it would "be different" for me. She meant that after the vulgar fleshpots of New York a little plain Bostonian living would do me good. It was different, all right. The big old house had never had electricity put in and the one bath had been installed in a huge room with four doors. Every time I went in I ran around bolting those doors lest some jolly member of the family pop in on my ablutions; and then I never remembered to unbolt them. But it certainly was good for Jimmy, if not for me. He ran wild on the dunes and the beaches and bossed the little girls shamefully. They adored him. I wonder if Lorraine remembers anything of that summer? She couldn't have been more than five, if she was that. But she followed Jimmy doggedly wherever her legs would take her.

Well, I left Jimmy there and went. As I remember, I took the North Cape cruise so that I wouldn't have to decide anything—how long to stay here, where to go next, what to see. I wanted Mother to come, but she wouldn't. "You have to strike out by yourself," she said to me. "The longer you wait, the harder it will be. I learned that after your father died. Mary moved in on me and wouldn't let me alone. It was before the girls were born, of course, and she plagued me to come back to Boston with her—you wouldn't remember. You were abroad." (So I had been—on Capri.) "Anyway, I knew I had to do something to keep her from running my life and so one day I just packed up and left."

"Where did you go?" I asked, fascinated.

"California," said my mother calmly. "I sent Mary a wire when I was on the train. Oh, she was wild! It was a wonderful trip. There are Burney cousins in San Francisco, you know, and I called them when I got there. They were delighted to see me. And I met such interesting people! One woman was starting a shop in Carmel and wanted me to use your father's insurance money to come in with her. I thought about it, but in the end I decided against it, California is really quite a ways away. Indian things, she was planning to sell, and I understand from Alice Burney that she's done quite well, though Mary always maintained it was a hoax. But I learned quite a bit about Indian ceremonials from her, the dances and all, and I went to Santa Fe, and to Taos—— My, it was interesting! I wrote it all up for one of the Theosophist publications, didn't I ever show it to you?"

"Never. I never even knew you'd gone, Mum."

"No, you were away. And then it makes Mary so mad I don't talk about it much. But you do what I tell you. You go off by yourself. I'll come another time."

She never did. There was always a reason not to. I wonder if she thought I'd got too grand for her? She'd loved James dearly, but she would never come down to a formal dinner when she was staying with us, she always had a tray upstairs when the butler got the gold service plates out and Miss Dyer started writing place cards and fussing with the table arrangements and the bank sent my diamonds home from the vault. (I never wore pearls again.) I wish she had come! She would have enjoyed it so, she always kept that open, childlike curiosity of hers. But she didn't. I had to go alone and make my new life up as I went along, telling myself, Remember, now, you're a rich American widow. You're thirty-four and a rich widow. If you're not sure what to do next, do what a rich widow would do.

It's a horrible way to put it, isn't it? I don't know that I would have thought of myself so at any other time in my life. Why did I do it then, why do I use the word now? I think because I know now—and felt then—that there is something contemptible about the kind of life which I succeeded in making up for myself. I was indulging myself, amusing myself, living by no standards except what pleased me. After a while this becomes very hard work. One must erect one's whims into categorical imperatives and one's taste into canons of morality, and then frivolity becomes really exhausting. Besides, I could not quite believe in myself. The flaw in the world which the war had exposed, the crippling in me that I owed to Gerald—they almost masked each other, but not quite. I could not forget that once nothing in the world had been impossible for me, nothing too big, nothing out of reach. Against all odds I had got free, I had struggled and won. And now—now I was free, I seemed in command, but I would not have dared again to undertake the struggles of the past. I distracted myself well, I was gay and entertained good company and traveled and stayed at smart resorts, but after a while a faint uneasiness traveled with me and sometimes I sensed a possibility of boredom in being a rich widow.

Still, I stayed one for five years. I stayed rich partly by accident, because the bank, settling James's estate in the summer of 1929, sold his equities out at the top of the market and put the proceeds into government bonds and annuities and other storm cellars. I didn't pay any attention, but the trust officers and all the vice-presidents and the president and the chairman of the board were bound and determined that the Greene millions were going to be safe as houses, and safe they were. I lost some, of course, but so little compared to what most people lost that I got to be rather ashamed of being so well off. As for being a widow—who was to take James's place? One way or another, I'd been married very thoroughly; and very young, too. Marriage meant James and not-James meant not-marriage for a long, long time. This was one thing that I was completely serious about.

I won't pretend, though, that I didn't have affairs. I did, and enjoyed them. It was self-indulgence, yes, but you see I hadn't had time to be a belle when I was a girl before I married, and my five years of belle-dom all over Europe and the United States were, in a way, therapeutic. I got rid of any hankering for wild oats and frivolity then and it's never bothered me again. I wasn't indiscreet. Mrs. Ford gnashed her teeth at me, but though there was gossip aplenty, it was good-natured. Actually, my name was "linked" (as they said then) with that of so many men, some of whom I'd never even met, that in the end the whole thing reduced itself to absurdity. Besides, I had Jimmy to think of, and James's name, and I put them first, far ahead of my self-indulgences.

Once when I was in Antibes Gerald tried to see me. I had one moment of panic and then I remembered who I was—a rich widow, able to indulge my whims, responsible to no one but myself. Still, though I was consumed with curiosity, I thought, Better not, and I sent word that I was engaged— I wanted to be rude enough to ensure his not coming back, for I could not trust the creature who ran my life, I could not be sure that one day she might not—whimsically, frivolously—agree to see him, find him attractive—— No. I won't go on. He was quite angry, the butler said. I stood behind the blind in one of the second-floor rooms and watched him come out the door of the villa and stride over to his car. It was a Bugatti, so he didn't seem to be doing too badly. Though of course he'd only have come to see me in the best he could beg, borrow or steal. He looks old, I told myself; but his back, his profile, that remembered walk, his hands on the wheel as he swung the car round too fast—they made my heart turn over and the ache of unshed tears told me what a pathetic thing my life was then. I kept my ears pricked for his name but I didn't hear it, so I guess he left Antibes.

Then in 1934 all my self-indulgent nonsense ended and I got married again to John Florence Delacruyz Belchamber. We'd known each other forever—well, anyway, since the war—but the first Mrs. Belchamber didn't die until 1933. I remembered her as lovely with a fey, drifty quality, and I was right. She drifted into a nursing home, poor dear, after a baby born dead. John went to see her faithfully, and sometimes she was coherent and anxious to get well and planning what to do with the gardens when she came home. He couldn't bear to tell her he'd let the place in Hampshire and she'd plan and plan. Then when he went again she'd be sucking her fingers, three years old. There was no reason why she shouldn't live to be eighty, they told him cheerfully, and we talked and talked about a divorce for him, which was frightfully difficult then and would very probably have meant the end of his career at the Bar, and whether if there was a divorce she would ever know. We went round and round in circles, first one of us on one side and then the other. Then one day in

January 1933 she got away from the place where she was staying, which was a big old house and rather remote. She'd never "needed restraint" and John had felt she was happiest in the country. It was lovely country; but not easy to find her in for, even distraite, she was a good countrywoman. When they did, she was ten miles away and dead of exposure.

John was very sensible about it. It happened at a time when he and I had reached a decision that he could not divorce her, but we kept reaching that decision periodically, it didn't affect our relationship particularly. He'd been at Davos for the skiing over Christmas, and so had Jimmy and I— I put it that way because that's the way it was. We stayed at different places and were very careful. Soon after he got back to England he went to see her, and it had all been quite normally abnormal. She wanted a dog, why couldn't she have a dog, then they could go for lovely walks together. John said of course she could have a dog, it was a fine idea, only it might be a little difficult for her to begin training a dog till the weather was better. Suppose they waited till spring and in the meantime decided which breed she wanted, he'd write to a kennel or two—— He knew she'd forget all about it, that was one of the troubles, her span of attention was so terribly short. She'd been very pleased about it all and he'd left her quite happy. But of course the good times never lasted, and she began to get restless and then, a few days later, she was gone. Poor, poor soul! He telephoned me at Davos to tell me, his voice was shocked and saddened, but of course she had died for him really years before and he could not mourn her as a man would mourn a wife.

Such a dear man! We fitted together like right-hand and left-hand glove. He had a great manner. When he went on the bench in 1936 he looked like the majesty of the law personified—noble, leonine head, massive shoulders, the robe sweeping down from them, and the top curl of his wig quite six and a half feet from the floor. But behind the manner was the dearest, funniest, most delightful companion I've ever had. We had always been friends, had always known that in a roomful of people we were on the same side, had always been able to talk together elliptically. But in the summer of 1930 when I was in England with Jimmy we met again, and—I don't know— everything was so easy and sweet—— He came to tea to have Jimmy introduced to him and we got laughing so hard, all three of us, that the tears ran down our cheeks and Jimmy, leaning against his shoulder, gave him a lapful of cake crumbs. Knowing the usual English attitude toward the manners of American children, I had a moment of horror, but John just pulled out a handkerchief and wiped Jimmy's paws for him and hoisted him up next to him on the sofa, and gave him his watch. "Mind you don't dip it in the tea," he said, and this delighted Jimmy, who had just been reading in *Alice* about the Mad Tea Party, and the watch was a repeater and Jimmy fiddled and fiddled and finally got it to strike, and by that time he was John's slave and adorer.

He was a serious child—not solemn, but reserved and thoughtful and with something of his father's quiet watchfulness; except with John. John he trusted utterly, with John he had all the boyhood things he could have missed so easily. He hated to make a fool of himself in front of anyone else, even me. But with John he'd indulge in laughing fits and outrageous romps and boisterous games, John gave him lessons in how to kick a football or hold a cricket bat. In the in-between years before John and I could marry, Jim was at school in Switzerland. I ached every time I left him there, but I knew it would have been a wrong thing to keep him with me, a hotel child, an appendage. And I *couldn't* settle, not then. But we always had his vacations together and, as at Davos, John often managed to spend a part of the holidays near us, so that Jim had that kind, undemanding, warm, jovial presence as a recurrence to count on in his life.

Then John was free and we knew we could marry. I came to England in February and we began to settle how things should be. I realized that I was becoming middle-aged because I enjoyed the planning and was not in the least impatient for the plans to happen before it was right for them to happen. We agreed that I must go back to America and see that everything was in order there and wind up all that I could. I saw a house agent and set him looking for a place for me to let in the fall, and though John would have loved to have Jimmy go to his old school, he quite understood how I felt about having him with me for a little while and told me how to go about entering him at Westminster as a day boy.

So I came home. How funny! I see that when I was talking "in the past" I said, "I went back to America." But now I must truly be an

American again—I was always a hybrid and never remembered, as I did not remember just now, to say "autumn" instead of "fall." I came home, then, to wind up my affairs, in 1933 just in time for the bank closings and the business collapses and Frank Roosevelt singing at me (he always sang his speeches, not spoke them) that I had nothing to fear but fear itself. It was indeed a dreadful time. When I told my dear friends at the bank what I wanted to do, they began fainting away in droves. They wouldn't touch the trust funds, but I made them put some of my own money that James had left to me myself back in the market, for it was perfectly clear that either *everything* was going, bonds and insurance and annuities and all, or else things had to get better, so again almost by accident we bought back at the bottom as we had sold at the top.

I enjoyed the battles about money, but I didn't enjoy in the least dealing with the actual physical remnants of my life with James. There was a lot to do. I'd left both the New York house and the castle standing much as they had been, with caretakers when I was away, and of course I'd been back a number of times, though never for very long. Now I had to close them, get rid of clothes, furniture, cars, the horses I'd kept—and papers and papers and papers. Once the executors had gone through them I'd just left them to gather dust. I put both places on the market, but there wasn't a nibble. Still, I had to clear them out so they could be sold when things picked up.

I did what I could in New York during the spring, and then moved out to the castle in June. Jimmy's school found a young man to travel with him and he came to me there, and Mary sent me a nice boy from Harvard who looked after him that summer, riding and swimming with him and taking him off for a couple of weeks to Maine. Mrs. Ford was suffering from arthritis, thank God, and though she called me up twice a week and sent an embarrassed young lawyer out several times, she was not underfoot. I told her she could have anything in the world she wanted out of the place, or take the whole thing over for the taxes until Jimmy came of age, but that wasn't the point, she didn't want the castle, but it was maddening for her to think of me disposing of it. Mother moved in and sat on the terrace reading, and kept me up to date with Theosophist circles at meals, but she was growing very frail, almost more of an aura than a person;

and it was I and I alone who had to tie up my past life in bales and decide what to burn and forget and what to take with me to another continent.

Thank God it was so for one day in July at ten o'clock in the morning I began on the drawer of the file in James's study that contained correspondence with people whose names began with V. He had had rather an acrid exchange with one of the Vanderbilts, which I put in the carton for burning, and there was an inch-thick stack of communications from someone in Seattle named Vernon about some of the timberland. I was sure the lawyers must know all about it, but I put it aside for them to check on anyway, and next came a folder marked Villeneuve. When I opened it I was confronted with a photograph of a little girl. She was a very pretty little girl, in a white dress and a little veil and wreath. I turned it over, puzzled, and saw that on the back was written, "Claire, sept ans, le premier mai, 1928."

It was my daughter, dressed for her first communion.

The light shimmered and went out. When I could see again my throat was sore from not moaning, but I was still holding the picture. There was a letter under it, in a vile French hand on thin paper, and it seemed to take me hours to decipher it. When I managed to read it, it turned out to be a yearly report on Claire's progress.

James had known all along where she was, with whom, when she made her communion, when she started school; known and not told me. Known and let me believe that she had vanished beyond reach. I should have known, I should have known, but I hadn't. Even when I thought I at last understood him, James had still kept this secret. I had thought he would want her hidden from himself as well as me, I had thought her name taboo and unmentionable, but I had again underestimated James's sense of duty and his strength, just as I had before, and before, and before. He had taken her from me and cut the connection between us, and *therefore* he had felt himself responsible for her. God knows what it must have cost him to read those letters every year! But it had been his duty, and so he had done it.

"Bright, affectionate," said the report. "Not, perhaps, the best of scholars, but of a sweet nature——" I couldn't make out who was writing to whom, the name at the beginning of the letter, M.

Villeneuve, meant nothing, and I couldn't read the signature. But underneath was the carbon of a typewritten letter from James thanking the addressee for passing on word about the child, and I realized that of course he had used an agent so that his name would not come into it. He would never have been so irresponsible as to tempt those who might be susceptible to the idea of blackmail by letting them know how many millions they were dealing with. I worked it out, finally. There were two agents. Every year, apparently, the curé of the village where Claire had been placed had written to a M. Villeneuve in Brussels and M. Villeneuve forwarded the letter to James. They were all there, the record of my child's growth from 1921 to 1929. In the latter year they were terminated by a letter to M. Villeneuve from James saying that he would be unable to receive any more reports. It was written about six weeks before he died.

What would you have done? I stood up, trembling, with all the letters in my hands and went to the telephone and gave orders to get me a passage to Europe on the first fast boat. She was twelve and a half now. I could remember myself at twelve being dragged reluctantly toward womanhood, furious, violent, unreconciled to the world I could never believe I had been born to. How much more must Claire feel this! For her, it was true! She was what so many angry children have dreamed themselves to be, the child of other-where and other-folk, caught in a net of mediocrity. How could I not have looked for her before! I cried to myself. How could I have been so thoughtless, so selfish, so stupid as not to realize that of course James would keep his eye on her! How could I have believed what James said instead of what James was! I felt the kind of shattering grief and guilt one feels in nightmares. I had deserted my child not once, but twice. Without stopping to think, in the grip of agony, I felt only that I must find her, find her, find her, snatch her back, and heal the wound that had crippled me.

Fortunately, a quick trip to Europe was the kind of thing that all my friends and relations quite expected of me. Jimmy was perfectly well looked after between Mother and his Harvard mentor, and I sailed on the *Aquitania* at three days' notice with no luggage but a couple of suitcases. I simply hadn't brought enough frocks to sit at the captain's table, so I put it about that my doctor had insisted I get away for a brief trip because I'd been overworking, and that I was supposed to rest. I didn't talk to anyone except a few young people who were much more interested in each other than in me, but who were gay and amusing and got in the habit of coming to have cocktails on the terrace that went with my suite—I hadn't meant to be so grand, but in the summer of 1933 that was what was easiest to get on short notice, the Royal Suite, or its equivalent. The rest of the time I lay out on my terrace alone, reading over the curé's letters, looking at the pictures of Claire, and scheming. Why on earth shouldn't I adopt a Belgian child, a war orphan, perhaps? Who was to say me nay? John? Of course I'd have to tell John more than that, but I could certainly manage, I was sure I could manage. My dear Claire had charmed the curé and surely now, four years later, she must be prettier and more charming than ever. I could hardly sleep on that crossing, I was so anxious to dock at Cherbourg and start running toward my child.

I debated whether or not to go to M. Villeneuve in Brussels, or direct to Claire, but there really wasn't a choice. I had to see her. I had never seen her. Once I had, once I had feasted my eyes and fallen into chance conversation with her, once we had begun to make friends, I could go back to Brussels and dispatch M. Villeneuve to the rescue. I had her picture, I had the name of the people who had adopted her——

Feeling, somehow, that I had best cover my tracks a bit till I knew where I was on this first surreptitious journey, I went to Antwerp to hire a car and drive south. We came to the village I was seeking in the early afternoon and I had myself driven to the Mairie and went in to inquire for the farm of the Morels.

There was no one named Morel in the village.

Would you have taken it as a warning and turned back then? I didn't; but I must have staggered, for the hired chauffeur, whom I'd brought in to get the directions, took my arm. "When did they leave?" I asked.

Never. They had never been there.

"It's impossible!" I said shrilly. "They were here four years ago, they have always been here, where is the farm of Morel, I will pay you whatever is necessary for the information."

But there was no way, there were no Morels. I had lost her again.

Someone had lied. Who? I stood thinking rapidly. Villeneuve, Villeneuve must have lied, to hold up money, somehow, or send it somewhere else, he had given the wrong family name or the wrong village. Why? I couldn't work it out, but he must have seen some advantage in keeping the knowledge to himself. Perhaps he had planned to sell it to James, and James had died first—— It must be another village, I thought, for the curé's letters had not been headed and no envelopes were in the files to show postmarks.

And yet, since I was there—— "Where will I find the curé?" I asked. There was just a chance——

They directed the chauffeur and we found the little stone vicarage next to the church, crouched under the bell tower, but the curé wasn't there. His housekeeper was all for keeping me out and the chauffeur was all for driving me on to Liége where we could get a decent meal, and coming back, but I wouldn't budge. Finally the old woman let me into the parlor, which had a dank stuffiness that got into my bones and my sinus cavities and led me to judge that the Goddess Pneumonia still had devotees in the land of Belgium, and the chauffeur went off grumbling to get what he could at the inn. He was a Fleming in Walloon country and hating it. And I waited and waited and waited. The car came back and I thought I would be more comfortable if I went and sat in it, but I was afraid to give up the beachhead I had established in the curé's parlor.

Finally he rode up wobbling on a bicycle. There was a movie, a year or two ago, in which Fernandel played a priest with a bicycle. I don't know whether it was humor or horror that made me hoot like a loon when I saw him, but at any rate, he was the image of the priest in that Belgian village. I could hear the old woman telling him all about me, furiously. Finally he came in and greeted me quite politely.

I had made up my mind what to do, waiting. I handed him Claire's last picture and said, "I am looking for this child." He was looking at me as he took it, it wasn't till seconds later that he looked down at the photograph. He preserved his expression very carefully, but my heart leaped up. Why, unless he knew her, did he need to preserve it at all?

"Why do you come to me, madame?" he asked, and then I handed him the letter.

He just glanced at it and folded it up and handed it back to me with the picture. If he'd known I'd never been able to puzzle out the signature—but he didn't. He said, "The girl is well and happy. If you would like me to continue the reports, I shall be glad to write to M. Villeneuve, as before. She had scarlet fever two years ago, but recovered perfectly. Since then her health has been excellent."

"She has not, however, been adopted by a family named Morel."

"She has been adopted by most responsible people who treat her quite as their daughter."

"I am anxious to see her," I said, sounding as unanxious as I could, which I'm afraid wasn't very.

"I'm afraid that's impossible."

"Ah," I said calmly. "But I come from her mother."

Then we had an eye-duel. He stood, I sat, and we tried facing each other down. Alas, he was as stubborn as I. "Her mother," he said finally, "might have remembered her before."

"That is very possible," I said, for the one thing I wasn't going to do was to lose my temper and defend myself. "As it happens, there were many reasons why her mother has not been able to act until now, but for the child's sake, perhaps we can let the past lie. I am here now."

"To do what, madame?"

"As I said, to see the child."

He thought for a long time and then he shook his head. "I am sorry," he said. "I regret your disappointment, and her mother's, but it is still impossible. It will be best that she is not disturbed."

I said, "Does your church give you the right to come between a mother and her child?"

"Certainly," said the curé. "In any case, madame, are you of my church? More important, is the child's mother?"

Then we had another eye-duel. I lost because I had begun to panic. He was going to save Claire's soul from me, I had run aground on the rocks of theology. I went sick and shaky inside and I could hear my voice saying what I didn't want it to say, threatening, pleading. He listened and grew more and more adamant. "No, madame. No, madame."

I was trembling and crying, "You will hear from your bishop," I kept repeating. "You will be ordered to let me see her!"

276

CHAPTER TWENTY-TWO

He said, "Very well, madame. When I am ordered you shall see her." And so I stumbled out in total defeat.

Well, I saw her finally. I went to Brussels and introduced myself to M. Villeneuve, who was a lawyer and grew colder and colder as I told him my story. To burst in that way on Père Amedée, unannounced, with no papers, no preparation, no negotiation, to threaten a priest with the power of his own church which was not my church—there was hardly a sin in the decalogue of the avocat that I had not committed. M. Villeneuve agreed stiffly to investigate the situation and attempt a rapprochement, but he said over and over that he could promise nothing, he seemed to enjoy saying it. I thrust a bundle of francs at him to make him stop, and he pushed them back distastefully, giving the impression that he was resisting a bribe. Finally we settled on the modest, usual sum for which he would undertake to look into this unfortunate situation. I paid him and he stood up and said that he would get in touch with me when he had something to lay before me. I asked him please to hurry, to telephone, to go at once in person, I would pay all expenses, and he stood perfectly silent until I ran down and then he bowed me out; and once more I was all alone in Brussels.

I stood in the street and raged. If hate and disgust and fury and loathing could still destroy a city as in the days of the Prophets, the Boulevard Adolphe Max would have started to crumble about me. What am I to do? I thought and there was nothing to do. London was so close, my dearest John was so near, and I couldn't even let him know where I was. I'd written before I left that I was going away for a rest, but I'd told John that I was going west to the Canadian Rockies. No, I would have to stay in Brussels and wait. The curé would trust no one but Villeneuve, if indeed he would trust *him*, and Villeneuve might negotiate for days or weeks. In the meantime I was sentenced to my hotel suite. I could see myself there, waiting, growing impatient, growing a little mad, reaching for the telephone, calling—calling whom? I didn't know, but surely my imagination would trick me into believing that someone could help and I would call, and the someone would only hinder.

So I went back to the hotel and sent for the manager and asked him to provide me with the best and most thorough guide who could be found in Brussels, and that very afternoon I started my sight-seeing, an occupation that I have never since undertaken any-where. Miles of churches, acres of painting, the guildhouses, the old squares and the new suburbs— I walked and walked and walked until I had to take three pairs of shoes to a cobbler, the heels were run over. I went out early every morning and telephoned the hotel before lunch to see if there was a message, and there wasn't. I went back for an hour's rest after lunch, and there was no message, and I called again in the afternoon—no message—and that was my life for nine mortal days.

Then one afternoon Villeneuve was waiting to see me. I took him upstairs to my rooms and poured him an apéritif and we sat down—— If I would sign an agreement promising not to reveal anything to Claire of her background, nor to upset her, I would be allowed to visit her. If this visit seemed to go off quietly, I could come again in a year.

I put down the glass of vermouth I was holding and stared at him.

"You see, madame," he said, "you have no legal rights in this child at all. Legally, you must realize that you are begging for a favor. The girl is the adopted daughter of—of a family whose name I am not yet permitted to tell you. She believes herself to be their child. She has had a Catholic upbringing and is a communicant. M. le Curé, I must tell you, has been very reluctant to consider any arrangement at all. Frankly, he is doubtful that you could see Claire without disturbing her in her present life where she is quite content. He spoke of the blessings of a quiet heart, madame, and in addition, he has the force of the law on his side."

I started to speak, but he held up his hand. "I prevailed upon him to offer this concession by appealing to his sense of duty. Has he, I asked, the right to deny the child an opportunity which may turn out to her good, if no spiritual danger ensues? The—family which I may still best call Morel are worthy people, but not well to do, and even in our countryside the difficult times are being felt. Claire's dowry, the farm which came to the Morels with her, will ensure a marriage for her, but not a grand one. Perhaps something might be added, another farm purchased or a small fund set up in the rentes. Père Amedée would not feel that he could deny this chance to Claire if her peace of mind were in no way disturbed by your visits."

"So I am to buy the right to see her," I said. "These are the terms of a procurer!"

M. Villeneuve's face grew flinty. He put down his glass and stood up.

"Don't go!" I gasped. "I—I had no choice! I couldn't keep her! I only learned where she was when I found the letters three weeks ago! Please, wait, let me think, let me speak, please——"

"I suggest you come to my chambers tomorrow, madame, when you have considered the situation and can speak with more calm."

"No, please, M. Villeneuve, listen to me, I know I spoke rudely, badly, it was shock, I apologize! But one visit a year! Not to know each other! To come as a stranger to my own child! Oh, M. Villeneuve, it's too much!"

"It is all that is possible," he said. But something must have touched him a little, for he added rapidly and a little guiltily, "It is all that is possible *now*. Mme. Greene, I advise you to accept this offer. What can you lose? At least you will see Claire. And I will see that reports are sent, as before. Who knows? By next year or the year after, things may change. Anything is possible."

"Do you think so?" I said. "Do you think so? I'll be much closer now, M. Villeneuve, I am to be married again and I shall be living in London. Something may be done, don't you think, when I am settled there?"

"Slowly," he said, "patiently, bit by bit, perhaps. Who can say? But you must move gently, madame. The first hurdle is this first visit. You must be calm, calm. Can you do that, do you think? Can you speak quietly to a little stranger? I suggested to Père Amedée that Claire—and the family as well—be told that you had been in some way connected with the relief mission of M. Hoover during the war and that you are now interested in meeting and talking with some of the families that you helped in those dark days. This family was helped then. Can you play such a role, madame, interested but impersonal?"

"Any role," I said. He looked at me for a while, not believing me, but what did I care? It was not he but the curé I had to fear. Villeneuve could dislike and distrust me all he wanted as long as he liked and trusted my money. So unwillingly he drew out the agreement for me to sign. I pretended to read it through in order not to shock him, but all I could think was that now, somehow, I would be able to have my child. I would cheat, steal, kidnap—— Oh, not right away, of course not. This time I would be good as gold. But soon. But soon. Next year I would be marrying John and with him all the magic irresistible power of the English law and somehow, I was sure, this would bring Claire back to me.

Of all the fools that I have been, that fool was the darkest. Not the most foolish, the one who loved Gerald was that. But the one who was wrong most grievously, who did the worst harm, who conspired blindly with herself toward the most tragic ends, was the one who wrote Diana Greene on that paper just twenty-three years ago. Because——

23

The door creaked, opening. Startled, Mrs. Belchamber looked up and her pen left a trail of ink next to the last word she had written. Lorraine came in and shut the door behind her.

"What——" Mrs. Belchamber began, and then changed this to "Well!" Her voice softened from its first asperity at being interrupted. "Well, my dear, where have you been? I couldn't make out from Tucker what had happened. You're just in time for lunch. Do you want some sherry?"

But Lorraine, leaning against the door, seemed not to hear. "What a lot you've written, Aunt Di," she said irrelevantly. "Your book is nearly full."

Slowly, carefully, Mrs. Belchamber put the cap on her pen and closed the thick notebook on the writing stand. Only when she had taken her glasses off did she look at her niece. "Come and sit down," she said. Lorraine pushed herself away from the door with an effort. "Something has happened," said her aunt. "Something is wrong. What is it?"

"Herbert tried to kill himself," said Lorraine. The flat words rang in the silence, and she sat down on a chair by the window. "Well, at least you didn't know. It's in the papers. One of the nightmares I had, driving out, was that you would have seen the papers, or Hilda would, out in the kitchen, and say something to the children. But it seems I got here first. He stabbed himself. He's in the hospital. The doctors say he'll be all right."

Her aunt's hand moved up to her mouth in a curious, wavering gesture, the distressed and frightened movement of an old woman. "He stabbed himself," she said softly. At once, recovering herself, she went on more loudly, "Lorraine, you—— My God, I'd as soon see the papers, they couldn't be more abrupt! Why? Where? Is he still in Germany?"

"He's here. He flew in yesterday. I——"

"Have you seen him?"

"This morning before I came out."

"But what—but why? It can't be—— Is it money?"

"Money?"

"Yes, of course, money," said her aunt. "Money, money, the stuff we live on! Is he bankrupt?"

"Why no, I don't think so. I mean—I told him I was going to leave him." There was another abyss of silence. Across it Mrs. Belchamber threw a sudden loop of incredulous laughter. "I'm doing this so badly!" cried Lorraine. "I'm so sorry, Aunt Di! It doesn't seem real to me either. He came back to the apartment last night, he'd flown in in the morning and gone to the office, I missed him then, I didn't know he was back at all. I told him I—I couldn't live with him again, be his wife. There was a little knife on the bar that I'd been using to cut limes for drinks. We talked, I knew he was upset, but I didn't think—— Anyway, I left, in the end, to come back here. He picked up the knife and followed me out to the elevator and— and he stabbed himself. In the chest. What saved him was luck, or anatomy—he missed the heart and the big artery. The knife hit a rib once, and then went into the lung. That's serious but not fatal. The doorman got an ambulance——"

"Lorraine, Lorraine! For pity's sake! Wait a minute, never mind the doorman and the ambulance! I don't understand one word you're saying. Why did this happen? Why are you proposing to leave your husband? What's been going on? You've been here with me all summer and you've never said a word! What's happened between you? Is there someone else?"

"There's no one else," said Lorraine at once, and at once licked the lie off her lips. Her aunt's face was white, her dark eyes burned in a mask that looked every year of her age. Does she believe me? thought Lorraine—but the mask had been wiped clean of expression by shock. "It seemed to me I couldn't live with him," she said helplessly, "that's all. What can I say? I didn't mean to hide things from you. I was just trying to find my way."

"You seem to have done a very poor job."

Now it was Lorraine's turn to be shocked into silence, to stare.

"I'm sorry," said Mrs. Belchamber and covered her eyes with her hand. "Forgive me. I didn't mean that."

"It's all right," said Lorraine. "I suppose it's true."

"Never mind. True or not, it was a stupid thing to say. But leave it for a minute, we must think. Have you talked to a lawyer? Have you been in touch with Herbert's partner, what's his name?"

"Cole. No, I——"

"You must. What's this about the papers? Should there be a statement to them? If you haven't talked to a lawyer, I'll call Duncan right away. What about the reporters, have they been after you? Then we'd better make sure no one can get into the grounds." She picked up the little bell that she always kept by her and shook it vigorously. For the minute or two before Tucker bustled in, she sat staring in front of her, paying no attention to her niece, while her lips moved, framing words, testing phrases. Her orders came out crisply—to have the gates closed on the drives, to set the gardeners and stable boys patrolling against trespassers. "Answer the phone yourself," she ended. "If anyone wants Mrs. de Koning, she's away. You'll take a message, but she's not here. And put a call in to Mr. Duncan at the Rector number. I suppose he's out to lunch now, there are no worse lunchers than lawyers, they sit for hours telling each other about their triumphs while their clients suffer to provide them with new opportunities. Leave word for him to call when he comes in. At once, it's urgent. Yes, Tucker, I'm sure you want to know what's urgent. There's been a very sad accident, that's what's urgent, and that's all that anyone needs to know. Lunch? Not now. In half an hour. But tell them to send in the sherry. No, tell them today I want whisky and ice."

"Tucker," said Lorraine, "are the children all right?"

"Why yes, Mrs. de Koning. Jane didn't eat much lunch, Hilda said, but that's no surprise. She put them down for their naps half an hour ago."

"Thank you." She leaned back and shut her eyes and Tucker, after one shrewd look, went out. "She'll read all about it," said Lorraine, still with her eyes shut. "Or at least she'll read what they print. We could have told her. They got a photograph of me last night, and the hospital told them he'd recover. The rest of the story is what they had in the files, mostly what they ran about Faith two years ago. Do you suppose they'll really chase me out here? I suppose

I should have thought of that. You can't live in a state of siege. I'd better go back to town."

"My dear, it won't last, someone in Newport will create a more spectacular scandal and distract them. And Duncan will put the fear of God and the libel laws in them, if anyone can. But about Herbert's office——"

"His secretary called me at eight this morning in hysterics, she'd bought the paper on the way to the subway and opened it up and there it was staring at her. I know I must talk to Mr. Cole—— What can I say? The hospital can tell him all I know. Herbert wouldn't speak to me this morning. Of course it's hard for him to speak at all with that injury to the lung. He's in an oxygen tent most of the time. They took it away when I came, and he lay and hated me with his eyes. The nurse stood there and chirruped at him like a robin calling for rain, and I talked nonsense, I kept telling him he was going to be all right. Then I couldn't stand it and I left. They smuggled me out the back way and I came back here. Half the time I drove ninety trying to beat the papers, half the time I thought how much worse everything would be if I cracked the car up, and I drove forty. I kept looking in the mirror to see if anyone was after me. You don't want to hear this. I'm just babbling. Oh, here are the drinks, do you want water with yours?"

"Please. That's all right, Charles, just leave the tray," said Mrs. Belchamber to the houseman. "We'll fix our own cocktails." She waited till he went out. "My dear," she said, "don't misunderstand me. But you've led rather a sheltered life. I—— Other people have had to go through this kind of thing, poor Faith had a bad dose of it, as you say. I don't—I wouldn't minimize it, but it isn't the end of the world. You'll find that people will understand, and even sympathize."

Lorraine handed a glass to her aunt and took one herself. "Shall I?" she asked, sipping it. "I wonder. Oh, they sympathize, you're right about that, they couldn't be kinder. It's the worst thing of all."

"Child——"

"Those kind, worried, interested faces!" Holding her glass she walked restlessly to the window, to the mirror over the mantel, and there stopped and peered at herself. "Do I look any different?" she asked. "Not a drop."

"You're young," said her aunt flatly.

"Not that young." She put her arms on the mantel and rested her head on them. "I feel exactly a million and two. At five minutes past eight this morning, with the telephone exploding, the doorbell rang and there was the doorman, the one who got the ambulance and helped me last night, Charlie, do you remember him? He always asks for you. Well, he'd imported his sister from New Jersey to look after me, wasn't that kind? And she'd left her husband to shift for himself and come in to do it, bringing a dozen eggs and a pound of country bacon, most of which she cooked for my breakfast, wasn't that kind? Only I couldn't eat it. It was a great disappointment to her. She lost a son in the war. She told me all about it while I wasn't eating. That's worse than this, God knows. But why did she think I wanted to hear about it? I don't think I understand people. Then a detective came from the police station to ask me how it happened, and he was very kind. Except to Charlie's sister, Mrs. Dingle. He wanted the knife and she'd cheerfully washed everything up. He was fit to be tied in a polite way, but he took it anyway. The phone kept ringing. The detective fixed that, he called the company and told them to disconnect the number, and I thanked him. The whole thing—I feel as if the world had vomited in my lap."

"Really, Lorraine——"

"I'm sorry, it's *exactly* what I feel like. Disgusting. Astounded. And the kindness is the worst. Even the reporters sound kind. Maybe someone in Newport will distract them eventually but in the meantime this is a great help to them, August is such a dull month unless there's a war. They're so happy to have a story they call me pet names. 'Look over here, sweetie,' a photographer said to me this morning as I came out. They followed me to the hospital and a woman called, 'Now don't run off, dear, we'll be waiting.' But I got out the back and one of Charlie's cohorts was waiting with the car for me. Charlie hasn't had such fun since he dropped bombs in postboxes for the IRA. Don't you be kind to me, Aunt Di, about my sad accident." Sitting down again, she leaned back and shut her eyes.

"My dear, the world has a fair quota of ghouls, I know, but——"

"Yes, it has. But I've never really been caught in the machinery before. Of course that's what you said, isn't it? That other people had been through it—— It doesn't help me to know that. I must be extraordinarily selfish, I keep feeling the pain and the horror and the amazement just the same. It *is* machinery, wheels and wheels and wheels going round, catching my clothes, pulling at me, battering me. The wheels are made out of people, and they sympathize and smile sadly and say how sorry they are and are kind—and I'll tell you something, Aunt Di, something I never knew before. It doesn't matter. Not what they say, nor how they feel, not whether they're sorry nor all their kindness. It doesn't *matter*. The wheels go around just the same, and I'm caught in them. Isn't that interesting? Or am I being naïve?"

"Child, we all have to find out, sooner or later, that kindness can't stop the machinery and love doesn't make the world go round! Never mind that now, Duncan will find something to stop it with. You're safe here, anyway. Don't think about going back to New York, if our own men can't keep the ghouls out, we'll hire guards."

"But I'll have to go back. I have to see Herbert."

"Why?" asked Mrs. Belchamber after a minute.

"Why?" Lorraine stared at her. "But—he's hurt. He needs——"

"He needs doctors and nurses and a good lawyer—which you are providing. Why does he need you, now, if he won't speak to you? If—forgive me—if something you told him drove him to this?"

Lorraine said, "It seems to me—surely I owe it to him!"

"Owe him what?" asked her aunt. "A hospital visit and a bunch of flowers?"

There was a pause. Mrs. Belchamber went on more gently, "Can you give him more than that, my dear? Can you go back to him?"

Lorraine's face crumpled toward tears and she hid it in her hands. "I don't know, I don't know, I don't know!" she cried.

"Then you've deceived him most cruelly," said her aunt, "because you told him you couldn't."

"Aunt Di——"

"No. No one can know this but you. Don't explain to me, don't ask me, I can't help you. Nor can Herbert help you. You can only do this yourself."

"I've been trying——" Lorraine began thickly. Then she stopped, dropped her hands to her lap and made herself take a breath and smile at her aunt. "All right, Aunt Di. I won't burst into tears of self-pity. I've been trying to work it out for weeks. I believed last night I knew what I could do, what I had to do. I very thoughtfully and calmly told Herbert it would be best for both of us to separate. He hasn't—— I haven't been the most satisfactory wife to him. That's not just my opinion, it's his. There was trouble last spring, I was upset and he was angry—— Oh, you can't explain these things, it had been going on for a long time. When he went to Europe I tried to face the whole thing, and he must have too. Then he wrote me about ten days ago, would I meet him, start over—— Well, I couldn't. It seemed to me it would just be more of the same and that he was fooling himself about our chances, about my changing and his changing. But then, then he did that." Her voice trailed off.

"Drink up your whisky," said Mrs. Belchamber. "You need it."

"I don't want it. I'm all right. Don't you see, Aunt Di—— When he did that, I knew I'd misjudged, I hadn't understood, because I'd never dreamed he could do such a thing. He wasn't—— He just wasn't Herbert, or whoever I'd thought Herbert was. He——"

"He was suddenly a stranger," said her aunt. "Yes, I know."

"Yes, exactly, how clever of you. He had changed, I didn't know him. It was—— Oh, it was horrible, but in a way it was the most intimate scene we'd ever had. And you see, there's something else. He had the knife. Couldn't it have turned either way? Didn't he choose to hurt himself and to spare me? Isn't it—isn't it an appeal to me? He begged me to stay, not for a reason or because it was right or sensible, but because he needed me. He never had before. He said he loved me—— It was all mixed up with threats, but he said it."

"My dear, my dear, he's himself too, the self you always knew and decided you couldn't live with, don't forget that! One moment of melodrama doesn't change the world. Does it?"

"Doesn't it? A little? I wish I knew!"

Mrs. Belchamber said wearily, "We all wish we knew. Alas, we don't."

"I thought if I saw Herbert again—that was all—it might help me to know."

"But would it help Herbert?"

"It was so dreadful to feel him hating me. Aunt Di, surely I can do something for him. I may owe him my life!"

"Perhaps you do. But there are some debts that can't be paid."

"I know, I know, but is this one? How am I to know? Everything you say sounds wise and sensible, but you weren't there, you weren't there! He had the knife, he had a choice——"

"Lorraine, don't go over it and over it! That's no use!"

"I'm sorry, Aunt Di. I'm sorry. I'm just trying to understand."

"But, dear child, that's just it, you can't, you know. You can't. Life keeps happening, it never stops to be understood. Don't you see that if you should go to see Herbert, trying to understand what has happened, you will make something else happen? You can't stop life and add it up like a column of figures, it flows. When you try to understand it, you're swimming upstream against the current. You can't do it. It's no good and worse than no good. You go back, you try to see where you went wrong, you try to cure it by doing it over and making it right—— No. It won't work. You will hurt yourself and everyone else concerned. If I know any one thing, I know that!"

"Aunt Di, perhaps that's all right for you. You feel things and know things. Life moves in the right direction for you and you're happy sailing downstream. But I—I've been trying to learn how to do that for so long! Forever, it seems, and it seems that I can't. I thought perhaps I had learned, it seemed to me right to leave Herbert. And see what happened! Today, all I know is that I don't know anything— right from left, good from bad, sense from nonsense. Tell me the world is flat and black is white, and I'll believe you, today. How do I know which is downstream and which is upstream? My feelings don't tell me anything, I can't trust them. I have to send everything round the long way through my brain. I *have* to think. I *have* to try and understand. Take Charlie, the doorman, the one who's helped me, sent me his sister, smuggled me through crowds of reporters and all—— He's enjoying himself, I told you. Well, that's all right. If he's playing that he's back in Ireland during the Troubles, and it helps me, why should I begrudge it to him? That's what I thought last night. But when I waked up this morning and there was Charlie again and his sister too, ready to take over, I didn't think so any more. I was scared. Faith had a maid once who was so devoted—do you remember her? Anna, her name was. Faith swore by her. Until one day it turned out that Anna had stolen two letters and wanted a thousand dollars for them. Faith had cried in Anna's arms over her troubles, and Anna had shown her pictures of her little boy who'd died in the fire raids on

Hamburg, and cried herself. It never occurred to me not to trust Charlie. But it never occurred to me that there would ever be any reason why I'd *have* to trust Charlie. I don't know anything, Aunt Di. Perhaps, right now, he and his sister are ransacking the apartment for pictures of me and Herbert and the children to sell to the tabloids. Perhaps I'm doing him the most dreadful injustice by even imagining the possibility. I don't know. Perhaps the best thing for Herbert will be never to see me again. But I don't know! I have to wait and let him tell me. Really I do. Truly. Or so it seems to me."

"It seems to *me*," said Mrs. Belchamber, "that what you have to do is go upstairs and get into bed and go to sleep. There's a choice of four kinds of sleeping pills in my bathroom."

"I don't want them. I slept—I think I did. The doctor at the hospital gave me something last night. I went up and down, in and out, all night. I don't want to go to sleep and pretend to dream it all away. It's all there. No pretense will change it. I must get used to it, not get away from it. Don't you see? What's the use of taking pills? They only change *me*, not what's happened. I woke up this morning and it was such a lovely day, and I lay and thought of people all over New York opening their newspapers and seeing my face. And it was unendurable. One of the women from the shelter came back to the apartment with me for a drink yesterday. She was there when Herbert arrived. Perhaps right now she's telling a reporter that he kissed me when he walked in and that I hadn't been expecting him. I thought of that, and it was unendurable. I thought of the children and—and other people I love—you, Faith—reading about it or hearing garbled gossip, and it was unendurable. I thought of Herbert waking up and realizing what he had done, what had happened and couldn't be changed, and that was the worst of all. I have pills too, Aunt Di, and I could have taken them then, enough to settle everything. I thought about it. I thought, Well, I've had a reasonably long life and a full enough life, a very lucky one, most people would say, and if I did what Herbert hadn't managed, I wouldn't feel really that I'd be missing a great deal. I'd had the best. It would be a reasonable act, not a bitter one nor an angry one nor a crazy one. It would get me and you and the children out of the machinery."

"It wouldn't have, of course. It would make it worse."

"I guess so, yes. It wouldn't help. I won't do it. I didn't do it. I got up and I could hear the phone ringing and Charlie and his sister arrived—wheels and wheels and wheels——"

"Lorraine, you're exhausted. I insist you lie down. I won't listen to you any more until you've had some rest. Now run——"

But here Tucker opened the door and said, "The doctor, m'lady." Lorraine, looking up, saw Savage looming behind the nurse and felt her heart lurch. Oh no, she thought, it's too much! Her hands wanted to knot together and she put them behind her, where they could do it out of sight. Tucker was saying, "Benson held him up at the gate with a shotgun and one of the men phoned up. That Benson! Shall I tell him to put the gun away?"

"Tell him to be sure it's loaded," said Mrs. Belchamber. She smiled at Savage as if he were about to take her picture, she flung out her charm like a flag. "Doctor, you're a miracle, you're just the man we want to see. My niece has—her husband has—suffered a sad accident and——"

But Savage was looking at Lorraine. "My nurse saw it in the paper," he said.

My head is heavy as lead, thought Lorraine, I'm bewitched, I can't move, I can't speak. She could only look back and say, in front of these people, the very least, the very most—"I'm all right."

"You don't look all right." He didn't move. Between them, shut out by their gaze, Mrs. Belchamber sat very still, her smile faded, her eyes widened. Not a soul stirred, only Lorraine and Savage looked to each other and the air between grew heavy, grew burning, with grief.

"I think I hear the telephone," said Mrs. Belchamber in a voice that was just too loud. "See to it, Tucker, please. Take messages." Savage moved to let Tucker by, the spell broke, the door shut.

He said, "I was very sorry to read about it. If there's anything I can do——"

"They say he'll be all right, thank you. It was Dr. Stone—no, Dr. Bryan, how stupid of me!—who operated last night, but Dr. Gruening saw him this morning too. Do you know him?"

"Know who he is. He's first class. If he says it's all right you—you mustn't worry." He tried to smile at her.

"It was such a little knife," said Lorraine. "I was cutting limes for drinks. You wouldn't think——"

Savage made an inarticulate noise. Lorraine saw herself, suddenly, cutting limes for *their* drinks two days before, the last time. Time spun, she was dizzy. "You wouldn't think anything so small could do such damage, but of course that's silly, isn't it?" she said rapidly, through the dizziness. "Thank you for asking about it, it was kind. I'll run off now, you'll want to check Aunt Di, and I'd better rest——"

"Just a minute," said Mrs. Belchamber; and Lorraine, who knew her voice so well, thought, Oh no! What is it? Something's wrong, something's—— Has she noticed something?

"What is it, dear?" she said, trying to speak gently, matter-of-factly. "Can I get you something? Oh, Doctor, would you like a drink?"

"No thanks," said Savage.

"No drink!" said Mrs. Belchamber, and under its mock surprise, her voice trembled. "This isn't a social call, then. It's an odd time for a professional one, though. You're not due till next week. I wonder why you came! Do you know, Lorraine?"

"No," said Lorraine, feeling her blood turn icy in her veins. Not now, not now! she thought. She's noticed, she's going to make trouble—— I can't stand it! Not right after she was so sweet, after she scolded me and helped me! Oh, not now, Aunt Di, please! Don't, don't!

"I beg your pardon?" said Savage—and said it wrong. Oh God, thought Lorraine, she'll hear it! I must stop her!

But she was just too late. "Indeed you should beg my pardon!" said Mrs. Belchamber, and laughed. Not an amused laugh, but a sharp, high angry one.

I must stop her! thought Lorraine still, desperately. Her tired body straightened. "What *are* you talking about, Aunt Di?" she said firmly, and then, as if in joke, "Have you been quarreling with Dr. Savage? Goodness, don't do that! Suppose he popped you back to Dr. Rushmore's! You wouldn't like that at all."

"I don't like this at all," said her aunt. "I don't like being fooled. Talking about! You know what I'm talking about! I'm talking about you and Savage. Good heavens! Why I've been blind as a bat!"

"What about me and Savage?" said Lorraine grimly. Out of the corner of her eye she could see that he moved suddenly. Be quiet, Peter! she thought at him. The only thing to do is to meet her head on and face her down.

"Look at his face," said Mrs. Belchamber contemptuously. "Who needs to know more than that? It's written all over it."

"What is written all over it?"

"What? Do you want me to say it?"

"Yes. Yes, I do."

"I shall certainly say it, then. You are lovers. You have been all summer. You lied to me, both of you. Is that what you wanted to hear?"

"I wanted to hear what you had to say. It isn't true. I'm sorry, Dr. Savage. I apologize."

"That's all right," said Savage helplessly. "I—— It's all right. Perhaps I'd better go."

"Perhaps you had," said Lorraine. Go, go, go! she thought at him, staring at her aunt, holding her eyes. Go quickly, get out, get out! I can't do this much longer. I'm tired.

But he wanted her to look at him. She could feel his hesitation. He had risked so much to come to her now, to see if she needed him! Of course he mustn't stay, it was dangerous, but surely she could throw him a look? Oh God, Peter, go! she thought. Then desperately and knowing how dangerous it was, she released her aunt's eyes and looked an appeal at him. His mouth tightened, he nodded his head an eighth of an inch, he started to the door——

The damage was done. Mrs. Belchamber's voice came low and furious, denying affection, sympathy, help. "How dare you, Lorraine! You apologize for me! And to this—this sheep in wolf's clothing! This hangdog who's afraid even to acknowledge your relationship! To lie for him, to me! How can you!"

"No one is lying——" Lorraine began again.

"Oh, be quiet! Of course you're lying, you're both lying, even though he's coward enough to let you do it for him. You've lied and lied and lied. I see it all now. Good heavens! This is why you've stayed with me all summer! To be near this creature! My kind thoughtful niece!"

"Aunt Di——"

"And Savage, my attentive doctor who came to see me so faithfully! What a fool I've been! What a fool you've made of me, between you! How you must have laughed! My dear, devoted niece, and that *nice* young man who came out to see me so regularly—only it wasn't to see me at all! Not at all! But you know, Lorraine, he never forgot to send his bill!"

"Mrs. Belchamber, I swear——"

"Oh, you do, do you, Savage! Then swear away! But it was a good fat bill, Lorraine, and I paid it every month, and he took the checks home to his wife and children without any moral qualms, I assure you of that. How many children is it, Savage? Five? You don't do things by halves, do you?"

"Oh Jesus," said Savage and turned away. He went over to the window and hit the frame with his fist. Then he stood there looking out.

Lorraine followed him with her eyes, twisting in her chair and turning her back on her aunt. "And you, Lorraine," cried Mrs. Belchamber at her niece's back. She leaned forward, gripping the arms of her chair. "You, you, you! What an actress was lost in you! What a talent! Why Duse couldn't have played the innocent better than you, right down to today, right down to five minutes ago! You nearly had me in tears, wanting to help you! And you've done it for two months, you've duped me for two months, what a fool, what a fool! Did you enjoy it—you and Savage laughing together at a crippled old woman? Butter wouldn't melt in your mouth, you only left me for your poor orphans—orphans named Savage, I suppose, one gross common ambitious slum-bred orphan with a bedside manner that didn't stop at the bedside, it got right in!"

Savage swung away from the window. At the fury in his face, Mrs. Belchamber laughed in triumph, with joy. "Look at him, look at him," she cried, pointing, "he's angry! I've said something I shouldn't! He's shocked. Am I shocking you too, Lorraine? You precious pair! You hypocrites! What a performance you put on today! It's a shame you came too late to see it, Savage—those great sad eyes, that touching distress about the scandal and the papers and the filthy world intruding on her private purity! And oh, her poor husband, her poor, poor husband! Should she leave him? Should she go back to him? She'd hurt him so, she couldn't stand it, and why had she left him in the first place? *I* don't know, but she had eighteen obscure reasons right out of Henry James—— Oh, excuse me, Savage, you don't know who Henry James is. Well, Lorraine, take a look at him. That's why you want to leave your husband, for that fat vulgar peasant over there with his five children and his devoted Catholic wife. Take a good look. Can you afford him? Is he worth it? A divorce won't be cheap, my dear, and you can't count on any help from me if *that* was in your mind—or in his. Do you hear me, Savage? Not one penny from me goes to her. Not one penny!"

Savage took one step. His hands were balled into fists and his voice was choking with rage. "Who wants your money, your damn dirty money?" he said. "Once I thought you were somebody besides your money, but now I guess that's all you can talk about because it's all you've got! I don't want your money, and what I got from you I worked for. But sweet Jesus, I'll pay every cent back before I'll stand here and take one more word of this, every red cent! Who in hell do you think you are? What gives you the right to sit there and talk to me like that? What——"

Lorraine had reached him. She laid her hands against his chest. "Stop it, stop it, stop it!" she cried. "No, no!"

"I won't take it," he said. "God damn it, don't try to stop me. I won't have you take it either. Let me——"

"No!"

"Let me go. She needs a lesson. Let me go. She can't talk to people like that. Laurie, let me go!"

For answer, Lorraine caught his wrists and, holding them apart, forced her body against his. He strained forward, his heart pounding, his breathing fast. How often like this in love, she thought. Will he remember? He can throw me across the room and kill her if he doesn't. She didn't say one word.

Then he said, "Oh my God!" and dropped his hands. He turned and leaned on the table by the chair where Lorraine had been sitting. His eyes were shut, his head bowed. Lorraine sat down weakly and for a long moment there was no sound at all in the room.

Mrs. Belchamber said in a hoarse whisper, "Get out of here!"

Savage didn't even look at her. Leaning forward, resting his hands on the table that creaked a little beneath his weight, he said, "Are you all right, Laurie? Did I hurt you?"

"No."

"Are you sure?"

"Yes."

"Get out of here," said Mrs. Belchamber, louder.

CHAPTER TWENTY-THREE

"What do you want me to do, Laurie?"

"Go, darling. It's all you can do."

"Will you come with me?"

"No."

"Go," said Mrs. Belchamber. "Go with him. Go. Go."

Savage lifted his head and looked at her. "Shut your mouth," he said. "You can do anything about me that you want, later, see? But while I'm here, you keep quiet." He finished with a glare. Then he went down on one knee by Lorraine's chair and took her hands. "Honey, I can't leave you here. Come along. This is busted wide open now anyway. Come on."

"No, darling."

"Why not? Did she say something that bothers you? Do you think I care about your dough?"

"No. No, of course not. But I can't come."

"No? Not worth it? All the mess? It will be one hell of a mess, that's right. Are you scared?"

"The only thing that could make me come," said Lorraine slowly, "would be you thinking I didn't want to. I want to. Do you believe me?"

"If you say so, Baby."

"But I won't. Too many people get hurt if I do."

"Won't they get hurt anyway?"

"Maybe. But not so badly. Things can be patched up."

"Is that all you want? Something patched up?"

"No. It's not what I want. But I guess it's all I can get. We'd be patched up too. And the children—I'd lose mine. You mightn't even be let see yours. That happens. We'd be patched up on top of that. I'm afraid it would bother me. I'm afraid it would bother us."

"Laurie, are you sure? This is a pretty big thing I have for you. Are you sure?"

"I love you. I always will. But I can't give Bobby and Jane away. Not possibly. It wouldn't work."

He still knelt looking in her face. But across their concentration came an indrawn breath, a muffled sob. Lorraine looked up. Savage turned his head. Twisted away from them in her chair, Mrs. Belchamber was crying. Her shoulders shook. A strand of her carefully arranged hair fell loose on her neck.

"I'll go," said Savage dully and stood up. "Tell her I'm sorry, or something. Tucker has sedatives for her if she needs them. She can always get Ingoldsby if she wants him. Laurie—it's up to you. You know what I want. You know where I'll be."

"Good-by, my darling," said Lorraine. She stood up and put her arms around him. He was rooted, solid, like a tree. His arms, she thought. His mouth. This is the last time now, and kissed him with all her self to last forever. He groaned, releasing himself. He took her by the shoulders and shook her gently and shook his head at her, frowning. She nodded, because she couldn't speak. He turned away and walked out and the door slammed behind him and Mrs. Belchamber wrenched herself upright in her chair and began to scream.

"Get out, get out, get out, get out," she shrieked. "Get out of here and don't come back. I will never see you again! Get out, get out!"

"I'm going," said Lorraine.

CHAPTER

24

August 19th

Peter—

The funny address on this letter is my sister's ranch. The children and I arrived three days ago and life has become suddenly very peaceful, a thing I had forgotten it could be. We are quite high here, looking northwest to broken hills that seem close enough to touch and are a day's ride away. Behind them are real mountains, but you can't always see them. When you can you don't believe it. I woke before sunrise this morning, mist around the house and everything gray, and thought— Why, there's a pink cloud in the sky! But it was a mountain that the sun had reached already. The air is wonderful. And though the country looks dry as dust, there are moutain gorges (arroyos? I'm not sure) where streams run down that are choked with green. We had a picnic supper in one last night.

My darling, this is the kind of news that I have to write you, there isn't any other. I'll stay here for a while, I think. Faith's husband, Julian, is very busy right now, this is the time for the roundups and the cattle sales, it seems. They have three ranches in different parts of the state, and he will be going from one to another for most of the next month, and I think I will stay that long anyway. Faith does quite a lot on the home ranch herself, and I ride out with her— western saddle, jeans, wide hat against the sun—and feel as if I'd escaped from someone's television screen. I couldn't bring the nurse I'd had, she thinks the West is full of guns and snakes, so I am quite busy too with the children. But the two Japanese houseboys that Faith has here adore them and I am able to leave Jane with them for a bit during the day. Bobby has to be plucked out of his saddle for meals. One of the men has already bought him a pair of boots, high heels and all. They stand on the table by his bed all night. This is a compromise. He wanted them under his pillow.

It's cold here at night because we are so high and we keep fires going and sleep under blankets. The big house and the two guest cabins stand around a pool and there are willows, just like in Connecticut. But the houses are made of logs and full of Indian things and the fires smell different because of the wood we burn—piñon, I think. I must learn all this, next week perhaps. How funny, I don't know at all whether you have ever been out in this country.

When I left my aunt's that afternoon I took the children and their nurse to Herbert's sister's in Bronxville. I simply walked in on her and told her I was fighting off reporters in the city and she would have to look after them until I could make plans. "Indeed I will, indeed I will," she kept saying, sort of gobbling it like a turkey and eying me as if I had something infectious, smallpox, maybe, which might with luck be fatal. But I managed not to say any more than I had to, and left—she didn't offer to take *me* in! When I got in the car again, though, I realized that I'd had it. Did you know there's a hotel in Bronxville? I didn't until I asked a policeman, but there is, and I went there and went to sleep. It was five o'clock in the afternoon and I slept till the next morning and when I woke up I lay there and figured out what I had to do, and coming here is what I did.

If the mess gets bad again I will come back. I hope it may not. I did what I could to stop it before I left. My aunt's lawyer, Mr. Duncan, seems very nice and good at suppressing things. He suppressed reporters right and left for me. Whether he can suppress *her* or not I don't know. At any rate, I didn't hear a word from her in New York before I left and I suppose no news is good news. I will write to her in a day or two and tell her where I am and see if this draws any fire.

It is ten days since I saw you. I know that sometime I shall stop counting like this but I haven't managed to yet. Every one of those days I have tried to think what I should have done differently, and there are a lot of things. But the interesting thing is that none of them is anything I did with you. I want to be sure you know this, because we were talking shorthand to each other at the end. I should have been cleverer and quicker and more understanding about a lot of things—and people—but not about you. I wouldn't change anything about it at all. Not from the first time I kissed you to the last time I kissed you. How funny that it began and ended just the same way, like a pair of brackets around a sentence! Except that the person kissing you was different—I grew up in between. Or I guess I should say, You grew me up. I don't know if that sounds like a compliment, but it is one. Here is another that sounds better. If ever you are angry again (Goodness! How unlikely!) or tired or unhappy, say, "For Laurie I was emeralds and pearls and all she ever wanted."

Darling, write me once and tell me how things are with you. I will let you know when I am coming east, but it would be a mistake for us to go about having great tragic meetings. For one thing you are too busy and I intend to be, and for another, this isn't a tragedy.

All my love,
Laurie

August 21st

Dear Aunt Di,

As you can see, or as Mr. Duncan may have told you, I am staying with Faith and expect to be for a month or so. The children adore it here and Bobby is seldom off a horse—there are two or three little old quiet cow ponies that he can manage very nicely. Jane pads about pursuing one of the dogs, carrying a rag doll or a kitten—she carries them both the same way but the kittens put up with it for some unknown reason—and pursued in turn by a giggling Japanese house-boy. We are all very well.

I was terribly distressed to leave you as I did. If you ask me why I left in that case, I will have to say that you told me to. You told me under a good deal of misapprehension, but it didn't seem like a very good time to try to argue it out.

I would like to tell you about it now.

Peter and I became lovers early in May. It came like a bolt from the blue and was very passionate and very wonderful. Neither of us hesitated for a minute. Neither of us planned or expected anything, either. What we felt was immediate and overwhelming. It had nothing to do with time—— I see I am being unclear, my besetting sin, brought on by trying to be precise. I mean that I knew perfectly well that it was not a permanent thing and so did Peter but we didn't think about endings because what we had was so intense. In fact the whole thing was not anything that could be thought about, but only something that had to be done.

We lied to you if hiding our feelings is lying, and in the end I certainly lied to you consciously with every bit of energy and ingenuity I could lay my hands on, but surely you see why. I was protecting him and he was protecting me, and we were both protecting all the other people involved with either of us. And, Aunt Di, that includes you.

We were not lying *against* you, laughing at you or being tricky or making fun. I would have spent the summer with you if your doctor was eighty-three and had a long white beard. When Peter came to see you, we sometimes had five minutes together if it seemed convenient for me to walk out to his car with him. Otherwise we sat in the same room and pretended not to care for each other, and if you think that is an easy thing to do with your lover, then you have never been in love, and that doesn't seem to me very probable. Our real meetings were always away from the house, when I drove to New York. Then I would go on and look after my "orphans."

Well, that is how it was with Peter and me. It is over now as it was always going to be over about this time. It ended in a mess and, as you and I would agree, this was my fault. But it was the fault of my relationship with Herbert, not of my relationship with Peter. I was worried about that, and I am worried about it, and what I said to you that day about it was all true, I wasn't play-acting. Really, Aunt Di, I couldn't if I'd wanted to. If you want to scold me, scold me about Herbert. You started to and I'm sure what you said is quite right. My dealings with Herbert have been clumsy and wrong and just wanting them to be right won't set them right. Perhaps they will never be right and could never have been and it was too late from the beginning.

Certainly there was a time last spring, before I could have told you what Peter's name was, when things had got so bad between Herbert and me that I think I was a little crazy. I felt like two different people and my life seemed to have got right out of control. Was that my fault? Was it Herbert's? Perhaps I will never know. Perhaps it means that I must never see him again for both our sakes. And yet, does it seem strange to you that I sympathize, and almost understand the thing that Herbert did because six months ago (no, it wasn't even that long) I was so lost, so close to violence myself? You were surely right when you told me to leave him alone, and I have. Even when I was in New York I just sent messages about the children and told him I was coming here, I didn't try to see him and I talked only to the nurse and to Miss Winters at the office.

If we should have a life together again (and how can I say it's impossible? Is anything impossible?), but if we should, it would have to be a life as different from the past as if we were two other people. But there you are—it seems to me that I am a different person, and that I have no right to say that Herbert may not become different too, no right to plan a life away from him until he tells me what he plans. I owe him something, Aunt Di. I'm not sure exactly what, but until I hear from him, I think I must just wait.

This is a good place to wait.

Aunt Di, I am writing you all this about my affairs because you are entitled to know the truth for your own sake. Because I don't want to think of you thinking that Peter and I, or I alone, used you and deceived you and teased you. We did not. There is another obvious reason too. That is, that if you think we tricked you meanly and behaved shabbily, you might be angry enough to tell people that we were lovers. This could wreck Peter's career and I suppose it would give Herbert grounds for divorcing me and taking the children.

Should I appeal to you not to do that? I have been turning this over in my mind ever since—well, ever since I left you, I guess. And I would do it—if I thought it was necessary. Because I would do everything I possibly could to stop such a thing happening. When Peter asked me to go with him he thought it was going to happen. He had never asked me to before, and he would not have asked me if he hadn't thought we were in the mess for good, anyway. I know that and I don't mind. We both have obligations that can only be ended by being hacked off, like arms and legs. That's a horrible simile, but it's true, and if I can prevent it I will. I refused to go with him because I thought it could be prevented. I know there are people who would say that I deserved to lose my children and suffer, but I don't believe you are one of them and so I shan't plead, but only say, it is up to you.

Would you ask Tucker whether I left behind Jane's blue gingham dress with the organdy apron? It is her favorite, and I can't find it.

Every now and then she remembers it's missing and roars at me. If Tucker finds it, I'd appreciate her sending it on.

Faith sends her love. So do I.

Lorraine

August 22nd

Dear Herbert,

The children and I are having an active healthy time here at Faith's. Bobby is becoming quite a cowboy and Jane is the apple of everybody's eye. She looks it too—pink cheeks, and what an appetite!

I expect to stay a month or so, and I'll send you a report on the children every week.

I hope you aren't too uncomfortable and that the air conditioner is helping. Mr. Cole's suggestion of sending you up to the Adirondacks when you get out of the hospital sounds like a fine idea. Such a nice man! He is very fond of you.

If, when you're stronger, you want me to come east and talk things over, I will of course. Just let me know.

Lorraine

P.S. Faith has just dropped the enclosed snapshots in my lap. Under the ten-gallon hat is Bobby. What Jane is clutching to her bosom are four kittens named (by Jane) Jelly, Kelly, Umbelly, and Fido.

L.

August 22

Laurie, you want to know how things are with me. Well, they aren't good.

They're quiet. I thought the old lady would see that hell started popping, but she hasn't. Not yet, anyway. Ingoldsby gave me a funny look when I told him I wasn't going out there again. He made with the eyebrows like he does and said, "By request?" And I said, "By mutual agreement." And he said, he was so sorry, Dear Boy. So I said, Shit. Well, no, I didn't, I just thought it. I suppose you'd know that anyway.

Maybe if I did say things when I thought them I'd have got you to come with me. What do you think? I used to be a real roughneck. Once I wanted to lay a girl—this was when I was in high school—and she didn't want to in spite of me being on the football team and a real hot shot. I guess she was religious. I twisted her arm until she said Yes and then I laid her and it felt fine. She cried all the time but I didn't care, it still felt fine for me. Maybe I should have twisted your arm.

Trouble is, I would mind now if you cried all the time. I guess I'm getting old and soft.

You can tell from all this dirty talk how mad I am at you for not coming. But I guess you can figure that out too.

I know how you feel about the kids. It's natural. I'm pretty gone on my own, particularly the five-year-old, Deedee. But Jesus, honey, the way it is now, I wake up in the morning and I try to think why it is I feel sort of low and then I remember I'm not going to be seeing you and it's like—I don't know—it's like not being able to get your breath. Why does it have to be like this? How come you can do this to me? You're good with words and I'm not and I suppose you know what you mean when you say this isn't a tragedy, I suppose it means something. I don't know what it means, though. All I know is I feel lousy. And I wonder if you do.

Oh hell, I suppose you do. I'm a bastard. But look, honey, don't sling those words around too fast and talk yourself into things. Don't get noble about not seeing me again. Let me know when you're coming back. We can work something out, Laurie—if you want to.

Honey, I'm a nicer fellow than this bastard of a letter sounds. Please remember it, after all it's your fault I have to write it at all. We could be talking. Call it talking, anyway.

Thinking of you,
Peter

August 24th

My dear child,
I don't know what to say to you. What you want to know first, of course, is whether I have talked to anyone about your affairs (or should I just say affair!) and you are quite right, I haven't and won't. No appeal is necessary. I wouldn't commit such an act of megalomaniac meddling even if I were beside myself, and certainly not in cold blood. Didn't I get Tucker out of the room, after all? I would have

thought Savage knew me better than that. But then (I hope this will not offend you. It's a simple statement of fact), he *did* come out of a slum, and there was certainly nothing in his breeding to teach him what honor or honorable dealing is.

You can tell him from me (don't tell me you're not in communication with him!) that I spoke highly of him to that old ass Ingoldsby. He can sink back safely into the bosom of his family and sleep peacefully of nights, since that seems to be what you both want.

As for the rest of it—well, I've read what you say. I'm an old woman but not *entirely* inexperienced. I'm willing to believe that you think you lied to me from the highest motives, and that going to bed with Savage seemed not only pleasant, but ordained from the beginning of the world. It's astonishing how often what we want to do seems the fated, the inevitable, and the *right* thing to do. Besides, I suppose that once you have got over the obvious difficulties in the way of finding him attractive, he is no doubt a more than adequate lover. What a lot of revelations you have enjoyed at thirty-two! Well, I can't pass judgment on you. You have to make your own life. I am glad, at any rate, that you feel my advice about Herbert was worth something.

At least rest assured that your life is yours to make and that I shan't interfere with your arrangements, whatever they may be.

Your affectionate aunt,

Diana Belchamber

August 24

Laurie darling,

I woke up sweating last night and thought what a stinker I was to write you the way I did. Half that stuff, I made it up. Not about missing you, wanting you, waking up and feeling like hell, that goes on all the time. The rest was my lousy temper.

Jesus, darling, I miss you. I tried saying what you wrote me, but I think I need you to say it to me. Please, honey, don't tell me you never will. And please forgive me for that lousy letter that didn't even say I love you. If I could have got it back from the post office I would.

Damn it, I haven't got time to write now, but I want to get a line

off anyway, and tell you to tear that other thing up, will you please?
It was from the roughneck. He loves you too, but he's pretty stupid
about how he says it.

Peter

August 27th

Darling,

I wrote you four letters and tore them all up. Two were noble and
priggish and one was as angry as yours at least, and one written late
at night was just about wanting you, so that you wouldn't have to
worry about how I felt. And you don't, you know. But the thing is
not how I feel, or you feel, but what we can do. I don't want to be
noble or sling words around, I just want to be practical. It wouldn't
be practical for me to lose my children, because I would go around
like the mother cat out here when Jane hides her kittens. Jane does
this every day (not in very difficult places, after all she won't be four
till next month), but the cat never learns. She goes crazy and tears
around hunting for them and making noises like a demented tea-
kettle. You don't want a demented teakettle-cat who biffs anything
that gets in her way leaping about through your life. Nor do I wish
to become such a creature. That isn't noble or priggish. It's selfish.

When you have lived as long and as thoroughly as you and I have,
you have just got yourself tied up in too many ways to be able to
untie the knots and start over. Even if I manage to untie my knot to
Herbert, you can't untie all yours. Being in love gives you a feeling
of beginning over and the world being new and a whole lot being
possible that wasn't, but, darling— I thing that is partly fake, a sort
of false youth and energy that can't last. Last time I wrote I said that
I changed, loving you, and so I did, but I am still the same person
really, even though I have learned a great deal, like how to be happy.
I said I had grown up (it was certainly time) but it was Lorraine
Forbes de Koning who grew up, not a sudden new creature born
of our love. Someone grown up can manage more things than someone who isn't. But partly this is because a grown-up person knows
what can't be managed and doesn't try.

That sounds sad, doesn't it, and sort of despairing. What I feel
isn't sadness, though. Part of it is just what you feel—and that I
don't need to describe. But partly I feel strong and determined and

anxious to undertake all I can, as if you had liberated me, somehow. And I suppose you have in a way, because knowing what you can't do makes it easier to do what you can do. You are not distracted by foolish wishing.

Am I getting priggish again? I think maybe I am. Blame it on my father's Boston ancestors, who were people who thought about their consciences all the time. Of course everybody had got over this by the time I came along, but one of my great-aunts was terribly full of family pride and she was always catching Faith and my cousins and me, and making us listen to old stories or read old letters and diaries. They gave me the creeps, they really did. The scruples those people had, and the reasons for not marrying, or marrying someone they didn't at all want to, it was awful! I was simply oppressed with their atmosphere—and yet you can see that I must have inherited a tendency to do the same thing. Though I used to hate them for taking themselves so seriously.

Darling, don't hate me, or be too angry at me for trying to see things from the outside. Life is not romantic. People mostly don't get what they want. But somehow I can't think this is sad. Think of what I got—you. And without wanting you, at least consciously. I don't remember now what it was I did want in those days, pre-you, but whatever it was it wasn't a patch on what I got. Wonderful, frustrating, maddening, surprising—no word is big enough to fit it. Life instead of dreaming, I guess, things that happen outside your own head. The thing about life is, it uses you, and that's good.

Ah, saying it's good doesn't mean that I'm happy! Loving you was satisfying, but I'm not satisfied! All the time you and I were able to see each other, I was telling myself that sometime we would have to stop seeing each other. At first I tried to fool myself into thinking this didn't matter. I tried to pretend that what we had was so important and wonderful that the memory of it would be as good as the actual reality. Well, that was pretty childish, the romantic childhood of my love for you, and it stopped. That last time with you, dear, I found that I was minding the idea of losing you very badly and that memory wasn't going to be any substitute for the actual thing, and I was bitter. That was the angry youth of my love. Now I have lost you, and I know that all that I felt before was true, but not all the truth. It was only emotion, only personal. Now my love is finished growing, I am accommodated to it and it to me. I am not foolish enough to think that being without you is the same as being with you, and yes, of course I am unhappy and angry and bitter. But also, I am a person with a life to live, I need to be used. Sometimes I am nearly sick with wanting you. But even if it turned out that we could see each other once in a while, and work something out, I am still a person with a life to live and I cannot live it with you. Whatever you or I feel, that is a fact. So I shall do the best I can by myself.

At present my best isn't very good, I admit. I——

Interruption. Mail arrives, your note and a letter from my aunt. First, don't wake up sweating, darling. And if you want to write, then do, but should you? It seems to me that trying to hang onto the past and make up a future is a terrible waste of the present, that's all. And the present is all people ever have. Now, in the present, what happened between us is over. If our lives should go one way, we might be able to see each other again, and that would be wonderful for me, but it would be a *new* thing, different from the old. And if they shouldn't go that way—darling, I won't, I can't, have you waking up and wanting me. I would rather be forgotten and gone than a drain on you now or a distortion of your future. I love you. I loved you. I always will.

Now, about my aunt's letter. It's thoroughly nasty, but never mind. On the practical side, which is what we're talking about, she says she hasn't and won't "talk to anyone about your affairs." So don't worry about hell popping any more. She also says that she spoke "nicely" about you to Ingoldsby. It's hard to remember right now that she ever speaks nicely, but she can when she wants to. That's a relief, isn't it?

Peter darling, good-by. I keep saying it over and over, don't I, like Sarah Bernhardt or whoever it was that made all those farewell tours. Would you like to know what I'm doing while I say it, so as to see it all? Somehow it might make it real, don't you think? I am sitting by the pool in front of the house and Faith has just come out on the porch. She has on a red dress, which means it is cocktail time, because we only put on dresses for dinner. She is now shouting "Martini?" at me and I shout back "Fine." I can have two now because I am getting used to the height. My first week here I got glassy-eyed after one. And Jane has just marched out of the kitchen with Sumi behind her to show me her supper dishes, all empty. She eats much better for him than for me. So I shall go and have one martini and read a Babar book to Jane (Bobby lies on the floor and pretends he is too old to listen, but if I skip anything he tells me) and put them to bed and have another martini and dinner. And then, since Julian is in town at a meeting of Republican cattlemen who want to hang Ezra Taft Benson, Faith and I will play cutthroat canasta for a couple of hours and then I will go to bed and this day will be over. And tomorrow there will be another and even though each takes me farther and farther from you, I can see you just as clear as ever, not blurred at all, only a little farther away, and so I always shall.

Laurie

August 28th

Dear Aunt Di,
Thank you for your letter. I appreciate your telling me that you will not say anything about Peter and me, and also about your conversation with Dr. Ingoldsby.

I send some pictures of the children, and will let you know what my plans for the future are when I know myself. I hope you will do the same.

Lorraine

August 29th

Dear Herbert,
Thank you for having Miss Winters write me. I am delighted to know that you will be going to Mr. Cole's next week. It's a lovely place, so restful and quiet. I hope you won't try to go back to work too soon.

Bobby never rides alone, and of course I won't let him. If I'm not with him myself, Earl, one of the hands, is. Earl is also teaching him how to use a rope, and it is astonishing how patiently Bobby will work at this. He roped an old stump back of the house three times running yesterday, and was bursting with pride.

I asked Julian what he thought about the trend of cattle prices, and he started to make me a speech about water, and how the water table is falling, or sinking, or whatever it does, and what California is doing to them by damming the rivers and stealing their water. If you would like to hear more about this, I am sure he will be enchanted to write you.

Jane asks me to tell you that she can skip rope forty-leven times. (She can't, it only seems like it when she does it on the porch and shakes the house.) Also, she has a new doll named Rumplepum. Miss Winters seemed surprised about Jane's names, so I will say at once that I don't know why the doll is named Rumplepum, nor the kitten Fido. Umbelly is Jane-ese for umbrella, and that kitten is called so because he is black on top and white on the bottom. Now you and Miss Winters know as much as I do!

I'll write you next week at Mr. Cole's.

Lorraine

September 1

My dear Lorraine,

I have picked up my pen and put it down again over and over for the last week, trying to start this letter, and I suppose that if I could put it off now I would, but putting it off has got to seem, finally, at least as difficult as writing it. No, nothing has happened, don't be afraid. Outwardly my life pursues the even tenor of its way. But inwardly——

Why did I burst out at you that way, scream, rave, lose control and goad poor Savage into losing it too? Why? Answering that question seems even more important than saying forgive me, though I am saying that too. All my life I have had moments of such sheer shrieking possession—but that's no answer. If one of the children had behaved so, you would have said it was a tantrum. Why, at the age of sixty-one, should I dare indulge in a tantrum? Because I am, in some part, still a child? After my behavior, I would be afraid to deny that, the words would stick in my throat. This is an old woman writing to you, who is still a child, writing in terror and agony of spirit, a lonely old woman who has lived on other people all her life, lived as a child does in the immediate moment. Now, reaching the natural end of such close ties, reaching the time too when I can hope for little pleasure from vivid experience, I should go on to another way of life—and I have been afraid to. Instead, in a fit of frenzy I sacrificed to my fear and my vanity the closest and warmest tie that was left to me—my relationship with you.

This I have begun to face. I can see it in the large, in principle. What hurts and humiliates is to remember exactly what I did and said—— Oh, Lorraine! Burn that letter I wrote, please do. And the hardest thing is to try to discover why it was at that moment that the furious child within me burst out at you—I know, of course, but that is not the same as saying it in words.

Let me begin by asking whether you remember saying to me that day, before the heavens fell (before I brought them down), that my book was nearly full? (This is not an irrelevancy.) I started writing it in the nursing home when I was beginning to see that a life of action had ended for me, ended a bit more abruptly than for most people, but not really a great deal earlier than it would have anyway. I realized, that is, that I could not live as I had in the past and that I would have to go on to something else, and so I began to set down my memories. Vanity had nothing to do with it. I was trying to face myself honestly and understand my limitations and my strengths by reviewing the things I had done and not done, the dangers I had brazened my way through and the idiocies I had committed. It was my hope that this exercise in hindsight would teach me what I might hope from the future by fixing the hazard of my faults in my mind and reconciling me to what I would have to leave behind. Well, it didn't, did it?

First I thought I would destroy my book, it had failed of its purpose. But I made myself read it over, and then I thought I would not destroy it, I'll tell you why in a minute. The reading was a lesson. Staring out at me over and over again—and, Lorraine, I knew it, knew it while I read and had known it while I wrote—was my great fault that has made and marred my life. If it has a name I'm too close to it to know it, but greed is one side of it and irresponsibility the other. I want too much. And when I find that I am expected to pay for what I have taken, why—I fly into a tantrum. I *enjoy* tantrums. To feel myself getting ready to cease being an adult, to break rules, to shout anything at anyone, is hatefully, thrillingly delicious. I am an addict of hysteria.

Heavens, how hard it is to write this! And it is going to be harder to go on. Harder than writing my book, certainly, because now I am writing for someone else and I know it—you will read this in two or three days' time. But I am going to go on because I want, literally, to do penance. I want to see if it has a deterrent effect. I want to find out whether, the next time I feel myself slipping toward the seductive whirlpools of fury, I will remember the very unpleasant time I am having now, writing to you. So I am going to tell you why I lost my temper and my manners and my control just when I did, and screamed like a fishwife at you and Savage.

I was jealous.

Does that surprise you? Do you find it faintly disgusting and rather incredible because of my age? If you do, my dear, you may be surprised yourself one day.

Or perhaps you think that I mean it symbolically. Well, so I do. But I mean it quite simply, too, just as simply and physically as if I were thirty, not sixty. I am an old woman and I can still find a young man attractive. Oh, of course I had felt quite sure that I was "sublimating" it nicely and that he had no idea that I felt it (and I hope *that* at least is true). But I was fooling myself, you see. I told myself that it was perfectly possible for me to exert an attraction for him too (sublimated and platonic also), the attraction of a wise and witty older woman who's seen the world and still knows how to handle a man. It seemed to me that he enjoyed being with me, and that his faithful trips to Woodbury were inspired by a *little* more than duty.

Then I saw his face and knew who he cared about. For the last time I was seeing that great helpless wonderful male passion that I had known so well and provoked so often—and it wasn't directed at me at all, and never would be again. What I felt for poor Savage himself, I suppose, is not really very important—but the passion, the tension, the game, the secret laughter, the wildness at the quiet core of life—— Ah, Lorraine, I'd always had it. All I had to do, ever, was reach my hand out. Even when I didn't (and I'm capable of renunciation) I knew it was *there*. And though I'd told myself often enough that it was over, some habit of the flesh still assumed that I had only to reach out my hand. Well, that day I learned better. I wasn't even part of a triangle, I was a bystander. You didn't do anything I hadn't done, Lorraine, there was no reason for me to say what I did. I lied and cheated someone finer than me for someone hardly fit to black Savage's boots, and made such a song and dance about it that you would have thought I was Helen of Troy. I tell you this now, but at the time I wanted to destroy you both. I wanted to degrade you in front of him, and disgust you with him. There was more, too. I wanted to make some kind of contact with him. I wanted to be noticed if I couldn't be loved—like a bad child, Lorraine. Like a bad child in a tantrum.

The only result was that I was obliged to sit there and watch you together, to see acted out what I would not have again. My dear, if I hurt you, be sure you hurt me; and I have no one to be angry at or to blame but myself. No one, no one but myself.

Well, this isn't quite the end of my confession or apologia, or whatever you want to call it, but instead of trying to abbreviate the rest, I am going to send out to you what I wrote for myself, my book. I hope you will not mind reading it. I said somewhere in it that it is an attempt at exorcism—and now I see that such attempts cannot be private. I have sat in stern judgment on myself and set down the record of my folly, and this is not enough. Someone else must read it too, no one can judge himself, and for one reason or another, I have appointed you to the task. There is just a little more to write, and I shall begin at once. Then you will know, I think, why (though I was furious at Savage) it was you I wanted to hurt.

How cold that sounds! How stupidly proud I am still! Reading this over I see that I have talked only of myself, and that the word "forgive" is mentioned just once, in passing. Dear Lorraine, I have no children now, you are all I have left, and I need forgiveness, I need you. I ask for things badly, I have always hated to ask for things, but I ask you now to try to forgive me—yes, even for the things I do not forgive myself. I hope you will manage it.

Write me in any case. I'll be in Connecticut for a while longer. But I have sent the horses to be sold and closed the stables. And I shall put the house on the market. I am going to take an apartment in New York for a while, till Tucker and I can see what the Rehabilitation Center there can do for me. I am a cripple, it is one of the numerous things I have begun to face, but I would like to be as spry and able a cripple as possible. The only weakness that I shall cater to is that I refuse to live in one of those old ladies' residential hotels. Bridge, yes. Gossip, yes. But better bridge, please, and gossip that is more than tittle-tattle. What do you think of my moving to

Washington and challenging Mrs. Cafritz and Mrs. Mesta for the National Hostess Stakes?

Thank you for the pictures of the children, though I wish you'd see they gave Bobby an English saddle, that confounded western armchair will ruin his seat. I hope Jane's dress arrived and appeased her. Don't let her roar at you, Lorraine, I would so like to be the last temperamental female in the family!

Diana B.

25

Lorraine, now that I know I am writing this for you, I wonder if it will change. Perhaps not. Perhaps, in a way, I have been writing it for you all along. I remember the day I started it quite distinctly. It was the day I lost my temper at you and Savage for the first time, and I think it was the day you two met. What an odd coincidence! Or is it more? Most other civilizations would think *ours* very odd to imagine that these events are only coincidence. And yet, believing in Fate has been bred out of us so thoroughly that I am aware I am writing this suggestion of more-than-coincidence partly as a joke, partly for show——

But only partly.

Now it is more important than ever to write honestly. How can you understand me if I lie and evade and leave things out? What I have to give you is only experience, and so it must be accurate. How much I want to give it! We all do, we old people, we want to offer you our wisdom, save you from our mistakes. We are told that this is futile and that one generation can't learn from another, but I don't think I believe it. Or, what is true about it is a small shabby bit of truth, and what is untrue about it is the important thing. For surely all our wisdom is learned and built up little by little from echoes and memories. Perhaps I shan't make everything clear no matter how I try, and perhaps you will forget much of what I say, or it will seem useless at the time, now, which is certainly a hard time for you. Is it presumptuous to think I might help you? I don't mean it so. I don't mean that I think you can simply learn from my experience, listen to me and be better off than if you followed your own bent. I mean—— Well, I suppose I just mean that, if it's any use to you, here it is, as honest as I can make it. Who knows? Later you may find yourself remembering more than you think you know and my forgotten words will echo. To say the young can never learn from the old is a mean excuse for not trying to reach each other. So I shall try.

What I was beginning to write the other day was that I should have let Claire alone. Her life was set in one mold, and if it was to be changed, I should have let her change it herself. It was not really her need, it was my guilt that set me to meddling. Perhaps she *had* needs, but they were not really what I thought of, and now I cannot even be sure. When I think back to that first meeting and try to experience it freshly, what I find myself remembering is not that she stood out from her family—her adoptive family, of course—but that she did not. She fitted them and they her. She was very pretty—sturdy, with Gerald's eyes and lovely golden-brown hair. I couldn't see any resemblance to myself at all, and I was thankful, for if I was ever to manage to adopt her it would be best if we did not look alike. She was almost entirely silent, and I told myself how well behaved she was, but actually I found it difficult to make contact. The curé, Père Amedée, who was present, realized my difficulty and after an internal struggle (it was perfectly clear on his face) did what I could not do—he suggested that Claire show me over the farm. So we went out together and she took me about the barns and the runs for the hens and the duckpond. I had to throw my shoes away when I got back to Brussels. I kept asking her about her life, but it was hard to get anything out of her— Yes, she enjoyed school, no, there was no particular subject that she enjoyed more than another, yes, of course arithmetic was difficult but no, she couldn't say that she enjoyed composition or history more—— Well, she enjoyed school because it wasn't so hard as the work she had to do on the farm when she wasn't in school—— I told myself that naturally she was shy, that I was a stranger, and that I wouldn't want her to be the kind of simple idiot who made friends at once, or the kind of calculating creature who would try to launch herself at a rich opportunity (namely me), but still I was—unsatisfied. I couldn't help feeling that there should be some way into her for me, some way we could talk more easily, my child and I.

I went away with Père Amedée. I asked him whether I might not take Claire out with me the next day, alone.

He was *dreadfully* suspicious of this request. I don't know what he thought I was going to do to her. I kept wondering what kind of confessions he must hear, or whether they had taught him so thoroughly about evil at the Seminary that he had never got over it. Of course, he may just have thought that I might be going to abscond with her to a Protestant minister and get her baptized into heresy, that would have been evil enough for him.

So I offered to take Claire's elder sister—foster sister—along too, and tell them both some cock-and-bull story about wanting to see the countryside and the villages that I had heard so much about when I was (supposedly) working for M. Hoover, et cetera, et cetera.

Another severe internal struggle shook him, but finally he agreed.

So the next day, off I went with Claire and Lucie. They were both thrilled to go driving out in a car grander than any ever seen in the village, and delighted to be let off work for the day, too, though Lucie told me they had to be back in time to milk the cows. With Lucie along, Claire was more talkative. Little by little the two girls got chattering about the neighbors and all the village gossip, and Claire teased Lucie about a young widower who was quite a catch and owned the biggest sow in the village, and Lucie sighed and blushed and giggled and wished she had Claire's dowry— I got quite fond of Lucie, as a matter of fact, and after I left I wrote the curé and asked him to see if the match could be arranged, and how much Lucie would need, and he fixed it all. It cost me very little and it bought me the good will of Père Amedée.

Well, we drove about and looked at a church here and a farm there, and then I suggested we drive into Louvain and have lunch. You should have seen the girls' faces. The distance was only something like thirty miles, but they'd never been there in their lives. As we came into that lovely little city they fell absolutely silent and when the driver stopped at the restaurant just off the Place Foch that I'd inquired about, Lucie took Claire's hand before they got out of the car. It was just one shock after another—the plumbing, the dining room, the flowers on the table, the menu, the silverware—and they withdrew into such simple-minded terror that I began to be afraid I had overdone it. I ordered an apéritif, however, and a bottle of moselle, and the wine helped. Of course they *drank* wine at home, I don't want you to think I was corrupting them! But it was harsh stuff and this was different. In fact, they wanted another bottle, Claire nudged Lucie to make her ask, but I wouldn't let them have it. They weren't tipsy, but the wine and the excitement and the lovely food went to their heads and their cheeks and they giggled and perspired and Claire began to ask questions.

I answered them very simply, where I lived, was I married, had I any children? Lucie listened popeyed. *She* was romantic and wanted to hear all about the man I was engaged to and how we had met and how I had met my first husband, but Claire wanted details. How big was my house in America? How many hectares in the property, (an impossible question, I told her in acres). What animals did I keep? Would I miss it when I moved to London? Where would I live there? How many rooms? It upset me a little but I put it down to difference in age. Lucie was old enough to be in love with her widower, Claire was still a ruthless child. Then Claire sighed and said, "You see, I am a property owner too," and Lucie said, "Yes, it is her dowry," very solemnly, and I realized that it was solemn. Claire was trying to place herself in relation to me. Or rather, in relation to the world through me. A property owner too! I was very touched.

So it seemed successful and I took them home. Lucie fell asleep on the way back, but Claire sat up straight watching everything we passed, looking and looking. She is curious, I thought, that's good, that's very good. They haven't managed to make a peasant of her.

Père Amedée was waiting for us when we came back, he hailed us in the village street and announced he would drive out to the farm with us. I imagine he wanted to forestall any emotions or revelations at our parting. He asked the girls how they had enjoyed the day, and Lucie told him all about it. His eyes kept moving from Claire to me as Lucie talked, trying to surprise some reaction in us. I don't think he was successful.

When we arrived (a flock of geese greeted us like the dragon in *Siegfried*), the girls got out and were received with shouts instructing them to change their clothes at once and see to the cows, so we parted in haste. But Lucie called out, "Oh, do send us word when you are married, won't you? And a picture perhaps in your wedding dress?"

I laughed and said, "Of course I will, children, and some of the cake too, if you think they won't eat it at the Douane. Good-by, good-by." Père Amedée didn't like the idea of my writing, but he couldn't stop it, after that. And after I paid for Lucie to marry her widower, he became almost friendly. Not friendly, of course, but almost.

Now, how can I explain the next years? Claire was very real to me, but she existed only in pockets of time. It was as if I had a second, secret personality tucked away within me. When that personality came out, I was Claire's mother. But most of the time all that was like a dream, a dream vaguely remembered after you have wakened. I told John about her—and I didn't tell John about her. I told him there was a child that I was interested in and had an obligation to and then—— Yes, I'll have to say it. I either let him assume or I implied—that she was James's daughter, not mine. Lorraine, this is one of the things I can't (not won't) tell you, I just don't know how intentional that lie was. I told him, you see, that I had only discovered her (did I say existence or whereabouts?) while I was going through James's papers. It seems to me that I was trying to protect myself from the untrue assumption that I had willingly let her languish on a Belgian farm for twelve years, but I may very well be deceiving myself.

I don't know why I didn't tell John the truth. Or do I? Why should I have been afraid of John, my dear good companion, my generous friend, who suffered from none of James's sensitivities? And yet, I had a nightmarish picture of his asking me who the father was, of Gerald turning up somewhere, raffish and raddled, of John's face as he looked from Gerald to me, not quite believing it possible—— At any rate, I didn't tell him.

Then once I had seen Claire and she was real to me, she ceased to be someone I could manipulate in my imagination. She was flesh and blood. She could milk a cow. She was a property owner, concerned for her future. I wanted to give her a new future, but I understood that I could not turn her from Cinderella to a princess by waving a magic wand. Nor could I have plucked her away from her village to the center of London on a flying carpet. But I hoped to get her there more prosaically one day, and so I suppose I was trying to preserve the possibility of an unembarrassed relationship with John.

What I could do I did, as fast as I could do it. I helped Lucie. Later I helped one of the brothers. My help to Claire was thus "covered," so to speak, I was a family fairy godmother. I arranged (always via the curé with a copy to M. Villeneuve) for Claire to have English lessons—not very good, but better than nothing. I wrote her occasionally, but I wrote Lucie too. I bought Papa Morel (I'll go on calling him that, there's a reason) two new milch cows. Some things I didn't do. Claire wanted to keep rabbits and I wouldn't let her. If she had time to keep rabbits, she had time to play the piano. Père Amedée and Claire and I battled over piano lessons versus rabbits for three months and, in the end, I'm afraid Claire won. No piano. No rabbits either, though.

By this time she was fifteen. You were eleven or twelve, Lorraine. You can remember my visiting you then. Do you remember my taking you and Faith to matinées when I came to Boston? I always thought, as the lights went down, that Claire had never seen a play. The curé let me take her about alone now, on my visits, but never overnight. I took her to Brussels and bought her some clothes that year, and we had an enormous dinner at La Taverne Royale, but I would never have dared suggest the theater or stopping at a hotel.

What I did suggest was boarding school. A convent school, of course. Some of the best teaching orders in the whole world are based in Belgium. And now we had a battle royal. Claire didn't want to go. This time, however, I won, though I never could have done it without Père Amedée's help. It was terrifying to listen to him: he told her that she was ungrateful and that God would not forgive her for refusing such an opportunity. She got whiter and whiter and more and more stubborn and then he asked her in a tone of—well, really of contempt —*why* she didn't want to go. I was sitting holding my breath, quiet as a mouse (this was all going on in Père Amedée's horrible parlor) and trying not to interfere. Claire wouldn't answer. I recognized the expression on that mutinous face, I'd seen it in a mirror a quarter of a century before. "Is it because of Jean Brunel?" asked the curé. "Or Pierre Arnaut? Or Henri Monnet?" And his voice went down and down, darker and darker, as if he were Calvin (different church, I know, but it's what he sounded like), and he began telling her that he wasn't blind to her little ways, her glances, her smiles, who she strolled out with—in short, her flirting with half the boys in the village. He told her about herself and evil, and she listened in a white silent fury and I—I was half sympathetic and half horrified. Evidently I had acted just in time. Another year, even the few months to her sixteenth birthday, and Claire and her dowry would have been bundled into the arms of some village lout.

Well, we got her to go. Then we had the problem of getting her to stay. She wouldn't work, she wasn't popular with the other girls, who were all of much better background, she sulked, she misbehaved—— The Mother Superior, a woman of real intellectual and administrative ability, told me finally that she sympathized with my aspirations for the girl and my generosity in assuming responsibility for her (Yes, I'd told her Claire was James's daughter too, I'm afraid), but that the girl would have to leave. She was a disturbing influence.

I asked if I might speak to Claire. If I failed to persuade her to behave, then I would take her away. "She isn't a stupid girl," I said.

"I know she isn't," said Mother Ignatius. "She is an unhappy girl, and I suspect that she is a frightened one. You (and I too) are asking her to step out of a world she knows and is confident and successful in and prepare herself for a world that she knows nothing about. And we have given her no reason. Why shouldn't she be allowed to go back to her village where she was happy and flirt with the young men and make the marriage she was brought up to expect, as her sister did? She can't understand why we are interfering with this simple desire. Tell me, Mme. Belchamber" (she pronounced it Belle-chambre though her English was better than my French), "does she know anything at all of her history? I would never suggest telling her if I could see any other way, but frankly I can't. Claire will not do what Claire does not see a good and sufficient reason to do. Suppose you were to tell her—naturally it must be your decision—that she really belongs in the other world, the world you and I are trying to fit her for?"

I sat and looked at Mother Ignatius's placid face, and thought, You're not stupid either. Of course, it wasn't as easy as she thought. Claire wasn't James's daughter, she was mine. "Let me consider," I said, and I considered. Finally I said, "Well, if I can see her and feel my way a little—perhaps, perhaps——"

"I understand your hesitation, it is a sad story," said Mother Ignatius. "I know that relating old sin must be a somber task, but think, my dear, if good can come of it, if we can turn Claire into the happy and useful girl she might be, it is in a way an expiation of that old error." She smiled at me—— You know, I wonder if she saw through me all the time and knew Claire was mine? No one else ever saw it (only I myself, in that one flash when Claire was furious, and then the resemblance I saw was twenty years old), but Mother Ignatius had spent a lifetime looking at girls, watching them grow up and turn into women and receiving their daughters in turn. Claire was Gerald's child, I always thought, but perhaps Mother Ignatius saw more. In which case, she was setting my Protestant self (she would have said pagan self) a pretty penance.

So I told Claire. To Claire I told the truth. I told her she was mine. We sat on tapestry armchairs under a monstrous wall crucifix in a little interview room and I told her all about it, except that I said, when she asked about her father, that he was dead. "You see now," I finished, "why I had hoped you would go to school here and learn all these things that seem so nonsensical and get on with the other girls, yes, and learn from them too. I want to take you back. I want you to come to me in London. I want you to have the life that ought to be yours."

Claire had fallen into her silence. Her eyes were enormous, looking past me. "Lucie was right, then," she said finally.

"Lucie!" I said. "Lucie knew?"

"She guessed. She remembered when they brought me home. She was only seven, but she knew that I wasn't born to my mother—her mother, I mean. And she knew——"

"What?" I asked.

"That it was me you wanted. You helped Papa and Lucie and Georges, but she said it was me you cared about."

"I'm very fond of Lucie," I said, quite indignantly.

"Oh, fond," said Claire. And went back to her silence. "It would be in London?" she asked at last.

"In London, yes. Then we have an old house in Hampshire, in the country, that is. We go there often and always in the summer, when my son Jimmy is home for his holidays."

"Jimmy," said Claire, her voice was as cold as spring water.

"You would like Jimmy," I said, though I wasn't at all sure of this. "He is very simple, very kind. He is two years younger—Claire, you know all this, I've shown you pictures. I'm still the same person, you know!"

"No," she said, "now you are my mother." And she looked at me—measuring, weighing. How could I be angry? But Jimmy never looked at me like that.

"Claire," I said, "you must have thought about this at least a little if Lucie—if Lucie suggested it to you. Haven't you?"

"Oh yes. Yes. I've *thought* about it. But——"

"But what, my dear?"

"I don't know," said Claire and shut her eyes. "I can't see it," she said pathetically. "I don't know—London is even bigger than Brussels, you said. And to have no one, no one of my own—I would be lonesome."

"Claire," I cried, "Claire, you would have me, dear child!" And I did what I had never let myself do, I leaned forward and took her hand. I pressed it to my bosom, I pressed it to my cheek. "Claire darling, I wouldn't let you be lonesome!"

Ah, but she looked at me then, and I read it all in her eyes! But you left me, they were saying. First you gave me away. Then, when you came at last, you came as a stranger, you came and went and never told. Why didn't you take me in your arms the first day you came? asked those eyes. Why were you so cold and distant, why did you pretend?

"And there would be other people," I rushed on, for how could I excuse myself? "You would like Jimmy and my husband, everyone likes him, and there would be young men and other girls, you would have friends—why, a month or two after you came to London, you'd forget all about being lonesome!"

She put her head in her hands, her lovely hair tumbled forward.

"You would marry in London," I told her. "How can you go back to the village? Think of Lucie's husband——"

Claire muttered something.

"What?" I asked.

She looked up, flushed. "He couldn't help losing his teeth," she said, "the horse kicked him."

"My dear child! Even with his teeth, even granting his good nature, he's gross, he's a peasant——" My God, Lorraine, did I say something like that to you? I did, I think I did—— Oh my God!

Then perhaps you know how she felt. She said, "But I am a peasant too."

I said very coldly, "Only by choice."

Her color faded. Lorraine, when I said these things to her, she was just sixteen, it was the spring of 1937. Surely I needn't have done that to a sixteen-year-old girl? But I did. I said, "You can go back and be a peasant if that is what you feel you are fitted to be. Or you can stay here and learn to be something else."

"Your daughter?" asked Claire. Her voice matched mine, I promise you, and I winced.

"Whatever you want to make of yourself. Yes, my daughter of course and always, even if you go back to the village, Claire." I did say that, Lorraine, give me credit for that at least.

She turned away. "Claire dear," I said, "don't waste yourself. I have no right to speak to you as a mother. I forfeited it, and you are angry at me. How can I blame you for that? I blame myself. I did what I thought best, but no doubt I was wrong. I have been wrong before. But let's forget that, let's forget me. Let us think of you, only of you. Don't waste yourself, Claire. Don't bury yourself. Imagine yourself my age, Claire, I am forty-two, think of yourself looking back at this choice from your forty-second birthday. Will you scold yourself for what you were afraid to do? Will you say, 'Why didn't I dare? Why didn't I try?' Will you? Think, Claire. Since you came here you have been behaving like a child, you have nearly succeeded in losing this chance, Mother Superior wanted to send you away. Will you let a child decide your life and destroy your chance? You will be a woman soon, my dear. Some things that seem hard now will seem easy then. Will that woman look back at this child in anger and regret? I know all about that, Claire, and I wouldn't wish it to happen to you."

But she was back in her silence for all my eloquence. All she said was, "I don't know. I don't know."

"Is that what you want me to tell Mother Superior?" I asked. "That you don't know?"

"I don't know. I don't know."

"Claire——"

"No. Don't say anything more. I am a peasant, I'm slow, I can't speak the way you do—— My farm. Did it come from you? My dowry?"

"Yes. More or less. From my first husband."

"So even that isn't mine."

"Of course it's yours. My dear——"

"You helped Lucie get married, you bought Papa the cows—— I don't understand it. I don't understand what you want!"

"Claire, I want my daughter, I want you."

"But not now. And not four years ago when you came. Only when they have made me a lady, fit to marry a lord. Only when I can play the piano. Only——"

"Claire, that is all for you! It's not for me! Of course I wanted you when I came. I'd take you to London with me this minute, if I could, but good heavens, Père Amedée wouldn't even let me be alone with you until last year! Did you think I didn't want you?"

"You never said," said Claire.

I've thought and I've thought, Lorraine, and now I don't know what to think. Could I have done something—not better—but right? Or did everything I did have to be wrong because the first injury could never be set right? Is it possible that I could have healed the wound if I'd done what she couldn't forgive me for not doing, come openly as her mother, swept her up in my arms, screamed and howled and run off with her? How could I have, with M. Villeneuve and Père Amedée fearing just that and prepared against it? And aside from that, wouldn't I have frightened the child? What I did was wrong, oh yes, but the question is, Was there any right possible? It's like an equation that can yield only negative solutions—— Isn't it? I wish I knew! Anyway, what I said then was, "I was a stranger to you, Claire. I wanted you all the time, but I didn't want to hurt or frighten you. You didn't know me and you were a child and I—I had no right to you, dear. I would have had to kidnap you!"

"I would have come," she said, not looking at me.

"And hidden? Until you came of age? I'm afraid that wouldn't have been very practical. Claire dear, this way we are working toward something permanent, do you see? Père Amedée, your family, are happy to have you here, and if you decide to come to me when you are old enough, well, they will miss you, but they will understand that you have made your own decision, and there will be no resentment or trouble. We will be starting on a practical basis, do you see?"

"I suppose so," she said, after a while.

"Will you stay here then and work? It's just for a little while. It will seem like such a short time later. Even if you came to me now, you would just be at another school and really, you know, this is a very good one. There are things that everyone has to learn and here——"

"How long must I stay?" she said.

"A year or two. You will have to be eighteen, anyway. But, Claire——"

"That's two years. I'm only sixteen now. Mother Superior will make me finish that year and so it will be two and a half——"

"Claire, listen to me. This is not just time to be got through. It is a foundation for a life. Mother Superior sent me to talk to you today because she knows how unhappy you have been here. This was her idea, because she believes that you need to understand things and to know the truth. She felt that if you knew why we were asking you to prepare yourself for a kind of life that you didn't know about, you would work at it, and you would be happier too. No one can make you stay here, she can't, nor can I. We hoped that you would want to stay, when you understood. She knows the trouble you've had here, and I doubt that she would keep you a day after she honestly believes it will be best for you to go. She can make it very easy for you to come to me, you know, if she's satisfied that you are ready. Or she can make it very, very difficult. I'm sure she doesn't want to make it difficult. After all, dear, all the girls your age in England are in school, you know."

She looked at me.

"And the boys, too," I told her, smiling.

She never liked to be laughed at, Claire. And I suppose Père Amedée on evil had made her sensitive. Anyway, she flushed and said something that I took to mean her acknowledgment of defeat because it seemed so desperate and so childish. "What if there's a war?" said Claire.

"Oh," I said cheerily, "if there's a war I'll come and get you."

Well, Lorraine, that's more or less the end of the story. Because there was a war and I didn't come and get her. I lost her in it, just as I lost Jimmy—or rather, not as I lost Jimmy at all, but just as completely. Not only Claire but the whole school vanished when the Germans crossed the Belgian frontier in May of 1940 and the war in the west began. Vanished without a trace.

I took Claire's past away from her in order to give her a future. Then I took the future away from her. Yes, I did. If I'd fought harder I might have got her away to England in the summer of 1939 before the war ever began. It would have been a fight, for Mother Ignatius wanted her to stay for her last year and the old woman assured me, when I asked about the threatening situation, that she had been through the whole thing before in 1914 when the Germans were very correct, and after a few months the school had been evacuated via Italy to Canada. Yes, I would have had to fight, but Claire was eighteen, and we might very well have won. But you see—I wanted to bring Jimmy home that summer. He was almost seventeen and it seemed to me that I owed it to his father to show him America and give him a chance to decide to be American, go to Princeton as James had, and get to know his own country. I was caught. How could I sacrifice Jimmy to Claire? And Claire had an invitation to spend her holidays at Grenoble with a school friend, I was so pleased that she was making friends, it seemed like a sign of progress—— Well, there you are. There were only negative solutions, and I sacrificed Claire to Jimmy.

I could go on writing justifications for ten pages—don't worry, I won't. Sometimes I think that hell, for me, will be to spend eternity arguing the case back and forth as I argued in those months when I didn't know what had happened to Claire. And I couldn't tell anyone about it. I had lost a child that no one knew was mine, lost her off the face of the earth, into horror. I almost wrote "unimaginable horror," but I imagined sufficient. The newspapers were full of German atrocities. This was a particularly dreadful turn of the screw for people of my age, because we'd read them all before during the First War, and then had been told that they were only propaganda, and had come to disbelieve them. But who could believe that the Nazis were incapable of them? So every time I read another eyewitness account of refugees machine-gunned on the roads I went through the same series of spasms: Oh no! And then, Oh, but we know better now, it's not true. And then finally, Ah, but you're wrong, this time it is true, this time it's happening. And it was.

I've had good times and I've had bad times, and I've had times that were just queer. In a way I went numb when I lost Claire, and in a way I saw more than I ever had, noticed little things, specks of dust and odd expressions. It was because I felt differently from everyone else in England. The English, after Dunkirk, were oddly exalted. If the Germans had landed, they would really have fought on the beaches and in the hills and all the other places Churchill talked about, fought to the death with pitchforks and fire irons and spanners. There was an old boy who lived near us in Hampshire who took the African assagais off his wall, relics of his father's campaign in the Zulu war, and had them sharpened. All around me people were living as if that was a commonsensical thing to do. John was. Jimmy was. He'd agreed not to enlist until his eighteenth birthday, but along with half of the rest of the sixth form he was taking flying lessons. I didn't know it. John did. Only I and Claire were not part of this mood. It was as if my heart had shriveled up and I was living with my brain and could see very clearly, like the little boy in the fairy tale, that the king had no clothes on. Everyone else was soaking in this great mutual rising-to-a-climax, but I was immune. I felt as if I were living in a lunatic asylum. I hated the English. They couldn't win, it seemed to me, and by not admitting it they were indulging in fantasy, perilous, perverted, wrongheaded, sentimental fantasy that was going to bring the end of the world down on our heads. The bloody earth was going to eat its young again, as it had done twenty-five years before, and my child was gone already, into the dark.

I asked Jimmy whether he wouldn't go back to America—it was stupid of me, but you see—negative solutions again. I had never seen him so angry. He said I talked like an appeaser and a defeatist and he was ashamed of me and ashamed of his American citizenship, which I'd been so careful to preserve. He looked just like his father, standing in front of me in a cold rage, vowing to renounce his country at once. I said, "Jimmy, you are all I have and I would like you to live," and he said the twentieth-century equivalent of Death before Dishonor, and John came in and got him away and for a couple of weeks he barely spoke to me and wouldn't listen to the news in the same room. It was better later, after he'd joined the RAF and started to grow one of those idiotic mustaches and talked incomprehensible slang, for the idea was to be offhand about the whole thing, and I heard no more about Death before Dishonor. He did renounce his citizenship, though. I think you had to, then. Later, a lot of Americans who had, transferred to our Air Corps and there was some kind of arrangement to restore their rights. But Jimmy was dead by then. He was dead. Well, of course you remember.

I think we live too long nowadays. Women, particularly. Pray that you won't outlive your children, Lorraine. Pray that you won't find yourself someday a useless, worn-out husk condemned to the hell of individuality within your personal self with no way to get out, no way to participate in the future, a dusty piece of bric-a-brac on a shelf waiting to be swept off and broken. An old woman, talking to myself —and if I talk nonsense or if I talk truth, does it matter? Who listens? Who cares? We live too long and there are too many of us. We are poisoning each other, and this wild green earth as well.

I'm tired tonight. I must stop writing. I'm not, after all, the Queen of Sorrows, but only an ordinary human being whose life, from the outside, must seem comfortable, lucky, and to be envied. So are you, my dear. And what, after all, am I trying to say to you, what exactly? It's something about living—something about acceptance. Something about experience.

It eludes me tonight. All I can see is what I have lost. I am writing in the shadow and everything around me seems so fragile and in such peril! Everything, everything, in jeopardy! I wanted to finish this tonight, but I'm too tired. I can't write what is true. The shadow has taken the color from everything. The shadow is true. But I must believe that the color is true, too, and tonight I can't see it.

I've let two days pass. You have my letter now, anyway, and there is really no hurry about this record, the only urgency is within me. Time will not run away, not for a long while. My hands are full of the stuff. I'll have to decide soon what to make out of it, when I'm through with this.

Yesterday I saw Savage.

I went into New Haven for some X-rays and testing and so on, to be sent in to New York, and on a sudden impulse I asked if he were at the hospital and if I could speak to him for a moment "to say good-by." I made that very clear. He came finally, looking very tired, and we had a most extraordinary conversation sitting at the end of a corridor with patients in bathrobes wandering past to be X-rayed.

I began by apologizing and he said wearily that it was all right.

"No, it isn't," I said. "I wish I could make it all right, but I suppose I can't."

"It doesn't matter," he said.

I wanted to argue still but I decided against it and oddly, for me,

I found myself with nothing to say. It was embarrassing. He just sat. Finally I blurted out, "Savage, can't we part friends? I have a lot to be grateful to you for. If we wipe out that last bit, could you think of me with kindness?"

And he said, "No."

Maybe I shouldn't tell you this. What can you do, after all? But I respected him, I suppose that's why I want to tell you. I'd never really respected him before and now I do. He said, "There wasn't any kindness about any of it. You weren't kind to me and she wasn't kind to me. Maybe I thought I was kind to her, but I doubt if she thinks so and maybe she's right. Why bring kindness into it? Leave it the way it is. She's gone and she says don't write, so let's leave it alone."

"I'm sorry," I said—and God knows I meant it.

"Yeah, we're all sorry. I'm sorry too."

"Sorry it happened?"

"Sure. Sorry it happened." But he wouldn't look at me as he said it. "It was crazy. How could anything come of it? There's nothing to do now but be sorry, and forget all about it. Well, I'll manage to, I guess. I'm going away for a month, end of this week, driving to Canada. I was born there, you know, but I've never been back. I'm taking my oldest boy and we're going to fish."

"Oh, Savage," I said, "don't be sorry! Later——"

But he said, "Leave it alone. I'll be what I have to be, I guess," and got up. "Well——"

"Good-by," I said helplessly. "I'll be in New York. I'll send you my address. Perhaps——"

"No," he said. "Don't do that." He took my hand and shook it solemnly and went off, a big burly figure in a white coat, looking tired.

I don't know whether you'll write to him or not, and there's no need for you to tell me. But that is what I said to him and he to me yesterday. Perhaps he is right and there was no kindness in it, that is your story, not mine, and I don't know nor want to. I hope, though, that there can be kindness between you and me, and I send you this word of him kindly, I believe, because I know what it means to hear nothing of someone you love.

Now I will finish my story as quickly as I can and then settle down to wait for whatever you feel you can write me back. I worked during the war as hard as I could. Do you remember writing to me at the hospital in Cornwall? I didn't want to tell you much about the work then, but we specialized in plastic surgery, particularly for the burned. We gave men back faces and made hands out of claws. It was long slow work—and never mind it now. John went to India first, and Jimmy to North Africa. He was killed in 1942 when he was twenty. After that my only desire was to go to bed every night in a state of physical exhaustion. That kind of work (plus money and pull, I'm sure) got me made administrative head of the hospital in 1943. Another factor was probably that I didn't care what I said to anyone, and could get supplies when everyone swore up and down that they didn't exist. John and I saw each other once in a great while and went to London and were as gay as two exhausted middle-aged people could be. We were there in the spring of '44, and he teased me about the Americans' successful invasion of England, and how, as soon as I heard American voices in a restaurant, I started switching my fork from hand to hand and eating like a Yankee.

Well, and then came the Normandy landings and then came the terrible fighting in June and July. It wasn't until August that our troops broke out and the liberation of Europe really began. Then, of course, they went fast, two weeks to Paris and in another week the Belgian frontier. I tried so hard not to hope that there might be some word of Claire, for the last four years had taught me how dangerous hope is. But for Claire's sake, not for mine because I didn't deserve anything, I asked someone on Montgomery's staff to see that she was looked for and then I told myself not to hope and I waited.

When Jimmy was killed I at least knew, his squadron leader saw the plane go down, on fire, into the Mediterranean. But after four years, I had to wait a last extra month before Claire was found. They found her finally, though. She was in prison. Not put there by the Germans, the Germans were gone. Put there by our friends of the resistance.

She had worked with the Germans.

I said I had imagined horrors but of all the horrors that was the one I had never conceived. She was never negligible, never someone who could be disguised, but what I had dreaded was the exposure that her beauty and her temper and her stubbornness might subject her to. I had seen her in my nightmares defying the Germans, caught by them, intransigeant. "Claire, be sensible, be prudent!" I had pleaded to her nightly ghost. Well, she had been prudent indeed. She had been the mistress of two successive commandants of occupation troops, passed with the job from one to the other. Everyone knew it and in addition she had been used to interrogate, in her nice school-English, three American fliers who had bailed out of a crippled B-17 and been caught trying to get to the coast. They did not live to tell the tale, nor did the farmer who'd given them some old jackets, but his neighbors and his wife's sisters remembered it all very clearly. The German commander might have got Claire out—if he'd been able to get out himself. But he wasn't. He surrendered to an advance group of exhausted Canadians, and then the women moved in. Before the Canadians knew what had happened they had shaved off Claire's lovely hair and beaten her, naked, with a chain from someone's well bucket. The Canadians got her away and put her in a hospital, but they couldn't save her left eye.

What did she know of America or England—except me? And I betrayed her. Over and over again. Lied to her. Promised her love and left her behind to terror. Why in the name of God shouldn't she have worked with the Germans? I don't know whether her lovers were kind to her, but for the first time in years she must have felt security with them and enjoyed power. My child. My Claire.

She was tried as a collaborationist and given a three-year sentence. I went to see her when John was at Nuremberg. She did not speak to me. Not once. Not a word. Her left cheek was scarred and pitted— my Claire, mine. I told her it could be made whole if she would come to me in England and she looked at the wall and didn't speak. I said I would give her a home anywhere, with me, without me, doing whatever she wanted, and she didn't speak and I went away finally crying and crying, but Claire never cried.

She is in a convent now. She went in as soon as she was freed. One of the cloistered orders. I won't tell you where, just as I've never called her anything but Morel. One of her brothers is living and so is Lucie. It was Lucie who wrote me that Claire was taking her vows. And I have never seen her since and never will. "She is dead to the world," they told me when I tried to see her after John's death, before I came home. My child, my Claire.

Two hours ago I put down my pen, for I had come to the end of my living and I was ready to write The End. Yes, when I pick my book up and weigh it in my hand, it is full. But have I come quite to the end of the writing? That is different from the living, quite as surprising to me, I assure you, but different. What will you make of it, I wonder? Will anything come through? Or do my words grasp at moment and meaning and miss both, clumsy, too big tools that only hide immediacy when they try to reveal it? What have I hidden and forgotten? What lies have I told? I'm sure a number must lurk in this landscape of fifty years! Well, I shall have to trust you with them, to see through them or ignore them as you want. But then, I am trusting you with it all.

You won't see it as I do. No matter how I try to sum it up, you will arrive at a different total. I should let it go, then, without a word and end the writing with the living. But I can't, quite. If this is a tale with a moral (and it may be), it's not a plain, barefaced moral. If I send it to you for a reason (and no doubt I have my reasons), it's not a simple one.

You said to Savage that you couldn't leave your children, so that over-obvious moral is one that I don't need to point out. You wrote me that you sympathized with Herbert's violence, having felt lost yourself. Then I don't have to apologize for the loss and the violence that is here. And I can't be trying to justify myself, for I believe to the bottom of my heart that what I did was unforgivable. What am I trying to tell you, then? The answer seems to be simple, for the story all sets one way—into the shadow.

But do I believe that? I ought to. I seem to have written it to this conclusion: defeat and betrayal. Pain and terror. Regret. The memories that wake you at night and lie with you, unappeasable. For you, perhaps, the memory of Herbert's gesture, and his turning from you in the hospital, the mess and the scandal. And for both of us, Savage, sorry that it ever happened, his poor face bruised under the eyes with weariness.

Would we refuse it, though? Suppose we had a choice, waiting to be born. Suppose we were told: You will do wrong and live in pain, you will sacrifice love to greed, you will live to curse this moment, just now, the first "now" you will ever know, the moment you are born, which locks you to the wheel. Would we refuse? The Buddhists, isn't it, say that we would and that we live only in order to learn how not to.

But I—I should not refuse. Not even now. Never, never. This now, this little needle's eye through which Time moves, and my hand across this paper, is all I ask, is punishment and reward and, it seems to me, enough. What I've remembered, all this brightly colored stuff, was woven by this tiny now, and now is all the time we have to turn it over under our eyes and try to understand it. No, I would not refuse. I would wake again in the night, at the beginning, and hear my parents confronting the future that comes always in disguise, themselves as strangers, and I would face my own fear as I face my sorrow, and begin over, contrive that third choice. I would always do it.

What can I tell you then, but this? Begin. Begin, my dear, who are all the child that I have now. Oh, give my love to Faith, of course, but you and I have fought each other hard enough and intimately enough to have come to be, a little, parent and child. Begin. I am not asking what you will do, nor suggesting. I had thought of trying to talk to Herbert for you, and then I thought, Why, what a foolishness! Haven't you done yet with managing for other people who can manage without you? Lorraine is grown up, she doesn't need anyone to live her life for her, she can make her own decisions. We have both learned that, I think, in these months, and I shan't interfere. Do what you want, whatever you think is best—but begin! I shan't even say, Don't be afraid, for of course you will be afraid.

I do say, Trust yourself. Not to do right, how can we ever hope to do right? But you have strength and stature and when you act, you will act in accordance with them. Begin. Don't try to do too little. Don't nag yourself about mistakes, of course you will make them, you can only do your best and no one's best is really very impressive. You will be sorry and be ashamed, you will say: How could I have done this or that! How could I hurt Herbert! How could I leave Savage! But there is someone to whom you owe at once a greater allegiance and a smaller respect, and that is yourself. Just as now is all you have of time, so yourself is the only instrument you have to live with. Use it. Begin. It's imperfect, they are never brave enough or persevering enough, these selves of ours, and they get hopelessly entangled with the poor bodies which are their pieds-à-terre, but they're all we have.

How foolish they are, and how audacious, probing the night sky beyond the galaxies and daring to love each other! Night before last I hated them, hating myself, and life seemed nothing but a swarm of gnats. Now—now I am, I think, a little proud of us. No, not proud. But moved. Tonight I feel you reading this, two thousand miles, and days, away; this old, unhappy mixed-up story that I could not change for any other even if I wanted to, this truth, whether it's lies or not. And whether it "helps" you or not, I see, is nonsense too, and another attempt at managing—will I never stop? You are at a pause in living, now, but your own story will go on, and tonight I am not even anxious to know what it will be. I trust you, my dear, not only with my life, but with your own. You have put it down for the moment, you are waiting, but I trust you to see where to pick it up and how to continue it. Just as tonight I know, for instance, that Savage isn't only sorry. He and his boy driving north together— how unexpected and how pleasant, somehow. Tonight, alone under the lamp (Tucker is knitting before the television set in the morning room), I am not alone. Tonight I don't have to retreat to the safety of the past where no more can happen to hurt, I can face tomorrow and the next day, the move to New York and beginning again. Tonight I can even think of Claire not in the past but in her mysterious present and pray that she prays for me, because she will have forgiven me if she does.

Good night, dear child. This untrustworthy, angry, baffled creature sends you her love with this great spate of words and waits, with the oddest confidence, for your reply.